SATANS
OF
SATURN

SATANS
OF
SATURN

by

OTIS ADELBERT KLINE

and

E. HOFFMANN PRICE

RAMBLE HOUSE

SOURCES

Introduction © 2012 by Richard A. Lupoff

Satans on Saturn © 1940 by Otis Adelbert Kline and E. Hoffmann Price; originally published in *Argosy* magazine.

Web of Wizardry © 1942 by E. Hoffmann Price; originally published in *Spicy Mystery Stories* magazine.

Selene Slays by Night © 1942 by E. Hoffmann Price; originally published in *Spicy Mystery Stories* magazine .

The Man from the Moon © 1930 by Otis Adelbert Kline; originally published in *Amazing Stories* magazine.

Satans of Saturn published 2012 by Surinam Turtle Press, an imprint of Ramble House, by permission of David Anthony Kraft, Executor of the Estate of Otis Adelbert Kline.

ISBN 13: 978-1-60543-635-7

ISBN 10: 1-60543-635-6

Cover Art: Allen Koszowski
Preparation: Richard A. Lupoff and Fender Tucker

Surinam Turtle Press #33

TABLE OF CONTENTS

A STREET IN MANILA,
AN APARTMENT IN CHICAGO

Richard A. Lupoff

The last time I saw E. Hoffmann Price we were sitting in
the living room of his comfortable, modest house in the hills
above Redwood City, California. Redwood City is a pleasant
middle-class suburb of San Francisco. I believe this was the
last interview that Price ever gave, shortly before his death
on June 18, 1988, fifteen days before what would have been
his ninetieth birthday.

We had spent much of the afternoon taping an interview
for a local radio station. I had two partners with me, making
for an overcrowded air sound. Normally only one or two of
us would have done the show with Mr. Price, but nobody
wanted to miss out on this opportunity.

Mrs. Price, a gracious hostess, served Turkish coffee to
the guests. It was, to coin a phrase, so dense that a spoon
would stand up in it and so strong that it nearly melted the
spoons. I don't think I slept for three nights after drinking a
tiny cup of that fierce brew.

The room was furnished with a lifetime of memorabilia.
On one shelf stood a row of miniature sculptures, created by
Clark Ashton Smith as gifts for his friend Ed Price. A magnificently carved antique wooden throne stood against one
wall. Ed Price warned us that no one was allowed to sit
there. It was reserved for the Son of Heaven, should he ever
deign to visit. Crossed swords — not the display variety, but
actual weapons that might once have inflicted fatal wounds
— were hung upon the wall.

Price was a great raconteur, and in a long life had known
an astonishing who's-who of the pulp world. On one occa-

sion, while driving from California to Louisiana, he had stopped at Cross Plains, Texas, to visit Robert E. Howard. Once ensconced in New Orleans he had entertained Howard Phillips Lovecraft, serving him a bowl of homemade chili that, in Price's words, "would have raised blisters on a saddle." Even Lovecraft, who prided himself in his fondness for hot, hot dishes, admitted that Price's chili was an outstanding brew.

Shortly before my colleagues and I were to leave, Ed Price drew me aside. He was a onetime army man, a West Point graduate and veteran of the First World War. He had traveled all over the world. He knew that I, too, was ex-military, a onetime enlisted man and then again an officer and a gentleman. My two associates had never served in uniform.

Indicating the others with a tilt of his head, Ed spoke to me *sotto voce*. "They've never been in the service, they wouldn't understand. But you and I — listen, if you'd like the address of the best whorehouse in Manila —"

Then he interrupted himself. "Hmm, come to think of it, the last time I was there was 1915."

That's the kind of guy Edgar Hoffmann Price was. A unique character. And a real writer.

~ ~ ~ ~ ~

In his posthumously published memoir, *Book of the Dead* (2001), Price describes his first meeting with Otis Adelbert Kline. It was summer of 1926. Price was visiting the offices of *Weird Tales* in Chicago. The editor of that magazine, Farnsworth Wright, summoned Kline from an adjacent room.

The two writers were already familiar with each other's work. Kline had been a *Weird Tales* regular since its first issue, which published his novelette "The Thing of a Thousand Shapes." Kline was a sometime unofficial staff member at *Weird Tales,* while holding down a day job at a food and spice importing company.

Both Kline and Price had been prolific pulp writers, working in a variety of genres. Both had an interest in Middle

Eastern and Arabic culture. Both had rejected traditional Christianity, Price becoming a lifelong Buddhist and Kline a Muslim of sorts. He could certainly not have practiced any orthodox variety of Islam, as Price was shortly to discover.

That very night Kline invited Price, Wright, and *Weird Tales'* business manager, William Springer, to his apartment to meet Mrs. Kline and their children, and to share a generous meal and a variety of tasty concoctions. Obviously the then-official Prohibition Amendment was widely and thoroughly ignored.

Price had been a member of an intercollegiate dueling team; Kline, also, was an amateur swordsman. Late that night, having consumed copious and varied alcoholic beverages and after Wright and Springer had taken their leave and the rest of the Kline family had retired, Kline and Price engaged in an impromptu duel. They used sabers rather than *epées* and dispensed with such protective paraphernalia as masks and pads. How both emerged unscathed from this contest remains a mystery. The encounter, however, led to a friendship which lasted until Kline's untimely death in 1946 at the age of fifty-five.

The initial collaboration between the two men also grew from this first meeting. It was a novelette, "Thirsty Blades," which they sold to *Weird Tales.*

Kline was a busy and versatile writer. His best known works were a series of fantastic novels serialized in *Argosy* magazine, one of the most prestigious and lucrative of pulp markets. Between 1929 and 1935 he placed eight such works with *Argosy.* They closely paralleled the interplanetary romances and jungle adventure tales written by Edgar Rice Burroughs. Kline even wrote a novel called *Maza of the Moon,* matching Burroughs' *The Moon Maid.*

A lengthy dispute eventually arose in the fan press, as to whether Kline was attempting to capitalize on Burroughs' popularity by imitating his *oeuvre.*

In the January, 1930 edition of *The Writer,* Kline published an essay, "Writing the Fantastic Story." In this piece he recounted the story of his father, an amateur astronomer, instructing him in the wonders of the night sky.

> *"He told me of the vast distances which, according to the computations of scientists, lay between our world and these twinkling celestial bodies – that the stars were suns, some smaller than our own, and others so large that if they were hollow, our entire Solar System could operate inside them without danger of the planet farthest from the sun striking the shell. He told me of the nebulae, which might be giant universes in the making, and that beyond the known limits of our universe it was possible that there were countless others, stretching on into infinity."*

~ ~ ~ ~ ~

Such, Kline averred, was the long-remembered inspiration of his interplanetary romances. He made no mention of Burroughs' immensely successful stories of John Carter, the Warlord of Barsoom. It is hard to believe that he was totally unaware of them, and yet . . .

Decades later, during the massive Burroughs revival of the 1960s and long after the demise of both authors, Robert A. W. Lowndes of Avalon Books and Donald Wollheim of Ace Books resurrected Kline's interplanetary romances and jungle adventures. Wollheim told me personally that he had tried to obtain publication rights to the Burroughs novels but been unable to get any response from the Burroughs interests, and published the Kline titles instead. In any case, once Kline's interplanetaries were available to a mass market the bonfire of controversy was reignited.

Throughout the 1930s Kline and Price maintained their friendship and collaborated from time to time on literary and even culinary projects. By this time Kline had established himself as a literary agent, and was one of his own more popular clients. In the same era, Price recalled,

"Otis sent me the synopsis and character sketches of several stories he had long hoped to write. There was ever less chance for him to get at these projects. One was a space opera serial Satans on Saturn, widely damned as the worst of Kline and the worst of Price."

~　~　~　~　~

In his memoir, Price goes on to relate Kline's unsuccessful attempts to market the serial. His prime market, *Argosy,* turned it down. Working his way through more conventional science fiction outlets, Kline finally reached *Thrilling Wonder Stories,* where he pleaded with editor Leo Margulies to take the novel for a token price of $250.

"Leo said, 'I'd not publish this God-damned mess if you paid me $250!' "

~　~　~　~　~

By this time, however, a new editor had arrived at *Argosy* so Kline gave that magazine another try and sold *Satans on Saturn* for $750! The story was serialized in five weekly installments starting with the issue of *Argosy* dated November 2, 1940.

Despite Price's own poor opinion of *Satans on Saturn,* it reads as a perfectly respectable and enjoyable example of its type. Space opera? Of course! On a par with the very best works of Jack Williamson, Edmond Hamilton, or Edward Elmer Smith? Perhaps not, but certainly far better than Price's own description and light-years superior to some of the inferior works produced in the US and UK during the "mushroom" years of out-of-hand publishing in the 1950s and '60s.

How much of the text is Price's work and how much is Kline's is subject to speculation. Price records that the original idea was Kline's. The rhythm and style of the prose seems to sway between the two, and one might speculate that since the narrative involves two major protagonists, each author penned the chapters narrated from the viewpoint of each.

Satans on Saturn takes place in the traditional version of the solar system, in which all the planets are pretty much like the Earth — only more so. In this model, Mars is cold and dry, rather like the Gobi desert. Venus is hot and moist, rather like the Amazon rain forest. Mercury is hot on one side, frigid on the other, with a livable, temperate, twilight zone separating the two. And so on.

In *Satans on Saturn* the planet Jupiter has a solid surface and a hot climate, while its moons are frigid but habitable. The Saturnians are giant, bat-winged, and horned. They bear a remarkable resemblance to the Overlords in Arthur C. Clarke's important novel *Childhood's End* (1953). The novel was developed from an earlier Clarke short story first published in 1946.

Could Clarke, an avid science fiction fan in his early twenties when *Satans on Saturn* was serialized in *Argosy,* have come across a run of issues and read the story in its serial form? It is entirely possible that he had read *Satans on Saturn* and developed his Overlords from Kline and Price's Saturnians. A caveat, however, must be expressed. This notion is purely speculative; should any evidence emerge to support it, the science fiction world will surely take note with great surprise.

Another aspect of *Satans on Saturn* which causes the modern reader to shudder is the recurring theme of humans being sent "to the ovens" by the Saturnians, and the Saturnians using "privileged" humans — in effect, turncoats — as overseers of human slave laborers in exchange for being spared "the ovens."

By the time Kline and Price were working on *Satans on Saturn,* Adolf Hitler's "final solution" had not yet come into being, and one may be sure that neither Kline nor Price would have wished to borrow this monstrous crime for use in a lightweight science fiction novel.

Otis Kline died long before the pulp magazine field withered and died. Ed Price enjoyed a long and productive life. He pursued a number of professions after his chosen literary markets had disappeared. He was a professional photographer of note. But he never lost his fondness for telling fantastic tales.

In 1967 a small collection of his short stories was issued by Arkham house under the title *Strange Gateways.* In 1975 a much larger collection, *Far Lands, Other Days,* was published by Carcosa. The stories in both of these books were gleaned from his contributions to the pulps.

Then in 1979, at the age of eighty one, he returned to writing and between 1979 and 1986 he produced six novels. Two of these are classified as fantasies: *The Devil Wives of Li Fong* and *The Jade Enchantress.* The others are a science fiction tetralogy: *Operation Misfit, Operation Longlife, Operation Exile,* and *Operation Isis.*

The day he departed this vale of tears, Edgar Hoffmann Price was found slumped over his typewriter, a partial manuscript on the platen.

The present Surinam Turtle Press edition is the first book edition of *Satans on Saturn,* and as far as we have been able to determine, the first republication, ever, of the 1940 serial. As such, it makes a valuable addition to the world library of science fiction.

As lagniappe, we have added two short stories by E. Hoffmann Price and a novelette by Otis Adelbert Kline.

"Web of Wizardry" is an example of the so-called Oriental Story of which Price was a master. Adventure tales set in the Middle East or in Asia, these stories are marked by their exotic settings and by a fascination with Eastern cultures, in this case those of the Arab-Muslim world. They are often, although not always, laced with elements of fantasy.

"Selene Slays by Night" is another fantasy by Price, but far different from "Web of Wizardry." A skillful blending of whimsy and horror, "Selene" has a realistic, contemporary setting, an unusual venue for a Price story.

Both of these stories appeared in 1942 *Spicy Mystery Stories,* a pulp magazine that was ultimately suppressed because of its risqué contents. To the modern reader, a typical *Spicy* story would read like a tepid romance, but in its day attitudes were very different.

Otis Adelbert Kline's "The Man from the Moon" was first published in 1930 in *Amazing Stories,* Hugo Gernsback's pioneering science fiction magazine, although by 1930 Gernsback had lost control of *Amazing* and was publishing the *Wonder* group of magazines.

An odd story in its structure, "The Man from the Moon" is half earthbound exotic adventure tale, half space opera. The latter half is especially significant in that it describes an ancient solar system and the circumstances under which both Mars and Earth's moon were brought to the condition in which modern astronomers know them.

We have noted elsewhere that Edgar Rice Burroughs' version of Mars — Barsoom — is warmer, wetter, and more densely atmospheric than the present Mars. This has led to an exercise in Higher Criticism that suggests that Burroughs' heroic earthmen were transported not merely across space but through time as well, to find themselves on ancient Barsoom. While most of Kline's interplanetaries are set on Venus, he did transport an earthly adventurer to the red planet in *Outlaws of Mars* and his rationale for the differences between that planet's ancient condition and its modern state is convincingly presented in "The Man from the Moon. "

The alert reader will have noticed that this book is titled *Satans of Saturn,* in keeping with many novels by Otis Adelbert Kline. The novel, *Satans on Saturn,* is as titled in its serial form in *Argosy.* The spectacular cover illustration is the work of Allen Koszowski. The black and white illustrations originally appeared in *Argosy* magazine; they were, regrettably, not credited.

— Richard A. Lupoff

SATANS OF SATURN

CHAPTER I

FISH THAT BREATHES FIRE

"BRADLEY! What's that up there?" John Parker gripped my arm and pointed toward a gleaming shape just visible in the gray mists that hid the peaks of the far-off Parima Mountains. "It's not a dirigible!"

Nothing less than a nest of tropical ants ever made Parker get on his feet in such a hurry. But there he stood, tiptoeing in his excitement, his head thrust far forward.

I squinted into the haze that was settling over Venezuela. "Take it easy, John; that's a dirigible. You've seen them before, huh?"

He ignored that; his agitation and incredulity were infectious. "No dirigible ever made a dive so steep," he insisted. "And now look!"

But I was stretching my legs toward our tent. For some strange reason, it occurred to me that Parker might have something there. As I returned, I jerked my binoculars out of their case. Even before I had the focus well adjusted, I picked out details that left me gaping.

The fish-shaped hull was of bronze-colored alloy. The horizontal rays of the sun brought out deep dents and pits in the metal. With my powerful glasses, there was no mistaking these scars, and long, ragged gashes that furrowed the ship's hull. The implications of armor so thick that abrasions were visible at that range made me grope for words.

Parker plucked the binoculars from my fingers, just as I said, "Uh—never was a dirigible that heavy."

"That is the least of it," Parker dryly remarked. He had re-lapsed into his usual slow speech, but his long face was tense, and his hand trembled a little. After a moment he added, "It has no propellers. Judging from the fumes and flash out of those ports—"

He stopped short. He must have picked up another detail which I had missed. The way he dropped his horn-rimmed spectacles to a camp chair convinced me that something was about to happen. Parker was usually fussy about trifles.

"New airship," I went on. "Some nut invented a rocket propulsion dingus; and for a wonder, it works. Simple, not having a propeller."

"They've dropped a net. They're hovering. Motionless," he said.

"Gimme those glasses."

I took over before he could object.

The strange craft had descended to about fifty feet above the tree tops that girdled the bottom of the mountain. A mesh device of gleaming yellow alloy fanned out as it fell. When the net come up, it sagged with a wriggling mass that I could not identify, even with high magnification.

Then the ship settled, and trees hid it from view. Presently it rose straight up; and having gained altitude, it swooped into the settling clouds.

"But what'd they catch?" I demanded, after telling Parker what he had missed. "There's no pond or pool within miles that's large enough to be dredged by a net that size."

Parker's face was peculiarly gray, and he stood there, rub-bing his long jaw. "The forest," he slowly said, "is likewise too dense for anyone to snare animals in that fashion."

~ ~ ~ ~ ~

I BEGAN to understand; and suddenly I felt weak, dizzy. "There's a clearing around that neighborhood," I said. "The only one for quite a distance. That Maku Indian village."

"That's right." Parker sighed and sat down. He polished his glasses, very carefully. He stared for a moment at his feet, then looked up. "And there is only one kind of game that can be captured in quantities enough to fill such a large net. Human beings. Our Indian neighbors."

He was all too right, but I said, *"Couldn't* be, John."

"I wish you could convince me," he said.

Just that. I didn't even try. I was thinking of the small community of Makus. We had visited them only two days before. And now—They would all have flocked out of their huts and into the center of the clearing to get a look at the shining fish of the air. Inevitably, curiosity would have made them gather in a cluster. They would have had no fear; not until it was too late. Not until the gigantic net swiftly fell, spreading out, cutting off retreat for all but perhaps a few at the fringe of the crowd.

They were our friends. For the past months, they had been daily visitors to our camp, bringing fruit and fish and farina in exchange for trinkets from our stock of trade goods.

"The turtle stew, she is ready, *señores."* This from Miguel, our Venezuelan cook and man of all work.

Having taken a sizeable turtle from the river that morning, he had promised us a masterpiece. His attention to the final seasoning had made him ignore our excitement, and entirely miss our exchange of surmises.

Like most of his kind, Miguel considered us mildly insane in coming so far inland when we were wealthy enough to live in town, on the coast. Pedro, his assistant, shared this opinion. So, had he been in camp, he would have paid no more attention to our chatter than Miguel did.

But Miguel's broad grin faded a little when he saw our faces. We did not look as pleased as we should have at his announcement. Then Parker brightened.

"We've been waiting for that," he said. "It smells good."

That was like John. He would not let his speculations rob Miguel of his well-earned approval. And the steaming bowls somehow convinced me that what I had seen must have been an illusion; that Parker's reasoning had more theory than sense. The odor of food does bring one back to earth. I was inclined to feel foolish at our speculations.

Miguel, with an empty sugar sack draped over his arm in the manner of a waiter, thoroughly enjoyed our appreciation. There was farina bread, Bogota coffee that he had roasted, dark and ground in a hand mill, just a few moments earlier. He topped it off with papaya melons and slices of limes.

~ ~ ~ ~ ~

PARKER and I had planned this trip to Venezuela even before we finished college, where his coaching dragged me through a succession of nearly fatal examinations.

"Bradley," he would say when I tried to thank him for his thankless work, "it's good practice, coaching a numbskull. I think I'll teach chemistry and physics and maybe math at U.C."

"With your training, you should," I agreed, and that was the way it worked out.

His stooped shoulders made him seem shorter than he was. Actually, he was nearly my height, a matter of two yards. From the chin down, I must have outweighed him by fifty pounds. So having won my diploma by a combination of football and Parker's studious habits, I started out as a cub reporter. Three years later, I landed at the rewrite desk of a New York paper; and about then, Parker got the chair of mathematics at a small Eastern university.

All of which led to my applying for a three months' leave of absence, without pay. His uninterrupted salary, which was considerably more than mine, convinced me, somewhat too late, that Parker's angle had its merits. So we came to Venezuela, to follow the Orinoco to its source.

~ ~ ~ ~ ~

WE WERE through eating before Pedro returned to camp.

Parker got his pipe going. I set fire to a cigarette. "I think," was my opener, "that we'd better take some more quinine. Collective hallucination, that's what—"

I was interrupted by a crashing in the underbrush, and had barely gotten to my feet when Pedro stumbled into camp. His face and arms were scratched and bleeding. His brown skin was slate colored now.

"What's wrong, Pedro?" Parker demanded.

For a moment he could not speak.

"See a ghost?" I asked—mostly to keep my own nerves in place.

"There are more ocelots than ghosts in Venezuela," Parker said. This was his view because he had mathematically proven that nothing as thin as a specter could possibly howl or tip tables.

Pedro let go the tent pole he had seized for support. "No ghost!" he panted. "No tiger. More worse, *señores!*" He crossed himself. "The devil is chasing us. Nothing will help."

I caught his shoulder and spun him halfway around. "Who?"

"Satanas and his devils. They come to the village in a brass airship. The people, they run out to see. This devil drops the net, he catches many and drags them up. Into big doors on the bottom.

"Some of the devils come out to get us when we run. When we get away from the big net."

"What'd they look like?"

"*Demonios!* Ten feet high! They breathe the fire from the nose—the mouth. Some of us they eat when they catch us in the jungle. Where they breathe, the green leaves are on fire."

"Incredible!" But Parker did not reach for his slide rule.

I'd forgotten about collective hallucinations. I said, "Pedro, how did you get away?"

"I was leave the village when they come. I hide. When I am not too scared, I run like hell. *Señor,* is terrible."

I could not doubt any longer. Venezuela was offering us a lot more than we had anticipated.

~ ~ ~ ~ ~

THE SILENCE that followed Pedro's narrative was more eloquent than any comment. Miguel, with the savage's ready acceptance of wonders, took the story for granted. Everything in the jungle that did not eat others was itself eaten; and if any creature was eccentric enough to breathe smoke, it at least had ample precedent: locomotives and steamboats had that same trait.

As for devouring half a village—well, it had not devoured Miguel; and thus the problem was not yet personal.

Parker's face was a study. Warm-hearted and kindly as he was by nature, Parker was too much the scientist to let horror overcome his habits of orderly reasoning and speculation.

Had Parker, living two centuries ago, learned that his grandmother was to be burned as a witch, he would have been grieved and shocked; but if there were nothing to be done toward rescuing the aged relative, he would reach for his notebook, record his observations of the *auto-da-fe,* and file them.

And were he himself at the stake, he would gain some consolation out of knowing that a fellow scientist was making careful observation.

"After all," he abruptly began, breaking the silence, "every living organism functions by virtue of a process of combustion. You eat a chunk of walrus meat up in the Arctic regions where the temperature is eighty below zero. Your body maintains its usual ninety-eight point two, plus or minus a few tenths, from the oxidation of the meat you've eaten. You exhale carbon dioxide. That proves something has been burned up.

"The only difference is that you don't oxidize your food rapidly enough to produce smoke or flames. Those monsters, I would conclude, are no more than creatures with an extremely high rate of internal combustion. I might say, with a hyper-metabolism. If your body oxidized a pound of meat in a tenth of a second, you'd burst into flames—"

He reached for the slide rule which he carried in his pocket, and used, regardless of flood, fire, or famine.

"Skip it," I said nervously. "You're giving me the creeps. Eating human beings is just a problem in dietetics to you."

The slide rule zipped for several minutes. Parker finally thrust it back into his pocket and declared, "To emit flame, those creatures must have a rate of metabolism many times greater than any known living creature. Their energy must therefore be correspondingly greater. And I might add as a corollary that their tissues must be composed of silicious substances which, while incombustible, are nevertheless comparable to our own bodies.

"There is nothing intrinsically impossible about the manifestations which Pedro reports."

"Those poor devils he saw devoured," I interrupted, "came to that conclusion without a slide rule."

Parker ignored that. In an instant he was on his feet. He moved with amazing agility for a person who has become slightly stoop-shouldered and near-sighted from study. He reached for a rifle.

"Hey! What the—"

"I am about to investigate," he explained. "These creatures must have a highly organized nervous system to have devised the method of aerial locomotion. A well-placed shot should knock them out of commission. A few holes bored with expanding bullets should cause such a leakage of thermal energy that the creature would not be able to function."

"Nuts!" I protested. "You're crazy."

"It's purely in the interests of science."

And that settled it. The idiot was setting out for the Maku village with a high-powered rifle, a slide rule, and a notebook.

~ ~ ~ ~ ~

I RATHER liked Parker; and furthermore, I couldn't let Pedro and Miguel think I was upset by the menace. So I picked up my .405 Winchester—a dainty little weapon which will slap an elephant back on his haunches—and followed him.

We had scarcely reached the edge of the clearing when I noticed that Pedro and Miguel were following. The former had a small-bore shotgun, and the latter carried a long-bladed machete. I wish now I'd given them both a swift kick and told them to mind their own business.

An hour's stealthy advance through the jungle brought us to the edge of the clearing in the center of which was the Maku village. Parker halted.

The place was deserted. Smoldering embers marked the spot where the chief's palm-thatched hut had been. By the bright moonlight we could see that the surrounding foliage had been scorched as if by fierce blasts of flame. The lingering stench of burned flesh was all too perceptible.

Death and doom brooded over the village whose inhabitants had but a few hours ago brought us farina and bananas.

Here and there we saw palm thatch that had been seared just short of the burning point.

"About ten feet from the ground," Parker reasoned. "Exhalation from the nostrils of the monsters. And look at the footprints!"

Huge webbed feet had left their marks in the damp earth of the clearing. Feet armed with long, curved talons. The claws, judging from one particularly clear print, must be highly articulated: six or eight joints at least.

"Too late to get any specimens here," was Parker's regretful comment.

"Let's go downstream and warn the next village," I said. "We might save those poor fellows from being wiped out."

"Just the idea!" Parker brightened.

"And maybe I'll get a chance at one of these fire-breathers while we're at it. Fire-breathing creatures with feet obviously designed for locomotion in quicksand and oozing marshes. Man, man, what a find this is going to be! The National Society of—"

Parker had set out across the clearing as he began pointing out the contradictory combination; but he did not complete his remarks. He abruptly halted. I joined him, and Pedro and Miguel caught up with us.

"What the devil is that?"

Parker cocked his head to listen. There was a faint hissing and whirring which we could not localize. It was not the voice of any jungle insect. It vaguely reminded me of the escape of a fine jet of gas under high pressure—or of the singing lament of an electrical transformer. The sound came from overhead.

Miguel's savage instinct was the first to react.

"Run! *For amor de Dios*—" He plunged headlong toward the sheltering jungle. Parker, startled, glanced up. I followed his gaze instead of Miguel's example.

A hundred yards over our heads hovered the monstrous, brazen ichthyform object which we had that evening viewed through our field glasses. It seemed larger than any zeppelin we had ever seen.

"Parker!" I yelled, snatching him by the arm. But it was too late.

CHAPTER II

THE FLYING FURNACE

AND THEN I UNDERSTOOD the ever-sharpening pitch of the sound we had heard. A monstrous net was enveloping us. It was settling over the entire village. I saw Miguel's frantic rush sharply checked by silvery, gleaming metallic meshes and heard his terrified shriek.

Miguel's instinct functioned more quickly than our thoughts. It was only a split second later that I fully realized that we had been snared, that the weighted fringe of the trap, drawn toward the center in the same way that a shrimp net is closed, had scooped us up like a handful of crustaceans.

I tore my hands cruelly, clawing at the flexible metallic strands. I kicked and twisted, trying to force the contracting mouth of the net to open enough to release us. But it had so swiftly closed that for an instant it held us by the legs; and then, as the contracting center was drawn up toward the crown of the net, we toppled backward, our own weight jerking us clear of the constricting circle. We fell into the annular pouch formed by the outer wall and the rising of the center.

I was still struggling when I heard Parker say, as he pulled himself clear of me, "Most ingenious device; a shrimp net that functions on a solid surface."

"Shut up," I growled. "You and your science! We're a hundred yards up in the air, bound for nowhere—and still going!"

Our net was rapidly being drawn back to the brazen quasi-zeppelin. The vessel had no propellers, as far as we could see. The whirring increased, and we could smell the pungent fumes of ozone, the result of some high-frequency electrical discharge. Now that we were clear of the tree tops, we perceived the swiftly accelerating horizontal motion as our captors headed approximately westward.

We were so close to the flying fish that its monstrous hulk blotted out the sky. In another moment, as the head of our net reached the hull of the vessel, a circular port swung open.

We were whisked into a compartment; the port lifted back into place, and grappling hooks engaged our net. There was a whirring of gears as the metallic meshes were drawn back. Presently we were free. And we were still armed.

~ ~ ~ ~ ~

MIGUEL stolidly gripped his machete.

Pedro dropped his shotgun, crossed himself, and began invoking every saint on the calendar. Parker, however, reached for his slide rule. He seemed to ignore the stifling, almost unbearable heat of our compartment.

The nearest comparison I could recall was the time I took a hand at pipe-line welding with an acetylene torch; yet there the scorching waves emanating from a pool of white-hot iron struck only my face, whereas here my entire body was subjected to a comparable blast. The walls of the compartment were fairly simmering. Miguel yelled and jerked his hand from the bulkhead he had touched.

A panel on the wall hinted at intricate electro-chemical equipment. There were thermostats, dials and gauges; also a nozzle-valve the lever of which was actuated by two metallic rods hinged to a fixed base and joined to form a triangle, the apex of which was a link joint.

"Put away your slide rule," I demanded, "and have a look at this gadget."

Parker squinted at the valve lever. Then he explained, "Legs of the triangle are of dissimilar metals. Their rates of expansion are unequal. See the apex of the triangle moving to the right? It's changing shape, because one leg is expanding faster than the other. That's what opens the valve and lets in more hot air. The opening of the port to admit us admitted cold air, so the temperature is being built up. Get it?"

"Do I get it? I'm half cooked now. It looks like we're at the receiving end of a culinary experiment."

Parker shook his head. "I doubt it, Bradley. One hundred and forty-four degrees will not coagulate proteins to the extent demanded by good cookery. The temperature has ceased rising. Note that there is no more hot air entering by that jet.

"And what is much more to the point, observe that there is an acoustical hook-up on the panel. Microphones. Vacuum tubes. A frequency converter. Hmmm . . . Unusual."

Something had bereft him of his facility at explanation. He was frowning and squinting until I was certain that one of the dials on the panel would record the force of his stare.

One of the indicators did move! It dropped back as Parker turned to eye me and shake his head. He was muttering.

"Bradley," he suddenly said, "you stare at that device, while I watch it. Think about something. Anything."

I began thinking about ice cold beer, electric fans, and polar bears.

"Now we'll both try it," said Parker. There was a note of excitement in his voice. "Let's get together. Concentrate on what you think of this situation."

I exploded. I expressed myself at length. Parker's eyes widened.

"Very unscientific attitude," he reproved. "And in addition, profane, obscene, and blasphemous. But let's try it."

We did. The indicator jumped to three times its first amplitude. It rose and smacked violently against the stop pin. And then it suddenly swung back to zero.

"You've burned out a fuse," Parker explained. "This is a mental vibration-recording device. Our captors undoubtedly have been listening in. Now that we have blown it out of action, we might plan our next move, and without their learning it. We're undoubtedly heading for the marshes further inland. While we can't escape yet—"

A panel of the bulkhead swung open, and Parker's discourse was cut short.

~ ~ ~ ~ ~

IN THE companionway was a creature fully ten feet tall. Its shape and face were human, after the fashion of a masquerade costume Satan. Webbed, bat-like wings grew from its shoulders. The feet were likewise webbed; but the hands, eight-taloned and super-articulated, had thumbs and seemed more facile than human members. .

The body was bright red; but whether the scaly covering was a close-fitting jerkin and doublet or the creature's skin, I could not tell in the wavering glow.

It wore a broad belt which supported and holstered small arms roughly resembling horse pistols.

It eyed us as if quite familiar with humans. Then it shuddered as from intense cold, rasped a command over its shoulder. A similar creature came from the companionway with a heavy cloak and gauntlets, which the first one donned. It was shivering as from the chill of the compartment in which we were being rendered like a chunk of pork fat.

Suitably clothed, Satan's duplicate stepped to the instrument panel, made several adjustments, and closed a switch. The odor of ozone charged the searing air. Satan began speaking in rasping, guttural syllables.

From a transmitter on the panel a metallic, uninfected human voice droned, "I am Thorgulu, commander of the Saturnian fleet. We are on the way to Saturn, where our scientists will question you.

"If you have anything to say, you may address the microphone. Your remarks will be converted into the Saturnian speech. En route you may avail yourselves of textbooks in the bulkhead lockers and learn some of our language and customs."

Thorgulu, having completed his address, turned to regard us. His sharp features were stern, impersonal, and soldierly. Our capture was no more than military routine. His narrow, topaz eyes shifted from face to face.

He nodded as he appraised me. He cocked his head, squinted, and stroked his chin as he studied Parker. He muttered a few words, and the transmitter on the instrument panel murmured in mechanical accents, "Unusual mental force, blowing out a fuse of the telepathic converter."

Miguel and Pedro next caught his attention. They were in the last paralysis of terror.

"Bardas!" Thorgulu's voice shook the compartment. His shivering attendant stood at attention. "This dark fellow is stupid but he looks edible. Take him to the cooks' galley and tell Shangro to grill him. Serve him with *luka* sauce!"

Bardas saluted. Despite the blistering heat, I shivered, watching a human being sent to the cooks' galley. I remembered the odor of seared flesh that had pervaded the Maku village, and I stood there wavering between horror and a sense of unreality.

Thorgulu watched Bardas cross the compartment toward Miguel. The poor fellow was beyond fright. It was no more than the jungle life: the eater and the eaten. All living things are either one or the other. And Miguel could not have understood the translations of Thorgulu's speech.

"Wait a minute," interposed Thorgulu, cocking an epicurean eye. "Don't grill him. Stuff him with *mongwe* and roast him. Yes, you fool, of course I want him basted with *sherboos.*"

That touched me off. I still clutched my .405 Winchester. I fired from the hip. In that close compartment the heavy rifle roared like a siege gun.

CHAPTER III

CONSIGNMENT FOR SATURN

THORGULU recoiled from the impact of the soft-nosed bullet. I heard the *smack* as the slug spattered to bits against the bulkhead behind him. I jerked another shot, and another, and yet another.

Thorgulu's ten-foot, broad-shouldered bulk crashed against the steel plates, smoke and flame jetting from the bullet holes in his chest.

Thorgulu was amazed and indignant—as a colonel might be if a recruit had spit tobacco juice on his boots. He coughed a wrathful burst of Saturnian oaths that the converter could not render into English.

He snatched the .405 from my grasp. His fist caught me full in the chest. It sent me sprawling into a corner. My shirt was smoldering from the fiery contact.

And as I struggled to my feet, Thorgulu scooped up the shotgun, jerked the rifle from Parker, and stalked out of the compartment.

Bardas caught Miguel by the nape of the neck, and strode after his chief.

"Roast Indian with *sherboos* sauce!" The bulkheads echoed my laugh. I gritted my teeth and tried to pull myself together. My own voice told me how near the ragged edge of sanity I had slipped. Parker, for once, had not reached for his slide rule. He was muttering to himself.

But Parker came out of it, true to type. "Bradley," he said, "those fellows are really taking us to Saturn. I've been watching the altimeter and the instrument that gauges the inflow of air. We're no longer getting terrestrial atmosphere. And a peep out the porthole gave me a hint of our position.

"Furthermore, the pull of gravity is lessening. Sitting on this iron deck isn't as weighty a matter as it was at the start."

"That," I grumbled, "is great. But it doesn't compensate for being served *au gratin.*"

"We're going to interview Saturnian scientists." Parker went on placidly. "We'll have enough in common with them to keep us from the soup kettles. Do you know, I'm beginning to get a few interesting sidelights on this."

I swore under my breath.

"Nothing like calm analysis," continued Parker, "for getting to the bottom of things. This convinces me that we've found a verification of numerous ancient legends; also, a logical explanation of mysterious and unaccountable disappearances. Belated wayfarers snatched by these Saturnians. The anthropological societies would give their right hands to be in on this."

I had my doubts. A right hand wouldn't be so bad, but when it threatened to include spare ribs and cutlets, the learned doctors would hardly be enthusiastic.

~ ~ ~ ~ ~

"YOU'VE heard of Talos, the Brazen Man of Crete," Parker said. "When he saw a stranger land on the island he spouted fire and smoke until his brazen body reached a red heat and then he embraced his victim. For centuries that has been considered a myth. But I'm convinced it was founded on fact.

"The tales must have resulted from an encounter with a Saturnian. And Satan, the fiery angel—isn't that another reflex of a Saturnian visit to earth, millennia ago?

"The salamander is still further confirmation: a creature unaffected by fire. Terrestrial salamanders are so obviously a recent effort to account for an old legend to which these Saturnians give the true background. Furthermore, the tales of fire elementals are now reasonably accounted for. Bradley, this is great!"

"I've lost my appetite, but I could do with a drink," I said. In another hour we'd be dry as mummies. My lips were cracking, and spitting had become a lost art.

I fished for a cigarette; but before I located a match, the bulkhead panel opened. A ruddy Saturnian was bringing us a copper jar of water.

"He must have been listening in on the thought vocalizer," hazarded Parker.

The Saturnian nodded, and made way for another who followed with a tray of small spherical-shaped buns. I was glad there was no meat, and said as much.

The one who brought us water smiled thinly, drew his heavy cloak about him, and said, via the mechanical translator, "Your remarks on Saturnian invasions of the earth are substantially correct. But this is our first big expedition: a survey preliminary to securing a steady source of meat. This necessity is constantly becoming scarce on Saturn."

"If you're so clever, why do you want us to talk to your scientists?" I wondered.

Our jailer replied, "We don't insist. All three of you look like tasty morsels. But the Arch-Mogok, Thorgulu, likes to humor the scientists of Saturn. He'll be decorated for this trip when he returns, and we'll all of us get extra meat rations."

He took no notice of my wry grimace, and continued, "There are beasts very much like yourselves on Titan, our sixth and largest moon. The climate there is just right, but our flocks are terribly depleted; and the resultant inbreeding will eventually cause deterioration of the stock. Choice specimens are already scarce, and those intelligent enough to act as power-plant engineers and agriculturists on Saturn are deplorably rare.

"If this continues, Saturnians will soon have to degrade themselves by manual labor, and eat quadrupeds and reptiles from the smaller moons."

He was distressed at that thought. He sighed a searing blast of fumes reeking with resin and creosote. I caught my breath and turned my head.

"It's awfully embarrassing," he explained. "The food we've had to eat leaves the taint of vegetable distillation products on the breath. The Mogok's sister, Mora-nala, won't look at me any more, now that I'm on a cellulose diet.

"But it'll be different when our colonies and breeding pens are expanded. With sound fellows like you two added to our flock—"

He grinned, snorted a streamer of bluish flame and stamped out of the room. He was shivering. The gust of air from the passage toward which he hurried was like the blast from a Bessemer converter.

~ ~ ~ ~ ~

AS SOON as the jug of water ceased steaming, and the rolls cooled off enough not to blister my fingers, I sampled our fare. The bread, hard enough to try the strongest teeth, seemed a mixture of corn and some leguminous substance, perhaps chick-peas coarsely pulverized.

One finally becomes inured to horror. And it was my turn to ruffle Parker's nerves; so I said with a jauntiness that I by no means felt, "After all, there might be *some* compensation. If the Titanians are at all like us, I'll be interested in looking over the gals. Mutual sympathy, and all that. I sort of go for brunettes, but I'll divide the redheads with you."

Parker turned the color of a cordovan boot. He was no woman-hater, but since those delightful creatures are not susceptible to mathematical analysis, they had never occupied much of his thought.

"Shut up!" he snapped. "I'm working on a scheme to make human flesh inedible. And if you'd get your mind off frivolity, you might take a hand in my calculations. You have a good head, when you care to use it!"

"Sorry, old man," I said. "But I didn't bring my slide rule."

Whereupon I struck light to a cigarette. Life on our world was after all a matter of the eaten versus the eater. If you escaped the larger devourers for three score odd years, you still died of old age, and the ultimate destroyers invaded your coffin. Unless you beat them by cremation.

In the meanwhile, millions of human beings had died as inevitably as had the slaves of Saturn: and not one of that horde had ever set out on the eight hundred and eighty-six-million-mile trip for ringed and many-mooned Saturn.

There was not a fighting chance left. There remained but that of relishing the marvels of whatever was ahead.

"To the ladies of Saturn," I proposed, lowering the level of our jar of water. But Parker was engrossed with his calculations; so I picked a soft spot on the metal deck, tossed Pedro a cigarette, and counseled him to get some sleep.

~　~　~　~　~

FOR two weeks we went flashing through space. We passed red Mars, threaded our way through swarms of asteroids, felt countless meteoric fragments spatter like one-pounder shells against the hull of the space ship.

Had we maintained full speed, the tiniest of those pieces of cosmic substance would have torn through the six-inch steel plates and insulation of the hull.

"And that," explained Thorgulu, who at times braved what to him was the terrific cold of our compartment, "would wipe us out as quickly as the vacuum would disrupt your bodies."

He was now speaking the Saturnian patois used in communicating with slaves. For lack of any other occupation Parker and I devoted ourselves to the work on grammar we found in the locker; thus we understood him well enough. This book was the work of a savant who upon his return from a terrestrial expedition had written in classical Greek and the Saturnian language.

"So you're that sensitive to cold?" Parker's tone was casually curious, but I wonder whether Thorgulu suspected his motive in asking. I could not read Parker's mind, and neither could Thorgulu, now that the thought-converter was no longer needed for communication.

"Surprisingly so," affirmed the Arch-Mogok. "It's our only weakness. Normally, we live about four thousand of your terrestrial years—that is to say, about one hundred and thirty Saturnian years. Low temperatures have a cumulatively destructive effect on our organism. Extremes of cold kill us instantly, just as my breath would shrivel you up like a piece of leather on a red-hot stove."

He chuckled pleasantly. Thorgulu was not such a bad fellow, and surprisingly amiable. His thoughts and sentiments were admirable from a philosophic standpoint, except where the matter of food was concerned. I remarked to that effect, and Thorgulu laughed heartily.

"You fellows are naive! The scholar who wrote that grammar you two have mastered in such a short time left copious notes on the Terrestrial diets, and he commented on the barbarity of the cold-blooded creatures who eat each other without the least scruple. Though your race devours fellow mammals, you have a horror of us. Yet in all our millions of Saturnian years, we've never eaten a fellow fire-breather.

"Terrestrian shepherds," he continued, "call their flocks by name, and then without compunction devour them. And yet you are much more closely akin to your quadrupeds than we fire-breathers are to your race.

"You Terrestrians mature in about a Saturnian year. Those yearlings which we don't eat then become unpalatable before the end or middle of the second year—that is, at the end of forty-odd terrestrial years. And by that time, you begin to develop all manner of ailments. Being cooked at your prime spares you a miserable old age.

"It's quite painless, our process of converting you into food. And it's much more aesthetic, I think, than the processes of decay which prevail on your earth. And finally, the Terrestrians inhabiting the part of the earth on which our first expedition landed cremated their dead—a process quite similar to our digestive processes."

I shuddered at the suave discourse. Thorgulu was perplexed.

"Terrestrians," he observed, "plunge live crustaceans into pots of boiling water, and think only of the savory odors. And they eat very young quadrupeds—an example of childish shiftlessness—whereas we send to the community kitchens only full-grown yearlings who have had a fair chance to enjoy the really pleasant climate of Titan."

That left me groggy. I gulped and reached for a cigarette. Thorgulu's topaz-colored eyes widened as I struck light and exhaled a cloud of smoke.

"By Nagaroth!" he exclaimed. "The scholars will be interested in this example of evolution." Then he frowned and somberly shook his head, "If the news leaks out that you have certain fire-breathing tendencies, those sentimentalists will ban you and your offspring as food. The whole expedition will be a total failure except for the scientists. Is it hereditary?"

I hastily explained that it wasn't. Any other answer might hasten my acquaintance with the Saturnian chef.

~ ~ ~ ~ ~

. . . FINALLY through our porthole we saw Saturn, large as the terrestrial full moon; and Titan, the largest satellite, was just visible to the naked eye.

But our enthusiasm at the magnificent spectacle was dimmed by the thought of Saturnian ovens. Parker and I might not at once become roasts and ragouts, but fellow beings would. So we drank our blood-warm water, chewed our spherical loaves, and cursed each other. Weeks of confinement in a blistering hot house wrenches the stoutest nerves.

The night before we reached Saturn, Parker hurled his slide rule into a corner.

CHAPTER IV

FIND VALENE!

NINE moons whirled across the black sky. The tenth and outermost was far behind us. We were hovering over the flattened polar regions. Beneath us were the three concentric rings, a hundred and seventy-two thousand Terrestrial miles from edge to edge.

As we veered at an angle, we could see light from the distant sun filtering through the fifty-mile thickness of millions of tiny meteoroids and impalpable star dust.

Finally we nosed toward the glowing whiteness of Saturn's surface. We were heading downward at a terrific clip. Though we had confidence in the skipper's skill, we gripped the flanges of the bulkhead members in anticipation of a crash.

Despite the terrific baking of the past six or eight weeks, sweat cropped out of my skin. The skipper must be crazy! He must have lost control.

Parker chuckled, and suddenly relaxed. "The outer gaseous envelope of Saturn," he explained.

An instant later we were whistling through dense vapors that left impenetrable mists on the porthole panes. But those mists presently thinned in the terrific heat of the planet. Despite the insulating space between the inner and outer panes, a scrap of Parker's note book turned brown from contact with the glass.

Thorgulu stalked into the compartment. For the first time he was not shivering.

"Good old Saturn, where a man can breathe without getting icicles on his beard! But what I came to tell you was that we'll have to move you fellows into an insulating cell. In another few moments you'd be cooked."

Bardas, his orderly, ushered us down the stifling passageway. In the next compartment were huge jars of clear glass. To the cover of each were attached copper tubes and cables leading from an instrument panel attached by metal rivets to the inner surface of the jar. The outer terminals of the tubes and cables led to the air conditioning and other equipment fixed to the wheel-mounted pedestals on which the jars were mounted.

"The controls," explained Thorgulu as block and tackle hoisted us into position, "are automatic, for the sake of the more stupid specimens. But you two can use the manual controls and get greater comfort."

As the lid was clamped down over my jar, I saw the captives from the Maku Indian village being hoisted into containers further down the passage. The preparations for our safety had scarcely been completed when I felt the gradual deceleration of the space ship. Being in line with a porthole, I got a preliminary glimpse of the Saturnian landscape.

~ ~ ~ ~ ~

WE WERE approaching a city of uncounted domes and hexagonal pinnacles imposed upon polygonal bulks whose metallic surfaces glowed and flamed in the steaming atmosphere.

I caught passing glimpses of monstrous and grotesque vegetation: a fantastic blend of orchid and cactus with the rigidity of a petrified forest. The colors were of spectral intensity, and the luster distinctly mineral.

As we swung toward a clearing, I had a momentary view of terrific crags, and volcanoes from whose craters rose higher and newer cones, smoking and belching forth flame and incandescent lava. Only a glimpse, but it was a peep into uttermost hell. Then the walls of the Saturnian capital cut off my view.

We had settled in the center of a vast plaza. Hordes of Saturnian Satans were drawn up in military formation.

Before I could half view the spectacle, Thorgulu gestured. A squad of his subordinates began rolling our jars toward the loading hatch. It swung open as we approached it. In a moment we were being wheeled down a ramp toward the gleaming tiles of a lordly square.

We were pushed across the plaza and toward the archway of the building which commanded the parade ground. Saturnians presented arms as the Arch Mogok, leading the procession, cleared the threshold. He led the way down the red glow of a vaulted passage, and thence into a vast hall whose ceiling was an ellipsoidal dome.

The doors were swung shut behind us. An attendant handed Thorgulu his cape and gauntlets. Others opened valves, and adjusted the controls on a panel near the door-jamb.

From another door came a file of Saturnians dressed as Thorgulu was. Their faces were wrinkled. Instead of rich red, theirs were a dull plum color; and they walked with halting strides. They were the savants, whose dying vitality was betokened by their subdued coloring.

They gathered around as our jars were uncapped. Chain hoists lifted us from our jars and into the steaming air which chilled the bones of all but hardy Thorgulu.

~ ~ ~ ~ ~

WE WERE lined up before the board of savants. They inspected us, one by one. They drew to one side to confer; and my knowledge of the slave patois made their learned diction fairly intelligible.

Thorgulu, moreover, spoke with the directness of a soldier; so the learned fellows had to tolerate his lack of culture and use somewhat elementary language.

"These dark specimens," said Thorgulu, "are insufferably stupid. And while they look edible, the flavor is distinctly second-rate."

Then, indicating Pedro, he continued, "This is another interesting variation; but I doubt if Your Excellencies will find him suitable. The other two, however, should go to the farm."

The scientists conferred for a moment. They acquainted Thorgulu with their decision. He rasped an order. A file of guardsmen advanced from the smoking wall against which they had huddled to get a bit of warmth, seized Pedro and the screaming Indians, and marched toward a door at the far end of the hall.

I caught a glimpse of what was beyond that door. Only a glimpse, but I barely kept my stomach under control. The fumes of roasting flesh billowed from the lurid glare of grills. Saturnians in heavy aprons scurried from carving tables to great copper kettles. I saw on the chopping block evidence of Thorgulu's contention that only prime yearlings were served.

Then the doors closed on the struggling Indians and the Saturnian kitchen.

"Ho, there, Bardas! Stuff these back into the insulated jars and ship them to Titan—certainly, you oaf! Give them double rations, and some books to read on the way. And if any of you poke them with your fingers to see if they burn easily, I'll have you dumped into the ice caps of Japetus!"

Bardas blinked and saluted. Thorgulu was not to be annoyed with foolish questions. But the Mogok had a warm heart, and that is no play on words. As we were hoisted into our insulated jars, he said in a gruff, not unkindly voice, "If you fellows make good in the breeding pens, you may be pensioned instead of being sent to the ovens when the Titanians—"

And the closing of the lid cut off his faintly consoling assurance.

~ ~ ~ ~ ~

ONCE our insulated jars were in the hold of the *Lumari,* one of the freighters that ply between Titan and Saturn, we were released in one of the refrigerating compartments.

Parker and I, once we had shaken off the horror of our glimpse of the kitchens in the left wing of the Saturnian palace, stepped to the porthole to view the moon-clustered sky; but rushing through space at around fifty thousand miles an hour, the cruising speed of the *Lumari,* we lost the effect of watching the Saturnian satellites moving across the heavens at nearly five times the apparent speed of the Terrestrial moon.

But Mimas, Enceladus, and Tethus, whirling about their parent planet at rates varying from fifteen to thirty times that of Luna about the Earth, progressed from one phase to the next so rapidly that we could see the change as we watched them rise.

Omar, I reflected, would have had the devil's own time of it, figuring just which was the *moon of my delight.* He'd have had to give some Persian beauty an astronomical chart to consult as she listened to his verses.

Parker, however, had to put a damper on that fancy.

"Omar," he grumbled, "would have been too busy patching leaks in his asbestos jacket to bother with verses. Moreover you couldn't see a damn one of those moons through the Saturnian vapor blanket."

We were heading for Titan at a rate which would make our trip last something like sixteen hours, not allowing for having to swing wide of our course to avoid the gravitational fields of intervening satellites, and those of half a dozen minor moons too small to be picked up by Terrestrial telescopes.

Our sun, eight hundred and eighty-six million miles distant, was a tiny speck of light in the blackness of space. Titan, Parker estimated, would get scarcely more than one percent of the solar radiation received by the earth.

We pictured a sunless globe about half as large again as the Terrestrial moon, and illuminated mainly by the reflection from the cloud stratum of Saturn. That monstrous bulk, viewed from Titan, would have twelve times the apparent size of the Earth moon we might never again see stealing over the crest of distant hills, or silvering a broad path on an earthly ocean.

But our speculations were checked when, some fifteen hours later, we decelerated as we approached the stratosphere of Titan. Our goal was a circle of apparently vitreous substance which glowed phosphorescently.

When we flattened out to land in the plain that surrounded the circle, we noted that it was made up of domes of glass, which surmounted heavily buttressed walls of masonry.

It was night on Titan. Like our own Luna, Saturn's chief satellite revolved on its own axis in exactly the same time required for a circuit of its parent planet. Thus our days and nights would each be somewhat longer than a terrestrial week.

Our captors donned heavily insulated space suits, flung open the loading ports, and hustled us down the gangplank.

The Titanian chill bit us to the bone before we could reach the airlock which opened into the circumvallation of what we assumed was the capital of the satellite. The atmosphere of our new home, while thin, seemed quite earthly except for a certain pungent tang.

~ ~ ~ ~ ~

WHEN the gates of Vallanu closed behind us, we were in a warm, thick atmosphere illuminated by the phosphorescence of the foliage that lined the walks, and stood in pots aligned on the cornice of the wall.

Several miles nearer the center of this hothouse world, we saw the granite bulk of the administration building, a miniature of the one in the Saturnian capital. Far beyond our destination were spectrally glowing fields that outreached our range of vision.

It was uncanny, this hothouse which covered uncounted square miles of Titan's surface; but before I could comment to Parker, we saw that the *Lumari* would return to Saturn with meat for the palace kitchens.

Vermillion-skinned Satans herded a group of Titanians down the avenue at our left. They seemed indifferent to their doom. I marveled at the stoicism of those stalwart men and lovely women.

Then I remembered that since time immemorial, Titanians in their prime had been marched to the space ships. The prospect had through the centuries become no more awful than the thought of natural death is to us on earth.

"They'll bake or stew the tougher ones—only tender meat for the grill."

A lovely, copper-haired woman in a pale blue smock regarded me with wide violet eyes. I knew that she was marveling at my outlandish costume and the horror that must have branded my face. She nudged the man at her side, whispered a few words. Then she again caught my eye, smiled, and made a gesture of reassurance and farewell.

"Move along!" snapped the Saturnian sentry, prodding me lightly with his goad. I moved; but I looked back. The others were eyeing Parker and me. They were all perplexed at the sight of us. The copper-haired woman bounded from the edge of the herd. She was at my side before their herdsman or our guards could block the move. Her arm closed about my neck and she whispered in the now familiar patois, *"Find Valene—Valene—"*

Even in that dome of horror I thrilled at the contact of flesh destined for the grill. But the fleeting touch of her lips against my cheek was terminated by the gloved hand of the sentry. He jerked her aside. The herdsman prodded her back into the flock.

Humanity marching to the ovens was no longer an abstraction. That last sweetly somber smile as she passed out of sight was like nails driven through my brain. As I staggered up the stairs to the entrance of the administration building, I wondered who or what *Valene* might be. A place, a person, a chemical—what?

And why that eager note in her voice, that momentary gleam of her eyes? That flame from the ashes of almost extinguished emotion?

"Halt!" commanded the guard.

~ ~ ~ ~ ~

WE WERE in front of a desk fashioned of silver-bluish metal. The heavily muffled Saturnian shook aside the upraised collar of his jacket, consulted our papers—noninflammable, flexible substance similar to asbestos, I later learned—and said:

"Because of the labor shortage, you two will divide your time between the breeding pens and the tasks of the other cattle.

"You, Parker, will serve in the engine-room of the *Karamanu*. Between cruises you will devote a suitable portion of your time to the female Titanians we will assign you. We will aim to accommodate your personal tastes as much as practicable.

"You will therefore between watches aboard ship prepare a set of blueprints and specifications clearly defining your preferences as to weight, color, curvature, and whatever other features you may think important."

Without waiting for Parker to catch his breath, the Saturnian personnel manager turned to me: "You, Bradley, seem to be too scatter-brained for the hazards of spatial navigation. Your levity and unscientific attitude compel me to assign you to agricultural work. And if you don't tend to business, you go to the subterranean power vaults.

"You, like Parker, will likewise submit a set of specifications—"

"Stop that gang boarding the *Lumari!*" I interrupted. "Hold out the red-haired one with the violet—"

"Idiot!" barked the Saturnian. "If you think you can save a prime yearling from the grill, your intelligence rating was grossly exaggerated!"

The accumulated madness of that cruise came to the surface. I leaped forward, hunched my shoulder under the edge of the desk, and heaved. It toppled over, sending the personnel manager and his chair crashing to the floor.

The guard, caught flatfooted by the unheard-of resistance, lost a split second in swinging at my head with his goad. As I ducked the delayed blow, I made a dive for the weapon that had clattered from the manager's holster and skated across the tiled floor. I evaded his leap, snatched and leveled the weapon.

I jerked the trigger. The concussion nearly tore the weapon from my grasp. The guard yelled and dropped to the floor, wrapping his membranous wings about him as if for protection.

Then I saw where my missile had landed: a chunk of white, frosty substance clung to the further cornice. There was a perceptible chill in the air. The intense cold of the projectile was condensing the moisture of the warm, humid atmosphere. I whipped the weapon into line, and fired.

The blast caught the guard as he recovered and tried to close in. I heard a terrific sizzling, and saw him turning lead color. The manager, untangling himself from his chair, jerked his second pistol from its holster. A blast of stinging cold screamed past my cheek.

And then I caught him squarely in the stomach. He doubled in the middle. For an instant he flailed and threshed in the clouds of vapor that billowed about him. Then he slumped to the tiles.

~ ~ ~ ~ ~

THERE was a pattering of webbed feet, hoarse yells, the clank of accoutrements. A squad of Saturnians charged from the airlock. The gates, however, were closed. There was no chance to break through and capture the ship bound for the ovens.

I slammed the front door of the administration building and slipped the bolt, just as the Saturnians crashed headlong against it.

"Let's go!" I yelled to Parker as I whirled toward a passage leading to the rear.

"What's the use?" he demanded. "You'll get much further by headwork than this sort of foolishness."

The door was bulging inward as the Saturnians massed forces and again charged it.

"You blockhead," I shouted, "you can suit yourself. I'm going!"

I cleared the room at a bound. Gravitation on Titan is such that my two hundred terrestrial pounds were about thirty-three on this small sphere. The Saturnians piled headlong into the office as I cleared the further door jamb.

Before they could collect themselves, I had the ice projector, hosing them with blasts of interstellar frost. They were armed only with staves; frost pistols, I later learned, were carried only by military Saturnians and by officials. Cattle guards had only their searing breath and their goads.

And their flaming breath could not carry across the hall I had cleared in three leaps. Icicles were already hanging from the eaves. But my pistol was empty, and a pair of frost-bitten Saturnians scrambled from the steaming heap that now hid the manager's desk. One began coughing flame, and as he revived, he reached for his goad.

I did not wait for him to get his joints warmed up. There was no chance of saving the copper-haired girl; I heard the whirr and drone of the *Lumari's* engines overhead. But I could dive into the dim depths of this monstrous hothouse. If Parker preferred strategy, all power to Parker!

It was night on Titan, and the Saturnians were hugging the furnaces in their barracks. I tore down an endless hall, and plunged into the further shadows as the first of the surviving sentries thawed out enough to bawl for reinforcements.

CHAPTER V

PARKER LEARNS THE ROPES

At this point in the story the paths of our two Terrestrians diverge; and in order that the reader may keep track of both, the editors have considered it necessary to leave Bradley's personal account. For a time, then, we shall devote ourselves to the story of what happened to Parker, letting Bradley himself pick up his own experiences later.

~ ~ ~ ~ ~

AS THE Saturnian guards recovered from the blasting administered by Kent Bradley's awkwardly directed frost barrage, they saw no reason for pursuit. They knew that he could not escape from the hermetically sealed enclosure of Vallanu.

Recalcitrant cattle, they reflected with Saturnian philosophy, inevitably reach the ovens before they become too tough; so why be unduly concerned?

They found John Parker huddled near a rapidly melting pyramid of frost. They shuddered, and routed out the assistant personnel manager. With sulphurous Saturnian curses, he tore himself away from his radiant heater, wrapped his insulating jacket tightly about him, and stepped into the office.

"This fellow seems docile enough," he observed, scrutinizing Parker's slightly stooped shoulders, thin face, and studious expression. "Take him to the engine room of the *Karamanu.* And tell the commander—"

He was interrupted by the whirring of a buzzer. He stepped to the extension visiphone, saluted as he recognized the stern face of the Arch-Mogok, Thorgulu, phoning from Saturn.

"Keep a close watch on those Terrestrians," began Thorgulu. And then in the screen of the visiphone he saw Parker and the wreckage of the office. For a moment the room shook with Saturnian wrath that came across seven hundred thousand miles of space.

Finally Thorgulu became articulate. He demanded and received an explanation. He commanded, "You chair-polishing oafs have no need of strutting side arms anyway! Publish an order that no official will wear frost projectors. Put them in storage. And the same applies to the sidearms of transport commanders.

"Another outbreak like this, and I'll give you a seven-stage frosting, thaw you out, and then kick you off the poop deck of the flagship. Just to give you a taste of real cold!"

The visiphone screen darkened as Thorgulu broke connection. Karadis saluted just for good measure, swore at the guards, and turned back to the instrument to obey the Arch-Mogok's orders.

The guards donned a second insulated jacket and hustled Parker to the main entrance, where they halted while awaiting the arrival of a deputy gate keeper.

Parker watched him jab one button after another of the thirty-six that formed the combination of the gate. As he touched the last one, the massive valves swung open. They prodded Parker into the airlock which kept the chill of Titanian night from invading the sealed city. The process was repeated, and the outer valve lifted like a portcullis.

"What are we going to tell the commander about this fellow?" wondered one of the guards as they plunged into the frosty blackness and headed for the lights of the hangar which loomed up from the far side of the landing field.

"To the everlasting ice pits with Karadis!" growled his fellow. "Let the commander figure that out. If Thorgulu doesn't tend to him first."

~ ~ ~ ~ ~

STAMPING and shivering, they hammered for admittance to the hangar. Again they passed through airlocks. By the greenish glow of glass tubes filled with the sap of the phosphorescent *lukâri* plant, Parker saw a score of space transports dry-docked for overhauling.

Saturnians stood guard. They watched the thousand or more Titanian slaves cleaning exhaust flues, polishing corroded hull plates, replacing cracked porthole covers, hurrying about with buckets of paint, power drills, and riveting hammers.

At the further side of the hangar was a group of instrument makers, busily checking gauges and indicators that had become inaccurate from the stresses of high-speed flight.

But for the horror that ate at Parker, he would have been enthusiastic at the prospect of taking part in technical work utterly unknown on earth. Terrestrial developments, while not a great deal less advanced—save in actual space flying— had branched in other directions.

The workers, Parker observed, were Titanian men and women, all of them younger than the ill-fated yearlings who had that evening been embarked for the Saturnian ovens. They wore soft leather boots and gray smocks.

Their features, fine and regular, were singularly alike in expression. This Parker took to be one of the evidences of the inbreeding which had caused the savants of Saturn such concern.

Here and there, however, were piquant diversions from type; an occasional milk-white skin and red or pale gold hair

that strikingly stood out from the predominating olive com-
plexion.

The men wore their hair cut square on line with the ear
lobes. The coiffure of the women was similar to that of the
Terrestrial Burmese: coiled and pyramidally arranged on the
top of the head, and occasionally adorned with glistening
combs.

The guards halted and saluted Quman, the commander of
the *Karamanu.* He stroked his bristling red beard, eyed
Parker from head to foot, and demanded, "What are those
odd devices on your eyes?"

Parker took off his horn-rimmed spectacles and explained,
"They give me unusual sharpness of vision."

He glanced about, caught a glimpse of a placard on the
distant wall of the hangar. With his spectacles he could just
contrive to read the large characters of the heading. These
were the first words of the standard text enjoining Saturnians
against undue roughness in handling valuable livestock.

The fine print was utterly beyond the sharpest vision, but
Parker recited from memory. It never occurred to Quman
that a newly arrived captive would have memorized the text
en route.

"By the horns of Nagaroth!" he roared. "Letter perfect,
and the best man of my crew couldn't read at half that distance! Take him to the navigating compartment. You ought
to be able to dodge uncharted satellites. You'd better, or I'll
know you've been asleep at your post!

"Take him away and—certainly, whom do you think I'd
have break him in but Shadra?"

~ ~ ~ ~ ~

THE guards prodded Parker toward the gangplank of the
Karamanu. As he set foot on the ramp, Quman roared, "Hey,
you, Terrestrian! If you can get along with that tow-headed
female, you might both beat the ovens. She's got eyes nearly
as sharp as yours, and we need a good breed of navigators."

Parker was unscientific enough to borrow as much as he could recollect of Bradley's profanity. A female navigator.

Some wench with a face like a battle ax and a voice like a fog-horn. Her eyesight kept her from the ovens.

"Move on!" barked the guard; and his goad, catching Parker just south of his belt, sent him diving headlong into the navigating compartment.

Parker was redder than a Saturnian oven when he clambered to his feet and saw who was laughing at him. She was tall and well-proportioned, with the merest hint of squareness in shoulders and chin—a warning hint, as Parker should have noticed. Not beautiful, no—not exactly; but in her profound blue eyes there was a quick intelligence that acted on Parker very strangely indeed. He was irritated by this unusual circumstance—and by the laughter that was now in those eyes.

"Who the hell are you?" he snapped. Then he repeated it in slave patois.

Her wide, generous mouth, pleasantly upturned a moment before, now became straight—but with a slight, hardly-suppressed twitching in one corner. "I'm Shadra, Prince Charming. Your new admirer. What are those things on your eyes?"

Without bothering to wait for an answer, she took the spectacles off his nose, glanced at the silvered visiphone screen, and grimaced; then handed them back with a shrug. "They make me look almost as funny as you do."

"Shut up," growled Parker, "and show me how you navigate this cruiser."

"In words of one syllable, I suppose. All right, Genius—watch closely."

~ ~ ~ ~ ~

SHADRA, he quickly decided, knew her business. Her explanations kept him on his toes. Spatial navigation required a mental gymnast as well as hair-trigger nerves and perfect coordination.

She had scarcely completed her remarks—a matter of several hours—when a siren screamed.

"What the devil?"

"Getting ready to shove off," said Shadra. "The inspectors have found everything in order. Bound for Saturn—"

Parker groaned. "Do you mean we'll have to haul a lot of fellow humans to the ovens?"

"You'll get used to it," Shadra told him. "It's not a bad life. They try to keep us contented so we'll not lose weight. Though I think I'll dodge the ovens. Navigation is a bit of a strain, and I'm considerably underweight—"

Parker's approving glance contradicted Shadra's explanatory gesture, which was intended to indicate just where and how much the lack was. For the life of him, he couldn't see anything wrong with the structure enclosed by her pastel green smock.

"Follow me around," she directed, "and watch me handle the observing instruments when we get under way."

The ports were being locked, cables fastened, and the *Karamanu* towed from the hangar and into the Titanian gloom.

They were not, as Shadra had expected, to take on a cargo of slaves. The port captain, after having handed the skipper his orders, supplemented them by a few words of instruction. These, coming in on the visiphone in the navigation compartment, told Shadra and Parker that they were to hasten out to rescue the crew of a transport which was disabled.

Parker was wrestling with more details than he could grasp; yet as he followed Shadra from one panel to the next, he contrived to interpolate between her observations and signals to the bridge, "Look here! I thought you were a navigator."

"I am," she said as her sharp eyes and alert fingers automatically shifted from instrument to signaling mechanism. "While the skipper actually has the helm, I'm working the integrator that combines all the dial readings into single code-expressions. The skipper recognizes them as indicating a certain setting of the controls. He of course in his turn signals to the engine room for the proper speed control.

"While you can navigate these ships through outer space without such intricate calculations, the presence of so many satellites and satelloids would slow us down to a thousand miles an hour. Watch . . ."

Parker did his best to follow the dervish dance of the dials that indicated ether-drift, velocity, gravitational influence of the nearest six satellites, and the progress of Saturn along its orbit. Presently he began to catch the point of Shadra's integrating device.

"Nothing more than an overgrown slide rule," he decided. "Just a lot more complex, and power driven."

"How you do catch on." Shadra was laughing at him again. Then her expression changed; she cleared the integrator, reset, and signaled a correction.

"One more like that, and we'd have been pulled off our course!"

"The skipper must trust you pretty far," said Parker.

"He's safe enough. Cracking up would be no more fun for me than for the crew."

"What," he whispered in her ear, "makes these Saturnians function? Is there anything besides intense cold that puts them out of action?"

She shook her head.

"If there is, I've never heard of it. Unless they fell into a heap of something that robbed them of their oxygen-absorbing power. In which case their temperature would drop and—"

~ ~ ~ ~ ~

BUT Parker had heard enough. Leaving Shadra to her work, he began a careful inspection of the navigation compartment.

From there he went to the machine shop where a crew of Saturnian mechanics welded a fractured inductor shaft for one of the generators which produced the magnetic impulse to hold the ship in space while the backlash of the atomic disintegrators gave it headway.

They were shaping a mould about the aligned ends of the broken shaft. That done, they poured a drum of silvery-greenish, metallic powder into the gap. The foreman, after inspecting the job, ordered Parker to the further bulkhead. Then he touched off the powder in the mould.

Something like thermite, Parker decided, flinging up his forearm to protect his eyes from the terrific glare and spatter of incandescent metal. He glanced at a dial and saw that the oxygen content of the compartment had dropped many points. Then he heard the hissing as the foreman cracked a valve and admitted enough gas to restore equilibrium.

While waiting for the welded joint to solidify, the Saturnians went to the engine-room. Parker, however, did not follow them. He loaded his pockets with the greenish welding powder. The stuff functioned only because of its greediness for oxygen. And that, coupled with Shadra's remarks, was food for speculation.

If you dumped a load of this compound on one of our fiery friends, he pondered as he returned to the navigation compartment, it might soak up every atom of oxygen in his organism. And though the compound would burst into flames, the insides of Mr. Saturnian would suffocate. . . .

Now if that idiot of a Bradley had stayed around instead of getting excited about one more or less red-headed woman, we might start something.

The gleam in Parker's somewhat owlish eyes was one seldom seen in scientific circles.

CHAPTER VI

RUNAWAY SHIP

AFTER six hours of cruising, the *Karamanu* began decelerating. "We're approaching the crippled transport," said Shadra. "It'll be pitching from either drift. Their stabilizers can't keep it under control, now that the impulsion engines are out of action. Watch for sharp turns, or you'll be piled up against a bulkhead."

"What will they do?" asked Parker. "Repair the engines, or tow the ship back to Titan?"

But before Shadra could suggest the skipper's probable decision, the radio-visiphone interrupted: *"Karamanu,* ahoy! Prepare to trans-ship our crew. Starboard bulkheads disintegrating. Oxidation rapidly getting out of control. Skipper disabled. Nugarat, second in command, taking charge."

"Some of the radioactive fuel must have leaked out of the disintegrators," Shadra explained, "and the bulkheads are crumbling. And that means finish for the crew if a hull plate gives way under the pressure."

"How do they trans-ship?" said Parker.

Shadra wondered at the tensity of his voice. She had never heard the like among the Titanians. They had for unaccounted generations been resigned to slavery and the ovens.

"Maneuver the *Karamanu* alongside, put a gasket between their loading ports, then lash the two ships together and open the hatches. If the transport is in bad shape, they'll probably cut the cables and abandon it in space. It'll disintegrate."

Parker pressed a signal button of the visiphone that interconnected the compartments of the *Karamanu.* He saw Saturnians donning space suits, and heard the second in command rasping orders. He broke connection and cut in on the artificer's compartment. Titanian slaves were breaking out space suits.

Parker's face hardened.

"I'm going to try it!" he muttered in English. Shadra did not understand, but she sensed his sudden resolve, and regarded him with narrowed eyes. They were now close to the disabled transport. The skipper was maneuvering the *Karamanu* by direct observation.

"What's eating you?" Shadra demanded. At this moment the ship, sharply responding to the helm, flung her against Parker; she straightened at once. "Well, what?"

"Capture this boat!" he whispered. "With all the crew diving for space suits, they're going to be busy outside. Can you drive it from this compartment?"

"No. Not as long as the skipper is at the bridge," replied Shadra. "And don't be an idiot."

"Stand by!" said Parker. "I'm starting a circus."

~ ~ ~ ~ ~

HE DASHED down the passageway toward the artificer's compartment, struggled into a space suit, and joined the squad of Titanians as they stood by to swarm through the hatch to lash the ships together.

They were sturdy, intelligent looking fellows; but Parker feared that too many generations of slavery had robbed them of the nerve to venture all on a single throw. He kept his counsel.

The space suits were something like a Terrestrial diver's outfit, except that there was a self-contained air supply, there were magnetic anchors to keep the wearer from slipping off the outside of the hull.

Once Parker donned the suit, he was not to be distinguished from his fellow slaves. The Saturnian second mate did not even count that section of the crew. The transport was slowly being gutted by the disintegration of the leaking radioactive compounds. Both crew and slaves were in peril.

Parker followed his fellows out the hatchway and into the absolute zero of space. Hanging by his magnetic anchors, he helped pay out the cables from the lockers, and stood by to leap to the deck of the transport when the *Karamanu* was maneuvered into position.

A Titanian stood by with a broad-bladed ax, ready to cut the cables when the crew and as much as possible of the cargo had been trans-shipped. Some of the plates of the transport glowed dull red, and from many of its portholes came the greenish glow that was spreading from one compartment to the next. Luminous fumes were leaking from seams sprung by the expansion of the plates.

Saturnian officers and men made gestured signals as they supervised the lashing. Elastic gaskets were dropped into position. A windlass took up the cables. And a cold sweat cropped from every pore of Parker's body. The odds were insane; but a surprise move might give him enough of a start.

Directly below him was the bridge. Through the portholes of the housing he saw Quman, the skipper, manipulate the controls as the winches took up the cable slack. A Saturnian armed with a flue cleaner was jamming the gasket into place about the hatchway flange.

Once the hatches were butted together and sealed against the vacuum and cold of outer space, Parker's chance would vanish.

Shadra was expecting something—but whatever Parker did would catch her off guard. For an instant longer he watched Quman. Direct navigation seemed simple as operating the throttle of a locomotive or the joystick of those archaic airplanes on earth.

Parker edged over to the Titanian who had the broad-bladed ax. The *Karamanu's* tail swung a foot closer.

Parker snatched the ax. Swinging it with both hands, he cut half through the flexible metallic cable. The Saturnian mate startled by the sharp impact, whirled from the crew that manned the cables. For an instant he stared, perplexed by the variation from the often-rehearsed drill.

Then he saw Parker's ax rise and drive home. Sparks showered as it sheared the cable and bounded back from the tempered plates of the deck. He leaped forward, lashing out with the twelve-foot flue cleaner.

Parker ducked the blow, saw the sudden spurt of flame from the exhaust port of the Saturnian's space suit, and sank to one knee. The Saturnian mate, cursing a jet of fire, flashed past. Parker's ax licked out.

~ ~ ~ ~ ~

THE sharp blade sheared a long slash in the Saturnian's armor. Parker was enveloped in the backlash of white-hot gas expanding into the frosty vacuum. A blinding haze of flame enveloped him. He felt the contraction of his suit as it crinkled in the fiery blast.

Through the hell-mist he saw figures leaping about the deck. A pair of Saturnians, armed with grappling hooks, bounded toward him.

Others, panic-stricken at the unexpected surge of flame from the punctured space suit, were diving for the after hatch. They thought that the transport would at any instant explode.

Parker parried the grappling hook of the foremost Saturnian, swung with his ax, and dropped the second stumbling across the deck. Then, energizing his magnetic anchors, he leaned back as if from a trapeze and drove his ax against a porthole glass of the bridge housing.

The heavy plate spattered to shards. Another blow. The inner plate was knocked in fragments as the skipper, hearing the first impact, left his controls to leap to the port.

A jet of flame roared from his mouth and ears and nostrils as the air of the bridge house was sucked into the vacuum of space. For an age-long instant Parker clung to the plates of the bridge housing, wondering whether the rush of gas would drag him into the void or burn his insulated suit.

A grappling hook clutched his arm. He lashed out with his ax, sheared the rod, and plunged headlong into the bridge house. The commander, first distended by the sudden expansion of gas, had flattened into a fuming heap.

Parker snatched the throttle lever and jammed it to down. The *Karamanu* lurched from the blast of power, jerked clear of the severed cable, and plunged into space.

As he bore down on the helm, Parker glanced at the visiphone. He saw Shadra at her instrument panels, saw her lips move, but could not hear a word she said. Then he understood her gesture, and leaned down until his head touched the transmitter.

"Swing to the starboard, idiot," she screamed. "Full speed ahead, before the transport explodes! I've locked the after bulkhead; the whole crew is caged there—those that weren't jerked from the deck when you jammed home the throttle!"

~ ~ ~ ~ ~

SHE faded from the visiphone. Parker, tense and trembling, held his course. He cut in station after station of the visiphone, viewing the compartments of his stolen craft. In one, a handful of Saturnians dashed down a passageway toward the engine room. A chill shot down his spine.

Then he saw the compartment door slide into place, blocking the rush to disable the power plant. Shadra had given him another moment of respite.

Presently she returned to the navigation compartment. She wore a space suit, and was dragging after her an insulated cable to which was attached a welding device. She flung open the door that separated the navigating compartment from the bridge, and handed Parker the electrode and a plate of metal.

He understood her gesture. As she held the controls, he sealed the porthole.

That task completed, Shadra opened the air valve. When full pressure was built up in both compartments, she stripped off her space suit and took the wheel. Then—and only then—she drew a long breath, let it out slowly, and turned on Parker with a tight little grin:

"Impulsive fellows, you Terrestrians. Want to get us blown out of the Cosmos?" She shrugged and went on before he had a chance to answer. "Well, it's ours—until they get organized and drill through the compartment locks."

"Think nothing of it," was Parker's grim retort as he slid aside the badly pitted port of his helmet. "You hold the course while I give our Saturnian friends their chance to surrender."

Shadra, giving close attention to the wheel, favored him with a polite snicker. "My, but you make things simple! What if they don't *want* to surrender?"

"An experiment," Parker said imperturbably. "You wouldn't understand."

He made his voice sound bored, but patient: "I take a pocketful of this thermite powder, burn a hole through the hatchway of their compartment, and let them see whether they can break out of their prison before the air supply of their space suits gives out."

"Hmmm. Interesting, I'm sure. So then what?"

"Back to Terra," said Parker, "to warn the governments of the proposed Saturnian raids. To equip a counter-attack that will clear every Saturnian from the face of Titan. I wish to Heaven Bradley hadn't dashed off like a madman—"

"Listen, idiot!" Shadra's cry cut piercingly through Parker's remark.

And then he heard the broadcast from the radio-visiphone. The commander of the doomed transport, still at the bridge, was reporting the plight of the *Karamanu!* Space cruisers, patrolling the satellite belt, were answering his frantic calls for help.

CHAPTER VII

BRADLEY RESUMES HIS STORY

AS I CLEARED the back door of the administration building and plunged into shadows which were broken only by the phosphorescent dome lights of the hothouse, I realized that there was no pursuit. This, however, convinced me that the Saturnians were so certain of my ultimate capture that they had not bothered to turn out the guard.

Parker was right in preferring strategy to crack-brained moves. Here I was an outlaw, without any chance of co-operating with Parker in a well organized escape. Not so good; but it was too late to go back and apologize

That eerie alternation of black shadows and wavering, greenish glow was oppressive. Tall fungoid growths lined the broad avenue that wound endlessly into the Titanian night. Being conspicuous in the roadway was preferable to plunging into that close-packed vegetation.

It reminded me of an insane cross between a tropical jungle and the Arizona deserts: the shapes were like monstrous *sahuraos,* lifting menacing arms not from clean sand, but out of spongy humus that exhaled pungent vapors. Among the taller fungi was a tangle of vines which bore gourd-like fruit. Some were shaped like serpents, others oddly resembled crustaceans; and all were of repulsively reptilian hues.

And then the avenue forked, each branch losing itself in darkness. For a moment there seemed no choice, until—just off the paving of the left fork—I saw the imprint of a human foot. Some Titanian had walked in the direction of headquarters.

Half a dozen yards further I noted another print, and on the paving were bits of fresh mud. Directly beneath the circle of illumination cast by a dome light I distinguished the trace of a Saturnian webbed foot. The convoy of slaves bound for the ovens had marched up this road.

That made my choice. The red-haired girl who had inspired my futile break had spoken of *Valene.* My best chance of finding this *Valene*—whether person, place, or substance—would be to backtrack on the trail of the Titanian slaves.

So I proceeded to do that, as rapidly as possible.

Far ahead, the phosphorescence became more intense. The fungoid growths no longer lined the path. After an hour's march, I saw signs of cultivated soil, neatly checked off by dikes, and partially submerged in water. Narrow dirt roads branched from the paved avenue.

In the quivering haze of light I saw clusters of low, dome-like objects that resembled overgrown beehives. Then came the smell of smoke from a wood fire, and the faint murmur of voices.

~ ~ ~ ~ ~

TO THE right was a towering hexagonal structure of bluish white metal. I ducked into the first dirt road in the opposite direction. That metallic bulk reminded me entirely too much of the headquarters building.

As I approached the nearest group of what resembled hay-cocks, I saw that they were surrounded by a palisade of dried fungus stalks lashed together with lianas, both of which probably came from the jungle that I had passed early in my flight.

I crept up to the stockade and peeped between the stakes. A group of Titanians were clustered about a fire in the center of the enclosure. Two of the group were men about my own age; the others were women and children.

Two kettles hung over a smoldering fire. The fumes were savory; and after that interminable diet of luke-warm water and bullet-hard spheres of bread, I realized that a square meal would be worth any risk.

"We'll be next," someone said.

"They took forty from *Annilu,*" another answered. "Don't be so gloomy about it, Hetro; we may not be next, after all . . ."

The kettles were removed from the crude wooden cranes. A man and six women gathered about each of the messes of stew. They were plump, well fed, and in a somber way con-tented enough. They spoke of the fields they were tilling; they gossiped about the inhabitants of the neighboring com-pounds, complained about the overseers—arrogant fellows exempt from the ovens.

These were the noncommissioned officers of the Satur-nian lords. Trusties, you might say, or straw bosses, who for personal exemption had become more severe than the man-eating Saturnians. Not much different, after all, from the setup that existed on Terra, some eight hundred million miles away.

And that was a warning hint; running into an overseer would be the height of bad luck. Those zealous fellows would turn me in in an instant.

This pause for stew, I gathered, was to break the day's work in the fields. Day, however, was on this gloomy satellite no more than an arbitrary time division: for the astronomical day of Titan was the equal of a terrestrial week.

The fungoid growths were stimulated by the dome lights. Shifts of Titanians were constantly at work, tilling the fields and working the factories which I inferred must lie further to the left. Day and night, moreover, would show little difference in temperature, since the radiation from the distant sun was trifling. The gigantic disc of Saturn was spectacular in its march across the sky, but it would have little effect on vegetable or animal life as we know them on earth.

This was no place to ask for food. These Titanians, debating as to the next draft for the Saturnian ovens, might not be such reliable hosts. Betraying me could gain them days of grace.

I marched on, skirting other compounds, hearing the "noonday" chatter of other two-family stockades. Men, it seemed, were in the minority—in the ratio of one to five or six women. That to a degree accounted for the marked similarity in physique and expression of the Titanians. Too late, the Saturnians saw the need of new blood. Saturnian efficiency in sending surplus males to the ovens was kicking back.

Monorail systems and overhead cable conveyors crisscrossed the hothouse. At times I had to duck to the shelter of dense vegetation to escape observation from the cars that shuttled back and forth in phosphorescent twilight.

Saturnian guards were in charge of some of the intramural transport units, and Titanians in crimson smocks rode others. Crimson, I judged, marked the human overseers.

As I passed a quarry, I again caught the odor of food and fire. The pit, approached by a steeply inclined ramp, seemed deserted. A hundred yards beyond I heard the voices of laborers. A raid on the abandoned quarry might net me food.

~ ~ ~ ~ ~

I DUCKED among the partly squared blocks that littered the ramp, and worked my way into the pit. It was honeycombed with drifts, and from the floor yawned a winze that led into the black depths of Titan.

As I approached, I failed to see signs of the fire I had smelled; nor was there any smoke to guide me. The Titanian cooking fires burned with a quiet, smoldering glow, emitting no visible fumes.

It was odd, that distinct trace of hidden cookery. The Titanians ate in family groups, as far as I had been able to observe. . . . Suddenly my observations were cut short. I flattened to the ramp, taking cover behind a block of the greenish mineral that had been cut from the pit.

A broad-shouldered Titanian overseer was prowling among the abandoned machinery at the bottom of the pit. He walked with the arrogance of authority. His features were grim and purposeful. While I liked his face less the more I saw of it, there was no denying that he was the manliest-seeming Titanian I had yet seen.

He was looking for something, peering here and there into drifts, pausing to sniff the humid air. He was armed with a copper mace which hung from a broad girdle. He wore a knee-length tunic, and his gloved hand gripped a scourge with many lashes. Altogether, this was a person of consequence.

He halted, chin thrust forward, eyes narrowing; then he bounded forward with a triumphant snort. There was a cry from the drift into which he plunged. He had discovered some fugitive female slave.

As I bounded from cover and dashed across the pit, I heard him saying, "Well! So you thought I wouldn't find you!"

There was a cry of feminine wrath. The overseer yelled with pain, cursed, and soundly slapped the fugitive. I heard the *chunk* of a body dropping to the floor of the drift, and a metallic tinkle.

The overseer emerged, carrying a slender, dark-haired girl of uncommon loveliness. She was partly conscious, but still helpless from the blow that had floored her.

She differed in face and stature from the Titanians I had thus far seen. Her features were more finely drawn, faintly aquiline; her hair was blue-black, and she wore a shimmering tunic that outlined her figure. She was shapely and high-breasted; her ankles and wrists were adorned with red-gold bracelets.

"Hold it!" I yelled. "You and I are going to take time out, right now!"

He started: My unceremonious address and outlandish costume had worried him for a moment. Then he dropped the girl, unlimbered his scourge, and growled, "Back on the job, or I'll skin you alive!"

~ ~ ~ ~ ~

THE lash crackled. I ducked, picked up a flinty rock the size of my fist and hurled it. He jerked aside. The jagged missile ploughed through his thick hair, shook him, but did not drop him.

He stared in sheer amazement as I closed the gap. My leap, tuned to Terrestrial gravity, caught him utterly off guard. He had never heard of anyone assaulting an overseer. Before he could again use his whip, or drop it and unhook his mace, it was hand to hand.

My flying tackle knocked him crashing against the rocky wall of the quarry. The shock should have hammered him senseless; but he was burly as an ox, and as hard-muscled. I wrenched clear of his crushing grip, ducked his blow, and cracked him one on the jaw. That shook him, but failed to lay him out.

As he recovered, he jerked the mace from his belt. Instead of retreating, I got inside his guard. The handle of the weapon crashed down on my shoulder with a numbing impact. Then I back-heeled him, dropping him like a sack of meal. The mace clattered to the rocks as his head smashed against the foot of the wall.

He was out. I stepped back, instinctively giving him a chance to regain his feet, now that he was disarmed. But that was not the custom on Titan. The dark-haired girl had recovered. She cried out and snatched the mace.

Chunk! The first blow crushed his head. I caught her wrist as she lifted the weapon for a second swing. She stared at me, her dark eyes wide with wonder. Then she relaxed, flung her arms about me and burst into tears.

"Oh, I was so frightened. When you stood there, looking at him—I thought you were hurt, and he'd get up and kill you. What were you waiting for? And now you've killed him, and they'll take you to the simmering oven—oh!"

"Wait a minute, wait a minute," I cut in. "First, *you* killed him. Second, let's duck into your cave and talk this over."

I shouldered the remains of the overseer and followed the girl, some fifty or sixty feet into the drift. There I saw a smoldering fire and a small kettle.

"I'm starving, lady. How's for a handout?"

She gave me a wooden ladle. "Okay, pal"—or words to that effect: Her Saturnian slave vernacular was as crude as my own. That set me thinking. I wondered if she might, like myself, be a recent captive from Terra. This matter of killing an overseer seemed to cause her undue terror on my account.

She was still in the grip of fear now. She tried feebly to hide it, but her body was trembling, and then she began to cry.

"Take it easy," I said. "I've pulled so many wrongies already that one more or less won't have any effect. After hosing a Saturnian official with concentrated frost, this last tangle is nothing at all.

"Anyway, this guy's clothes will come in handy. I'll put them on, you bandage my face as if I'd been injured, and I'll carry on in his place."

She eyed me, smiled through her tears, and said, "Oh, that'll be just *wonderful!* I know we'll get along splendidly."

We might as well begin calling each other by our first names. That always helps. To say that I just dropped in from Terra would be too much, so I introduced myself and made no reference to origins.

"Kent Bradley," she said. "How awfully nice. I'm Valene—from Japetus."

"And that," said I, "makes us old friends. I've been looking for Valene, and it's a real treat to learn you're not a chemical or a town."

CHAPTER VIII

MEETIN' WITH A JAPETAN

VALENE spent the next hour or so coaching me in the duties of the Titanian overseer, and giving me lots of handy advice about the local situation.

My first move after eating would be to dress the dead overseer in my clothes and drop his body into some other quarry. That should throw the Saturnians off the track by making them think that in my flight I had taken a fatal dive. Things looked much better than they had an hour ago.

A quiet evening with Valene was worth any reasonable risk, even though what she told me of the penalty for assaulting an overseer did make me draw a long face. As for my succession of crimes—

"Let's talk about something else," I suggested, as I worked my way to the bottom of the pot of stewed gourds and fungi. "About yourself. A lot more pleasant."

"Well, there's not much to tell," Valene began. "I'm the daughter of Guraz, chief of the cave dwellers of Japetus. According to our traditions, we all come from some far-off planet, captives of a Saturnian raid of ages ago. The Saturnians brought our ancestors to Titan, and penned us up in this combination of farm and breeding station.

"My father's remote ancestor stole a space ship loaded with a cargo of slaves bound for the ovens of Saturn. The details of how he did it have been lost in legends, but the fact that we populated Japetus proves the story.

"Japetus is honeycombed with caverns, some of them larger even than the space under this dome. With the machine ship, laboratory, and the supplies in the Saturnian space ship, we entrenched ourselves in the caves of Japetus.

"The Saturnians sent an expedition to recapture us, but with the crags that rise from the surface, their cruisers could not come close enough to the bottoms of the valleys to pick off our outposts. And when the Saturnians put on their space suits to fight on foot, and of course without benefit of their wings, we dropped rocks on them. That tore their space armor, which let in cold air and put them out of action.

"And when the second expedition came to Japetus, several years later, we were ready for their preparations to invade our caverns. In the laboratory of the stranded space ship one of our leaders invented a chemical that dissolves the fireproof Saturnians and their armor. It's terrible stuff: it eats into rocks, glass, and metals. We can't keep it in anything but wax containers."

It must be, I concluded, some form of hydrofluoric acid. But this was no time to discuss chemistry.

"Why don't the Saturnians dope out the same kind of weapon to recapture the Japetans?" I wondered.

Valene explained, "We wear a wax-impregnated armor, so we're not injured by the fumes of our own weapons. The Saturnians can't wear anything of the kind because of their high temperature."

~ ~ ~ ~ ~

THAT was food for thought. Too bad Parker was not on hand. He could make use of such information. But what most interested me was why the Japetans did not leave their tiny satellite and fly back to Earth, or some other planet.

Valene, however, shook her head. "We have no fuel for the atomic disintegrators of the stolen ship. We can't produce it on Japetus. So we are stranded. We can not return to Titan to rescue any more of our distant relatives.

"Our entrenchment on Japetus is a standing insult to the Saturnians. Every once in a while they make raids, and capture Japetans. It served me right, I guess; but I was just starving for a glimpse of the outer air, and I took one chance too many.

"So here I am. I think they tried to use me as a hostage, but the Japetans figure that one more or less of the chief family is not enough to risk the enslavement of the entire satellite. The Saturnians treated me very nicely while the negotiations were in progress, though I was heavily guarded.

"But I managed to make a break, and I ran to one of the slave compounds. Then that overseer began getting fresh. I crisscrossed his face with a lot of first class scratches. Then I left the compound and came to this deserted quarry. It reminded me of our Japetan caves.

"And he's been hunting me ever since. I couldn't eat raw fungi. I had to risk a fire, and that's what attracted his attention. Oh, I hate to think of what would have happened to me if you'd not interfered. He was going to drag me away to his compound, to take the place of one of the women they recently sent to the ovens . . ."

"Hmm. And that accounts for *find Valene?*"

"Yes. That girl," she explained, "thought you must be a Japetan; you looked too independent and pugnacious for a Titanian. She wanted you to find me. She thought that two of us might stir up some trouble here on Titan. The legend of the Japetan flight has been the one hope among the slaves of Titan. Though most of them have become docile, a few planned revolt."

~ ~ ~ ~ ~

THAT evening—I should say, "rest period," which comprises about sixteen Terrestrial days—Valene and I completed our preparations for my impersonating the dead overseer, Gul-Sharan. I objected to going to his compound; for despite our similarity in stature, and the bandages that would disguise my face as well as voice, there were too many chances for a slip.

"And furthermore," I concluded, "with his half dozen gal friends, someone is bound to get wise."

"Mmm, yes," admitted Valene, "and I'd hate to have those stupid Titanian females pawing you. But don't you see that if there is no one to take Gul-Sharan's place, the body of the supposed Kent Bradley will get a much closer look? Someone will discover the trick. But if you appear as Gul-Sharan, everything will seem quite regular."

That sounded reasonable. Furthermore, Valene's knowledge of the routine of the colony might enable us to make an early escape, while if we hid in the abandoned quarry we would at the best be merely on the defensive, unable to make any moves toward liberty.

"And don't worry too much about Gul-Sharan's companions. He was a high-tempered, arrogant fellow and they all stood pretty much in awe of him. So crack the whip—literally as well as figuratively—and keep them in order."

I shouldered the body of Gul-Sharan and carried it up the ramp, skirted the lip of the quarry, and heaved it over the side. So much for the end of Kent Bradley's trail. And then Valene led the way to Gul-Sharan's compound: six thatched huts enclosed in a stockade.

Valene had nerve to spare, but I could plainly hear the pounding of my own heart as I stalked up to the entrance with what I hoped was the dead overseer's stride. Five young women were gathered about a copper kettle: all slender and shapely, and younger than the hapless victims I had met marching toward the gates of the colony. I ignored their greetings, brusquely repulsed the two who wondered at my bandaged head, and followed Valene to the hut farthest from the gate of the compound.

The hut was illuminated by a phosphorescent globe, a concession accorded only to overseers. That had guided Valene to the right place. The furnishings were simple: reed matting on the floor, two benches of wrought metal, several pots, and a low desk at which Gul-Sharan kept the accounts of the farms and quarry in his district.

I ruffled the thin metallic sheets on which he marked up his production reports, and Valene's low-voiced comments helped me form a sketchy picture of my duties.

"You'll be getting six carloads of *nari* ore ready for hauling to the Saturnian transport," Valene explained.

"And that's not all I'm going to prepare for loading," I said. "Among other things, you and I are going to try to stow away on the ship, and make a break for Japetus. I'm going to find out about those acid bombs, and there's going to be a house-cleaning on Titan."

We sat up late that "night," perfecting the plan which Gul-Sharan's reports had suggested. When Valene had finally cleared up complications against which we would have to guard, I saw that our chances were better than fair.

"I'll sleep for a week," I said, hitching the reed mat around in a futile effort to find a soft spot. "This everlasting artificial illumination won't wake me—"

"I'm used to it. I'll see that you don't oversleep," Valene assured me.

CHAPTER IX

WRONG BUCKET TO KICK

I ALMOST yelled when someone shook me by the shoulder. Valene was doing her best to wake me from an attempt to make up for weeks of restless sleep in a furnace-like space ship.

"I'll join the women working in the *guri* field right next to the quarry," Valene whispered. "And do be careful."

Behind her smile I sensed the anxiety that she was trying to conceal. One slip, and we'd go straight to the kitchens of the Saturnian high command.

I began to doubt whether freedom was worth the risk. As I looked back toward my hut, I caught the look in Valene's dark eyes, and knew that she had been whistling to keep up my courage.

I strode past several compounds, mustered the laborers as they fell in, and marched them to the quarry. The women struggled in twos and threes toward the adjoining fields.

A Saturnian official was at the ramp that led into the pit. From the muttered comments of my crew I learned that this was Nuruk, the most critical and high tempered of the local officers. I saluted as we marched past; and under his fierce eye, there was no need of my supervision. The slaves filed into a drift, seized pickaxes and drills, and fell to hewing out blocks of the mineral.

"What happened to you, Gul-Sharan?" Nuruk demanded.

"I tripped and fell, Excellency," I explained, "while pursuing an odd-looking fugitive—he was wearing some strange disguise—"

Nuruk's wrathful cursing interrupted my remarks; then he demanded, "Where is he? What happened to him?"

"He ran over the edge of the abandoned quarry in section nine," I answered. "I'm pretty sure the fall killed him."

Nuruk stalked up the ramp. He was going to investigate. I ordered my crew into an adjoining drift to get sharper tools to replace those blunted by the glass-hard ore. During their absence, I dragged an ore bucket from a cross-cut, heaved it to the bottom of the car, and laid it on its side. Then I rolled fragments of the mineral over it. I had just completed my task when the miners returned with fresh implements.

I eyed the ore heaped high in the far end of the car.

"Roll it out!" I ordered. "And couple it up to the other four. Then get to work on the last one."

When leveled off, the load would be equal to the contents of the other cars. But before the tall heap at the front was distributed, Valene would be stowed away in the ore bucket. I, as overseer, would be riding the string of cars which the sweating slaves would push toward the Saturnian transport.

Women from the adjoining fields brought us pots of stew, and joined us at the mid-shift lunch period. They were all chattering and babbling about the discovery of the body of the rebellious prisoner. The story of my escape from the administration building had traveled from one end of the colony to the other by something akin to the Terrestrial grapevine telegraph.

I sat somewhat apart, perched on number five car. When I saw Valene descending the ramp with my pot of lunch, I brusquely hailed her. She drew herself to the coupling bar.

"Bring it over!" I snapped. "Do you expect me to come and get it?"

She clambered over the jagged chunks of ore. For good measure, I growled at her awkwardness in spilling some of the gravy.

Then, as I took the pot of stew, I whispered, "Watch your chance, and duck into the ore bucket. When I go back to work, I'll start the heap of *nari* rolling back to cover it. And you'll know how to carry on when the car is emptied into the hold of the transport."

~ ~ ~ ~ ~

SHE ducked below the edge of the car, and slipped into the ore bucket. While I was certain that the move had not been observed, sweat cropped out of my forehead. If anyone missed Valene, if any miner wondered at that ore bucket, it would be awkward to explain.

I started a miniature landslide, and half covered Valene's shelter. Then I seized my spoon and resumed eating my lunch. Some of the women were already gathering up the empty pots. I'd have to conceal mine before the end of the rest period.

Easy enough. Then I saw that Nurfik was eyeing me. He was frowning, and his brow was furrowed with deep wrinkles. The work, as far as I could determine, had progressed well enough. Gul-Sharan's detachment of slaves had an unchallenged record for high output.

Nuruk rose from the boulder on which he had been squatting and stalked toward me. "How much of this *nari* ore does the order call for?"

I told him. With little hesitation I answered the next half dozen questions. But for Valene's coaching, I would have been tripped up then and there. His narrowed eyes covered me from head to foot.

The situation was becoming more dangerous every moment. Despite my successful imposture, I sensed everincreasing peril. Once, as I groped for an answer, Valene prompted me from her place of concealment. I was certain that Nuruk could not have heard her whisper.

He bounded to the coupling bar and stood at the far end of the load. "What do you mean by taking Gul-Sharan's place?"

I managed to answer, "I am Gul-Sharan, your Excellency!"

"Rot!" growled Nuruk. "You do seem to know his business, but you're not Gul-Sharan. Among other things, he is left-handed. You've been eating right-handed, and the sling chains of your mace are suspended for a right-handed person"

In the heat of my battle with Gul-Sharan, I had not noticed with which hand he used his weapons. Neither had Valene noted his left-handedness. It was worse than bad—it was fatal. But I made one desperate play.

"Excellency," I explained, "Gul-Sharan was tracking down a fugitive prisoner. He asked me to bandage my face and take his place, saying that his crew would carry on perfectly as long as they did not know the difference."

Nuruk eyed me, nodded, and muttered. Flames jetted from his nostrils as he scowled and pondered on my answer. It was a serious breach of discipline; but unless punishment was immediate, there was still a chance. Valene and I might even carry on with our scheme.

"Not so bad," he grumbled, scrutinizing the heap of ore we had mined and loaded.

~ ~ ~ ~ ~

I WAS prepared for his demanding my true name, and was ready to give him one that would ring true. His next move caught me entirely off guard. He snatched at the knot that secured my bandages. His sharp nails sheared the cloth. It smouldered from the heat of his finger tips, but he unwound it before it charred in his grip. In an instant I was barefaced.

My coloring betrayed me; that I knew before his wrath could find words. The Titanians have either black or copper-blonde hair. None had close-cropped, sandy hair, nor were any of them deeply suntanned. My coloring was neither olive-pallor, nor paper-whiteness.

"So—you're the Terrestrian who turned the administration building inside out, eh?" he howled. "By Nagarreth, you've got some explaining to do!"

He stepped forward as if to grip me by the shoulder. Then he checked his stride, recollecting that his smoking hot fingers would be dangerous. His lunge shifted the crest of the heaped-up mineral. Half a dozen lumps rolled from under his feet and clattered toward the empty end. Nuruk, feet slipping from beneath him, pitched headlong with the sliding ore.

Though half buried in lumps of *nari,* he noted the almost buried ore bucket. He snatched the rim and jerked it loose.

"Now what?" he demanded, wrathful at his undignified nose dive.

Then he saw the stowaway, and recognized the captive from Japetus. Valene's distinctive features and coloring betrayed her. The published descriptions of that prized prisoner had put all the Saturnians on guard.

Nuruk bawled an order. A Titanian sprang to a switch panel. Presently a conveyor came whirring along the overhead cable and halted at the head of the mine ramp. Half a dozen of our fellow slaves hustled us to the car.

Resistance was useless. Nuruk followed us. The door slammed. The engineer shifted the controller, and we set out for headquarters.

"This," said Valene as we picked up speed, "is so final that there is no sense in moaning about it. Absolutely nothing we can say will do a bit of good. Nuruk just files a report, has it stamped by the personnel manager, and we are locked up in the refrigerating compartment of the next ship bound for Saturn.

"And no one has ever escaped?"

I could not dig up enough bravado to convince her that we could upset old precedents.

CHAPTER X

BACK TO PARKER

PARKER'S face lengthened as he heard the commander of the disintegrating transport whip the ether into whirlpools.

"Can we outrun the patrol boats?"

Shadra shrugged.

"Either that, or we will become a Saturnian delicacy," she replied with a wry gesture. Her eyes, however, were level and unafraid. She glanced into the televisiphone mirror, brushed a stray wisp of gold bronze hair into place, and wiped a smudge from her cheek. "Take the controls, playboy, and no funny business this time. I've got an idea."

She stepped to the radio-visiphone, shifted several rheostat levers, closed a switch, and watched the indicator on an ammeter jump to the needle. The entire bridge house began vibrating and humming as if it would at any instant disintegrate.

"What on earth—" Parker began, bearing down on the helm, ducking a satelloid by a sudden upward swoop.

"Wave vortex," said Shadra. "Blotting out the transport message with power gone crazy. They'll know something is wrong, but they won't be able to track us down as quickly as they might otherwise. All right—you take the integrator and give me the wheel."

Shadra nosed the ship sharply up from the plane of the ecliptic and fed it full power. Far to the rear, Parker detected signs of rapidly converging pursuit. In response to Shadra's instructions from the bridge, he cut off the power vortex.

Strategy would no longer help. It had settled to a matter of speed and deftness of maneuvering. And there Shadra justified the high esteem with which the Saturnian overlords had regarded her as a pilot.

The pursuing cruisers had more powerful engines than the *Karamanu;* but the transport, hurrying to the rescue of a vessel in distress, had carried not even ballast. The cruisers had greater top speeds, but their acceleration was not as sharp.

The course Shadra set was erratic, zigzagging, a nightmare that kept Parker's hair standing on end. Zooming dizzily in a perpendicular rise from the ecliptic, she tricked the pursuers into taking up full speed. Before they reached effective artillery range, she had picked the next ether "hole," or the next gap in the dangerous shoals of satelloids that reached out far from Saturn.

Then, a dive that sent Parker's stomach lurching up to his collarbone. In the tele-visiphone he saw the pursuit carried several thousand lengths beyond their mark before they could wheel.

When they did wheel, they had overshot the clear areas in the shoals, and had to pick their way, wasting ruinous amounts of energy in putting out repulsion screens to deflect satelloids and meteor swarms.

As long as the pursuit was kept roughly in the ecliptic, the velocity of the ship made the relative speed of the obstructions to navigation comparatively negligible.

Shadra was gaining. Then, having pulled the Saturnian cruisers through the ecliptic, she picked the next channel, again zoomed upward, and reversed the direction of flight. This forced the pursuit to slacken speed to neutralize the dangerous *relative* increase in meteoroid speeds, whose orbital rotation now opposed the flight of the ship.

~ ~ ~ ~ ~

HOURS later, they reached the outer zones, where the satellites of Saturn have a retrograde motion. There a final shift of direction hopelessly delayed the Saturnian cruisers.

They were out in clear space, beyond the dangerous Saturnian ether-ocean.

"Holy jumping cats!" Parker said fervently, as he stepped at last from the integrator. "Like driving ninety miles an hour through a Manhattan traffic jam—and getting away with it."

"And now," Shadra suggested, "take the wheel while I open the loading ports. They work from master controls. That'll dispose of our Saturnian passengers in such a way that we'll be *sure* they won't try to recapture us. It's a bit more practical than fussing around with any of your experiments."

Parker grinned and let it go at that; and presently they settled down to top speed flights.

"We'll have to work in watches," said Shadra. "Get some sleep while I hold the course. Don't need the integrators any more."

It was hard, grueling work, Parker discovered, long before the *Karamanu* nosed inside the Martian orbit. They were both worn and haggard, and Shadra's eyes seemed as large as saucers in her drawn, weary face. Parker assured her that she was becoming lovelier every day.

"Liar!" Her tone was tart, but the lines of her face relaxed when she said it.

Later, when observations revealed clear stretches, Parker locked the controls, threw out a repulsion screen, and let the *Karamanu* go flashing on its course. He and Shadra won a few hours of rest from the strain of navigation.

The inductor-bearings were hammering, and the exhaust tubes were clogging with atomic ash—but they'd make it. Saturnian pursuit was so far behind that finding the *Karamanu* in that vast gulf of space was beyond the finest instruments.

~ ~ ~ ~ ~

IT WAS shortly after sunrise, a month after Parker's break for freedom, that he landed the *Karamanu* at an airport near Washington, D. C.

The guard turned out, and so did the officer of the day. His first impression was that a new model army blimp had made an emergency landing. Then he looked a good look at Parker and said, "You do not look like an officer to me, and if you are a civilian test pilot, I'll have to have your credentials."

"Sorry, Captain; we've just returned from Saturn, and I have only these." He reached into his pocket to get something of identification value out of the tangle of memoranda. "I am John Parker, formerly—"

"You returned from where?"

"From Saturn." Just then Shadra stepped from the hatchway. "To be exact, from the satellite, Titan. This lady—"

The captain's annoyed and puzzled look changed, and a little too abruptly to please Parker. "Oh, to be sure! I'm afraid the commanding officer didn't tell us about you. Very glad to meet you, Mr. Parker. And you too, Miss . . . umm . . ."

"Shadra, and I'm not crazy!" she flared. "Neither is he. Well, anyway," she added with sly malice, "not *very.*" Parker nudged her, viciously.

"Why, of course you're not," the too-affable captain continued. "This way, please. The colonel will be very happy to welcome you."

This distracted Parker just enough for the voice and hands behind him to come as a surprise. Two men caught his arms from the rear, and someone said, "Don't move, or I'll conk you! So it's from Saturn you've come, is it? Don't worry, lady, we won't let him hurt you."

"Nice work, Sergeant," the captain said in his natural military voice. "Always gives the service a black eye, roughing up civilians. March them to headquarters. Corporal Smith, report to the adjutant that we have arrested two suspected spies—though possibly this fellow is a maniac who's stolen a dirigible from some experimental station."

"Very well, sir." The corporal saluted and left at the double time.

"I'm not crazy," Parker protested. "You're the weak-minded one. Look at the marks of meteors on that hull. You blockhead, does that really look like a dirigible to you?"

"Shut up, or I'll bust a gun butt over your head," the sergeant grumbled. "Watch him, men. These maniacs sometimes have more beef than a whole squad of sane guys."

The captain stalked grandly on to report to the adjutant, and then to the commanding officer.

~ ~ ~ ~ ~

COLONEL WATSON was gray and red-faced and stocky. He had a double row of campaign badges on his tunic, and his shrewd eyes looked from under shaggy brows. His interest was evenly divided between Parker and the tall woman at his side. He shook his head and said to the adjutant, "This man may be a little upset, but he does look like the John Parker who disappeared—"

"Right! I am the one who was last heard of on the Orinoco. If you'll listen to us, Colonel, perhaps I can convince you we are not spies, and are not mad."

His earnestness impressed the commanding officer, who said to the adjutant, "Please get the newspaper files at the post library and compare the details with whatever identification this gentleman can give us."

Parker went on, "Here are notes and my wallet. And if you'll be so good as to listen, I'll tell you what happened to me and Kent Bradley. It was in the jungle, and little wonder no one ever gave a straight account, for there were few survivors, and those were Indians. But first of all, you must get that space ship under cover. Into a dirigible hangar."

Colonel Watson picked up his cigar. "Ah . . . *must*, Mr. Parker? Please relax now, I am intensely interested. Do sit down."

"You may suit yourself, Colonel Watson. Saturnian patrols may be following us. If they see the familiar shape and color of a stolen ship, be assured that they will try to recapture it. And that ship is the one thing this country needs. As a model, I mean, for others like it, to drive the Saturnians out."

Parker's level glance as well as his words made the officer frown perplexedly, then rise and say, "Very well, Mr. Parker. Please come with me, and we shall move your ship under cover. I fancy your ship would be useful against—ah— Terrestrial enemies."

The adjutant, who had returned with the file, broke in. As the papers rustled, Parker heard the adjutant whisper, "This undoubtedly is the man, sir. But you mustn't board that crazy thing with him, sir. It's a trap! You'll be kidnapped."

"Nonsense, Captain!" Then, to Parker, "Let us go at once. And tell me what happened in the Orinoco."

The officer of the day and the adjutant, Parker saw when he glanced over his shoulder, were in a huddle at the guard-house. They were worried about the colonel. Parker went into his story, touching only the highlights as he crossed the parade ground, and went toward the hangar.

"They scooped us up with monstrous nets," Parker concluded. "Bullets did not harm these winged devils. Luckily, Shadra and I were able to escape from captivity. I've had to skip details, simply because I must show you this vessel before I tell you anything else."

"Bullets would not hurt them, eh? Very well, Parker, we'll go into that later. Let me see the inside of your ship."

He gestured for Parker and Shadra to precede him. The guard came forward with fixed bayonets, and the officer of the day had a drawn pistol. They still could not believe that their weapons would be quite useless against the Saturnian ship.

"Well, well," Colonel Watson said, as he stepped in through the hatch. "This is remarkably thick armor. Captain! Get a look at these plates, and see for yourself."

With that, he hurried after Parker and Shadra. At the end of the passageway, Parker turned to gesture and say, "Here is the control room. Do you wish to inspect the propulsion mechanism, or do you wish to see me move her into the hangar?"

The instrument panel was bewildering, for in addition to the unintelligibility of the markings on the dials, there were many whose indicators, shape and fluorescent glow made them utterly unlike anything on earth.

The plotting room was even more confusing. The colonel stood there, making inarticulate sounds and shaking his head as Parker explained, "These are much like your conventional coast artillery plotting devices, except that they are tri-dimensional, and much more complete. And, of course,

suited for the complexities of radio-beam sounding for meteor shoals and satelloids. If there are no questions, suppose I
set her into the hangar? And tell your guard to keep clear of
the hull, front and rear."

Colonel Watson was frank about it: "Questions? Young
man, I'd not know what to ask you." He leaned out of the
port: "Captain, get the guard away, we are taking off."

Parker pressed a button, and the hatch slid ponderously
into place. He moved a control lever. The deck shivered
from the poundings of the worn inductor bearings, and a
great cloud of dust surged over the parade ground when the
exhaust blast hit into the ground.

She needed a thorough overhauling, but there was enough
mileage left in the captured *Karamanu* to give Colonel Watson an eye-opening demonstration.

She took off, and none too smoothly; but no Terrestrian
would notice that. Parker cut the power down to a minimum,
and circled lazily toward the gleaming tip of Washington
Monument.

"Get back to the post. I'm quite convinced, and I'll accept
the responsibility for giving you temporary hangar space. It
is quite possible that the War Department will be interested
in your invention, Mr. Parker."

"Shadra, show the colonel around the ship; while I swing
her back."

Shadra flashed him a knowing look over her shoulder.
Parker, for all his slide-rule principles, seemed every once in
a while to stumble across sound bits of human psychology.

CHAPTER XI

INVASION!

BEFORE Parker swung back to the dirigible hangar, the adjutant's inquiries had started a dozen newspaper men for the
post. They came with the idea of getting an interview with
the unexpectedly returned survivor of the Parker-Bradley

expedition in South America; but when the fish-shaped and bronze-colored space ship leveled off and settled to the floor of the hangar, they did not know what to say.

The guard told them that Parker claimed to have returned from Saturn with a personable young woman in an outlandish dress. "And if you don't believe it, buddy, just have a look when she comes out. Sure, he's crazy, every inventor goes whacky, but a gal like that—aw right, *I'm* crazy, then; and he didn't say that!"

Guards posted by the zealous officer of the day kept the charging journalists out of the hangar; but no one cared what happened to Parker and Shadra. The colonel shouted above the uproar, "This new type of ship is not sponsored by the Government, but you may quote me as saying that it seems to work."

"How about Saturn?"

"We did not go to Saturn, and I am unable to discuss that."

Parker and Shadra had to face camera men at the steps of headquarters. The colonel said, "Don't release all the details. A panic might start; people might believe what the press considers and offers as a hoax."

Parker did not mention the motive that led Saturnians to seek human prey. That Shadra had given the colonel a hint— as she must have—without reviving his queries as to her sanity, testified to her command of English. Parker had given her instructions on their long trip; and she learned rapidly.

When the newspapermen had gone, most of them were bewildered from trying to figure where fact stopped and fake began. But they were certain of one thing: that the strangely shaped ship did have a theretofore unheard-of propulsion device; and that was something to tie to.

For the next few days, feature writers and cartoonists and columnists had their turn. Alienists and anthropologists and scientists were interviewed: since Parker and Shadra, now accepted by Government officials as sane refugees from an outlying planet, were in conference with War Department and State Department heads. Fashion designers had the show windows of the capital blossoming with Titanian motifs; photographs of Shadra were all that they needed.

From time to time, some foreign scientist damned Parker as a fraud, and declared that the atomic propulsion devices were a hoax, a mere buildup for a stock promotion swindle. Others were just as convinced that Parker's experiences were authentic; and some persisted in considering him a mad inventor.

Bit by bit, he had released further details. The Government was watching every news item; and investigators were working over the entire country, ready to report the first sign of panic.

There was a buzz of coast-to-coast interest, but no terror. The story, even toned down, was simply incredible. Parker in the meanwhile had little time to catch up sleep, as Colonel Watson, making a second flight in the *Karamanu,* submitted a report advising that ordnance experts and other specialists make a detailed study of the propulsion devices.

As a result, Parker blistered his tongue from caffeine tablets; and finally, in spite of all stimulants, fell asleep over his slide rule.

He had barely awakened from a forty-eight hour sleep when the renewed conference with officers from technical branches of the army and navy was broken up by a radio-visiphone message from Vera Cruz.

~ ~ ~ ~ ~

THREE ichthyform ships, described as substantially identical with the one Parker had brought to Washington, had raided the city, scooped up hundreds of natives, and soared away quite unharmed by anti-aircraft shells and machine gun bullets.

This message had scarcely reached the conference room when the President's secretary arrived to demand strictest secrecy, with no more newspaper interviews by anyone taking part in the investigation of the ship and Parker's data.

Then came a conclave of ambassadors from the Associated Governments of the world; this meeting was at a private estate outside of Washington. Strict censorship suppressed the alarming dispatches from Vera Cruz, for the initial incredulity was shaken by code messages from the home governments. The reports, in code, of depredations in Eastern Europe, Malaya, and parts of South America left no doubters.

In spite of these messages, a few of the more conservative delegates suspected that some government was using a newly discovered scientific principle to terrorize the world and win a redistribution of power.

"Gentlemen," Parker said when he took the floor, "if the majority of you, who are convinced, will vote me an appropriation for experimental purposes, I will develop arms that can to a degree cope with these invaders. In making my escape from Titan, I was unable to bring a captive Saturnian to convince you.

"However, an expedition under your supervision might result in at least a few prisoners to convince you that these alarming reports are made by people who have actually witnessed the like of what Kent Bradley and I saw. That these invading ships, like the one I brought to Terra, actually do come from Saturn. I am sure—"

His appeal was interrupted by a low-pitched whirring and a humming that quickly became shrill and greater in volume. There was a scraping of chairs, a confusion of voices. "That's the sound he described!" one shouted and others clamored, "I heard him demonstrate that ship; it's the same note!"

Then all spoke at once. There was no more order, and the chairman stopped pounding with his gavel. He joined the rush to the door, and the meeting poured out into the grounds of the estate.

A long, ichthyform craft was hovering over the city, slowly circling at a level appreciably lower than the peak of the Washington Monument. The voice of the city soon was loud enough to reach into the suburb where the conference

had met. Sirens tore into the shouting; and traffic, for a moment paralyzed, now insanely dashed toward the outskirts of
the city capital.

~ ~ ~ ~ ~

THEN came the ear-splitting *whack* of three-inch field
pieces, the heavy boom of larger artillery, the scream of
shells that missed the mark, and the concussion of those that
burst against the armor of the low flying space cruiser. Every
piece of ordnance in the artillery park out toward Alexandria
was bombarding the invader.

The heavier projectiles, moving with muzzle velocities
low enough to permit direct visual observation of their trajectories, swerved erratically from their courses. They flew
off into space, along the branches of insane hyperbolas.

The anti-meteoric repulsion screen was deflecting the
bombardment. Some of the assembled diplomats stood
calmly by, regarding the bewildering display with the unruffled calm of veterans under fire. They realized that no
amount of haste could evade the attack. They watched the
monster circling, settling down, lowering a grappling net.

Others made a concerted rush for their cars. The parking
space became a tangle of locked fenders, rammed vehicles,
and engines frantically spun by drivers who had forgotten
their ignition switches.

Dense fumes poured from the lower ports of the space
ship. The net was dropping—dropping. The monster hovered, deliberately spreading terror. Then the net flashed
home, vanished below the cornice level of the taller buildings.

The whirl became a whining, and the delegates of the Associated Governments saw the web rising, bit by bit, packed
to bulging, like an uncommonly successful cast of a shrimp
net. Field glasses directed toward the ichthyform monster
dropped from shaking fingers.

"My God!" muttered a silk-hatted dignitary at Parker's
right. "Like Satan—in person—breathing fire—"

Another, paper-white, said in a low, hoarse voice: "They're eating them—raw—I thought you said—they cooked them—"

"They do," said Parker, "when they're at home. Under campaign conditions, they are not so fussy."

The hatch cover rose into place behind the net. The space cruiser rose, nosed toward Yucatan, and slipped through the air like a streamlined silver bullet.

Visual proof again made Parker the man of the hour. Every War Department scoffer who had survived with his sanity fairly intact assured Parker that no one had ever doubted him.

Parker was put in charge of the ordnance proving-ground at Aberdeen, with a full corps of scientists and commissioned specialists to work along half a dozen separate lines of attacks and defense. The research departments of each of the Continental Scientific Unions began independent experiments, with a radio network to keep each other posted.

Industries were pooled; tailings dumps of mines and slag heaps of smelters were combed for substances thus far considered as commercially useless.

Refrigeration engineers developed gases which combined extreme combustibility with freezing points within a few decimals of absolute zero.

To amuse the public while all this work was going on in a thousand laboratories in unrevealed centers, rallying songs were composed, and headline platitudes about Terrestrial unity. Propaganda experts took charge of the drive to muster every man, every dollar, and every weapon to make the solar system safe for Terrestrians.

Shadra found the three-minute pep speakers the most novel persons she had met on earth, next to the cheering audiences. She canceled her radio contracts in order to miss none of them.

But after a few days of it, she donned an asbestos smock and a gas mask and joined Parker in his underground laboratory.

CHAPTER XII

BRADLEY CARRIES ON

NO INDICTMENTS are required to get Terrestrial crayfish from a bayou to a kettle of boiling water seasoned *a la Creole,* with garlic, lemon, bay, thyme and cayenne.

Similarly Valene and I were not even questioned at the Titanian headquarters building. We were merely discussed, with humiliating brevity, by the personnel manager.

He initialed an order. A methodical Saturnian clerk made a suitable entry in a running inventory system. We weren't *sentenced* for our plotting, and my two attempts at rebellion and escape. We were merely dangerous livestock that had best be eaten at once.

I've heard judges pronounce sentences of death. They are impressed with the solemnity of the occasion. So is the condemned. At military executions, troops parade, bugles sound, the firing squad marches to its post. Then, *present arms!* A salute . . . There is dignity in a Terrestrial sentence.

But we were accorded less ceremony than a chicken at the chopping block. That affronted every instinct. And strangely enough, we could hardly realize that we were doomed. Our emotions were paralyzed when we heard, "Kent Bradley and Valene will be cooked in sixteen hours."

It could not mean me. It couldn't mean that shapely, dark-eyed girl. Not even when we were marched out the same avenue which has been a one-way street for hundreds of generations of Titanians.

Saturnian guards saluted our escort. The commander of the gate pressed a succession of buttons that operated the inner valve of the airlock. It rose like a portcullis. We cleared the threshold, and heard the humming of the motors that lowered it into place.

"Got any ideas, Valene?" I whispered.

"Nothing." She smiled wanly. "Except a lot of perfectly splendid ones that could have prevented this. I'm awfully sorry, Kent. It's all my fault. I really killed the overseer. You didn't."

"I would have." Which was the truth, and she liked that.

The outer valve was rising. We shivered from the first chill of the thin outer atmosphere. Our ears whirred and buzzed from the sudden drop in pressure. Our captors were muffled in insulated suits. Their exhaust flames suddenly lengthened.

Accustomed as we were to the tropical humidity of the hothouse domes, the frosty air lanced through our smocks. Valene's lips were already slate-colored.

I wondered how her remote ancestor had managed to steal a space ship. I wondered what cunning, what tenacious clinging to sanity had given him the clue to freedom: what momentary slip of his captors had given him that instant which blossomed into victory.

~ ~ ~ ~ ~

THE sun was rising. The week-long Titanian night would in a few hours brighten into a grayish blue pallor. A tiny white disc was beginning to show its upper edge over the unbroken horizon. Its motion was imperceptible to eyes attuned to the sudden glory of a broad copper disc swooping up from behind the Terrestrial hills.

There were only four of us in the airlock: Valene and I, our guard, and the Saturnian engineer who was working the controls of the ponderous valves.

The enemy wore insulated suits to keep out the chill. The engineer's gloved hands groped among the massive switch blades and levers to cut in the floodlight which would illuminate our path from the hothouse to the smaller dome of the hangar. There the satelloid express awaited its cargo.

There must be other prisoners, I reasoned. They would hardly send a special convoy for two rebels. We were not important enough.

I still wondered how Valene's remote ancestor had turned the trick. Could it be repeated?

Then I caught the first play. "Look the other way," I whispered to Valene. "I'm starting a show. Be ready to hop."

Before her fingers closed on my left arm, I was in motion. I still wore my overseer's mace. To Saturnians it was an insignium of office and not a weapon. Against them, it was utterly harmless, though it would crush a human skull at one blow—as its original owner had learned. Yet it served a purpose our captors never anticipated.

I hurled the copper weapon over the engineer's averted head and at the master switch. The heavy copper handle and the sling chains short-circuited the entire power supply. An eye-searing flash, a blinding billow of metallic vapors; a fierce lash of flame, a scorching shower of molten copper—and in an instant, there was darkness broken only by the lingering haze and afterglow of energy that had evaporated several pounds of copper in an instant.

I caught Valene's hand and bounded forward into the blackness. The air lock was jammed. The entire front sector of the hothouse dome was without electrical power. The Saturnians, though unharmed by the heat and metallic vapors, were dazed by the unexpected blast. The engineer was cursing. Our guard was still fuzzy-witted.

Thus Valene and I gained twenty yards—fifty—a hundred—Lord, how that girl could run! In the tensity of that moment, she matched my Terrestrian strides, which carried us sailing like kangaroos.

We cut to the right, our herder after us. His long legs stretched out. Jets of flame poured from the exhaust ports of his insulated suit. But he was handicapped by his protective armor.

We were running for our lives. He was pursuing groceries. That made a difference. But running in that frosty ghost of an atmosphere was torture. Our inhalations were stabbing gulps that left us empty. Our nostrils were seared by the cold.

My Terrestrially attuned muscles enabled me to take prodigious leaps; but the pursuer was accustomed to Saturnian gravity, slightly in excess of that on earth, and his bounds took no odds from ours.

"Head for that ravine!" Valene gasped. "Get away from the level ground—our only—chance—like they do —on— Japetus."

~ ~ ~ ~ ~

THE Saturnian engineer, true to type, had kept his post. He cursed and fumed and wondered what alibi he could offer the works manager. Our herder, bent on running us down, did not take time out to signal to the hangar for a general hunt. Our escape was utterly without precedent, and a Saturnian without rules is hampered.

Our pursuer could not use his wings. That was our salvation, and his handicap. Accustomed as Saturnians were to the coordination of wings and feet, to be deprived of the use of either set of members hindered the other entirely out of apparent proportion.

Deadly as the frosty air was to Valene and me, it was worse for the Saturnian. It lowered his internal temperature at every gasp.

But we felt the fumes that eddied from his exhaust ports, and wondered if we could reach that ravine.

"Separate," said Valene. "You go on—I'll duck. We're mountaineers at home!"

She wheeled. I swerved. The thick-witted Saturnian cattle herder was confused. He could not pursue in two directions at once, and he had to decide which captive to get first.

He did not waste much time in thought—but split instants counted. I gained two long leaps that carried me clear of the mouth of the ravine, and toward its left wall.

As I bounded, I risked a backward glance. Valene was skirting the lip of the deeply eroded cleft that stretched into the darkness.

I leaped to the right. And inertia works on Titan just as it does elsewhere. The heavy Saturnian could not wheel as quickly us I could. He crashed headlong into the rocky wall.

The shock knocked a jet of flame out of him. For an instant his gasp illuminated the ravine for fifty yards. Valene gestured and cried out.

~ ~ ~ ~ ~

I COULDN'T get it. But it was time to move. My ears were roaring, and my nose was bleeding from the low pressure of the atmosphere. The ovens of Saturn, however, were an inspiration. I gathered myself and zigzagged again, heading toward Valene's side of the ravine.

The Saturnian stumbled, and measured his length on the rocks. The crash was impressive and encouraging. I remembered how Terrestrial pigmies gang up on an elephant and finally overwhelm the monster. I gained fifty yards as the Saturnian clambered to his feet.

"Work your way along this wall," screamed Valene. "Toward that narrow fork."

A crevice gaped from the gloom. I had lost time, listening and trying to whip my wits into action. The Saturnian lunged.

Valene and her insane notion! How could I maneuver in that cramped crevice? But it was too late to retreat. I worked my way in and up, cutting myself to ribbons on the ragged ledges. Flame from the pursuer's exhaust ports illuminated my advance. He was gaining.

Then I caught the point: the Saturnian was fairly jammed in the narrow cleft. He was tearing at great tongues of rock, seeking to work his way toward me. Clever girls, these Japetan ladies.

Then I learned just how clever. I risked an upward glance.

"Wait a second!" I yelled.

Valene, however, needed no help. She was slender and supple. Peril gave her strength. She dislodged a boulder that hung balanced near the lip of the cleft.

The Saturnian, sensing his danger, jerked back, but not quickly enough. The chunk of granite crushed him to the floor of the ravine. A howling gust of flame poured from his insulated suit. His arms and legs threshed furiously, but he was pinned in place by the rock.

The pigmies had snared their elephant. Now kill him.

CHAPTER XIII

THE SENILE SATURNIAN

VALENE slid down from her perch. We approached our pin-
ioned enemy as closely as we dared, and warmed ourselves
in the fumes that surged from his insulated suit.

"Now what?" I demanded. "We can't last long in this thin
atmosphere. We'll freeze. And certainly starve. If in the
meanwhile we aren't picked up by a Saturnian patrol, as
soon as the jammed valves of the hothouse are opened."

"Look."

"Well, I'll be fried!" I said, following Valene's gesture. I
had not realized how far we had run. Far to our left were the
compound domes of the Titanian colony We had run some
five or six miles. The low gravitational pull of the satellite
had served us well.

Finding two fugitives in one of the ravines that seamed
the face of Titan would be a hopeless task.

"Freezing," said Valene, "is not so bad. Better than being
eaten. Though the docile Titanians of this day probably don't
think so."

"Maybe we can beat that," I suggested. "This fellow will
finally burn out, but until then he'll keep us warm. The worst
of it is we can't eat him. But maybe we can rustle up some
fungi to keep us alive until we find a cave, or some outcropping of the internal heat of Titan. Some hot spring—
something—"

Valene shook her head.

"That is possible," she said. "There are a few fumaroles in
Japetus, and the heat of the deeper caverns is appreciable.
But we're not fixed for exploring."

And then I took another look at our prisoner. He seemed
securely pinned down, but there was still the chance that he
might escape. I circled about, picking up one piece of rock

after another. Finally I found a lump of obs:dian. I struck it against a boulder. It broke, leaving a razor edge.

I slipped up to the intake side of the Saturnian and hacked the insulating suit. It was tough, but it yielded to the glassy edge of the flint. Another stroke. The Saturnian's renewed threshing convinced me I was on the right track. The boulder that pinned him seemed to shift as he struggled. I hacked again, slashed, drove home.

I jerked back just in time to keep from being burned to a crisp by the sudden surge of flame. For a moment the ravine was bright as a Terrestrial sunrise. Then the flames wavered. The hissing exhalation subsided to reeking fumes of vegetable distillation products.

The inrush of frosty air was congealing the Saturnian. Presently he would be a dull leaden color, numb and rigid as a piece of jerked beef. Or rather, as an inanimate piece of asbestos.

But I was encouraged. While baiting a solitary Saturnian whose wings had been rendered useless by his insulated suit was quite different from meeting hordes of them in battle formation, the moral effect was stimulating. They could be trapped.

~ ~ ~ ~ ~

"YOUNG lady," I said, "you and I are not doing any freezing. On the contrary: we're going places. I'm taking you back to Japetus; and your folks will have to show cause why they shouldn't set us up in a nice cozy cavern just for two."

"Kent! This is so *sudden!* But how on Saturn—"

"Here's the play," I said. "When this Saturnian is completely frozen, I'm going to peel him out of his suit, rig up some stilts for myself, and put it on. Then I'll drag you back to the hangar, report Kent Bradley vanished without a trace, and—"

"But that's crazy!"

"Sure it is," I admitted. "But we can't live on love and frosty air very long. It's all or nothing. Once we get into the hangar, maybe we can pick off one of the little space tugs or launches and make a getaway."

"But I can't operate one," said Valene. "And neither can you."

Which was as bad as it was true. I had forgotten that the Japetans had not for centuries operated space ships.

"How did your great-great-and-so-forth grandfather do it?" I asked, after a moment of thought.

Valene shook her head. "It's a tradition, ages old. You know how legends grow. The only fact left is that we are on Japetus, and must have come from Titan."

"Your ancestor pulled a fast one, and he didn't do it sitting around wondering,"

I said. "Let's do something about it. Freezing may be nicer than being eaten, but getting home for tea on Japetus is much better."

Our search for material to make stilts was futile.

"Why not put me on your shoulders?" suggested Valene. "That'll make us nearly the right size. And you know the signals the Saturnians use when they wear suits that don't have any radiophone equipment."

Not such a bad idea. Report or, better yet, go directly to the hangar, report to no one, and prowl about the shops and air docks as if engaged in some errand that would require an insulated suit for the supposed return trip to the Titanian colony.

During our debate, the Saturnian had died from the cold. Valene and I for a while despaired of getting the boulder off him; and it was not until I back-tracked to the mouth of the ravine and found his drover's goad that we were able gradually to lever the rock out of place.

~ ~ ~ ~ ~

GETTING our victim out of his insulated suit was easier. The outfit was shaped like Terrestrial overalls, except that it had a hood. This we punctured with a sharp rock, knocked the Saturnian's horns from his head, and thrust them through the openings.

Carrying Valene astride of my shoulders and maneuvering both of us into the heavy suit was awkward, but finally we succeeded.

The Saturnian's jerkin and doublet we hacked loose and used to fill out the very-much oversize hood and to round out the shoulders. I was none too confident that our stuffed Satan would pass muster. Valene's arms were entirely too short to make the sleeves of the suit convincing.

But the lady from Japetus had missed little during her brief stay in the Titanian colony.

"These fellows," she said, "spend a lot of time haughtily stalking about with their arms folded. Throw away that drover's goad and pretend that you're an inspector. And by moving slowly enough, you can make the absence of fumes and flames seem reasonable."

It was worth trying.

I had bored two little loopholes in the front of the suit, at the level of my eyes. I helped Valene stuff the sleeves and maneuver them into place. We lashed them into position and secured them by one of her jeweled clasps.

The quiet chill of the Titanian gloom seemed inviting and friendly as my feet moved the synthetic Satan toward the mouth of the ravine. Our venture was an insane blending of carnival masquerade and with empty hands going out to face a hungry tiger.

As I lurched and stumbled among the rocks, I doubted that I would ever get any control of those oversize foot coverings. When we reached the open plain, carrying on became easier.

Our problem, however, was just beginning. To get past the airlocks of the hangar was the stumbling block. There was only one logical approach: to lurk in the gloom and fall in at the rear of the next party of Saturnians coming from the colony, or else to await the departure of a space cruiser, skipping in as it was towed out.

Valene and I compared opinions as I stalked across the barren plain. Presently we realized all our speculation had been wasted. To the left front, we saw the gates of the Titanian colony rise. A glaring floodlight lanced the darkness between the hothouse entrance and the domes of the hangar.

A siren howled. An answering screech came from the hangar. Colored flares shot up and burst in mid air.

~ ~ ~ ~ ~

MY COPPER-HANDLED mace, it seemed, had done more damage than I had expected. In addition to blowing the fuses, the dead short must have melted or volatilized the switch blades, crippled the devices that controlled the airlocks, and for a time blocked all communication with the hangar. This outburst was the first wave of the alarm.

The Saturnians were turning out in force to track us down. Revolt had gone so far that Valene and I could not be abandoned to perish in the dismal wastes of Titan. We had to be captured as an example to the cattle folk of the colony. It was too late to retreat.

Flares were burst in clusters: dazzling blue white, smoldering red, blinding green. A hangar airlock opened, and the glare of the inner illumination reached far out into the Titanian dawn.

"To your right," said Valene. "A hummock—or a boulder—over there."

The synthetic Satan crouched in the shadow cast by the mound of earth excavated from a nearby prospecting shaft.

That blocked my view, but Valene could peep over the edge. She kept me posted. Voices and the *pad-padding* of many feet gave me a clear picture of the general search that the Saturnians were organizing.

"Kent," said Valene, "do you think you can join the pursuit? They aren't in march order. Just pouring out in irregular groups. Others are rounding up the slaves; and I see—*wait a minute!*"

It seemed that I waited a year. Then she resumed, "Way back in the hangar, I caught a gleam of metal. A space cruiser slipping its moorings. We'll have to risk it—once they take the air with searchlights we'll not have a chance."

"How about this pit?"

"All or nothing, Kent! Get ready—"

I edged toward the fringe of the shadow. As a flare settled close to the earth, vastly distorting the patch of obscurity that concealed us, I strode from cover. The cross lighting helped us.

I had walked a dozen strides when the favoring flare blinked out, obliterating the shadow extension. That left us in the much weaker glow from the hangar gates.

No one could have seen us emerging from concealment. In that deceptive light and ghost dawn of Titan, all shapes were grotesque.

With arms folded, a stooped and aged Saturnian stretched uncertain legs toward the general muster at the hangar.

CHAPTER XIV

MEET THE NEW SKIPPER

THEN came the most ticklish two hundred yards I ever covered in my life. I told myself a thousand times over during that short walk that not one of these Saturnians who came out could imagine that a Japetan girl and a bare-handed Terrestrian had baited a cattle guard to a finish. But I was dripping with perspiration when I edged in at the right of the gate.

I made a sharp turn to avoid blocking the advance of a company of Saturnian troops who had just been marched from the Arch-Mogok's flagship. I skirted the wall of the hangar.

Valene whispered, "See that patrol boat—the long, slim one air-docked near the battleship?"

I headed for it. Order was being restored. Saturnians and Titanians were resuming their interrupted duties. The whine of the air pumps and heating units dominated the subsiding tumult.

The airlock through which we had entered was closing; but toward another they were towing a light cruiser. I noted its signal lights, and caught the answering signals at the gate.

That gave me a hint.

I paused at the patrol ship, saw that all but a few plates near the stern had been ground smooth, that only a single pair of exhaust flues had to be reamed and swabbed.

"If you've got any ideas," I said to Valene, "sound off. I'm going to take command of this boat."

"It's up to you, Kent. No one's pulled a trick like that for Lord knows how many centuries."

I would have given my right hand for a five-minute huddle with John Parker and his slide rule. Then it occurred to me that Valene's remote ancestor must have been a stout fellow who didn't know a logarithm from a marlin-spike. And he'd made it.

I stalked up the gangplank, and hoped Valene would see to it that the venerable Saturnian inspector nodded sagely while I supplied the deep-chested, taciturn grumbling.

I headed for the engine room. The chatter of the Titanian mechanics subsided as I entered.

"Old hatchet-puss is back," said one, gripping his hammer and belaboring the inductor shaft they had set up in a straightening jig.

Valene pinched me—angrily, I thought: and I pinched back a warning. I didn't mind the aspersions they cast at our collective Saturnian; but what if that less-than-popular inspector returned while I was prowling around!

"The dirty such-and-such spends so much time hugging the heating coils, it's a wonder he didn't tell us to throw a disintegrator out of whack so we'd not have to take the air," muttered another.

The fellow I was impersonating must be deaf, judging from the colorful and disrespectful words used to describe him. But what was more to the point, I had learned that this patrol boat was not only ready for action, but that it was likely to be called out.

"Go to the bridge," Valene whispered.

I strode down the passageway, halted in a compartment that looked like the instrument panels of six terrestrial airplanes and the control room of as many submarines jammed into a piano box. It was a nightmare of dials, levers, gauges, and indicators.

I should navigate a thing like that, impromptu. They had them simpler eleven thousand years ago or Valene's ancestor was a genius.

Or maybe a fool for luck.

~ ~ ~ ~ ~

A SLENDER Titanian in a black smock with gilt braid stepped into the compartment. He began pressing buttons, closing switches, watching pilot lights blink on and off, and listening for the whirr of buzzers and the tinkle of warning gongs.

"Now what's the idea?" I boomed in as deep and Saturnian a voice as I could muster.

He snapped to attention, knocked a few charts from a plotting table, and saluted. "Just checking up, your Excellency! Our number is going up in a few minutes."

"Is everything right?" I growled.

He assured me that it was—shouted it at me, in fact.

"You take the helm, and stand by," I ordered. "I'm half frozen now, with all that cold air coming in. Get ready to cast off."

He saluted again, picked up the charts, and headed for the compartment forward of the instrument room. That, I decided, must be the bridge. And in a moment I heard his voice from the visiphones in the after compartments of the ship. The mechanics were dropping their tools and hurrying to their stations.

"Never mind reaming the other flues," he concluded. "All hands stand by. The old scum is in a hurry!"

"They have no right to talk that way about us!" Valene whispered indignantly, as the after and forward hatches were battened. Only the main hatch, squarely amidships, was open. Deck hands were preparing to drag aside the gang plank.

And then I saw a stoop-shouldered Saturnian tottering down a runway: arms folded, head hunched forward, he was muffled in a baggy insulating suit to protect him from the chill of the hangar.

"Good Lord! That's the commander of this ship!"

~ ~ ~ ~ ~

HIS head jerked erect. His face was concealed by his hood, but the sudden tensity of his body warned me that he was startled by the flurry of preparation to get under way.

He eyed the towing cables and cranes that were to drag us to the air lock. Then he noted the gangplank, all ready to be pulled clear. His hoarse voice boomed a muffled, rumbling query.

Valene froze and stifled a cry of dismay.

"Get out of this masquerade!" I said. "Quick!"

I ducked into the angle of a bulkhead. Trembling Saturnians explained their actions. The tottering old navigator growled, "Where's that blistering son of a this and that who thinks he's in command of this tub?"

He broke out in simmering Saturnian oaths that made the best efforts of the mate of an ancient Terrestrial windjammer sound like sewing circle chat.

Valene wriggled clear of the insulating suit. I opened a locker and thrust her into it, then kicked our masquerade after her. I slammed the door and plucked a swab from a corner, just as the fuming skipper cleared the hatch.

"And what the curdling crust of chaos are you doing?" he bellowed.

"Getting ready to swab the deck, your Excellency!"

"Where's that *kraklin snardu?*" he demanded. "I'll show 'em if I'm too old to navigate! All of 'em." His language there was, happily, untranslatable; but he was inquiring after the usurper, who had presumably been crowding him out of his command.

It never occurred to him that I was not a member of his crew. If he had any thought at all for the appearance of a human being, he might have attributed my comparatively swarthy skin and sandy hair to oxide dust from the flues. Certainly no one would expect to find the fugitives in the hangar.

But if he failed to find the usurping skipper, the crew would be questioned and in the ensuing line-up they would pick me as a stranger. If he got as far as the bridge, my sailing orders would be countermanded.

"This way, your Excellency," I answered, gesturing down the passageway. "Inspecting the reserve fuel."

In my first trip aft I'd noticed the open door of the bunker loaded with mineral which, when disintegrated, furnished power for the patrol boat.

"Shall I go on with my work, your Excellency?" I inquired, standing aside for him to pass.

"Carry on," he growled. "Do you suppose I'm giving you a vacation?"

I turned, nodded and gestured to the men whose routine the skipper had interrupted.

"Go ahead," I said. "He means all of us."

As they fell to, I followed the skipper. His wrathful grumbling had set every last man of the crew into a blaze of activity. The Saturnian swung left, glared at the door of the bunker. It was now closed.

He seized the latch lever, jerked the door open, and thrust his head into the compartment.

It had but one exit. The reserve fuel, as nearly as I could determine, was let down to the power room through a chute opening from the floor, which was now stacked ten feet deep with the phosphorescent mineral.

Fumes billowed from the door. The stuff was violently radioactive, and the bulkheads that confined it were made up of a six-inch thickness of laminated metal.

The skipper's head jerked right, then left.

"Where is the scum?" he growled.

I did not answer. I shifted my deck swab until I held it like a lance at rest. As the skipper began to turn from the companionway, I charged, catching him off balance. He pitched headlong into the bunker. I slammed the door, dropped the latch into place, and whirled the locking disc. The metal trembled from an inaudible concussion.

~ ~ ~ ~ ~

I HAD no idea how long the skipper would remain bottled up, or whether any branch of the intercommunication system of the ship would enable him to give the alarm. At all events, I had gained a moment's grace.

The towing blocks were lowered into place. All hatches were battened, and we were drawn toward one of the airlocks. The cluster of lights blazing at the left of the rising valve matched the signal bank I had a few minutes ago noted on the prow of the patrol boat. And in another moment we were out in the gray Titanian dawn. The sun had just cleared the horizon.

I dashed forward as the towing blocks were cast off. A radio-visiphone in the instrument room was droning orders from headquarters. The Titanian at the helm was nosing the boat into its course. We had a certain area to patrol, and we had to maintain communication with vessels covering the adjacent areas.

That would be bad.

I stepped into the bridge house.

"Forget that stuff," I said to the Titanian at the helm. "Head this boat to Japetus or I'll take you to pieces by hand."

He eyed me. I repeated my command, and added, "Don't worry about the skipper. He's bottled up in a fuel bunker. Now give 'er the gun. And be mighty sure you don't attract attention before we're out of the patrolled area."

CHAPTER XV

GET HIT AND RUN

FOR local navigation, it seemed, the skipper did not need the help of the operator in the instrument room. But Jarus—the Titanian at the helm—was in a blue funk.

"We can't ever make it! I tell you, it's insane. We'll be overhauled before we can make a break from the patrolled area. They'll cook every last one of us for a trick like that."

"Listen, Jarus," I interrupted, "being cooked is nothing to what I'll do to you if you don't carry on. Where do you Titanians keep your guts?"

"That's not the question," he snapped. "We skilled mechanics and navigators are exempt from the ovens, and why should we take part in this crack-brained conspiracy?"

"Because," I said, "if any Saturnian ship signals us to heave to, I'm taking you to the reserve fuel bunker. I'll kick you right into it. And that stuff will give you such a cooking as no Saturnian ever dreamed of. Your exemption is over. Earn a brand new one by going to Japetus. Right?"

Jarus sized me up from head to foot. His face was a sickly green. My guess as to the fuel bunkers and the sixty-odd pounds by which I outweighed him seemed to have turned the trick. Or maybe it was because my voice wasn't sweet.

He bore down on the controls, and sent the patrol boat zooming upward and out of the level covered by the searching parties.

I ran back to the corridor from which the main hatch opened, and lifted the latch of the door behind which Valene was concealed. "A *nice* way to treat a lady—" she began; but I said, "It's all for the cause, honey. Listen . . ."

I told her what had happened and concluded, "You round up the crew. Sell them on our idea. I've got to keep an eye on the pilot. These gutless lads will sell us out at the drop of a hat unless we buck up their morale. Do your stuff. I'm scouting around for weapons and a few ideas on navigation, and then I'm keeping Jarus under my thumb."

Valene went aft. I opened a succession of lockers, found no side arms, and abandoned the search in favor of trying to find what if any armament the boat itself had. I had gathered from scraps of conversation that it corresponded roughly to a Terrestrial coast guard vessel, or revenue cutter. But it should have some light ordnance.

By glancing through the portholes, I checked the outer contours of the hall and noted what seemed to be gun turrets. The doors of those compartments, however, seemed locked.

I returned to the bridge. Jarus was glum and resigned. I glanced at a bank of dials before him and ordered, "Faster, or I'll break you in two!"

An indicator jumped forward another thousand units. I noted the lever which operated the velocity control.

"Bank left, then nose up."

He obeyed. I watched. Though the elementary operations were simple enough, the bewildering maze in the instrument room gave me a rough idea of the grief I'd have when it came to real navigation, once we got beyond the atmosphere of Titan.

"Now bear on Japetus, again," I ordered.

Whether he did or not, I could not tell. Aiming at a tiny globe not as large as the Terrestrial moon, and six times further from Titan than Luna is from Earth, could not visually be checked. While Jarus might be spineless, there was every chance that he would risk selling us out to the enemy.

And then the radio-visiphone crackled to life. What I saw in the screen was bad enough, but what I heard was worse.

"All ships, attention! Close in on Satelloid Guard *Nilara!*"

The glare of a searchlight blazed from the screen. We were spotted. Jarus looked sick.

~ ~ ~ ~ ~

"SHAKE them!" I growled. "Yank 'er up on her tail and get clear of that light—but fast!"

He obeyed. The glare in the screen flickered out at the bottom. But the transmitter droned. *"Nilara,* ahoy! Are you out of control? Heave to for inspection. By order of Karaku, Arch-Mogok."

"Answer him!"

Jarus turned to the transmitter and in a quavering voice explained that the stabilizers were out of sychronism. But in another moment two searchlights reappeared in the visiphone screen. They had picked us up again.

"Because we answered the call," Jarus hastened to assure me, "their directional apparatus spotted us."

It sounded reasonable, but it did not ring true. They could not possibly have picked us up so quickly and on such a short answer. I rammed the throttle lever home, swung the controls left and up. The sudden swerve flung Jarus into a corner, and only a strong grip kept me from following.

This might be insane navigating, but it ought to throw the pursuit off the track. If we crashed headlong into a satelloid—well, that would be an escape from the ovens at least.

As Jarus picked himself up, I said, "Feed me the data, and quick about it. I'm driving this thing as fast as it'll go; and if you give me the wrong information, you won't like it when we crash."

That should have finished Jarus, but it did not. Something was wrong. A threat like that should have worried him. I put the cutter over the hurdles, corkscrewing, diving, zooming, banking without pretense of pattern or sense. The velocity indicator slammed against the pin and stuck there. We were moving—I didn't know where, except that it was away from the Saturnian ovens.

Three searchlights blossomed out on our tail. Despite my efforts, they were picking us out of the black void, following our insane zigzagging course. They were gaining. Something dropped in a long, fire-trailing arc across our bow: a warning shell, seconded by a final command to heave to.

That shell took Jarus' appetite, then and there. And at that moment the door opened and Valene came to the bridge. Six Titanian mechanics and a pair of navigators followed her.

"They're with us, Kent," she said.

"Man the guns," I answered, giving the controls a twisting that looked like a conjuror's pass. As the atomic disintegrators warmed up we gained in speed. The indicators could no longer record it, but the high-pitched whine of the inductors told the story.

My wrench on the helm piled the new allies in a heap. But the visiphone screen was for a moment clear.

"And who's the navigator?" I demanded as they scrambled to their feet. "Finally, what's wrong here? How can those fellows manage to follow us the way— There they are on our tail again!"

"Easy," said the square-shouldered resolute Titanian. "Look at that."

He pointed to the pilot lights of the signal bank. The answer was simple: our clearing signals had not been cut off. And as final evidence of Jarus' trickery, it was the tail bank that was on.

But before I could make a move, the party broke up in two directions: one plunged to the signal bank switch, the others closed in on Jarus. Before he was entirely hammered to a pulp, two of the cooler heads dragged him aft to fling him into a locker.

~ ~ ~ ~ ~

AN IMPACT racked the cutter, pitching her abeam. The crash rattled every rivet in the hull. A shell had caught us amidship. In the screen I saw that a rapidly moving cruiser had slipped up from the left.

The square-shouldered Titanian leaped forward and snatched the controls.

"Let Kardok take them," said Valene. "He can get us out of it."

For the next five minutes the bridge house was a whirlpool of plotting tools, limbs, charts, and instruments upset by his jugglery of the controls. He hooked his belt to a stanchion, braced his legs, and howled for more power.

The mechanics ran back. They divided their time between the deck and the bulkheads. Any marksman who could pick that cutter out of space had to be a magician.

The visiphone had become a blank blackness. Once there was a furtive flicker as a searchlight pencil for an instant got in line with our viewing screen. We corkscrewed and then zoomed up to dodge the hail of shells that were fired at the reflected gleam of our hull.

Then Kardok flattened the nose. A navigator in the instrument room danced like a madman from one dial to the other, and droned into a speaking tube as he plotted our course.

"Forty-eight hours to Japetus," said Valene as we settled to a steady course. "Unless the enemy's faster boats guess our destination and go ahead to blast us out of the air when we try to land. So why not fool them and head for Terra instead?"

Valene's idea was natural. But there was one objection: the Japetans had developed sundry weapons against the Saturnians. Without that knowledge, the Terrestrial forces could not repel the inevitable successors of the raiders who had captured Parker and me. I explained it to Valene and concluded, "Now if you still want to head for Terra, instead of the risk of landing on Japetus, okay. Whatever you say."

"We'll go to Terra," said Valene, "on our vacation. Now let's find some food. I'm terribly hungry."

A drink, I figured, would be a lot better; but I compromised by following Valene to the galley. She'd probably be a terrible cook, but I could eat fuel from the bunkers—almost.

Then I got an idea.

"While you're busy here," I said, "I'm going to see if Jarus is conscious yet. And if he is, I'm going to kick him around the corridor a little while, just for luck."

CHAPTER XVI

HOMECOMING WITH FIREWORKS

VALENE and I divided the watches.

While our navigator's vigorous action had left us no doubt as to his honesty, the fact that we were actually clear of Titan and less than a million and a half miles from Japetus made us unwilling to take even the semblance of a chance.

A million miles without a sign of trouble. Another quarter of a million, and not an enemy in any quadrant of space. It began to look as if our drill and target practice with the five guns of the *Nilara* had served no more than to relieve the monotony of our flight—although, in thus blasting to pieces half a dozen satelloids, we did remove as many obstructions to navigation.

Saturnian artillery, I had ample opportunity to observe, had developed along lines not strikingly different from Terrestrial ordnance; but there were notable variations in the nature of the ammunition and in the structural details of the guns.

The shells were all provided with de-magnetizers so they were not affected by the repulsion of screens thrown around all craft to deflect small meteoric bodies. And the aiming and range-finding devices were considerably in advance of our Terrestrial anti-aircraft ordnance.

In general, however, a passable familiarity with field and coast artillery would enable one to do creditable work with Saturnian guns.

Instead of nitrous compounds, the Saturnians used an explosive based on the same radioactive mineral that propelled the ship itself. It was, roughly, just a matter of stepping up and controlling the rate of disintegration.

Finally, the shells themselves had a rocket propulsion charge. This enabled even a small cruiser to carry rifles which had extreme range without excessive recoil.

. . . Well! Some hundred thousand miles from Japetus, I found that my curiosity concerning Saturnian ordnance had not been wasted. Four light armored cruisers appeared from the starboard quarter. As Kardok's voice made the visiphone quiver, four others cropped up, far astern. They swung out of the customary wedge formation and spread into a crescent whose horns cut off our retreat.

They carried heavier armor than the *Nildra*. Their speed, however, was not much in excess of ours; and in view of the peculiar construction of Saturnian artillery we could equal their guns in range and hitting power. Nevertheless, our chances of being blasted to pieces were exceptionally good.

There was no exchange of signals, no command to heave to; just a rippling spurt of flame along the pursuing crescent. Kardok nosed down in a dive that racked the *Nildra* from stem to stern.

"Man the guns!" I yelled into the visiphone.

The first volley missed us. The shells burst far ahead of where we had been when Kardok nosed down; but the ranging shots gave the enemy a good observation.

A second volley burst short. They were trying to bracket us. But that trick is difficult when a target moves as fast as we were going—and in as many directions.

Kardok led them a devil's dance. But with all his skill at the controls, the enemy fleet would close in on us, unless our eccentric sweeping and spiraling hampered the pursuing fleet.

Each maneuver gained a certain distance. Once we dipped below the ragged peaks of Japetus, we were safe. But they were still nearly a hundred thousand miles away.

The *Nildra* quivered from the recoil of our five guns. Our fire, however, was wild. Our continuous change of course, which had thus far deceived expert Saturnian gunners, was even more fatal to our own marksmanship.

~ ~ ~ ~ ~

VALENE and I studied the charts and checked them against our time, distance and velocity gauges. The enemy was now beginning to close in on us. It was as if we were maneuvering in the inside of a monstrous funnel, the snout of which was pointing at our goal.

The further we advanced, the less maneuvering space we had. The eight cruisers were now swooping in great involute curves. Our position was becoming doubtful if we could not make a break for open space.

"Stop zigzagging and dive!" I commanded.

Kardok's jaw hardened and his color changed; but he obeyed. This dangerous trick was our only chance to gain headway. We would either reach our mark or be riddled. The fresh burst of ranging shots scored. A shell tore a stabilizing vane from the port side.

One of our stern guns caught the pursuer squarely on the nose. For an instant the cruiser on our tail was enveloped by a sheet of searing flame that hid the entire Saturnian squadron. Kardok bore down on the controls, and shifted the *Nildra* out of the course which the Saturnian gunners had on their plotting boards.

We gained by that exchange. Japetus now gleamed like a Terrestrial full moon on a frosty night. The answering blast from the pursuit squadron missed us by miles.

Our position, however, was still perilous. The Saturnians could again get us bottled up, and if our gunners failed to score another lucky hit, we were washed up.

Far on our left front was a tiny satelloid, one of the strays that go whirling about Japetus. If we could shift our course and time ourselves so that it would block the pursuit, we might gain enough to get through.

But before I could set off the velocities involved, our radio-visiphone transmitted the booming voice of the squadron commander: "*Nilara,* surrender. The Saturnian Council authorizes me to promise free pardon to entire crew if you will return to Titan. Free pardon, and exemption from the ovens. Fire suspended awaiting answer."

Valene and Kardok exchanged a glance.

"The Saturnians," said Kardok, "live up to their agreements."

Valene nodded, and supplemented, "They do. And as far as I can figure it out, they want us back on Titan to prove to the slaves that not even the most daring and luck can hope to escape. If they blow us to pieces in action, the Titanian slaves will think we made it. We've become valuable to the Saturnians."

"And a whole lot more valuable to ourselves," I added.

"Ten seconds," warned the Saturnian commander's voice, "and we resume fire."

~ ~ ~ ~ ~

A GLANCE at the visiphone screen told me the probable result of that fire. We were almost bottled up. And if we did make a sideslip and break through the hail of projectiles about to be directed toward us, the pursuit squadron would have us cut off from Japetus. We were now so close that a lateral move would be as suicidal as turning and attacking.

I made a fresh setting of the range-finding instrument, called for all possible speed, regardless of how long the engines could stand the overload. I saw a ghost of a chance, and decided to take it. My order to the gunners was simple.

"Three seconds," warned the Saturnian commander.

Our gunners reported that they had loaded and laid as directed.

Kardok and Valene eyed me for an instant, wondering at my orders. "One second!"

I brushed Kardok's hands from the controls, glanced once more at the dials and the visiphone screen, then bore hard on the helm. The *Nilara* swooped in a spiral curve that corkscrewed to the left. The Saturnian guns, laid to pick us off if we tried to dive and zigzag toward Japetus. were for a moment out of action.

Before they could shift either cruisers or guns, we were outside their enveloping spirals and heading for the tiny satelloid. It was a jagged mass not much larger than three or four space cruisers.

The squadron commander was now certain that our flight was cut off. He was equally certain that we were making a futile break for open space, that we could not be insane enough to try to take refuge on that tiny chunk of barren rock.

I swung over on the controls, flanking the approaching satelloid. For a moment its bulk, now quite close to the *Nilara,* loomed large in the visiphone screen and blotted out the Saturnian squadron. Then a reverse loop that centered the satelloid on the screen, and I signaled the gunners.

Our five rifles poured a broadside of high explosive shells into the satelloid which we were now chasing along its orbit. A sheet of flame blocked out the entire screen. The concentrated impact blasted the satelloid into uncounted fragments.

The pieces continued with their orbital velocity. It was as if a gigantic shrapnel shell had poured a hail of balls into the approaching squadron.

I nosed over and headed for Japetus. Smoke and flame and dust, expanding into the vacuum of space, formed a vast cloud that blocked the visiphone screens of the pursuers. The flying fragments of rock pounded and rattled against the hulls of the fleet. The result was like a concentration of artillery fire. It jarred their observing instruments out of action.

During that instant the *Nilara* gained out of all proportion to the time required for the maneuver. Our stern guns poured a steady fire into the cloud which enveloped the squadron.

Japetus was at hand. Mighty crags and savage gorges were already distinguishable. We flattened out, so that our path matched the curvature of the satellite. The enemy had reorganized the pursuit; but as the squadron emerged from the cloud on our tail, we saw only six cruisers. Satelloid fragments had taken their toll.

I nosed the *Nilara* into the atmosphere of Japetus, and then gave Kardok the controls. He made a dive for a long, narrow gorge. We settled in the blind angle of the wall.

But as we flung open a hatchway, a terrific explosion shook the gorge. Then came the long, rippling blast of a broadside. Fragments of rock screamed, and green fumes billowed down the narrow cleft.

~ ~ ~ ~ ~

WE CLEARED the hatchway and followed Valene toward one of the several tunnels that gaped blackly from the wall. The Saturnian cruisers were now circling over the gorge, systematically bombarding it. But as we reached cover, an explosion at our left knocked us flat. A spurt of flame lanced the ever-thickening green smoke. A shell roared and rumbled.

It connected: and as we picked ourselves up, a Saturnian cruiser dropped like a rock. Its engine still hissed and whirred. It flattened out of its dizzy dive.

Another blast from our left. But this time the Japetan artillery did not score a clean hit. A blaze and roar, a surge of smoke from the tail of the cruiser: it wavered, spiraled erratically, and pancaked. The remainder of the Saturnian squadron turned tail and fled.

The hatch of the wrecked cruiser swung open, and a platoon of Saturnians swarmed out. Their plan was obvious: to seize the *Nildra* and escape. The attempt, however, was cut short—not by the Japetan gunners, who could have turned their artillery on the *Nilara,* but by a company of footmen who emerged from a tunnel we had thus far not noticed.

The Saturnians deployed to use their flame projectors. The Japetans, wearing armor similar to the insulated suits of the enemy, hurled grenades as they advanced. Flame billowed from the line of Saturnians.

Half a dozen Japetans toppled over in a smoking crisp; and then as the survivors scattered, every man for himself, the bursting bombs enveloped the crew of the stranded cruiser. Haloid fumes drifted toward our tunnel.

We heard the dull coughing report of grenades that Japetans, lurking in ambush, hurled at the enemy. Oily clouds now all but filled the gorge. We could no longer see—but we heard the hoarse roars and choked gasps of the Saturnians.

Two of the platoon charged to within a few yards of the hatchway of the *Nilara.* Another shower of bombs. Through the corrosive mist we saw their bulky bodies pitch forward. Before our eyes, their insulating suits melted like sugar in a cloudburst The writhing bodies flattened into shapeless, soggy heaps.

"Good Lord!" I gasped, catching Valene's hand to drag her down the tunnel and out of range of the spreading cloud of corrosive poison. "Let's get out—"

"Don't bother," she said, smiling. "Watch."

The Japetans reappeared. Each carried on his back a metallic cylinder with a flexible nozzle, and as they advanced, they sprayed the ground and the air.

"Neutralizing the poison attack," Valene explained. "As soon as that is done, we'll go out and join them."

CHAPTER XVII

VALENE—GONE!

MARGOL, the commander of the Japetan troops, joined us aboard the *Nilara*—which had come down in a gorge several hundred miles from the main colony.

While the wrecked battle cruiser was being lashed to the *Nilara* to be towed along as a trophy, Margol fired a barrage of questions at us. We answered all we could, and fired back.

I said, "Just how did you happen to have your artillery on hand and ready to meet the Saturnians?"

Margol grinned, stroked his bristling beard, and answered, "Some of the long-range Saturnian shells that missed your stolen ship came crashing into the hilltops near headquarters. That gave us ample warning. From then on, we watched the combat, and estimated your probable landing place.

"We have all these gorges charged, and unless they blasted you to pieces in mid-space, this was your most likely landing field, coming at your velocity. So we moved some artillery through the subterranean tunnel system . . ."

He gave me considerable details concerning the corrosive gases used by the Japetans in fighting off Saturnian landing parties; then went on, "And with this cutter which you captured, we can look forward to a counter-attack against the Saturnians. The reserve fuel in the bunkers ought to be sufficient for a round trip. Furthermore, it is not impossible that our engineers may salvage the wrecked cruiser.

"One raid on the mines of Titan will replenish the stock. In the meanwhile, we may be able to build a small fleet of space ships, having two to use as patterns."

A short flight brought us to a much larger ravine. There we landed and went on foot into the maze of tunnels and caverns in which Valene's people had lived for centuries. I had little chance, however, to make any intense study of the lighting or ventilating system, the heating plants, or the cellars in which fungi were cultivated for food.

Valene's return to Japetus started an impromptu carnival that made the subterranean city a riot of festivity. It was not until late that night that Valene was allowed to retire, after giving her father's people assurance that she had indeed returned from Titan.

~ ~ ~ ~ ~

FINALLY, however, a council of war was called in the vaulted chamber in which Guraz, King of Japetus, held audience.

"I'm so tired; I'm perishing on my feet," said Valene, detaining me for a moment at the door of the throne room. "But I'll see you in the morning."

"Try and dodge me," I said, as I released her hand and joined the Titanian delegation.

Kardok and the gunners, all wearing the uniforms of Japetan generals, an honorary rank conferred upon them for their valor in action, were seated on a dais at the foot of Guraz' throne. The perils of the past forty-eight hours had eradicated every trace of Titanian docility from their faces. They sat there, grim and belligerent as their Japetan kinsmen.

I saluted Guraz, a broad-shouldered fellow with a face like a Balkan brigand. He was doing his best to conceal the joy behind his craggy mask.

"While I think of it," I finally managed to get in against the crossfire of deliberation, "why not question that Saturnian I kicked into the fuel bunkers? That is, if he hasn't evaporated."

Guraz laughed grimly. "The mineral in the bunkers hadn't hurt him a bit. He burned three men to a crisp when we opened the door. But he's quite beyond questioning now. Of course, the chemicals we poured on him did leave some stains on the deck of the *Nilara . . .*

"I was half thinking of keeping him as a hostage or messenger; but all done and said, I can't complain about his having been summarily dissolved."

That got a big hand. A group of scientists joined the council, and the meeting promised to last indefinitely. The Japetans seemed to think that because I had tricked a few Saturnians, I must be utterly inhuman and quite exempt from such trifles as weariness.

I contrived, however, to keep my eyes open and start another recital of my observations on Titan and the flame-breathing enemy. But when the learned doctors tried to draw me into an account of what had been happening on Earth since the first raid from Saturn, I decided that they had gone too far.

"Get my friend Parker," I advised. "Make a raid on Titan and sift him out of the crowd. Put him in your laboratories. I'll guarantee that inside of a month or two, not a Saturnian will venture beyond the rings of his home planet.

"And now—with your permission—I'm going to find myself a place to sleep for the next week or two. This is rotten etiquette on earth, and it may be worse on Japetus, but I'm plum corked. How about it, your Majesty?"

I bowed to him.

Guraz grinned, nodded, and whispered a few words to an official at his side. As I followed him from the council room, the scientists and the military men resumed their arguments, half a dozen groups talking at once. Each had a separate and distinct idea as to the quickest way to turn out a fleet of space ships.

There was another hot argument among the committees on strategy as to the best tactics to use in raiding the hothouse domes of Titan.

~ ~ ~ ~ ~

GURAZ's steward picked one out of a bewildering maze of dimly illuminated hallways, and branched down an arcaded cross passage. He halted in front of a curtained archway.

"His Majesty hopes that our primitive facilities will please you," was his courteous wish as he drew aside the curtain.

"Tell his Majesty to waste no worry on that score," I replied, crossing the threshold.

The room was hardly more than a cubicle hewn from greenish rock. The blankness of the walls was relieved by arched niches in which stood flagons and bowls of beaten metal, and tumblers of skillfully blown glass. In one corner lay a thick mat of woven fungus stalks and two stools of wrought metal, apparently of copper. Primitive, but acceptable.

I hefted a flagon and sniffed the contents. It contained some of the pungent liquor distilled from the fruit of a subterranean plant. The Japetans had emptied many a keg of it during the festivities that followed Valene's return. I filled a tumbler; but before I could drain it, there was a tapping at the doorjamb.

I brushed aside the curtain. A shapely Japetan girl stood at the threshold.

"Her Majesty would like to see you in her apartment," she said.

"Her Majesty?" That stopped me for a moment; and then I knew that she meant Valene. Meeting in the face of peril, and plunging from one danger to another and worse had given me little chance to have any thought of my lovely companion's rank. "Right away. Lead on."

"Her Majesty," explained the attendant, "has had such a trying day that she finds sleep quite impossible."

It hadn't struck me before, but that was exactly the way I felt. I followed her down the hall.

As a matter of fact, I had suddenly forgotten the fatigue that had brought me from the council room. Listening to wrangling generals and scientists is one thing, and having a few quiet words with a girl like Valene is something else entirely.

My guide passed the council room, crossed the main tunnel that led into the gorge in which we had landed the captured coast-guard boat, and then headed down a lateral passage.

Finding one's way about this maze, I reflected, must require considerable experience. From cross drifts I heard the distant shouting and chanting of the Japetan soldiers, still feasting, broaching keg after keg of *sherboos* and becoming more warlike every moment.

We turned left and into an arcaded passageway.

"Please wait here," said Valene's maid, "and I will announce you."

The troops were having a large time of it. The uproar became louder. Then I caught a note that was far from mirthful. An angry roar surged down the arcade. The solid rock quivered beneath my feet, and an explosion jarred my ears.

Artillery fire!

~ ~ ~ ~ ~

A SCREAM came from Valene's apartment. As I bounded toward the door the maid reappeared, shrieking at the top of her voice.

"Wait a minute!" I said, catching her by the arm. "What's up?"

She was quite beyond coherent speech. Another crash or artillery blotted out whatever sense her answer might have had. I tore the curtains aside and cleared the threshold at a leap.

Two Japetan girls, dressed like my guide in scarlet smocks, lay crumpled on the floor. One was unconscious. The other, though her head was bruised and battered and her black hair was clotted with blood, showed signs of recovery.

"Snap out of it!" I ordered. "Give her a drink of *sher-boos*—find out what's wrong."

Then I saw that there was no need of further information: a scrap of vermillion cloth, the color of Japetan royalty, and the sapphire bracelet which Valene had worn on her left wrist, lay on the green paving.

Some enemy had slipped into the underground city and had dragged Valene from her suite. I heard a roar of voices and the pounding of many feet, and the roar of artillery fire. The council room was disgorging its gathering of advisors.

"Take care of your friends," I said as I dashed down the hall to join the shooting crowd.

We emerged on the floor of the gorge. The artillery fire had subsided; but this was scarcely noticed in the rumble of the crowd. I followed the gestures of the Japetans. Far over-head, the gleaming shape of the *Nilara* mocked us. And as the crowd made way for Guraz and his officers, I saw that only the wrecked Saturnian battle cruiser remained.

Some traitor was piloting it back to Titan.

Valene's maid came screaming through the pack.

"She's gone! They took her—"

Neither of Valene's other two attendants could identify the daring invader. They had been knocked unconscious before they could give the alarm; but not a shred of hope was left. Some one or more among the Titanians of my crew had abducted Valene and was hastening to Saturn.

With only a wrecked cruiser left, we could not pursue. The fear of mass reprisal had undoubtedly induced some trai-tor to win immunity in advance. And Valene was gone!

CHAPTER XVIII

TURN OUT THE GUARD

I MUST have taken Valene's capture more to heart than did her hard-boiled father. At all events, when he saw my long face, he slapped me on the shoulder, and fairly telescoped my spine. Considering my weight, that was a hefty pat.

Guraz said, "Buck up, my friend! You've been through a tough siege of it, but we're depending on you to help us take the warpath."

His gruffness, I began to sense, was a bit put on. But the way he put it did snap me out of the jitters. His people were depending on him, and so he had to stand up under his loss.

A few centuries ago, on Terra, we had decided that kings were excess baggage; but then Guraz was an old-fashioned specimen, and he justified the breed by being steadier under fire than his subjects; a better man than any of them.

Guraz proved this during the days that followed. Never a word about, "If we can repair that wrecked cruiser in time, we may find Valene." The girl was something not to be mentioned in his presence. If I had not known the whole story, I would have concluded that he was so absorbed in rebuilding the wreck, in planning a raid on Titan and on Saturn, that he had not a thought for anything else.

Once I did catch him in a corner, muttering into a two-quart flagon of *sherboos.* He gulped and stuttered, "Here, you! Drink up." But I knew what was eating him, though I pretended I didn't. So I drained the stuff, and by the time I got it down, he was pacing and scowling and bawling out a scientist.

"Your Majesty," the white-haired scholar managed to cut in, "the cruiser *Sargoza* can be repaired. Completely rehabilitated."

"That's what I've heard right along," said Guraz. "Do you mean it this time?"

The clanging of the forges, the puff of blowers, the crash of trip hammers in the adjoining shop made the cavern tremble. "It will be risky perhaps," the scientist hedged. "But it can be navigated, provided—"

I cut him short. "I'll take care of the provisions. And nuts to the risk. Particularly if I have a good gun crew."

~ ~ ~ ~ ~

WE HAD the Titanian navigators. It was pretty well established that the only weak sisters in the lot had been the two who had been missing ever since Valene's abduction. And by the time the warped plates were replaced, the inductors trued up and balanced, and the instruments reconditioned, the morale on Japetus was reaching a peak.

People began to speak of Valene, and Guraz did not shut them up.

"What's your plan, Bradley?" he demanded.

"We haven't enough fuel to raid Saturn, and neither have we a chance in a dog fight with their big cruisers. So why not go to Titan? We'll make a secret landing. We'll slip into the hothouse and get Valene."

Guraz frowned.

"How do you know she's there?"

"She and I raised such a riot getting out," I reasoned, "that they'll make quite a show of her having been recaptured. If any other Titanians get the revolt bug, putting her on parade will cure them as nothing else would. Anyway, that's the way I size up the Saturnian way of thinking."

Guraz muttered in his grizzled beard. "Right. And you came all the way from Terra with them. You talked with the Arch-Mogok, Thorgulu."

"A nice chap, if it weren't for his diet," I said. "Yes. They do think in grooves deep as these ravines. A precedent for everything, and everything according to precedent. Otherwise Valene and I would never have made it.

"They're a lot like some of our Terrestrial tribes. Utterly thorough, utterly persistent—and utterly unable to see the other fellow's angle. So they don't anticipate how he'll put one over. And this fracas hasn't shaken their confidence, remember."

That decision rolled the council in the aisles. And that was the plan when the cruiser *Sargoza* finally took off.

~ ~ ~ ~ ~

WHEN we passed the orbit of the satelloid that Valene and I had blown to pieces, we had to make a wide detour. Otherwise the swarm of fragments would have punctured the hull.

"If we don't find her," I said to Ion, the chief officer we'd promoted from the Titanian crew, "she's at least got a permanent monument in space."

"We'll find her, Your Excellency."

"Skip the Excellency till you know how good I am. The name is Kent. Or Bradley."

"Very well, Your Excellency."

They go out for titles on Japetus; and finishing a Saturnian single-handed gives a fellow a case of permanent prestige, even if he had a woman to drop the boulder which conked the enemy.

We slipped up on Titan's dark side. This was easy, remember, since the satellite's "day" is equal to a Terrestrial week. And in the shadow, it was too cold for any Saturnian to venture unless he was driven to the hardship.

Except for a detachment left with the *Sargoza*—they had orders to duck back to Japetus if we got into any trouble that looked like an unhappy ending, since the ship was more valuable than we were—I led the crew toward the compound domes of the hothouse.

"If they get shaky," said Ion, whose second command could navigate passably well, "we'll be stranded. Any serious commotion will—"

"That's just the point," I told him. "You've got every reason now for being careful."

"Down," some one whispered from the rear. "There's a light."

"Where?"

"Our right."

We were on our faces before this last was spoken. In the direction mentioned, I saw an eerie glow; a reflection from a glass-hard ledge. My first thought was that some Saturnians had seen us land, and were creeping up a ravine.

"Spread out, and sneak toward them," I said. "Don't make any noise. If we blot them out before there's a disturbance, we can do a lot before another patrol sets out to find why the first one is missing."

We lost half an hour or more in creeping toward the glow. Even when I realized that it was not moving, I refused to let anyone take a reckless chance. It was not until we were right on the lip of the cleft that I learned the answer.

The joke was on us.

But it was a sweet one. Far down below was a bed of luminous mineral. What we had seen was its reflected glow. Had we passed during the gray Titanian day, we would never have noticed the outcropping.

Ion whispered—though there was no reason now for keeping his voice low—"It looks like fuel for the disintegrators."

"Precisely. If not that, then something like it. Like enough to be worth looking into."

We backtracked and found an easy approach to the bottom. This was not far from the level space where the *Sargoza* had landed. I set the crew to work digging at the vein of ore.

"Load her up to capacity," I told them. "Next to finding Valene, this is the best thing that could have happened. All of you stay here, except Ion."

Once they were at their next task, Ion and I set out alone for the hothouse. In addition to our side arms, we had some tools from the machine shop of the *Sargoza*. They were not especially suited for digging, but they were of tough, glass-hard alloy; they would do.

~ ~ ~ ~ ~

WE HAD more of a task than I had anticipated. The walls were set deep in the rocky skin of Titan. Tunneling would take days, since the thick barrier was nearly as solid as foundation rock. I had assumed that the hothouse had been built over a patch of thin earth; there were such, here and there, on the satellite.

But from every appearance, it now seemed that the earth inside had been hauled from considerable distances and concentrated; that its richness was the result of synthetic chemistry on an incredible scale.

I nudged Ion, whose shoulders were sagging. By the dim light from within, it was plain that all his optimism had sagged; his face had. "Get up on my shoulders! We're not whipped yet. Keep that chisel."

He obeyed. He was husky, and I was ready to call for a rest when he whispered, "I'm prying a pane loose. Won't have to break it."

And so we finally got in through the roof. It was ticklish work, dropping to the cantilever truss that supported the superstructure, but we made it. Then some more gymnastics. Hanging by my knees, I managed to reach down and out, and work the dislodged pane back into place.

Once we crawled down one of the supporting columns, I went back through the jungle of fungi and looked up. From the ground, the job looked right. I had some difficulty in deciding just which pane had admitted us. I had just one qualm, but that was none of Ion's business. He'd know soon enough, if anything slipped!

My familiarity with the general arrangement of the hothouse now served me well. Thus we quickly picked up one of the minor lanes, and likewise avoided the dangerous main roads, and the course of the overhead trolley system.

Crouched in a dense patch of fungi—certain varieties of these growths were planted to enrich soil drained by intensive cultivation—we watched a group of slaves and their Saturnian inspector.

Ion caught my arm. He was about to risk a whisper. I clamped my hand over his mouth. But no one could blame him for nearly losing control.

Valene had been paraded as a lesson to the slaves. The two traitors, Argol and Xanthos, were now chief overseers. The cattle-like placidity of the Titanian slaves who discussed the tragedy had changed to despair. Formerly resigned, they now knew that escape was possible; that for all of Valene's courage, that two of their own kind had betrayed her.

"We can't do a thing for her," muttered one of the several who were near us, and not at the moment under the taskmaster's eye. "But if I ever get a hand on Argol and Xanthos!"

"When does she go to Saturn, did you say?"

One answered, "Depends on how many groups see her each day."

~ ~ ~ ~ ~

THE Saturnian inspector came toward them. I caught Ion's shoulder, and signaled a slow retreat. We would hear no more from this group unless we waited; and we could afford no delay. Not when I knew that there was a chance of her still being in the colony.

"They figured it wrong again," I told Ion. "Instead of bluffing the slaves, parading Valene has made them mutter. And think. Which they didn't do before."

"Where is she now?" Ion asked.

"They parade her to a group at a time," I explained. "We have to do some more listening. I don't know how many groups there are."

"Neither do I. Working with the navigation gang," Ion said, "kept me from knowing a thing of what goes on in this hothouse."

But though we soon got additional information, it was far from pleasant. The last exhibition of the recaptured girl would be near the administration building. It might even now have been completed.

We raided a laborer's hut. The occupants were absent. Thus I got a slave tunic for Ion. In another place, I found an overseer's tunic for myself. With this distinction in rank, I could make a pretense of being on some special duty, with a common laborer to do the actual work.

The tools from the *Sargoza's* kit made such a story plausible, if we were forced to give an account of ourselves. Unhappily, I did not have a copper mace. They were not as common as a change of clothing. But whatever the risk, it could not be avoided.

Near the administration building we saw a regiment of slaves, male and female. They were grouped around a platform. A Saturnian addressed them. He warned them of the futility of revolt.

"Go out and see her board the ship to Saturn!" he was saying in conclusion. "She was smart enough to escape, but the long arm of the law reached to Japetus and caught her. See, and be warned."

Saturnian guards, muffled in insulating suits, herded the regiment toward the air locks. We joined. The shivering thousand went out into the cold and the dim gray of Titanian noon. Floodlights played on the gleaming side of a cruiser. A ramp was drawn up to its loading port.

Then Valene appeared. She wore a scarlet gown. Jewels sparkled on her throat and bare arms. The Saturnian treasuries had been turned inside out to adorn her. A tiara, something unknown on Japetus, blazed in a circle about her high piled black hair.

They were making a show of her, accentuating her loveliness and her rank so that the slaves would be all the more impressed by the fate she could have avoided for a dozen years.

The mutter of the slaves suddenly ceased. They looked up, silent. The Saturnians mistook this for awe in the presence of one about to face premature death. But I could read Ion's face, which was a reflection of those about us. There was wrath, not awe.

The only difference was that Ion had learned something about courage during his stay in Japetus. The others still had that lesson ahead of them, or there would have been a reckless rush, a vain and futile rush to overpower the guards.

~ ~ ~ ~ ~

WE WERE near the ramp, Ion and I. Valene did not see me. Her glance was high, reaching out over the crowd. She was shivering in that biting air, I knew; we all were.

She raised her hand in a gallant gesture. In the silence, her voice carried: "I'm sorry to keep you out in the cold," she said. "As for me, I like it."

Ion fiercely whispered, "Dash up and grab her!" He caught my arm, as if to pull me with him. "We can run for it. To the *Sargoza*. As you two did to the *Nilara.*"

"Shut up, you fool!"

"But we can! We can try!"

Then she caught my eye. Whether she heard, or merely sensed my presence, I do not know. But it was a long glance, before I had to kick Ion's shins and say, "I've got a better plan. We'd all be killed and not save her. Shut up!"

Valene smiled a little. She turned when her guard beckoned.

Then someone yelled, well in the rear. Saturnians roared and rumbled, spurted flame and smoke. A siren screeched. Guards were turning out! Saturnians in suits made for the most intense cold. They were running out, skirting the wall of the hothouse.

The news spread until voices near us made it plain. The leakage of cold air past the pane we had dislodged had attracted the attention of a Saturnian inspector. Now they were looking for the slaves who had supposedly escaped in a suicidal flight into the dark.

If they found the *Sargoza* we were finished!

"Let's go," I said to Ion.

But we were herded back into the hothouse; the ring of Saturnian guards kept us from slipping into the outer wastes. I wondered how long we could evade the inevitable check-up of slaves.

CHAPTER XIX

BOMBARDMENT ON TERRA

EARTH, meanwhile, was rapidly recognizing the genuine menace. Saturnian raids, staged like the one on Washington, had swooped down on other capitals; likewise, they had dipped into thickly populated rural districts, striking first at one continent, then at another.

"It looks," said Parker, thumbing the dispatches he and Shadra were examining as they took time out for a ham on rye at the laboratory, "as if the Saturnians are getting a cross section of the Earth's population."

She rose, glanced over his shoulder, and somberly shook her sleek head; a Terrestrian wave had enhanced its beauty. "Cape Town, Khartoum," she read. "Ankara. Khatmandu. Singapore. Moscow—and a raid on Outer Mongolia. That covers every color!"

"Ah—every flavor, my dear," Parker corrected, grimly.

An orderly dashed in, and the spectacled scientist hastily dropped Shadra's hand. Deep lines were making a network around his eyes and accentuating his mouth. "Now what?"

"The ordnance department report, Dr. Parker. Urgent!"

They had stepped him up in rank. With enough raids to authenticate his story, he had collected a basket of honorary Ph.D's, Sc.D's, and of course, some LL.D's though he knew nothing about law.

Parker studied the message for a moment. His eyes widened. He leaped to his feet, let out an unscholarly yell, and dropped his slide rule.

Shadra was puzzled. "Now what?"

He did not answer. He could not. He had her in both arms and he was kissing her. That was more than the orderly had expected; he had his own ideas on scientists.

Ruffled, flushed, and with a glow in her eyes, Shadra finally got a chance to gasp, "John—you might wait till after office hours!"

"It's the demagnetizing shells!" He waved the yellow sheet. "Corbin has succeeded! The deflectors can't turn the projectiles out of their trajectories any longer." Then he sobered up. "If it actually works."

He turned to his desk and forgot all about Shadra and the orderly. He spread out the papers that had accompanied the dispatch and reached for his slide rule.

~ ~ ~ ~ ~

GETTING the new armament under production took time. And the Saturnians redoubled their attacks. They were working from a base in the deadly Bolson de Mapimi, in northern Mexico; a blistering desert whose heart was inaccessible except from the air.

Spies were helping the invaders. As on Titan, they were panic-stricken people who thought that it would be better to win personal safety than to run the risk of being netted in the raids that now threatened North America and Europe.

The Saturnians apparently had made the most of their opportunity to take human specimens of all races to the home planet; and coming back, the raiders concentrated on the continents which offered the best stock for populating other satellites.

Parker and Shadra were now at the Canadian plant where duplicates of the captured *Karamanu* were being built. The big problem was to find substitutes for the alloys the Saturnians used; and particularly, a synthetic fuel to feed the disintegrators. Camouflage concealed the shops; supplies were hauled in by night over mountain trails.

"The first one," Parker said, "will be tested tomorrow. If it passes inspection, we will be able to fight them on their own terms."

"That's only half of it," Shadra said grimly. "A counterattack on their capital will give them something to think about; that's next!"

"If famine doesn't beat us first," Parker answered. "Raiding parties have been keeping such a close watch on the corn and wheat belt that the farmers are hiding."

He sighed. Fresh dispatches had dampened his enthusiasm. "There may be a general surrender. Thorgulu has been spreading propaganda. Listen to this one . . ."

He read the Arch-Mogok's persuasive argument, the same one that had been offered on the trip to Saturn; easy work, comfortable living, with no cares until the time for going to the ovens.

It sounded alluring, after months of terror, particularly when there seemed to be no chance of repelling the invincible invaders. The vast majority of the harassed population could not understand the delays in counter-attacking. They were hopeless and desperate.

Shadra shook her head. "That logic made cattle out of my people in the Titanian gardens," she sadly said. "It may work here, too."

"Let's go out into the assembly department," Parker said. "Sitting at a desk— Moving about is what we need."

And then he learned how civilization was crumbling. The first warning was an ominous humming; the familiar sound of a Saturnian cruiser, far overhead. The variation in the note told him how it was circling, how it had its target spotted. Despite camouflage, it had come directly to its goal. Spies had betrayed the carefully hidden plant.

Parker leaped to a telephone. "Lights out! Pass the word—"

~ ~ ~ ~ ~

A RUMBLING blast drowned his words.

The impact flung him against the wall. Glass shattered and the pungent reek of explosives surged down the hall. Sirens were screaming and the workers of the night shift yelled as they fled to their dugouts.

"Get under cover!" Parker shouted, as he helped Shadra to her feet.

He turned to run down the passage. She followed him. Another blast blotted out his protest. A girder, hurled high into the air by the first detonation, crashed down through the roof. It blocked the way. The lights no longer winked through smoke and dust. The power system had been knocked out.

Parker scrambled over the obstacle. Then he heard the sharp smack of artillery fire. A searchlight blazed to life. The portable generators of the anti-aircraft stations were in action, and great reflectors shot their million candlepower beams into the darkness. They picked out the yellow plates of the raiding cruisers.

Another bomb dropped. One wing of the plant was enveloped in a gust of flame. But the spreading smoke now masked the target, so that the Saturnians could no longer place their explosive with as much accuracy as at first.

Parker ploughed his way through the yelling workers. He stumbled over others who had been cut down by flying fragments.

Shadra would not let go of his hand. He fairly dragged her along. The attack had been in progress only for a matter of seconds, but it already seemed hours; the earth shook under his feet, and choking fumes seared his nostrils and eyes. He lurched into the casemate that sheltered the fixed guns.

An officer recognized him and gestured at the sentry who tried to bar the way. The plotting crew were unaware of the interruption; the gunners continued tracking, setting off the data.

Whack! The steeply inclined barrel flashed back, dipped into the recoil pit. All the while, the turntable was slowly moving, and the gunners were setting off the next elevation.

The gun had scarcely risen into battery when the breech opened. Fumes gushed back. A single blast of air flushed the bore, and one of the crew slammed a fresh shell into the breech.

Men yelled, and their voices could be heard even above the ear-splitting whip of the succeeding shot.

"Got him! Got him!" they cried as they saw the effect of the first projectile.

The other battery was blasting away. Parker saw the hovering invader yaw under the concentrated impact. Clouds of smoke half muffled the tail. The magnetic repulsion screen no longer deflected shots. A burst inside the hull of the cruiser had blown a plate loose from its rivets.

It dropped, twinkling in the searchlight glare. The ship spun, wallowed. Suddenly it raced after the falling fragments. Its disintegrators had been disabled.

Shadra was yelling triumphantly in mixed English and Saturnian. Parker held her with one arm and grinned at the artillery commander. Another Saturnian ship crashed. The last one fled.

But the grounded invaders were not waiting to have the wreckage blow about their ears. They poured out. The searchlights shifted.

"Direct fire!" the gun commander shouted into the telephone.

"Wait!" Parker yelled. "Wait!"

~ ~ ~ ~ ~

HIS voice hadn't a chance in the uproar.

The Saturnians, advancing on foot, spewed smoke and flame. Space suits confined their wings, and there was no time to get out of them, even if they had been able to endure the bitter northern cold.

They tramped through the snow. Small-arm bullets drilled their armor but did not stop the desperate rush.

The hastily armed workers broke before the towering monsters.

Then the field guns got into action.

Not even Saturnian insensibility to missiles could stand that. Shrapnel with fuses cut for muzzle bursts and explosive fused for contact detonation ploughed into them. They disintegrated in clouds of flame and fragments of mineral that but an instant before had been animate.

The last of the stranded invaders were almost at the gun muzzles before they were blown to bits. The raid was over, and thick smoke blanketed the entire plant site.

Finally Parker made himself heard. "I told you not to fire! Why didn't you wait until we tried the liquid hydrogen bullets?"

The officer in command chuckled indulgently. "This worked, didn't it?"

"Of course it did. But you can hardly use artillery to blow each individual Saturnian to pieces," Parker objected. "We needed these specimens for testing the effect of the new ammunition. It seems just the thing on paper, but we're not sure it will work in practice."

"I fancy you would have gone out to capture a few, if you'd had time?"

Parker shrugged. "Let's see what is left of the plant. We drove them off, but took a terrible setback in doing it."

He was all too right. The factory was a tangle of twisted wreckage. Every ship had been damaged by the bombs. The propaganda department could circulate the story of the first victory, but Parker wondered how much good that would do. People were now prone to believe bad news readily, and receive good tidings with skepticism.

But when the inspection was over, he brightened a little.

"There's one point that is in our favor," he told Shadra. "While the *Karamanu* is the only ship left, we've at least got a supply of fuel. So we can bomb the Saturnian headquarters in northern Mexico. The ships that crashed had enough in their bunkers for a long cruise."

"And will you go on that raid?" Shadra asked levelly.

"I ought to. I piloted her all the way from Saturn."

"Then I'm going, too."

"You'll not. One of us has to stay. In case of—well, accidents, someone should remain, to guide an expedition back to Saturn. To get Kent Bradley."

Shadra shook her head. "John, there's not a chance for your friend. Not with the way he made that insane break.

They must have hunted him down, to make an example of him."

"That's why I wanted to capture some Saturnians," he answered. "To question them. As well as to try those frozen hydrogen bullets on them. Seeing a few of their comrades punctured and frozen, then blow apart by the expanding gas, would make them willing to talk. And if we made a demonstration like that, we could release a few survivors, to carry the news to Saturn."

The artillery officer approached. He cut in, "That's a fine plan, Dr. Parker. But catch your rabbit first."

CHAPTER XX

STAND BY FOR BOARDERS!

THERE was not a chance of carrying out my plan for Valene's rescue. At the best, it had been slim enough; and the leakage of cold air, which had been detected by the unusual fluctuations of the thermostats that controlled the heating of the hothouse city, had warned the Saturnians that something was wrong.

When they found the dislodged pane, where Ion and I had slipped in, patrols turned out to search every slave village, every thicket of fungus, and every mine. We were on the dodge. The best we could expect was to escape detection. And there were plenty of overseers ready to betray us to pacify their furious masters.

"Looks as if there's going to be a general muster of all the slave pens," I whispered to Ion as I caught his arm and bit by bit nudged him toward the fringe of the crowd that had enveloped us. "If we aren't recognized as strangers right away, a count will spill it all."

"Their bookkeeping is too good," he gloomily muttered. "What'll we do?"

"Get busy before things quiet down too much," I advised.

Finally we detached ourselves from the crowd. Regardless of risk, we boldly set out on our way down the main avenue. A repair party was leaving headquarters. They had tool kits. An overseer marched them along. He turned back to answer the Saturnian who had some afterthoughts to add to orders just delivered.

"They're going to the leak," Ion said.

"We'll join them."

Ion thought I was crazy. There was a good deal of justice in that opinion, but there was no other course. While he had been willing to make a suicidal dash to pick Valene from the ramp of the space ship, he hesitated on a bold play to save himself.

"Listen," I told him. "We'll be caught here. Our crew out in the dark will be jumped before they know what's happening. Chin up, guy! It'll work."

As we stalked boldly along on an imaginary errand, I explained my plan. It was one of those simple things that are perfect if they work; though I had to use a lot of effort to make myself overlook the chances of failure. We made a roundabout march. I was in a sweat, but we had to play our part.

Every so often, I had my companion halt at a pipe line or valve house. I gravely watched him while he tapped and prodded around in the tangle of tubing. This was an old device that kept many a workman drawing pay on Terrestrial construction jobs; and there was no reason why it would not succeed on Titan.

"We're just about there," Ion said. He was getting shaky, and I did not blame him a great deal. "Suppose the overseer gets suspicious?"

I peeped through the thicket that separated us from the wall; we were now close to the leaking pane in the dome. "He looks like a nice fellow," I said, "and it'd be a shame to hurt him. Just be ready, and don't forget that a spanner is good for loosening nuts as well as tightening them."

Ion nodded and hefted the tool we had picked up on the way and added to our equipment.

~ ~ ~ ~ ~

I WALKED up as if I owned the place.

Ladders had been set up. A boatswain's chair swung from a girder. Without a word to the overseer I climbed up and watched the glaziers who were sealing the joint.

When he saw me he shouted, "Who are you? What are you doing here?"

I answered, "You're not doing it right. That's not the way, at all." Then, to Ion, "Bring up those tools."

One of the glaziers muttered. "Shut up."

I said, "Those are my orders, and here I am. Get out of my way."

Ion was now beside me on the girder. Its flange was two feet wide; it was broad enough to be a catwalk, but it did not offer the best footing in the world if one got a sudden push on the chin, which was the prospect one or more of the party faced.

The overseer, still not quite ready to believe his eyes, came up the ladder. Having someone cut in on his job was getting under his skin. "Come down, you! If I have to get you, I'll kick you down!"

Anger interfered with his judgment. The workmen were leaving the argument to their chief. They crept out on smaller girders, to be clear in case we began to grapple. The responsibility was not theirs, and they were risking nothing by quitting work and letting the overseer handle me.

As Ion stepped clear of the top rung, I cracked down on the boss of the repair squad. He crumpled, did a loop, and chunked down into the fungi. Before the gaping laborers knew what to say, Ion had knocked the partially caulked pane out of position. It dropped outside the wall.

I said, "If you fellows have any guts, you'll follow me. We're getting out of here."

That left them gulping. Ion seconded me: "You'll get small thanks for telling the Saturnian works manager you let us escape."

They exchanged glances, muttered, then agreed. Ion scrambled over the ledge. When the last laborer had followed him into the bitter cold, I went over the side.

We headed at a dead run toward the distant ridge which concealed the ship. Ion panted, "Why did you risk so much trouble? Suppose we'd had a fight?"

"The overseer won't be talking for quite some time. When the thermostats show cold air rushing in at the same spot as before, the heating engineer will just think that the crew is having difficulties in fixing the leak. If we'd broken through anywhere else, there'd have been a new leak, and then there *would* have been fun."

Far out in the treacherous grayness, we saw parties of Saturnians fuming and floundering over the uneven terrain. They were not making fast progress; they did not believe that fugitives could do anything but perish in the cold, and their main interest was getting back into the hothouse.

We ducked down steep slopes, crawled along the ragged bottoms of ravines. Sometimes the searchers, circling about, passed within a few yards of us. But finally we slipped between the outermost groups.

~ ~ ~ ~ ~

THE general alarm had aroused the crew of the *Sargoza*. They were ready to take off, but they had resolved to wait until detection was inevitable.

"How much fuel?" I demanded.

"Bunkers loaded," was the report.

"Where's Valene?" someone asked.

Then I stepped into the cabin and they saw my face. For a moment, no one spoke. Then Ion said, "I guess I was crazy, wanting to drag her off the ship. But I hate to go back and see Guraz and tell him I didn't try."

To blame him for accusing me was hardly fair; I knew how all the Japetans felt about Valene. Then someone asked, "What ship, Your Excellency?"

"The ship," I bitterly answered, "that's taking her to Saturn. We lost so much time coming back through the inside, instead of making a direct return, that there's not a chance of overtaking it. The *Sargoza's* not fast enough."

"But no ship left," the crew insisted. "We were watching for signs of you. We heard the disturbance. The sirens. We expected a cruiser to start circling with search lights."

"Look!" Ion gestured. "One is taking off now!"

He was right. The glow of the repulsion tubes was unmistakable.

It was not a ship sent to search for us. It was heading into space, in the general direction of Saturn.

"Cast off, right now!" I ordered. "Whether she's on that cruiser or not is something we can't tell without a look."

The news of a slave escape must have delayed Valene's departure until the Saturnians had time to check up and see whether a general break had been planned. While they would not fear an uprising of their human cattle, they had to consider the possibility of a mass suicide; hundreds of Titanians, stirred by Valene's bold escape and tragic recapture, might have decided to rush into the cold wastes and perish, rather than to submit to further slavery.

Or such was my estimate of whatever reason had delayed the departure of the cruiser. Though for the moment I was too busy at the controls to think much. Holding a low elevation, we maneuvered the *Sargoza* to the further extremity of the crater that had concealed her.

~ ~ ~ ~ ~

WE CLEARED the lip with hardly a foot to spare. Bysweeping close to the surface of the satelloid, we might escape observation. The glow of the disintegrators would not be so conspicuous.

Nonetheless, it was tense work for a few moments. An outcropping tongue of rock might slice our hull. Some Saturnian patrol, circling about in the gloom, might notice the glow.

Ion, however, insisted that our chances were good. "Your Excellency, if one of the patrols did happen to be on that ridge behind us and saw the disintegrator tubes, they'd mistake the lights for the breath of some member of one of their own searching gangs."

That was something I'd overlooked. I felt ten years younger.

"Saturn, here we come!" And the engineer got the full speed ahead signal.

We were not trying to pursue the ship which had just left the satelloid. We would be spotted, and the whole fleet would be on our tail. The play was to swing in a wide loop, and—

But first, we needed all the power we could crowd on. The *Sargoza* was shivering from the strain. As we gained elevation, we changed our course so that the satellite itself would shield us from chance observation by cruisers that might be coming into port.

"The inductors can't stand much more, Your Excellency," the engineer warned.

"Neither can I! Pour on some speed!" I told him.

Finally we straightened out. Titan was far behind us. Ahead was the ringed planet, with its inner moons. For a while, there was nothing but blackness riddled by swarms of meteoroids. They peppered the hull.

Despite our racing clip, we had lost time through our strategy; assuming that the cruiser which had left Titan was holding a normal pace, she would nevertheless have gained thousands of miles.

Our quarry was a mere speck in that moon-spattered gulf.

Finally our instruments detected the ether disturbances of a cruiser. I signaled for an upward swoop and prayed that the skipper ahead would not be looking for trouble. Unless he was unusually wary, he would pay little attention to the indicator that revealed the presence of a ship long before the visiphones or optical equipment could pick it up. There was not enough traffic to make that necessary, since we were still far from the thickly traveled routes between Saturn and the inner moons.

Bit by bit we overhauled her. I kept on the blind spot that all but the newer ships had. Her running lights and general shape identified her. This was the one which carried Valene to Saturn!

We cut off the power and coasted on our momentum. We no longer emitted any betraying glow. I played tricks with the controls. The *Sargoza* yawed and spun; ether drift added to the erratic twists of the course.

Then we got busy with the visiphone. I gave a false identification.

"Inductor burned out. Cargo disintegrating a weak plate," I told the skipper. "Tow us to Saturn."

The cruiser acknowledged our distress call. The skipper had no reason to doubt. The successful raid on Japetus, culminating in Valene's capture and the supposed destruction of the *Sargoza,* left little ground for suspicion.

Bit by bit, the cruiser came alongside. Both crews went into the routine of donning space suits and climbing out to adjust the gaskets and flanges that would permit the two vessels to effect a transshipping of cargo, and free passage of men and tools if repairs were possible.

I turned out the rest of the crew. "Take it easy," I cautioned them. "Act natural— until the acid squad gets into action. We've got to nail every Saturnian at once, or we're sunk."

CHAPTER XXI

ACID VS. FIRE

WE FACED a free-for-all, but with every advantage of surprise on our side. If we hadn't had to worry about anything but knocking off the other ship, everything would have been just dandy. As it was, every man of my crew realized the one great danger: Valene might be a goner when the acid and flame started flying.

Ion said, "There's no way we can find out where she is. She may be locked up in a compartment where she'll be perfectly safe. On the other hand, she may end up right in the midst of the show."

"I've been thinking of that," I told him. "And then there's the Titanian crew. We want to look out for them. Here's the way we'll do it . . ."

My plan depended on the number of Saturnians in command; also upon whether the crew was mixed or entirely made up of Titanian slaves. More than that, though, we needed a story that would sound reasonable all the way through. Ion shook his head, dubiously, when he heard what I had in mind.

"But suppose it won't work?" he objected. "Suppose you're in the midst of them and a riot breaks out?"

"That," I told him, "is just why I'm going. If I'm wrong, I'll be the first one to get a whiff of acid."

This was a grandstand play; but the natives of Japetus fell for it, very much like Terrestrians. However, since someone had to stick his head out, I figured it had better be mine; I had the most at stake. So when the details were arranged, and the airtight connections between the two ships secured, I boarded the *Mogok*.

The crew, as far as I could see, was entirely Saturnian. Whatever human slaves there were must be in the compartment aft, or perhaps at the control panels, forward.

But there was a chance that no Titanians had been taken along, if only because Valene's daring escape and her recapture might inspire even the favored slaves with notions of mutiny and trickery. A treacherous crew could make one suicidal move and destroy all hands, merely by opening a port which would let the air escape.

I saluted the officer who was in charge of the watch. "We have some perishable cargo," I told him, meaning that our compartments were loaded with human cattle. "And with bulkhead plates going to pieces—"

"How did that happen?" the officer demanded.

"Unusually active ore. Our skipper can't figure it out. He's in the bunker himself, investigating. He would like to have your captain come aboard to verify the state of affairs. He'd rather not face an inquiry alone."

"Afraid they'll demote him, eh?" the Saturnian officer snorted. Plumes of flame hissed from his nostrils. "This is going to be fun for the blending plant at the mine. Your skipper's got nothing to worry about."

"What's this?" A copper-red Saturnian stepped from the passage that led forward. He reminded me of Thorgulu, except that he was older; his insignia indicated that he was in command.

"Who's been getting fuel that's too active? Never heard of such a thing! Wish I could get some myself. The stuff we're carrying looks, smells, and works like mine tailings!"

~ ~ ~ ~ ~

HE WENT into a huddle with the officer, entirely ignoring me for a moment or two. The intense heat of the compartment indicated that the entire crew must be Saturnian.

Finally I managed to cut in, "Your Excellency, our perishable cargo is in danger. If the bulkhead gives way, they'll all be incinerated. Have you any insulated lockers where they could be stored?"

The captain nodded. He gestured, issued an order. The officer relayed it to the crew. "Wait a minute," the commander cut in, "till I get out of this infernal cold! Hold it!"

The crew stepped back from the sealed door. Valene and perhaps other slaves were behind it. Things were shaping up nicely. It all depended on the skipper's next move. I reminded him, "Our captain needs some help in the engine room. One of the fuel bunker plates has given way, and it's too hot for any Titanians."

"Take all hands with you," said the skipper. "Burned-out inductor, fuel that's too active, and half her plates ready to crumble—this is worth taking a look at. You, there! Get the perishable merchandise out of the way."

I went back, stepped to the visiphone to relay the word to our imaginary skipper, then had a few of our crew herd the others over. Outside, wearing their space suits, the remainder of my men were in place at the airlocks.

The Saturnian skipper and the second in command went into the *Sargoza*. The others crowded after them. Then I closed the port that had been opened only a little while ago.

The last Saturnian to board the *Sargoza* must have heard the sound, or felt the sudden compression of air. He whirled, yelled. The officers, who by now were near the engine room, looking for the nonexistent skipper of the derelict, echoed his shout.

Flames and choking fumes leaked past the port. Blows shook it. But the locking device was already engaged. In spite of the intense heat, we spun the hand wheel, cutting off the blazing breath of the enemy.

We had them bottled up. Or so we thought, until the door of a forward compartment slammed open. Three Saturnians lunged out. The noise had aroused them. They had evidently been dodging duty on the salvage job, but now that they sensed that something was seriously wrong, they came out of cover.

A gust of flame roared out a dozen feet. The nearest Titanian, unprotected by any armor, was enveloped by the deadly exhalation. Behind me, Ion and half a dozen Japetans wrestled with the door that opened aft.

And then the *Sargoza,* still firmly secured to the cruiser she had overhauled, took off under full power. The tricked Saturnians, getting to the controls, planned to take both ships back to Titan.

~ ~ ~ ~ ~

I CUT loose with my acid projector. The waxed fabric that should protect me was already thinning under the terrific heat, but there was little choice between roasting and corrosion.

The bullet connected with the leading Saturnian. The blistering liquid, attacking his mineral tissues, made him recoil.

For a moment he blocked his companions. That gave Ion a chance to get the door open. The *Sargoza,* under power and turning sharply, flung us all against a bulkhead. But that sudden change of direction tumbled the roaring Saturnians in a heap. Being more agile, we retreated before they could recover.

Acid fumes and smoke made the compartment a choking hell. I fired a second and a third shot. The second Saturnian, recovering, went down when the blast hit him. But I was half blinded when I pulled the door shut.

We were in the hold designed for human cargo. At the moment, however, this seemed little advantage. One of the enemy blocked our approach to the controls of the ship we had taken over; rather, had tried to take over, for it had now become a deadlock.

The last minute change of plans had kicked back. Encouraged by what had seemed to be a chance to get the entire Saturnian crew bottled up, I had gambled on an exchange of ships, and avoiding the risks of fighting it out with inadequate equipment.

Valene emerged from one of the insulated lockers. She still wore the colorful dress in which she had been exhibited to the Titanian slaves.

"I thought everything was lost," she cried. "And now you're here! I didn't see a chance. I might have known you'd find me!"

The fumes that followed us before we closed the door thickened the air, half blinded us. I hated to disillusion her. But the Saturnian who was at work in the adjoining compartment left me no choice.

"Maybe there is another move, but I don't know what it is," I said. "Instead of you, now it's the two of us, heading for the ovens of Saturn. Even if I can finish that fellow before he gets us."

She did not quite understand that, nor was it necessary. The Saturnians we had tricked could return. In the ensuing match with acid against flame, none of us could survive. The cramped space robbed us of any advantage. The fumes from our own weapons would destroy us, for the hot blasts of the expiring Saturnians would melt the wax layers of our acid-proof suits. And those of us who had no such protection—this included Valene as well as some of my crew—would go down at the first instant of encounter.

The hammering outside ceased. The enemy at our door seemed to have another plan. Valene was the first to notice that the temperature was rising. I glanced at an indicator. Ten degrees up, and climbing rapidly. He was trying to bake us to a finish, so that we would not have a chance with our destructive acid projectors.

"I'm going out," I decided, "and settle him. Close the door behind me, quick. When the show is over, take the controls, reverse the power on this ship, and break the bolts that tie us to the *Sargoza.* Then it will be a race, and this is the fastest boat."

After all, I did have a chance. Particularly if I slipped up on our persistent enemy. And something had to be done rapidly, before the tricked Saturnians aboard the *Sargoza* had time to think it over; for the moment, apparently, they were content to take us back and let the authorities deal with us.

I stood by the jamb, ready to dive out when Ion and the others opened the door.

~ ~ ~ ~ ~

SUDDENLY there was a shrill screaming. The metal plates vibrated like reeds of organ pipes. Valene, startled, dashed to a porthole glass.

"Look! Fire pouring out of the *Sargoza!* Like a comet!"

"Hold it," I yelled to Ion. "Don't open that door yet."

Valene was right. The whistling sound had subsided, but an incredibly long streamer of flame still gushed out of the nose of the *Sargoza;* it fanned out, spread in every direction.

Then I saw the men in space suits. They were members of our crew who had remained outside the hulls, staying at their posts after the two ships had been fastened together.

Sensing that something was wrong, one of them had gone forward with a heavy spanner to knock a porthole glass out of the control room. The sudden vacuum had finished the Saturnians we had tricked into the *Sargoza.*

I drew my acid projector. "Only one more enemy to settle, and I'm attending to him, right now. Open that door before we're roasted!"

It was just that simple. I caught him at the temperature controls and dissolved him before he could turn around with his fiery breath.

Though we had spent some trying moments, we not only had broken up the Saturnians' plans for Valene, but had also captured another ship. Now that things were under control, the men outside the *Sargoza* could climb in through the shattered port, replace it or seal the nearest airlock, and finally open the door that still separated the two ships.

CHAPTER XXII

FUEL STOP

"IF YOU keep this up," said Valene, once we had both ships under control, "you'll be an admiral. Or how many does it take to make a fleet?"

Coming from her, that sounded as good as her smile looked. In fact, everything looked fine until I began to consider that we were somewhere on the route between Titan and Saturn. "Your folks back home," I said, "are worried silly about you. And if we have another jam as close as this last one, I'll begin to wonder a bit myself."

"Then let's hurry back to Japetus. I never did like public mourning."

"They're too busy," I told her. "Building cruisers. There wasn't a chance for you, so your father quit thinking about the personal angles and went on the warpath."

"Oh! He's planning to raid Saturn?" Her eyes widened.

I shook my head. "Not a chance. We haven't enough fuel. The more ships he builds, the less there'll be to go around. But there's plenty for an attack on Titan."

"A surprise party, to rescue the slaves?"

"Perhaps even take over the satellite. It can be done. A lot of the ground is pretty much as on Japetus. Broken up, with plenty of caverns. Or so it seemed, when we landed to pick you up. Among other things, I found an ore deposit. High grade fuel, I'd say."

Valene's eyes brightened. "You never miss a chance, do you?"

"Well—the whole crew couldn't go with me, so I put them to work while they were waiting. The ore vein is in a ravine, not a great distance from the hothouse. I noticed it by sheer accident."

For a few moments, she did not say anything. I cut in the visiphone, and checked up with Ion, who was in charge of the captured *Mogok.* He had everything under control, and was awaiting orders.

He read his position as he had calculated it; the figures agreed with mine. Since we'd set out with nearly double the crew needed to navigate the *Sargoza,* neither ship was seriously short of hands; for in getting Valene back we'd lost fewer men than we had expected.

"Follow the present course," I ordered, "and in case we are separated, take the long route back to Japetus. No use in risking a direct run through the belt of satelloids."

"That's a mistake," Valene cut in, catching my hand before I could cut the visiphone switch. "Wait, Ion. Just a minute."

~ ~ ~ ~ ~

"WHAT'S that? Mutiny?" I grinned " and tried to give her a dirty look, but that didn't work at all. "Or do *you* want to navigate?"

"Oh, no, not at all. But we ought to go back to Titan, slip up on the dark side, as you did when you landed in the ravine. Load the *Mogok* with ore, too. Right up to—well, full to the top."

They didn't have plimsoll marks in space ships, but I got her idea. And cancelled it, then and there. I mean, I tried to. "Forget that. You're going home and staying home. What do you think this is?"

"It's wasting a lot of fuel: You'll have to make another round trip. Silly, it's perfectly safe. You did it before, didn't you?"

"Yeah. I did. And since then, what with broken panes in the hothouse, some slaves missing, Saturnian patrols hooting around in the hinterland, and the *Mogok*—I'm referring to this ship, just in case you don't remember—not being checked en route to Saturn—it's perfectly safe. Yes, we'll have tea and scones in the administration building."

"What's tea and scones?" She wouldn't listen to reason at all.

"An old Terrestrian custom. If you get those fool notions out of your head, you—well, both of us, for that matter— might live long enough to take a look at Terra, and find out if my old pal, John Parker, made it all the way back."

Ion's grin was filling the visiphone screen. He could not get a word into the argument.

"I'm not interested in Terrestrian customs!" she retorted. "We'll be perfectly satisfied on Japetus."

"Huh?" The way she said that took my breath. "Oh sure. We. You mean us. Or do you?"

She nodded. I said, "Then don't be silly. Your father would skin me alive if he heard that I took you back to Titan so we could dig a load of ore."

Valene eyed me for a moment, as if she had something important to say but doubted whether she should say it. Finally she decided. "He's not my father. Guraz isn't. And never was." Then to the visiphone, "Ion, head for the dark side of Titan. We're going that way!"

"Hold your course," I cut in. "Or I'll knock your head off!"

I snapped the switch. Valene protested, "I'm not a princess at all. I'm not important enough for all this special consideration. We do need fuel. You said enough to make me realize that. The sooner we make a raid, the fewer slaves will reach the ovens of Saturn."

"I don't care who you are! . . . Who are you anyway?"

"Oh, just nobody at all. My father was one of the defense council."

"Old soldier, huh? So was my granddad, back on Terra. Used filthy language and chewed tobacco and howled because his pension wasn't enough to keep him in rum. Nice family, darling. We'll get along swell."

"So you're not disappointed?"

"At what?"

"Because I'm a sort of impostor."

"I'm tickled silly," I truthfully told her. "Though Guraz is a nice fellow, for a king. But how come, this princess stuff?"

"Well, father was killed in a counterattack against the Saturnians, and Guraz adopted me as a companion for his young daughter. And when she died—well, I'd become one of the family, by then. And the Saturnians who captured me didn't know the difference."

"How about the traitors who were responsible?"

"You're awfully naive," she answered. "They couldn't gain any advantage by telling the Saturnians the truth, could they? Now, we're going to Titan, aren't we?"

"We are not. Especially since you're my personal discovery, and not a sort of Japetan symbol for something or other."

But I'd had a couple of tough days, and Valene was persistent as any Terrestrian woman ever dreamed of being; so we did head for Titan's dark side. Ion just grinned when I cut in the visiphone and countermanded my original order.

~ ~ ~ ~ ~

SOME time before we reached the satellite, the ether was thick with calls. The *Mogok,* bearing her lovely and supposedly distinguished prisoner, had not been checked in by the observation stations of the inner satellites.

Ever since my original break, and Parker's escape, the Saturnians had been worried about mutiny; which is why the *Mogok* had had none of the human crew that usually did the disagreeable work.

"Your bright idea," I said reproachfully, "has put us in a nice corner."

"You're awfully thick-headed, Kent, if you don't see that I've practically saved your two-ship fleet." She sighed. "At times I think you are as solid between the ears as a Saturnian admiral!"

"Thanks very much," I said frigidly. Though after all, a dame doesn't *openly* call a fellow a blockhead unless she's awfully sore at him, or quite fond and possessively inclined. "How are we so nicely situated, with those radio alarms keeping the ether boiling?"

"Silly! They'll never dream of searching the ravines of Titan. But patrols working from the outer satellites have gotten the messages, and they'll be looking for a ship bound for Japetus."

"We fought our way through once before, didn't we?"

She sighed. "Wasn't it fun, too?"

~ ~ ~ ~ ~

THEY MADE our landing, setting the *Mogok* down nearest the ore vein. Every broadcast band was hot with inquiries about the missing ship. Patrols were setting out from Titan, but not to circle the satellite.

"What did I tell you?" Valene said.

I picked up a pinch bar and joined the crew. The ore was definitely stratified, which made it easier to mine; just a matter of applying a lever to a layer and prying. It broke off in sheets several inches thick and a few feet square. The matrix, crumbled and eroded, was readily shoveled away; and since the vein did not dip sharply, our small gang had a simple problem in open cast mining.

We spent several Terrestrial days working the veins of *nari*. Then we saw the first signs of Titan's grayish dawn. It was time to leave; for, though we were in a ravine, a reflection from the hull of one of our ships might attract the attention of a Saturnian observer.

The patrols that had gone out to find the missing *Mogok* were returning, some singly, others in formation. As nearly as we could learn from intercepted signals and messages, the search had been abandoned.

We closed the ports and hatchways. We had ample time, since Titan's day, equal to a Terrestrial week, is gradual in its approach.

As we cleared the lip of the ravine, heading away from the sunrise, I got a visiphone flash from Ion. He said, "There's a cruiser being towed into the airlock of the hangar. A big one. She just limped in with a light patrol boat."

I reset the observing instruments, and looped back. He was right. The cruiser was a monster; one of the big ones used by the Saturnians in their flights to Terra. Why it was docking on Titan, I could not guess, and I had no time. Ion was shouting, "If we strike quickly, we can blow her up and block the gates."

The idea had its points. I gave him the okay and put on full power. As I swung sharply about, I saw the glow of the *Mogok's* repulsion tubes. Ion was giving her all she would take.

"Nose straight up," I told him, "and open fire as we dive."

There was no time for further orders. Our upward swoop had already attracted attention. Instead of pulling the crippled cruiser in through the gates, the patrol boat was trying to save time by backing her out. Until one move or the other was complete, none of the Saturnian warships inside the vast enclosure could get into action.

Then I pointed the *Sargoza's* nose straight down. Our gun crew was far from expert, but it was a simple problem in direct fire. It was a question of aiming the ship, rather than the artillery.

At my signal, the gunners cut loose in battery. The recoil nearly knocked us in half. Great clouds of dust and smoke mushroomed up to meet us. I could no longer see either the hangar and shops, or the brazen gleam of the long range cruiser.

As I leveled off, fragments of wreckage hammered the bottom of the hull.

And then the *Mogok* whistled past us. Just what Ion's marksmanship had accomplished, I could not say at the instant; nor was there any time to reconnoiter. We had to race away before an alarm attracted too many of the patrols which worked from other satellites. With both our ships overloaded with *nari* ore, we would be handicapped where fast going was in order.

"And that," said Valene, as we bored into space, "will give the Saturnians something to think about."

"It's nothing to what we can do, now that we have fuel enough for the Japetan fleet. Enough for one good show, at least."

The visiphone pilot lamp blinked. I cut in, and got a report from the *Mogok*. "Admiral," said Ion, "the hangar is a mess of wreckage. It'll take from now on for them to get their ships free."

"How do you know?"

"I looped back, once I passed you," he answered. "There was so much smoke I couldn't see much, the first time."

"The dope was curious," I said to Valene, when Ion broke contact. "Someone might have blown him out of the air. But I'm curious myself. That long range cruiser limping home has me thinking."

"Maybe they ran into a meteor swarm," Valene suggested.

And that was something which we could do ourselves, at the speed we were holding. So I settled down to navigation.

CHAPTER XXIII

STOWAWAY

WITH the return of Valene, the Japetan morale increased and shot right up. For one thing, we'd outsmarted the Saturnians; and that could be done again. Better still, we'd brought back a darn good supply of fuel.

The shops were working day and night, and the scientists were perfecting acid-throwing weapons and the protective armor needed at close quarters: proof against flames, and likewise able to resist the deadly fumes of the liquid hurled at the enemy.

Our nearly fatal hand-to-hand scrap with Saturnians in the close confines of the *Mogok,* made such equipment number one on our list. For we had planned a raid that was to liberate the Titanians at one swoop.

Guraz approved it. "We'll land in force. We'll surround the hothouse, blast the hangars and shops out of commission, and then round up and exterminate every Saturnian on the satellite!"

As he spoke, he paced up and down the high-ceiled cave, beard trailing and a flagon in his hairy fist. The assembled citizens and fighting men shook the cavern with their applause, and the scientists joined in.

"We have a hundred ships," the head of the construction department reported, when the clamor subsided. "But there is enough fuel for only fifty. We'll have to make another raid."

Several of the fighting detachment took the floor at once. Guraz roared them off their feet, and beckoned to me. I said, "We need a surprise party when we land. It's lucky that we've not had a whole Saturnian fleet trying to blow Japetus out of its orbit. Why that's not happened, I can't say. But it will if we make another trip and don't sweep the satellite clean."

This was conceded sound strategy. Several officers said, "We'll take fifty ships and keep the others as a reserve.

When we make the raid, we'll load up all fifty with *nari* ore and bring it back."

This had a splendid ring to it, but we needed more than morale. I countered, "You boys haven't been on Titan. Where one ship or two might by a lot of luck land and get away, a fleet of fifty could not make an impression. It's going to end up in a lot of hand-to-hand fighting. We can't clean up Titan with the crew of fifty ships."

"How about arming the Titanians?" someone proposed.

"Eventually yes. But they're too accustomed to being cattle," I explained, "to be relied upon. They might be great, they might be utterly worthless. They're an uncertain quantity, and quality, too."

"All right, let's hear *your* idea!" a red-bearded commander jibed.

I had known right along that this "admiral" business would get under a lot of skins; but Ion had spread it around, and Valene, with more loyalty than judgment, had seconded him. Nonetheless, the boy with the red beaver was making it too personal for me to swallow.

~ ~ ~ ~ ~

"YOU asked for it," I told him. "So here it is, and see if *you* like it!" Guraz was grinning and making gestures, being all for me. I went on, "Well take the whole hundred ships; and instead of fuel for the return trip, we'll take extra men and extra small arms for whatever Titanians are game to fight. We'll mop up Titan, absolutely clean, or else we won't need any fuel for the return. How do you like that?"

The read-bearded officer gulped, and his mouth sagged. The muttering quieted, and so did the approving comment. But nobody from Terra was bluffing these folks. He came back, "I think it's fine! I didn't know you had that much backbone, *Admiral!*"

He was on his feet. Others joined him. The gang went wild, and the news spread from cave to cave. I said to Guraz, "We're in for it. Are you with me? Whole hog?"

He did not know what a hog was, but it sounded good to him. So all hands left the council cavern to get the fleet ready for a quick descent on Titan.

Valene found me in the tangle. Her eyes were a little too bright, and she was blinking. "You're crazy." she said, gulping a bit. "Suppose you don't have time to dig more fuel, and can't get any from the Saturnian ships."

I laughed. "Why, then we'll stay on Titan. Can't walk back, can we?"

"And we can't go after you."

"That's a chance we'll have to take."

And after mature deliberation, it did seem to be somewhat of a risk!

But getting the fleet in order left little time for morbid notions. We took off in three groups, each in wedge-shaped flights. Scouts went ahead and others guarded our flanks. Their mission was not so much to prevent surprise as to engage and hold any Saturnian patrols until the fleet could blow them out of the air.

The idea was to see that no transport, cruiser, or other space ship got away with news of a Japetan fleet; otherwise, we would have to contend with everything Saturn could pour on us. And with limited fuel, we could not afford to waste any in maneuvering. Thus our descent was direct.

We timed the attack so that we would strike when the Titanian night was darkest. When I gave the order to get ready for action, I got the first surprise.

They found a stowaway in a locker of one of the gun turrets. Valene, evading the guards, had boarded the flagship.

CHAPTER XXIV

SUICIDE SQUAD

I DIDN'T know what to say, but Valene did. This was her argument: "Even if you did win, you might not be able to return. So I came along."

"You'll be a great help," I said, being annoyed and flattered at once. "You barely get out of one jam when you do your best to get right into another."

"If you think you're going to be marooned with that crowd of Titanian ladies, you're crazy," she retorted.

"So I see." The crew was grinning. They enjoyed the encounter immensely. My ears were getting red. "Listen, my chick! You dive for cover and keep out of everyone's way. We're going to be busy in a few more minutes."

Her eyelashes drooped. She demurely said, "I'm so sorry I'm in the way. If I'd known you'd feel this way about it, I'd have stayed at home."

She would not have, but there was nothing further to say. And that the crew thought this rare joke was a good sign. They were in high spirits and spoiling for a fight with the Saturnians. That counted a lot. But I began to realize that John Parker's ideas on women being pests did not need to be verified with a slide rule.

Our attack was a complete surprise. Far below, the opalescent domes of the hothouse glowed like great eyes from Titan's gloom. I could catch the sheen of the hangars, the metal-roofed shops, the network of glistening runways along which the space cruisers were drawn when they were moved from one department to the other.

No signals came in from any of the fleet. The ether was to be kept undisturbed unless the scouts had to notify us of an approaching Saturnian cruiser. Our arrival had been planned to fit into the lull in outgoing and inbound traffic from the ringed planet.

The leading flight swooped in perfect formation. Our searchlights blazed, long white fingers reaching down to the gleaming metal and glass. Then the long-drawn concussion as the first broadside let go.

Smoke and dust and flying debris blown from the buildings below made it hard for us to see. The leading flight nosed up, and the second one dipped down, guns blazing. As we came out of the low-hanging fumes, I saw the third wedge diving; the second, enveloped by gases and dust and fragments, was invisible. Only the rumble of explosives, and the scream of flying wreckage proved its existence.

There was no answering fire because the Saturnians, unprepared for a mass invasion, had no artillery except on their docked ships. And they were in the midst of the twisted tangle of girders and roofing.

We did not attack the hothouse proper. To do so would expose the Titanians to the mercy of the bitter chill outdoors.

Then a Saturnian cruiser rose from the swirling fumes. Despite our fire, the vast extent of the shops and hangars could not be covered in our first succession of dives. Another emerged, firing as she cleared the dense clouds of smoke.

~ ~ ~ ~ ~

ON THE ground, I could barely distinguish one of our flights, which had landed just as the others opened fire. Japetans poured from the hatches. They bounded into the surging fumes. Each wore fire- and acid-proof armor, and carried an acid projector.

This detachment was charging toward the administration building to keep the aroused Saturnians from summoning help from the ringed planet or notifying cruisers plying between satellites.

More ships escaped the concentrated fire than I had expected. As the first flight circled back to blast the riddled target with another broadside of explosive and acid, a disabled cruiser opened fire from the ground. Others, upended by our shells and kept from settling back because of girders and wall sections that had crumbled, thrust their noses through the clouds, and brought into play what guns had not been disabled.

The increasing reply to our attack convinced me that the Saturnians were rallying, manning the turrets of cruisers that had been disabled for flight. They were stubborn and desperate.

Ion's flight was on the tail of the first ship to pull clear of the wrecked air-dock. One of my flight was blown out of action by fire from the ground. And the fugitives, long streamers of flame pouring out of their propulsion tubes, were heading for Saturn.

One, swinging to avoid Ion's guns, crashed headlong into a ship trying to head him off. A lucky shell disabled another. But we had no fuel for further scouting. In the confusion, no one knew whether or not every fugitive had been overtaken and destroyed.

One by one, the flight swooped down into the clouds of smoke. This was no time for regrets. We had our work on the ground. The engineer reported, "Thirty seconds more fuel supply!"

A cruiser, lacking power, nosed down and crashed.

I don't know how many seconds more we could have stayed in the air; but it was probably just about as long as a man could hold his breath. Now that the observation compartment shield had been lifted, and we could see by direct vision, I learned that we had our hands full.

Hordes of Saturnians raced about. Some had edged weapons, others had flame throwers, and all were making the most of their naturally fiery breath. Without waiting for us to come out of our cruisers, they darted toward the dead spaces between gun turrets; these groups had cutting devices to pierce the hulls so that they could catch us at close quarters.

As our crews scrambled into fire-proof armor, I figured a way of handling these fire-breathing guys. The order went over the visiphone. With what power we had available, each cruiser was shifted so that when we were on the ground again, the guns of one would cover the dead spaces of the other.

Then, leaving some of the crew at their posts to maintain this defense, the rest of us went out to mop up.

Our idea was to exterminate the enemy; but it seemed they had the same idea about us. The Saturnians who had fled from the administration building and into the further reaches of the hothouses were rallying. They had rounded up Titanian slaves to march before them as human shields.

Behind this living barrier, they advanced. Others counter-attacking from the flanks, hurled rocks and pieces of shattered girders at the Japetan forces. Whenever flame-proof armor was torn, the wearer was finished by the backlash of the weapons of his own comrades, if not by the flaming breath of the towering Saturnians.

~ ~ ~ ~ ~

SOME, desperate, peeled off their armor and used their wings; with the exchange of flame, these winged Satans could endure what to them was terrific cold. Soaring overhead, they dropped wreckage on the advancing Japetans.

Some of these things I saw; others I learned later. During it all, I led a patrol into the smoking wreckage of the hangars and shops. We had to clean out every disabled ship, just in case some desperate Saturnian tried to get it into the air.

They rallied in groups. Tall, raging, exhaling flame and smoke; some wore space suits and faced acid until man and armor collapsed from corrosion. And when this happened, the disintegration of the dying Saturnian created such a vortex of heat as to drive us back, yards at a time.

My own men, raked and battered by the slave goads or the impromptu weapons snatched by the Saturnians, breathed in flame and acid that leaked through their slashed armor; they spun dizzily, dropped, and we hurdled them in our advance. There was no treating the fallen, for nothing could help anyone who had inhaled a gust of flame or corrosive gas.

Groups of Saturnians, literally going nuts, peeled off their armor, gathered in compact masses, and rushed us. They faced quick destruction; but in their frenzy they laughed at that and charged, flame gushing from mouths and nostrils. These suicidal attacks broke, but only after whole squads of Japetans had been roasted in their own armor, which had its limits.

But finally we fought out way through that smoky hell, clambering over girders, gun turrets, ribs and plates blown from cruisers. We cornered the last Saturnians. Some stood and faced us. Others, more cunning or less desperate, ran out into the frozen wastes of Titan.

These would perish, or else return for a final counter-attack. Whether they planned to steal a ship and escape, we did not know. But we did know that we were stranded on the satellite until we could salvage fuel from the wrecked cruisers in the hangars; the crude *nari* could not be used until it was treated and blended.

So with perhaps half of my detachment surviving, I turned back toward the administration building. A glance at the formation of ships reassured me. The ranks were unbroken. Valene and the guards were safe, though Saturnians were heaped in windrows all about the group.

CHAPTER XXV

CORNERED

WE ARMED as many Titanian slaves as we could, and put them at the head of each party that searched the huge interior of the hothouse. The idea was not to use them as shock troops but to increase their morale. Most of them were horrified at the vengeance to come, but some of the bolder ones needed little persuasion.

Not more than a few dozen Saturnians were routed out of hiding. They did not last long. The encounters were small-scale repetitions of the nasty fight we'd had in the shops and hangars; but these skirmishes made a new race out of the Titanians. The cattle had become men.

"Ion," I said when the last Saturnian in the hothouse had been cornered, "we've go to get some of these people out. Half the fleet will be used to carry them to Japetus. The other half will stay here, in case the alarm did get to Saturn."

"You mean to be on their tails, so they can't pursue?"

"Right on the nail!"

"The idea is fine," he went on, frowning. "Except that we need fuel."

He had forgotten the wrecked cruisers in the hangars. When I reminded him, he rounded up a gang to get to work. Now that the show was over, for the time, Valene came out of shelter. She caught me off guard, while I was watching Ion march his men to the smoking ruins.

"You look as if you've lost the fight," she said.

"Huh. The fight hasn't started yet," I told her. "Just to make your visit pleasant, I'll let you in on a secret. Our only chance of a getaway, or even of defense, is cutting up those twisted wrecks and salvaging the fuel for our cruisers. And that's not a matter of minutes."

She didn't bat an eyelash. I tried to give her a hard-boiled look and a growl to match; I was worried about her having poked her pert little nose into what promised to be a one-way trip if we didn't make good time in every move.

She laughed at me! "Quit that, sour-face! You've not failed yet. And I wouldn't have missed this for anything. Listen to them, in the hothouse!"

The Titanians were singing. Long files of them danced around in the eerie glow of the great dome. This was different from the night when they had watched Valene paraded before them as an example of what happened to rebels and fugitives.

"And I should be grinning, huh? Suppose something does let them down, at the last minute?"

"But look at how long it'll take for a messenger to get to Saturn, if one of those ships did escape," she insisted. "And then the trip back."

She was right. Just the same, I wasn't as cocky as I had been at first. I smelled trouble, and I didn't know just why. Maybe it made me the skeleton at the banquet, but I cut into the celebration and got the Titanians to work.

~ ~ ~ ~ ~

THEY formed a basket brigade; long lines of them, shoulder to shoulder, passing parcels of salvaged fuel from hand to hand. In that way each cruiser, served by its own line, was refueled as rapidly as the next.

Some, drunk with victory, grumbled at being marched back to the ore grinding and blending plant. But Ion and his officers put the fear of Saturn in their hearts.

Valene, for all her ready smile and back-talk, ended by standing on her tiptoes.

The race against an invisible enemy was getting her on edge. Finally she whispered, "I'm getting shaky myself. What are you holding back? Did a message get through? Didn't the first rush block the signal house in time? Tell me!"

"I don't know. It's a hunch."

Relief shifts of Titanians took the places of those who reeled as they stood there, merely releasing a basket before another one passed along to take its place. In spite of their exertions, they shivered in the bitter night. We reversed ventilation fans, so that hot air from the domes swept them, but the whistling winds scattered that warmth; we couldn't heat the whole satellite.

Blue-lipped, teeth chattering, they stumbled back into the domes, and new gangs, already shivering at the thought of what was ahead, took their places. The Saturnians had never worked them so mercilessly, and the liberated slaves cursed their freedom.

If they weren't ripe for mutiny, I was crazy. Since we weren't Saturnians, they felt that we had no right to drive them to exhaustion.

But when the surprise did come, it caught me off guard.

One of Ion's Japetans came dashing out of the administration building. He shouted and gestured as he ran, but I couldn't understand him. Valene and I turned to meet him. Those in the basket line nearest him were dropping their parcels of fuel and running toward the domes.

Then I caught it. He gasped, "Signals! Fleet from Saturn! Picked up signals! Coming this way!"

"You're crazy," I said. "They couldn't be out here already. Get back on the job, you! Ion, round those fellows up!" I caught the messenger by the shoulder. "Take your time and talk slow!"

He gulped, gestured some more, and repeated, "No mistaking it. Picked up orders passing from ship to ship."

The Titanians were trampling each other in their hurry to get back into the domes, which their Saturnians would probably hesitate to destroy. Others, with more spirit, were running to the weapons and armor they had discarded upon going to work. The messenger repeated, "I can't be mistaken! The voices weren't human."

~ ~ ~ ~ ~

WE HAD taken on enough fuel for maneuvering, even if not for retreat to Japetus. Ion passed the word along into the hangars. His men came running out. The invading crews, followed by the more pugnacious Titanians, headed for the cruisers. There was no time to make any plan or issue any order—not until the hatches were battened and we were ready to take the air.

Ion waved from the port of the control room of his ship. Then the screen was lowered. Communication was then carried on by visiphone. "Send out patrols," I said, and gave orders for the several flights. "And keep in touch. Don't risk any fights if you can help it. If we're outnumbered, we can do better on the ground."

The main reason for taking off was to be ready to settle any small detachment before its commander could become suspicious and send word back to Saturn. I still felt that whatever patrol was approaching could not be on the way in response to news of our attack.

Aside from scouting flights, the fleet hovered low, and near the outlying ravines and craters. If it came to the worst, we could shelter some of the ships against attack, and perhaps get the enemy to risk a landing party—which would be to our advantage.

The next few minutes verified the alarm. The air was hot with signals; Saturnian skippers announcing their intention to land. Then, though we were skimming low, they sighted us and we saw them.

These were not patrols nor transports, but long, bronze-colored monsters such as Parker and I had first seen in the valley of the Orinoco, the evening we learned that Saturnians were raiding Terra. The size, the shape, the color, all were revealed by the glow of the repulsion tubes.

Searchlights blazed. The skippers of the leading ships already sensed that something was wrong; they were not getting proper cooperation from the ground.

As we tuned in, a Saturnian voice made the visiphone shudder. I did as much myself. Thorgulu, the Arch-Mogok, was cursing the heavens and every satellite. He promised to blow us out of the air if someone did not explain in a hurry.

I never did learn who fired the first shot; whether one of our gunners or one of the enemy's. But in split seconds, the problem became, "Who isn't firing?"

The stars were hidden out by monstrous ships. We were outweighed and outnumbered. As we tried to scatter, Thorgulu's fleet spread in a vast crescent to surround us. He probably did not suspect that our fuel was too limited; that if we had fled, we would have become derelicts in space, to be picked off at will.

Disabled ships crashed against the jutting crags. Thorgulu, leading the center of the half-circle, was forced down by our returning scouts, who swooped from overhead. And then our fleet, stringing out, flattened into the ravine we had picked during our brief preparation for the emergency.

Some were blasted to junk as they landed. Others maneuvered into the shelter of overhanging ledges. And with crashes resulting from hasty landing, scarcely more than half of the Japetan fleet survived the running fight.

They had us bottled up.

~ ~ ~ ~ ~

ENOUGH of the Saturnians circled overhead to keep us under cover. The others landed on foot to inspect the wreckage of the hangars, and to regain control of the slaves in the hothouse domes.

Thorgulu, calling from his grounded flagship, demanded surrender. We recognized each other over the visiphone screens. That was natural enough, after our long cruise from Terra to Saturn.

"Turn over your arms and leave your ships, Bradley," he demanded, "and I'll give you transportation back to Earth."

"Why don't you send a crew over to me? Or us?" I countered. "You're not weakening, are you?"

Flame and smoke for a moment obscured his sharp face. Then he retorted, "We can blow up the whole ravine. Bury you and your mutineers."

"Just try it!" I yelled. "We'll get out on foot, and how will you like chasing us in this temperature? And you'll have to get us, or we'll cook up something else."

He turned a deep reddish purple, clenched his claws. He sputtered and roared with fury. Orderlies came from the signal compartment with messages. He listened a moment. I couldn't hear what they told him, but his remarks made it clear enough that the subdued Titanians had explained.

"I'll give you enough ships to take your whole party to Japetus, or back to Terra."

"You're too anxious to be friendly," I told him. "If you want us, come down in these ravines and get us."

No Saturnian ever liked to play in a network of caverns; the Japetans had convinced them that such tactics did not pay. I cut off the visiphone. That would finish what remained of Thorgulu's temper. There was a chance of tempting him to recklessness.

Meanwhile, all escape seemed to be cut off. Ion reminded me, quite needlessly, that this was the case. "Maybe he really wants us out of here before the slaves become too daring. The Saturnians don't want to kill them off to regain control. He doesn't want a suicidal rush. They're valuable property, and a lot of them have found new courage. It might spread."

He offered me this argument as we crept along sheltered ledges toward a cavern where we could meet the other officers in council.

"You're right," I had to admit. "That's reasonable. He could place some ships where we could get at them without running any risk of being nabbed. But he's too anxious to make peace with us. There's a catch somewhere."

The council spent some hours trying to figure out just what lay behind Thorgulu's desire for a truce. We arrived at no conclusion.

"I don't trust him," declared a gray-bearded Japetan. "It'd be a shame to let the Titanians down, after the good start we made."

Another said, "We've had good luck handling these fellows on foot. Maybe we can spring a surprise and get a fresh hold on things."

That was worth trying. While Thorgulu's forces had heard of our success in hand-to-hand work, and had seen the remains of their fellows, they had not witnessed our procedure in action; thus they would hardly expect counter-attack.

~ ~ ~ ~ ~

THE space cruisers that had circled overhead finally withdrew and landed. As Thorgulu got more details about our raid, he realized that before we could make a break, his fleet could overtake us and blow us to bits.

So without knowing it, he played into our hands. We left a small detachment with each cruiser, and then set out on foot to win what small chance we had of catching the enemy off guard.

If this succeeded, we could escape before Thorgulu decided to blast our hiding places about our ears. Trying to leave on our own initiative seemed far more prudent than accepting his terms. Or so we thought, as we crept into the darkness of the week-long Titanian night.

Saturnians were already at work repairing the damage done by our raid. According to our reckoning, forces from the ringed planet must already be on the way, unless our surprise attack had cut off every one of the few ships that had survived the initial blasting.

Then we saw the far-off glow.

"Bigger fleet than the one that drove us down," Ion groaned.

His words passed from man to man. For a moment we were frozen, beyond hope of despair. The sky held a red promise; and the nearer it came, the more we realized that thus far we had seen only the shadow of Saturnian power. Vengeance was on the way.

My thought was: They'll clean up here, and then knock Japetus out of its orbit. Blow it to dust.

If we had not been so shocked, there would have been a panic. Saturnians were manning their ships. We could see the dark masses silhouetted against the reflection of the hothouse dome lights from the bronze-colored hulls of the cruisers.

"Back to cover," I yelled. Then I changed that order. "Hold it!"

Something big was happening in space. Sheets of flame outlined the fleet that had been marked only by repulsion tube glow. We heard no sounds. In the thin layer of Titanian air, it should not take long for the vibration to reach us.

Silence meant that the explosions—those prodigious flashes could be nothing else—were far above the Titanian stratosphere; that the great expanse of the fleet had made us underestimate the distance.

"It's a battle!" Ion cried. "Revolution in Saturn! Civil war!"

CHAPTER XXVI

SLIDE-RULE PARKER

THE Saturnian attack on the space ship plant in north central Canada turned out not to be as ruinous as John Parker and Shadra had at first expected.

In the first place, while every one of the partially assembled ships had been damaged, the reconditioning was mainly a matter of working on the hulls and the propulsion machinery; for the complex and costly instruments for navigation, artillery fire, control, and visiphone communication had not yet been installed.

Furthermore, the Saturnians had been decisively defeated in a mass attack; the non-magnetic shells had pierced the repulsion screens and brought the icthyform space ships down; and field pieces, firing shells with fuses cut for muzzle bursts, blew the supposedly invulnerable Saturnians to pieces.

And—far too important for incidental mention—the wrecked space cruisers had bunkers loaded with disintegrator fuel.

Parker said to Colonel Watson, now officer in charge of the assembly plant, "Colonel, it is not as bad as it looked." He telescoped his slide rule, and put it into its worn and battered case. "As long as the propaganda department keeps up civilian morale, we can get those damaged space cruisers reconditioned, make a surprise attack on the Saturnian base in northern Mexico, and try the effect of our shells filled with frozen hydrogen."

Shadra retouched her make-up and tried to think of new arguments to keep Parker from personally leading the raid in Mexico. The hurry and roar of Terra, though fascinating enough, still kept the girl from Titan on edge; particularly the assembly plant where she and Parker had desks.

She regarded her mirrored reflection with dismay, for the Terrestrian scientists had not yet succeeded in eliminating the excess of blue from their heatless glow tubes. "Not bad, though," she had to admit, "except it makes one's lips almost mulberry. And those rings under my eyes—"

She looked up, and noted the necrotic pallor of Parker's long, thin face. The ruddy colonel was an outrageous blue-bronze-purple. Shadra brightened. *Everyone* was awful under Terrestrian cold light, though it was easy on the eyes—and in spite of the stroboscope effect which Parker threatened to eliminate once the Saturnian problem was solved.

The colonel was saying, "The electronic welding works out nicely, with a blanketing jet of argon to keep that touchy alloy from oxidizing before it's cooled. Don't worry, Dr. Parker; the Engineer Corps will get that squadron fixed up. And the Antarctic assembly plant has a number of units almost ready. To say nothing of the plant in Greenland."

Parker's face lengthened. He took his slide rule out of its case and made a few settings. They had nothing to do with the problem at hand, but after recording the result, he looked up and said, "As long as the propaganda department keeps up civilian morale, we're all right; but what assurance have we?"

The colonel laughed. "Don't borrow trouble. We'll even capture you a Saturnian for experimental purposes, so you'll know beyond any doubt that solidified hydrogen settles those fire-breathers."

Shadra still regarded her mirrored image, and not from any undue feminine vanity. She was weary, and the twitch at the corner of her eye told her that she would have to keep shorter office hours. She told herself, "That's just the stroboscope effect of that vapor lamp, I can't be jittering as much as all that!"

But to make sure, she switched on the photo-visotype. As the tape began to unreel, light reflected from polished keys flashed to the sensitized tape, and a vapor bath almost instantly developed the photographic image: a modernization of the noisy teletype that used to drive newspapermen mad, and made stock brokers dive out of windows.

~ ~ ~ ~ ~

THE blossoming out of a word at a time, instead of a letter at a stroke, made photo-visotype easy on the eyes, but it had this defect: it was just enough out of step with the vapor lights to require a light of its own. Some blamed this on the inventor's shrewdness, others on the profit-mindedness of manufacturers. At the moment, Shadra was not concerned with this detail.

She watched the words jerk, shift, shudder in the most eye-wrenching way. She shook her blond head and sighed. "Well, I am not as shaky as I thought. A visotype would hardly develop a twitch, and my eyelids just seem to flutter."

But Shadra saw enough of the words on the jerking tape to make her cry, "John, look at this! Colonel, you are missing something!"

She snapped on the reading light; there was no longer any twitch, and the tape flowed smoothly along, word after word coming up black on its surface. Parker rose, took one step, and then readjusted his glasses.

The colonel's face changed; he turned a deeper blue-plum color, cursed and said, "They're crazy! It can't be! Not after we beat them so decisively."

But there it was:

... *rioting* ... *Chicago out of hand* ... *Buenos Aires under mob rule* ... *Argentine dictatorship consolidating* ... *South American republics to treat with Saturnians* ... *Scientist Parker's hydrogen shell a delusion, scientific organizations discredited. Canadian victory pointless. South American congress plans compromise. Citizens owning less than a square kilometre of land or income less than one thousand pazoors annually liable to draft on Saturnian demand* ...

"No wonder they're revolting!" the colonel howled. "The air is full of proposals like that! Panic spreads, there is no telling when some crackpot will suggest something like that up here. And then we *will* have riots!"

Shadra said, "John, maybe it is quieter and safer back on Titan. If these beastly Terrestrials are calling you a delusion, after all your work, after all your study, after the way you have worn yourself to a shred, it'd serve them right if you left.

"And you too, Colonel, you and your silly conceited Army artillerymen; you could not take a chance on a hydrogen shell, you were afraid John would get a reputation, and that your antiquated pop guns would be condemned."

The colonel threw up his hands. "Now steady, young lady! You've put it just a little too strong. Well, maybe we were a little too eager to prove old-fashioned methods are the soundest. Unconsciously, I mean, not intentionally. Parker, I'll get in touch with the President at once; the Department of Propaganda must be armed with the very latest word from this plant."

The colonel eyed Parker; his jaw sagged, and he reached out. "You don't look as if you heard a word I said."

Shadra caught his arm. "Let him alone, Colonel; he gets that way every so often. Call the President, and I'll get the last minute reports."

~ ~ ~ ~ ~

A CALL from any assembly plant received preferred attention; the President's chief secretary was on the visiphone in less than a minute after the colonel had put through the code symbols.

Shadra pressed a switch and then waited little over a minute for a red blinker to light up on the panel of the automatic selector. She opened the magnetic conduit and removed the ferro-silicon container into which the reports had been rolled, down in the filing department.

Shadra removed the papers and stepped to the visiphone. "Here they are, Colonel. Our latest plan, and—"

Just then Parker interposed, absent-mindedly thrust the girl aside as if she had been a misplaced swivel chair, and said over the officer's shoulder, "Here's the answer, Your Excellency. Please ignore Colonel Watson's well-meant suggestion; we simply do not have time."

The President took that with a smile. His friendly, unruffled voice and twinkling eyes showed that he believed more in results than in rules. "Excuse me, Colonel Watson," he said. "Very well, Doctor Parker?"

"Be so good as to have Propaganda announce that the hydrogen shell has been tried and found good. That because of military secrecy, its success has been withheld, and is being released now only because the public is not giving us the confidence we deserve."

"Why—why didn't you tell me before, Doctor Parker?"

"Because I am merely anticipating success by a few days. According to thermodynamic principles"—he reached for his slide rule, and without breaking into his discussion—"the expansion of the gas is at the rate of—"

"I would scarcely deny that, Doctor Parker. Please make yourself clear on just one point. You propose to announce that the shell is effective, a solution to our problem, and before a final proof is made?"

"Exactly, Your Excellency. Judging from reports, it will be too late if we follow the chronological order."

The President for once frowned. He turned from the visiphone and for a moment neither his face nor his voice was transmitted; only the blurred murmur of speech, and vague office sounds, fifteen hundred miles south. Then he flashed to the screen again: "If your slide rule convinces you that frozen hydrogen in small arms bullets will beat the Saturnians, I shall consider the case proven. When do you leave for Saturn?"

"In less than forty-eight hours. The welding machines are working day and night, the reconditioning has gone unexpectedly well," Parker answered.

"When can we expect you to return?"

"When the Arch-Mogok Thorgulu and his party are settled."

"Very well, Doctor Parker."

The visiphone screen went blank. Shadra cried, "Now you've done it! You didn't have to—"

"I did and I do have to go out and personally back this gamble. I certainly cannot send someone else out to test, in actual service, a practically unproved device."

"But you may not come back. It may not work."

Parker smiled. "In that case, my dear, the President would be so annoyed that I'd much prefer not to return. To say nothing of the roasting the scientific associations would give me."

"Oh." Shadra's voice and smile sharpened. "Well, just imagine how I'd feel, listening to the wives and lady friends of the association—not to mention the female scientists. So I am going with you."

Parker knew that he had been out-maneuvered without even having raised a slide rule in defense. So he said, "All right; after all, it has to work; and if we surprise the Saturnians, there will not be too much danger."

CHAPTER XXVII

GET THORGULU!

EVERY assembly plant in the north and south polar zones contributed its quota of finished space cruisers; and a South African development company surprised Parker at the last moment by supplying a synthetic fuel which, while not as efficient as the natural ore of Titan, was available in quantities sufficient to cram the bunkers of the entire fleet.

And within a few minutes of M-hour, the mobilized space fleet took off; long and fish-formed, outwardly duplicating the Saturnian pattern, as a matter of strategy; while as to equipment and operation details, there were differences aplenty.

Parker was in command of the fleet, as technical expert, and the rehabilitated *Karamanu* was his flagship. Her sister ships had plates of bronze-colored alloy, but as they cleared the Terrestrial atmosphere and got well into the spaceways, Parker pressed a signal button. With scarcely a split second delay, the entire fleet glowed blue-white.

"Effective, I think," he told Shadra. "Until the last moment, we look precisely like Saturnian ships. Then, to avoid confusion and the danger of blowing each other out of the ether, we switch on the color change beam. And if you'll notice, this is not stroboscopic!"

Shadra laughed. "If it hadn't been for the quiver of glow lamps at the plant, you might not have gotten the news until the following morning and no telling what might have happened."

She picked up a few yards of photo-visotype tape and glanced at its text. "Your victory-to-be, and every Terrestrial town waiting for your triumphal return as if it had already been accomplished, is what staved off general revolution. Not just in South America, but all over."

So when Parker finally reached the Saturnian orbit, he had to win a victory that had been celebrated days before. The Terrestrial press correspondents had followed their usual routine of writing all the details of the battle before a shot was fired, and then doing two sets of statements of "far reaching results," according as the Terrestrians or the Saturnians actually won.

After centuries of practice, they had learned to claim, for instance, a brilliant victory and without any apparent inconsistency conclude with a summary of the number of human victims the defeated Saturnians expected each year.

. . . by forcing the Saturnians to take charge of all habitual criminals, the Terrestrians will solve two problems with one move . . .

Hours later, when Parker had finally finished sending code messages to Terra, he saw from the space charts that the Titanian orbit was near. The executive officer reported by visiphone, "An unusual number of Saturnian cruisers has just been sighted by scouts. Contact is impending."

"When do we sight the Titanian slave pens?"

"A little after we see the Saturnian patrols. They are reported concentrating on that spot."

This unusual gathering of the enemy's ships demanded an immediate revision of Parker's plans, for to continue to Saturn and leave so strong a force behind the Terrestrian expedition would be a dangerous experiment. It did not take an expert in strategy to see how grave the risk would be.

Without any slide rule exercises, Parker could see that while an immediate attack on the presumably unguarded Saturnian capital might result in a signal victory, it might also be followed by a fatal attack from the rear, launched on a fleet temporarily disorganized by mopping up the vast spread of the city.

Parker said, "Keep me posted. We'll have to settled the Titanian patrols."

~ ~ ~ ~ ~

THE fleet swooped into the long night of Titan. Incoming reports from the scouts took more and more of Parker's time. In the signal compartment, busy operators were intercepting messages passing between units of the Saturnian squadrons.

With every moment, Parker realized more fully what a dangerous trap he had outwitted by his decision not to drive directly into the capital.

The visiphone transmitter kept him in personal touch with the commander of each Terrestrian cruiser, while Shadra was busy at the photo-visotype, which recorded the reports of the scouts. But before many minutes passed, this close coordination of so many units, arranged in such great depth, became impossible.

"*K-12,* engaging Saturnian cruiser!" a squadron commander reported. "*K-15* disabled but carrying on."

Parker's mouth tightened, and when he looked up, he saw that Shadra's face was white and tense. His smile was short and bleak. "This is what we have been working toward," he said, and snapped on the illuminated chart which filled all of the space on one bulkhead.

The ships were represented by moving spots of color. Each Terrestrian was now sending a radio beam whose fluctuations gave its position in space, while photoelectric cells "saw" and transmitted corresponding information on all enemy cruisers within their angle of vision.

The Terrestrian fleet had avoided the confusion of names. Each had a number, and the initial preceding was a designation of size or type. Each *K,* for instance, was modeled after the captured *Karamanu,* Parker's flagship.

K15's spot of color winked out. She might be a smoking ruin, her crew already blown apart by the escape of her atmosphere into the vacuum of space. Perhaps only the oscillation transmitter had been damaged. But now details of battle were out of Parker's hands. He could only draw inferences. *K-12* was engaging two Saturnians. One of them dropped out of the field of vision.

Parker wiped sweat from his forehead, for no one had time now to give him any details, and while he could follow the swoop and flash of each vessel, he could only guess what was happening in those encounters, until the disappearance of a color spot showed—

"Yes, but what? Destruction—flight—maneuver?"

"They know what they are doing, John. You went into that so often, in so many drills. Do sit down. It has to go out of your hands for the time. You can't personally pilot each cruiser."

Shadra was right. He had prepared the plans, and he had selected men to execute them; and now that the two fleets were clashing, he could do nothing but watch and wait, wait for the time to send the second and the third squadrons into action.

The *Karamanu's* signal crew was piecing together the intercepted messages. The Saturnians had been taken by surprise by the bronze color and the shape of the Terrestrian ships, and only when the leading squadron had blazed out blue-white did they fully realize that war had come home to them.

"These reports are confusing," the signal chief said. "The enemy speaks of Japetan ships slipping around the rear of their fleet. They seem to refer to us. No reference to Terrestrian forces."

Parker brightened. "So they are guessing? Try and find out how and when anyone on Japetus built enough ships to turn out the Saturnian navy."

The second squadron swooped down. In spite of the false perspective of a two-dimensional chart, Parker could visualize the neatness of the attack. The enemy, alarmed, were rising swiftly; they still seemed, as far as he could judge from their formation, unaware of the lurking second and third line of Terrestrian capital ships. Apparently they had believed when breaking through the *L* and *M* scouts that there was only one line of the powerful *K* ships.

~ ~ ~ ~ ~

PARKER switched to direct vision. The *Karamanu* was now so close to the center of action that moving chart devices could no longer cover the field, for their angles of photoelectric vision were not wide enough.

Lines of flame rippled through the gloom. The glow was reflected, bronze-colored. The opposing forces swooped, dipped, wheeled about to blast each other out of the air.

In an instant, Terrestrian and Saturnian ships looked so nearly alike that friends might shoot each other down through inability to keep track of their companion ships on the right and left.

Parker passed along the signal, and the Terrestrians' fluorescent paint film began to glow blue-white. Thus, at a glance, he could see how far his squadron had penetrated, how many were fighting, how many were crippled, how many were sinking in a trail of flame.

The signal crew chief returned: "We intercepted a message asking Kent Bradley to surrender, under threat of immediate annihilation. If he surrenders, he gets a safe conduct to Japetus or Terra."

"What?"

The chief repeated the message. "There is no chance of a mistake. Bradley said—"

"Well, what did he say?" Parker demanded, when the man hesitated. "Bradley's alive! Bradley's revolting. What did he say?"

"Uh—well—Beg your pardon, sir, but these are the words he used—" The chief blurted it out, and it was impressive.

The precise scientist forgot discipline and slapped the man on the back. "Absolutely authentic! He would put it that way."

Shadra looked puzzled. "I never heard words like those. What do they mean? I thought you'd taught me English."

"Er—it's a peculiar dialect they speak in Bradley's state," Parker said. Then, to the signal chief, "Get me more of it! Who is the Saturnian? Can you arrange a direct hook-up?"

"Yes, sir. Thorgulu, the Arch-Mogok, speaking to Kent Bradley. At once, sir."

He ran from the compartment. Parker dashed after him. "Get the right band and tell Bradley not to surrender, not to make any terms, but to hang on."

While waiting, Parker ordered the commander of the third squadron into action. "I know we ought to keep a reserve, but go in anyway! Kent Bradley and some Japetan rebels are fighting off all the Saturnians. We have to help them make the most of their attempt."

He cut the visiphone and then turned to Shadra. "Imagine it: Bradley, stealing or building ships, leading a revolt instead of going to the ovens. That is why there is a concentration of Saturnians, and that is why we were able to steal up on them. They were expecting more reinforcements from the capital to help subdue rebel slaves."

The visiphone pilot light blinked red, and Parker cut in again. The screen clouded, then blurred colors took shape; the signal chief had tuned in the Saturnian wave band.

Thorgulu's ruddy face and sharp nose and blazing eyes filled the screen, and his harsh voice made the transmitter crackle: "If you don't accept my offer right now, I'll get you even if you are hiding in ravines, I'll blast down every peak and flatten the country, you—"

Then Kent Bradley came back at him. Parker chuckled. The signal chief had not exaggerated. "Very unscientific, but forceful." Parker pressed a button, and turned to a local circuit's transmitter.

When the executive officer's face appeared in the screen, Parker said, "Tell *KK-5* to take command of operations. The *Karamanu* is to follow radio beam directions and get direct contact with the ship of Thorgulu."

"But you can't," the officer protested. "You can't turn over command in the midst of an action like this. I'll send a cruiser, several cruisers—"

"I can and I am going to," Parker cut in. "Tell *KK-5* to take over. He helped me draft the plans, and if he does not know them as well as I do, someone should convene a court martial."

The officer saluted. Shadra asked, "John, what are you planning now? Do you mean to say you are going to go after Thorgulu as a private and personal adventure?"

"I am going to hunt that fellow down and make an example of him, but not as a personal adventure. It just happens that the *Karamanu* is the only ship equipped to pick out and follow Thorgulu's ship in all these hundreds milling around. There is no time to waste. Are there any other questions?"

Before Shadra had a chance to think of any, Parker went down the passage that led to the bridge. Slide rule work had its limit. Kent Bradley's gallant defiance had made Parker forget that he was a calm and cold-blooded scientist.

"Carry on," he said to the executive officer. "All you have to do is find Thorgulu's ship, and blow it out of the air. Chase him to Pluto and beyond if necessary."

CHAPTER XXVIII

THEY'LL LIKE VEGETABLES

THE action had become general. The upper air of Titan was a tri-dimensional traffic jam of ships, wreckage, and scout patrols dashing crazily among the heavy cruisers. The *Karamanu* ploughed through the confusion; and then for deadly instants she was in a zone of cross fire, as liable to destruction by friend as by enemy.

"Is the man crazy?" Shadra gasped, as a sharp turn flung her against a bulkhead. "We're dropping."

"Diving under power." Parker paused to glance at an instrument panel to verify this. "Thorgulu must be close to the surface of the satellite."

Shadra had turned to a port, and her face was pressed against the thick pane. "I can see the domed gardens and slave pens, the light of them, miles of them. But it's foggy."

"Smoke," Parker corrected. "Searchlights over here. Reaching through. Ground searchlights. Flame from the ground—*look!*"

A long wavering line of fire rippled red through the swirling vapors that blanketed the face of Titan and made the glow of its domed city seem farther away than the instruments indicated. An explosion blotted out half of the familiar curve of the airlock where Saturnian space cruisers docked.

In a few seconds, Parker was certain that an unheard-of thing had happened: fighting on foot, between Saturnians and slaves—slaves, and their Japetan allies.

Now the *Karamanu* was far below the dog fight of midspace. She skimmed low, swerved to avoid a tall tower which buttressed the domed city of Titan. The pilot said, "The ground is covered with ships, and our infra-red 'eyes' indicate large bodies of men maneuvering on foot, and in the ravines beyond the city."

He was getting this from a receiver clamped to one ear, but visual verification was available. He touched a switch and Parker saw figures on a screen: the weird distortion of fog-penetrating infra-red converted into visual wave lengths.

There was no doubt about it; tall Saturnians fumed and smoked in their space suits, and hordes of Titanians attacked them, singled them out, cornered them, overwhelmed them with devices whose gush of fumes soon blocked out even the infra-red rays.

Then the pilot shouted, "We've got him! Thorgulu's ship!"

He twisted the controls. This time Parker and Shadra had snapped on safety belts, or they would have been crushed against the bulkhead. Ahead, a great bronze-hued ship swooped out of the mist. The signal chief reported to the bridge, "Thorgulu's long-range communication system is out of commission. As nearly as we can make out from intercepted local messages, he is going to Saturn for reinforcements."

"Like hell he is!" Parker yelled. "More speed!"

No coordinated details from the satellite were available, nor were the messages exchanged between the *KK-5,* now flagship, and the cruisers in action, clear enough to give a picture of what actually was happening around the domed city of Titan, and in the deep ravines. But soon it was certain that the Saturnian fleet was beginning to lose. The only query was, "When do we win?"

"No, that's not the only question," Parker said. "Indeed, there are several more. First, how did Bradley fare, and second, is Thorgulu racing for reinforcements he can't summon otherwise, or is he merely trying to escape?"

The probability was that he needed reinforcements, or wished to take a warning to Saturn. The Arch-Mogok's valor had never been questioned.

~ ~ ~ ~ ~

THORGULU swooped up and through the confusion of cruisers. He would have made a clean escape but for the radio beam reflection from his hull, for the dense smoke rising from the satellite's face made all ships look alike. The Karamand put on more and more power as there were fewer maneuvering ships; but Thorgulu was losing no time.

"That's the fastest ship the Saturnians have," Shadra said.

"It is a long way to Saturn," Parker answered. Then, seeing that the satellite was already far behind, he asked the signal chief, "Any reports of the battle on Titan?"

"At B-hour plus twenty-nine, the Third Squadron started out to meet any possible Saturnian reinforcements, or to shell the capital. The Third was not needed in the action over Titan."

"Good for *KK-5!*"

Ahead, Saturn loomed up larger against the blackness, white and shimmering, its ring an arch of stardust and star fragments and vapor. Mists blanketed the planet's face, and only radio or infra-red could penetrate deeply enough to pick out the Saturnian capital.

Thorgulu's ship was losing speed. The flame from her repulsion tubes was irregular. The uneven propulsion made her twist and swerve crazily in her course. Parker pressed a button, and the *Fire at Will* signal flashed in each gun turret.

The *Karamanu* shuddered, and for all her insulation, the navigation compartment quivered from the blast. One of the shells grazed Thorgulu's ship, and fire streamed far after her. The Arch-Mogok answered, and then both ships settled down to maneuver; flight and pursuit were for the moment over: for one of the combatants, perhaps permanently.

"You and I watch, now," Parker said, glumly. "Slide rules are of no use."

Shadra's tense face relaxed in a smile. "Don't feel that way, John. Your calculations made all this possible."

The ring of Saturn now blocked out all the further stars and the blackness beyond. Thorgulu had to swoop sharply upward, or dive almost straight down and into the vapor blanket. The *Karamanu* flattened out to block that last move, and a broadside blasted up at the fugitive's hull. A gush of flame and a surge of smoke indicated a shattered compartment.

In open space, Thorgulu would still have had at least an even chance; but with his erratic propulsion and the deadly barrier of fragments that whirled with the vapors of Saturn's ring, his only choice was a steep upward swoop.

Parker reached for the visiphone and spun the dials. This was the first time in many months that he had direct speech with Thorgulu. "Surrender, as a hostage to guarantee good behavior of all Saturnians," Parker said to the Arch-Mogok, "or we'll blow you to pieces."

"Come and get me!" Flame and smoke obscured the visiphone screen, and almost blotted out the Saturnian's sharp, red face. "We do not surrender."

The half-crippled ship still had some artillery in action. A crashing and grinding broke communication for dragging seconds. One of the *Karamanu's* gun turrets was disabled by a shell. Thorgulu, still at the visiphone, yelled, "How do you like that? Come nearer and take us!"

"Our fleet is shelling your capital," Parker said. "And not all the smoke in your compartment is your breath. Your ship is breaking up, and your fuel bunkers are leaking."

The screen went blank. Fumes enveloped the Saturnian ship. Aboard the *Karamanu,* the maintenance crew raced about with welding equipment to patch the bent and torn armor of the jammed turret. At the same time, the other turrets continued their fire, pouring shells into the spreading cloud of smoke. The dense fumes were reaching out to the planet's whirling ring and blending with it.

~ ~ ~ ~ ~

THEN Parker saw how Thorgulu had tricked him. Rather than surrender, he had thrown out a smoke screen and now his ship was heading straight for the planet's outer ring; straight into destruction, for the thickest armor could not endure the combined impact of the millions of solid particles which mingled with the vapor and dust that made the fifty-mile thickness of Saturn's girdle.

There was a green blaze of vaporized metal, spreading so bright and broad that for seconds no one aboard the *Karamanu* could see the white of the planet's face. The space ship's hull had vanished from the shock of meeting all the meteorites in that band of planetary dust.

"The bravest of all those stiff-necked Saturnians," Parker said, when his eyes recovered from the glare. "Suicide, but not surrender."

Shadra's cry made him shake off the mood brought on by Thorgulu's gallant end. "Brave, but cunning! Look—over there."

Her voice made Parker and the pilot snap back to the instruments. A small, gleaming hull whisked from the edge of the smoke screen; the lower edge of the obscuring cloud from which Thorgulu's cruiser had dashed headlong into the ring of Saturn. The *Karamanu* swerved, and Parker shouted the bearings of the new target.

Thorgulu, he was certain, must be in that small life boat with the survivors of his crew. But the *Karamanu's* fire was wasted on such a small target. "Dive after him," Parker shouted. "Don't let him reach the vapor blanket! Keep him from the capital!"

Then Parker saw the final display of Saturnian courage. The life boat headed for the space between the concentric rings. She zigzagged and vanished. Pursuit was impossible, for no ship the size of the *Karamanu* could risk the deadliness of that seemingly clear zone between the outer and inner ring of Saturn.

The *Karamanu* depressed her nose and swooped down into the planet's vapor blanket. There was no way of learning whether Thorgulu's insane valor had ended in a burst of flame, or whether he had worked his way through the fifty-mile depth and to the other side of the ring.

One thing however was certain: in that light space-launch, Thorgulu could not travel fast enough to warn the capital.

And when the *Karamanu* leveled off in the steaming atmosphere of Saturn, Parker easily located the capital. There was sullen glow, a crisscrossing of searchlights, and a circling of space cruisers whose fluorescent blue-white identified them. The third squadron's work was almost over.

The mushrooms of dust and colored flame slowly settled down to the level of the dust which shrouded the domes and pinnacles of the Saturnian capital. Parker signaled the *KK-5*, and in a moment, the squadron commander reported, "We are preparing to land and mop up the city. The population has revolted, and all the leaders are barricaded in the citadel. Hydrogen shells are going to get their trial."

The *Karamanu* landed and her crew turned out with small arms. Parker went with the landing party. Shoulder to shoulder, shambling in heavily insulated suits, the Terrestrians crossed the smoking square. Saturnians charged from the citadel; hard-shells, defiant to the last, unable to believe that invaders could meet them and their gusts of flame face to face.

The hydrogen bullets stopped them. First the cold beyond any Saturnian imagination; then the expansion as the solid gas became liquid, and the liquid, hundreds of degrees below zero, began to boil and expand. The action was instantaneous, explosive, and each Saturnian became a bomb that burst. The flames that followed, almost on the very impact and burst, were really the aftermath, the fierce combination of hydrogen and oxygen.

But the Saturnian targets were already beyond any appreciation of the blaze that roared down their lines, wherever a Terrestrian bullet hit. They turned and fled, bewildered by the alternation of icy gusts and bursts of fire.

"They're working," Parker shouted behind his gas mask, and reloaded his hydrogen pistol. "I'm right, I was right, it's just as I calculated."

The survivors of the sortie reached their red hot palace. It was not until the story of Thorgulu's defeat and probable destruction was confirmed by his failure to reach the citadel that the stubborn defenders surrendered.

Revolt, the disappearance of the Arch-Mogok, the terror of frozen hydrogen, cracked their stubborn spirits. Parker said to the commander of the *KK-5,* "It's all done; they are resigned to a vegetable diet. Carry on. I have to go to Titan and find out about Kent Bradley."

CHAPTER XXIX

BACK TO A BUDGET

WHEN Ion pointed at the sheets of flame far up in the Titanian stratosphere, and shouted, "Revolution in Saturn! Civil war!" I called it wishful thinking. His guess didn't sound reasonable until I remembered the disabled ship I had seen on our return from taking Valene from her captors; a large one, bronze-colored, like the vessel that had carried Parker and me from Terra.

It was followed by similar ships in wedge formation, and far behind that squadron I saw the glow of what must be propulsion tubes. It made me think of the flicker and waver of Terrestrial northern lights; and trying to estimate the size of the successive waves was no job for this tense moment.

Apparently Saturnian ships were shooting each other down. I could now hear the dull rumble and roaring as the battle came into the thin upper atmosphere. There was a crashing and grinding; great cruisers lost way, began to spin and fall, smashing into each other, and flames stretched out like the tails of comets. A gun turret, blasted out of place, shook the earth when it fell into the twisted girders of the air-dock.

If this was revolution, no wonder Thorgulu wanted to compromise; no wonder he did not want our Japetan ships to counter-attack, with all that hell above him. Why there should be revolt in Saturn might be learned by the survivors of this insane tangle among the crags of Titan; but—

"Look—look at the blue ships!"

Ion's shout accompanied a strange sight: even as I looked up into the grinding and whirling tangle, wondering whether wild shots from the. maneuvering cruisers would not do more damage to us than the direct efforts of our enemies, I saw a score of bronze-colored ships turn a dazzling blue-white.

No signal could have caused such instant execution of an order to remove camouflage; some high-frequency impulse released from a master-oscillator must have activated the fluorescent pigments that covered the vessels whose color had changed.

Fluorescent? It had to be; nothing else could explain the peculiar wavering and ripple of the light that made the new-comers stand out against the black sky, against the smoke, and against the dust that rose in clouds when shells missed their aerial targets and exploded against the crags of Titan, or buried themselves in the soil and blew up tall geysers of fragments.

This change of color made the whole confusion clear. I caught Ion's arm and yelled, "See it? All the blues are one fleet. It makes sense; see them gang up on the bronze? A surprise trick—they didn't show their color until there was danger of friends' shooting each other down in the tangle!"

Ion began dancing around and waving his arms and yell-ing. The Titanians and Japetans nearest him passed the word along. I shouted, "Nail the Saturnians before they can get the rest of their ships off the ground. Don't let them join those in the air!"

That color change must be one of John Parker's carefully calculated devices. Parker, back from Terra, had come to clean house on Titan. A slide rule was on the warpath now, and the Saturnian fleet milled about, not yet recovered from the confusion.

~ ~ ~ ~ ~

WE BROKE into a run. The Saturnians, heading for the cruisers still lined up on the plain, saw us approach and wheeled to meet us. Acid projectors coughed their charges into the solid rank. The enemy outnumbered us, but they could not ignore the threat; particularly not with the roar and terror overhead. Whatever communication the fleet had with the ground could not be helpful, for things were happening too rapidly for signal crews to maintain anything like co-ordination. It was each ship for itself.

Hampered by their insulated suits, the Saturnians could not move quickly enough to spread out and overwhelm us by sheer weight.

The more aggressive Titanians saw their chance. They poured out of the hothouse. They snatched metal fragments from the hangar wreckage and belabored their oppressors from the rear. The blows did little damage, but the jagged bludgeons slashed the Saturnian insulation and let the biting chill sink in.

For every Saturnian who took it on the chin, a score of slaves dropped, scorched and stifled; but inspired frenzy made newcomers join the battle. They had seen one small victory, and they were going wild.

In the meanwhile, hell was whirling above us. The over-head battle made the sky a solid sheet of flame and glittering metal. We could now distinguish the pursuing ships from the Saturnian fugitives. Color and contour made that simple. Blue-white hulls rammed those with bronze plates.

Overwhelming force and superior numbers were telling. Saturnian ships crashed against far-off peaks; geysers of flame rose. Others were forced down by sheer weight. Their crews raced across the plain. And the Terrestrians landed. They came out in grotesque armor that made them look like deep-sea divers.

Our surprise party merged with the ever-increasing ranks of the Terrestrians. Isolated groups, fighting it out to a finish, dissolved in spurts of flame and gusts of acid. A few of the ships on the ground, despite our attempt to cut off the crews, took the air. And then the scattered clusters of Saturnians and Terrestrians tightened into lines.

~ ~ ~ ~ ~

OUR allies from home had a weapon that made acid projectors seem crude and ineffective. They fired bullets whose effect was dazzling; the fire-breathing Saturnians burst like bombs. There was a blinding sheet of flame, and the monster was gone. This was fighting the devil with fire!

I'd heard of that, but here it was, a figure of speech put into real and terrible practice.

The battle in the air was over. A pursuit squadron had headed for Saturn; whether to meet reinforcements, or to carry war to the heart of the Saturnian power, I couldn't guess. The week-long Titanian gloom was shaking with roars and rumbles and explosions; dark masses of our allies loomed up here and there against the bursts of flames that marked the end of another cornered group of the enemy.

A few Terrestrian cruisers circled overhead, in mid-space, while others, just visible, patrolled the stratosphere; their readiness to observe and give the alarm added to the uncertainty, the eeriness of the madman's battle on the dark plains of Titan, and in the ragged ranges and deep ravines that seamed the satellite.

One by one, the Terrestrian cruisers not on patrol duty landed near the airlock, and their crews joined the widely scattered landing parties.

A courier was dispatched to Japetus, for even with a possible counter-attack, we felt that we could spare one light cruiser to let the council of the further satellite share our triumph.

Hours passed before the mopping up was completed. Rather than surrender, many of the Saturnians plunged into deep ravines, and rising flames, soon extinguished, told how the Titanian chill had finished these obstinate fighters.

I hurried back to the domed city with Ion, for we both wanted a complete picture of what had been going on all around us.

A Terrestrian officer was checking up on ships absent, ships accounted for, ships demolished in action; it was still too soon to begin mustering the crews. He looked up from his desk in the flagship of the squadron that had made the first contact. He chewed a cigar, his lean face twitched, and his hand shook as he said, "I guess you're Bradley. Your friend, Doctor Parker—"

"Slide Rule Parker?" I forced a grin and tried to wise-crack. The officer nodded.

"Right. Turned command over to *KK-5,* after saying that he was chasing Thorgulu to Pluto and beyond, if necessary. He was not with the second squadron that went to bombard the Saturnian capital, and so far, we have not had any word of him."

Valene had rejoined me after order had been restored. "Try and get in touch! If he's lost, the victory is half wasted. If it hadn't been for him, not many of us would be here."

The officer sighed and shook his head. "Sit down and wait. Messages are coming in right along."

But there was no message to warn us of Parker's landing. Probably it had never occurred to him that anyone was particularly interested in his personal doings. Valene and I bobbed up from the bench and ran to the grounded cruiser's porthole when we heard the whine and hissing of another ship landing.

Flood lights played on it. A hatch opened. The officer looked up again from his work and said, "That's the *Karamanu,* Parker's flagship."

"Thanks a lot," I said. "Maybe if you went along, you could point Parker out to me; I'd love to have his autograph."

I caught Valene's hand and dragged her across the debris-littered landing field. The officer, I noted as we both stumbled and landed in a heap, was back at his work.

~ ~ ~ ~ ~

THEN I saw Parker. He halted as he reached the end of the gang plank. We faced each other, trying to think of something to say. He wore his usual unpressed tweeds.

The blonde who clung to his arm was wearing the first Terrestrian ensemble I'd seen in a long time, and she seemed to think Parker was well dressed. Her nose was smudged, and her bottle green outfit had suffered from the lack of space that goes with space travel, but she looked almost as good as Valene.

He poked out his hand, and then I thought of a brilliant greeting. "Hi, John. What'd you burn those Saturnians with? The landing parties did a nice job—slide rule stuff?"

A grin spread all over Parker's weary face. I could see he had lost a lot of weight and sleep. He answered, "Liquid hydrogen. Very simple. The intense cold froze their internal organs. Then the sudden expansion—"

Instinctively, he fumbled for the slide rule always in his pocket. "It released—"

"Never mind the B.T.U.'s," I cut in, and grabbed his hand. "Who's the girl friend?"

So I met Shadra, and then I learned that she knew Valene. Though all this took time. It was difficult to talk sense, and we did not succeed. Valene and I listened to Parker's account of what had happened back on earth; how the invention of projectiles that would go through magnetic repulsion screens had won the first advantage over the invaders, and how the liquid hydrogen bullets for small arms had solved the problem of fighting the devil with fire.

"What's the next act, John?" I asked him.

He sighed wearily, dug out a crumpled pack of cigarettes, and offered me one. Shadra, the devoted girl friend, found her monogrammed lighter; as a Terrestrian, she was a natural. "I always lose mine," Parker said, when she flicked the release. "So she's tracking along so I won't waste so much time hunting it."

"For a scientist," I said, "you've done pretty well. You act almost human."

Shadra smiled and looked pleased with herself, then offered me the lighter. Valene's eyes became round as saucers. She'd never seen a cigarette smoked, and she wondered if I was going Saturnian.

"Don't worry, darling," I told her. "Where you're going, you'll have to learn the trick yourself."

But the funny thing of it was, that long-anticipated ciga-rette was no treat at all. I dropped it on the deck and tramped on it. Then I said, "John, where are we going from here?"

"Back to Terra. We've shelled the Saturnian capital and the taste of hydrogen bullets broke their courage; cracked them far in excess of the actual casualties."

"They tell me you lit out to nail Thorgulu."

"We did not capture him," Parker said, wearily. "He dropped a smoke screen, and while we were looking for the cruiser he abandoned, Thorgulu slipped out in a space-launch, right for the space between the rings of Saturn. We could not follow, and we saw no sign to tell us whether his light boat was smashed or whether he made the almost im-possible passage. But regardless of that, he is marooned in space if he continues his flight; and if he tries to go home, he'll be imprisoned."

"Why? A brave fighter, I'd say. For an enemy, a pleasant chap."

Parker explained: "That is what his late friends said; but after we trounced them and blew half of their capital around their shoulders, and introduced them to Terrestrially frozen hydrogen, they remembered that he had pioneered these raids and so they want no more of him."

"He's the goat, eh?"

"Certainly. These Saturnians do have human traits. In a way, one could almost be sorry for him. A great leader, but he undertook just one enterprise too many. Very much like the crop of dictators who were bent on saving Terra by pay-ing the Saturnians a tribute of 'subnormal' humans. I am sure you see the great possibilities such a plan offered a ruling clique which had enemies to dispose of."

~ ~ ~ ~ ~

THIS told me that Terra had been playing pretty much true to form. When Parker went on to assure me that the various saviors of the people probably were now in secure jails to protect them from their public I asked, "How come? The news of this battle can't be in Terra already."

Parker's long face twisted in a grin, and he actually winked as he answered, "The newscasting services announced the unqualified success of the hydrogen shells before we left Terra. Probably they announced the capture of Thorgulu."

This was too much for me. I could not imagine precise and scientific Parker faking a story, and he had already told me that this Titanian battle had been the first test of the hydrogen projectile. He saw my amazement, and forestalled my question.

All he did was take his slide rule from the pocket of his greasy vest; he tapped the case, and said, "It was mathematically inevitable, and so I reported success. The wiping out of the Saturnian garrison in northern Mexico could not have taken place until a week after we took to space. More ships had to be built, for I needed every one I could get."

I did not ask him how he knew that Saturnian headquarters in the Western Hemisphere had actually been blown out of existence. He would have just strutted that slipstick and looked omniscient. Not that I begrudged him a bit of shining in the reflected splendor of calculus, but there were other things to discuss.

Among these were the details of the negotiations with the Saturnians who had survived the attack on their capital. Parker concluded these with his usual dry precision, and then said, "I think, Bradley, that you would find it tiresome to commute between Japetus and Terra. Well—"

"I'd love it," Valene cut in.

"What I meant was," he went on, "that the best way to remove temptation from the Saturnians is to transport the slaves of the satellite and the free people of Japetus back to their forgotten home on Terra. We have such a large fleet that not too many trips would be necessary."

"Your friend," Valene said, "is almost as smart as you are, darling. That's a perfectly wonderful idea. And if Shadra can get used to those funny clothes, I'm sure I can."

And that's the way it worked out. She did get used to those funny clothes. It keeps me broke buying her new ones. And Parker, having learned a lot of things his original scholarship had not included, has a similar report. He's invented a slide rule with setting for working out a household budget.

WEB OF WIZARDRY

By E. Hoffmann Price

1. The Weaver

THE GARDEN WAS PERSIAN; the fountain was silvered by the moon which rose over Shiraz, where Hafiz had once written a verse to the mole on the breast of a Turki dancing girl. And Barry Baylor should have done as well, for the girl on the silken soft rug was worth a poem in any language.

Marta stretched, reaching out with long, slim legs, and arched her bosom against the lace panel of her nightgown as she laced fingers behind her head and looked up from the cushions. "I'll have a mole tatooed . . . oh, almost any place you please, if you'll just stop looking so down in the mouth. Allan won't be back for a couple days!"

"That's just it!" Baylor rose, cat-quick, a tall and angular man with sun crisped hair and weary eyes; at the same move, he picked Marta to her feet. "Pack up now. Let's be honest and come out in the open."

For a moment she snuggled in his arms, her red hair pillowed against his shoulder. "Don't be silly, Barry. I can't leave Allan. We're not hurting him this way, we would the other way."

Her logic tempted him; then, resolutely, "We've got to quit."

"It was an accident—we didn't plan all this."

He nodded. "No . . . but we can stop it. All or nothing."

She looked up, wide eyed, and saw that he meant it. Then Marta laughed softly. "You'd better consult a magician, darling. With the right spell, Allan will be fed up with me, he'll kick me out, he'll fall in love with—oh, a Turki dancing girl, he'll send me to you with his compliments, please take the wench, Barry, be a good chap, won't you?"

~ ~ ~ ~ ~

THAT was how it started; that was why Barry Baylor, riding from Shiraz, stood in the entrance of the cavern in which webs of wizardry were woven; where a witch muttered spells, and bound them fast with knots of colored yarn.

Aisha was old beyond belief, and uglier than anything but time could make a human. For the moment, she squatted beside a smoldering fire instead of bending over a loom. Grizzled, greasy, a rag-bag with glittering eyes; but her voice amazed Baylor with its smoothness when she said, "O Man, you come to change the web of destiny, you come to change the patterns that Allah has made. The blessing you seek will become a doom and Satan the Damned will mock you. So rub your head and go your way, and the peace upon you."

But Baylor had come to rebuild the fate of three persons. For the duration of the war there would be no more rug buying; soon he would leave Iran, and without Marta, for he had stayed too long, trying to persuade her, and now he dared not tell her that tickets home would leave them with not enough to tip the stewards. And after so many nights of thinking in circles, it seemed logical to consult a magician.

Baylor said to the hag by the fire, "I know what I want, and it is not advice."

Aisha laughed softly. "You will not listen, yet I must warn you, for that is the law, the law that Allah has imposed on *djinni* and men and angels."

The murky cavern was larger than it had at first seemed to Baylor. He was puzzled and disturbed by the tricks his vision played, for despite the dimness of hearth and wavering torch, he could now see for a vast distance which must reach beyond the heart of the mountain, and further than any eyes should penetrate. Space stretched without limit, and luminous haze, drifting like wind driven mist, billowed about the small looms, the hundreds of looms, each with its partially completed rug.

He advanced further into the reek and eerie glow and said, "Then I am warned and what comes next is my business, not yours. Weave me a web, so that the days to come will be different from the days that have passed."

"There are three of you," she said.

Baylor started. "Who told you?"

Aisha sighed and tucked a greasy gray lock back under a greasy red velvet hood. "They come for love or gold or vengeance. Could I mistake one for the other?"

She gestured at the nearest looms. There might be other patterns, but these rugs were in the manner of Shiraz, with small figures of men and beasts and birds scattered among the arabesque lines of border and field. "I weave the symbols of your wish into the web, and what I weave becomes your destiny. I can have robbers waylay him, or an avalanche bury him, or a horse fall with him, or his servants slay him."

"Shut up, you old fool!" he cut in. "I could settle it that way myself."

She rose, lithe as a girl, which made her even more repulsive. She stepped to one of the many small looms and pointed at the tight stretched warp. Only enough weft had been cast to make the striped web. Thus far, not one knot of the pile had been tied. Aisha said, "Whatever I weave, that is the pattern of your tomorrows."

For a moment, Baylor forgot Marta and the gardens of Shiraz: The rock beneath his feet became clouds, and power intoxicated him; for he had lived in Iran too long to doubt that weird woman. Thus he knew that for all the yesterdays which ignorance had marred, there was a correction, and that the end would make a harmony of what had started in disorder.

When chilly caution crept into the drunkenness of that high moment, he told himself, "Try it, if it doesn't work right, stop the weaving. You can't lose!"

He wondered for a moment how one could pay the weaver of wizardry. He wondered why the mistress of destiny was ugly and greasy and old, and why she lived in a cave instead of in a palace with high tiled walls and gilded cupolas.

"What does this cost?"

"No more than you can pay, and no less. I will demand when you believe from knowing, and what can I ask that the master of his own fate cannot pay?"

He had no answer. She picked hanks of yarn, and began tying Senna knots, first of one color, then of another. Her skinny fingers danced like motes in a moonbeam; Baylor, who had seen many weavers, could not quite believe that any pattern could grow so swiftly.

Aisha muttered as she squatted there, swaying to the rhythm of her mumbling chant. She shot a weft thread across and back again, so swiftly that there was scarcely a break in the flicker of fingers tying knots. Small figures grew before his eyes. Tomorrow was being shaped. He protested, "I've not told you yet—you don't know—"

Aisha ignored him. Her eyes were half closed, as though she shaped a pattern that existed in her mind. That damnable mumbling, hissing, crooning; sometimes the sound made Baylor think of bats cheeping and birds twittering; again, he thought that he could distinguish words, some of them in languages which he understood. And the cavern's quivering haze tricked his eyes. There were momentary flashes of far off vistas.

"You don't know—" His voice became a croak. "Wait till I tell you—"

Her fingers danced on, the greasy red velvet cap with its golden coins and golden braid bobbed. Now her eyes were tightly closed, and when in fear and wrath, Baylor caught her shoulder, he yelled and let go.

That skinny frame beneath the rotting rags was no more to be checked than an avalanche. He was not even sure that he had actually touched the witch; his hand tingled as from a barrier of force which cut Aisha from the world of space and time. Small figures took shape, angular figures like a child's drawing on a wall, yet there was no denying their identity.

Allan Ostrom was there, and Marta, and Baylor. And then there were the symbols of events.

Baylor choked from cursing. He turned and stumbled from the cavern mouth, and lurched into the saddle. He spurred his horse down the steep trail and galloped toward the plain and Shiraz.

He was shivering and drenched with sweat. And when his panic dimmed, unease took its place. Out in the moonlight and the open, he told himself that old Zohrab's crazy tales had upset him, that he had been worrying too much about Marta: that wired-edged nerves had cracked when he forced himself to reach for that horrible recluse who squatted in a cave and mumbled.

But he could not shake off the depression, caused by feeling that a blind, mad thing was shaping his tomorrows. He began to understand, as he had never before, why Moslems in the presence of the uncanny recite,

"I betake me to the Lord of the Daybreak for refuge from Satan; and from the evils of the night; and from the spells of women who blow on knots."

He knew now that *blowing on knots* was more than an obscure expression to puzzle occidental scholars.

Then, as his long ride ended in the first light of dawn, new life came into him, and he laughed. Too much brandy, too much sleep lost, wondering if he could take Marta back to the States, wondering what a rug buyer could do, back home, after all these years of going from Shiraz to Kirman to Sulaimanya; he knew Iran, and nothing else. His panic proved that he'd come far too close to going native.

"If it works, good. If it doesn't, no harm done," he told himself, then shouted to Zohrab, the porter at the gate.

2. Pot of Gold

THAT very day, returning from an inspection of the truck and bus stations he was managing, Allan Ostrom dropped in for cocktails with Baylor; he brought Marta with him. She was part of his pride, part of a self-assurance and smugness which infuriated Baylor.

Ostrom, gray, distinguished, a leader in modernizing Iran, now that the Nazis had been interned; the man was good. And Baylor, with only one moth-eaten servant, old Zohrab, was the first to admit that Allan Ostrom had a right to be complacent about life. But now Baylor's wrath reached a new high. He was thinking, "I'm a flop. I consult magicians while this go-getter does things . . . Marta's right, she can't leave him, not for me."

Ostrom inquired about the rug business, as though he did not already know it was damned beyond any hope, at least until after the war. Shipping was too valuable, insurance rates were way up. Ostrom said, magnificently, "Too bad you're not a technical man, Barry. Ever so many openings for engineers today." He chuckled indulgently, made a grand gesture. "Oh, well—"

Marta cut in, "Allan! After all!"

Baylor was not becoming red. He sat there, smiling. "Times change. Ups and downs, you know."

But for a moment, he wondered if this was a working out of Aisha's magic. Ostrom had never been so tactless, so condescending. Baylor's unnatural calmness came from thinking of what he had told Aisha: "I could arrange it *that way* myself . . ." As though considering someone else's problem, he asked himself if, after all, that lordly fellow shouldn't be killed.

Ostrom went on, as he swirled his gin and bitters, "Artistic temperament, eh? But you're really a good business man, Barry."

Baylor rose, still smiling. "Yes, when there is some business."

"Ha! Philosophical."

Then Baylor flipped the dregs of his drink into Ostrom's face. "Get out of my house, you conceited—!"

Ostrom, sputtering and incredulous, leaped to his feet. Baylor uncorked the punch he had been saving for months, the punch delayed on Marta's account. The impact surprised him. He could hardly believe that he had struck with his fist. The pop sounded as though made by a hickory axe helve. Ostrom staggered back across the terrace. Out on his feet, he still moved, clawing blindly as he dropped.

He caught Marta, jerking her off balance. Her ankle twisted, and she toppled, thumped to the tiles, toes pointing skyward, and skirts bunching about her hips. Ostrom crashed, smacked his head against the coping of the fountain.

Baylor stood there, numb and cold and sick. Something devilish had maddened him; for an instant, he had counted on the impact of the man's head against the stone. Now it was over, and once more, he was the Baylor who absorbed Ostrom's condescending remarks as fair penance for what went on during Ostrom's tours of inspection.

He stumbled forward. Marta untangled herself and sat up. "I don't know what came over me," Baylor muttered, and knelt beside Ostrom. Then, "He's not hurt badly. But he would have been, if he'd not barged into you and spun instead of landing squarely against that coping."

In a few minutes, Ostrom had recovered enough to sit up. His eyes were normal; there was no fracture or severe concussion. He said, dazedly, "I don't know why I said that—I don't blame you much."

He refused assistance, and walked slowly toward his waiting car, while Marta went to get her hat. Baylor went with her. They had only a moment, and he had just time to say, "I'm scared. I never flew off the handle this way."

"He never was so nasty before," she countered, and clung to him, lip to lip, for a moment. Then, drawing away: "Barry—you do look worried. It's over. He's not hurt—"

"I went to see a magician," he told her, and without waiting for an answer, he turned his back.

When he heard the engine start, he returned to the garden, and yelled for Zohrab. "Brandy! And hurry up."

When the old man brought the liquor, he asked, "What else, sir?"

"Get out! Take the night off."

Baylor sat down to think it over. He had resented Ostrom ever since meeting him; but ever since that accidental meeting with Marta, and the kisses which had followed, he had controlled his resentment toward the man, mainly from his feeling of guilt. And this momentary urge toward murder frightened Baylor as much as the illusions of Aisha's cave had upset him. It was as though he had gotten his first real look into himself, and had gazed into horrifying depths whose existence he had never before suspected.

He was not the man to will another's death; urging Marta to leave was bad enough. This reversal of all principle could only be because of the symbols woven in Aisha's web. The accident of Marta's twisting ankle was all that had prevented the full working out of his murder-wish.

Aisha's magic was working, and that it had missed by a hair was no consolation. Such things took time to build up. The symbols of that which he was to do had merely been not quite complete enough for an irrevocable move.

Baylor poured a number of drinks. They did not help. Finally, he went into the house to stretch out on the lounge and clear his head. A strange half-sleep followed: a nightmarish state in which his thoughts fought among themselves. He was not sure whether he was awake or asleep, lying or walking.

Cold metal startled him. He was getting a pistol from his dresser, a weapon that had accumulated dust for months. Fully aroused, he dropped the gun and for moments stared at it.

There was only one thing to do. Luckily, Zohrab was out. For a sickening moment, Baylor knew why he had given the old man a night off; the answer was unpleasant.

He went into the garden and got a shovel. Then he pried a flagstone loose and began digging. He could finish his task before Zohrab returned. There was no place, except in the tiled area, where he could dig without later arousing the old man's curiosity. If Zohrab saw freshly turned earth, he would suspect a treasure cache made during his absence and he would surely dig, particularly after this unusual night off.

Seepage from the garden and fountain made the task easier. He did not need a pick. In a few minutes, the hole was better than knee deep.

Then a car drew up. Someone was tapping at the porter's lodge. There were few Europeans in Shiraz, and none of them would call at this hour. He resolved to ignore the summons, but curiosity whipped him as he stood there. At last a woman called, "Zohrab! Do wake up!"

He dropped his shovel and hurried to the gate.

Marta was waiting.

"Barry, let me in!"

In the moonlight he could see the tension of her face, the feverish brightness of her eyes, the tightness of the hands which clutched the grillwork. Marta wore only a gown under her robe. Always before now, she had arrived fully dressed; the negligee which she put on for lounging in the garden was what she had brought the first time she came to his house alone.

"Zohrab's out." Then, as he turned the key, "What's wrong?"

She flung herself into his arms. "Oh, Barry! I'm half mad!"

"How is Allan?" He pried himself loose from her clinging embrace, held her away from him. "Is he—?"

"Sleeping. It's not *that,* thank God! He's not badly hurt, just muttering. He took a sedative. It's me—"

She buried her face against his shoulder. "What's wrong?"

"Oh, I don't know. Nightmares, horrible things. Death all around. I had to see you."

As Barry Baylor went with her across the garden, he knew what had disturbed Marta. He said, "No use hiding it from me. You'd hardly gotten to sleep when you began to plan for your . . . freedom."

She stared, eyed him. "It was just a nightmare."

"I consulted a magician."

Then he told her all about his ride to Aisha's cave. Marta cut in, "I understand. Something terrible is driving us. I'd better leave. Before—before—"

She stopped when she saw the spade and the gaping black hole which looked up at the moon; her color receded. She did not need to speak the question in her eyes. Baylor said, "That pistol. I'm burying it deep, so deep I can't get at it quickly."

His purpose was so fixed that in spite of her having said that she had better leave, he resumed his work. The weirdness of the night pushed out all thought of kisses beside the fountain. He scarcely noticed the lovely legs exposed when the breeze whipped Marta's gown. He did not speak until the shovel struck something metallic.

It was the lid of a pot. He exclaimed and lifted it. At the gasp which followed, Marta sank to her knees and peered into the hole. "My God—Barry—it's gold!"

He had a handful of dull yellow coins: ancient mohurs, darics, pieces struck by forgotten Sassanian kings, and buried by a former owner of the villa. After wrenching at the pot, Baylor had to dig some more. At last he raised it to the surface.

The hoard weighed well over a hundred pounds.

"We can leave," he said, and laughed until the sound in his own ears restrained him. "We can go home!"

"Oh, Barry!" Marta cried, hysterically. "We're rich—the magic has worked— it's fantastic—"

They lugged the pot into the house. It took Baylor little time to refill the hole and tamp the flagstone back into place. With a broom he scattered the excess earth across the flower beds.

As they went back into the house, he caught her in his arms. "It's worked—it's a sign—all this craziness to make me dig, to make you come over and be with me when I found it!"

He hoped, during one chilly moment, that Allan Ostrom had suffered no more than a superficial concussion; that he had taken nothing but a sedative. The uncanny sequence of events still troubled him. But that qualm faded before Marta's kisses, and with her closely pressed against him, his forebodings faded.

At last she stirred drowsily in his arms, and sighed. "I must go back. I shouldn't have left him tonight. I'll think of a way of telling him in the morning, or the next day, when his head is clear."

3. *"Shoot and Be Damned!"*

THE weaver in the cave had many webs under her finger tips. Baylor scarcely expected Aisha to concentrate on the pattern which was to reshape three foreign lives. But the pot of Sassanian gold was just the start.

The government took over the truck line which employed Ostrom. High officials gave all the fancy jobs to their relatives, or to old employees who had enough cash salted down to enable them to dig up "presents." Now that the business was running at a profit, the men who had developed it had to pay a bribe to retain their jobs.

Their ability to pay was assumed: no one could imagine that Ostrom and his fellows had not embezzled or grafted themselves rich. The officials, according to their lights, were merely levying a roundabout income tax.

While all this was an old story to Baylor, it came as a shock to Ostrom, who, having lived up to his income, could not pay off.

"He's worried," Marta said, when she told Baylor the news. "Dead drunk—he's never done that before—Barry, I can't leave him now!"

"Oh, hell!" Baylor jerked himself clear of her, and leaped to his feet. "Can't leave him when he's on top of the heap, can't leave him when he's gotten a kick in the chin. Go back home where you belong!"

Marta snapped up, brushed her skirt into place. Then the angry flush faded from her cheeks. "It was his pride, Barry. That's why I couldn't leave him before—because he'd lose face. And now I've got to stick, till he gets a fresh start, somewhere, somehow."

"And he'll stay here, trying to beat the system, trying to prove he's good!"

She nodded. "So I can't ditch him, can I?"

Baylor shrugged, helplessly. "I guess not."

Marta came closer. "I'm scared, too. You've started something terrible. That witchcraft is real—it's working."

"Working, yes," he exclaimed, fiercely, and drew her to him. "Against me, against us!"

"Barry," she gasped. "Let me go. He might miss me."

But Baylor would not release her. The pressure of her shapely body inflamed him, made him reckless, intoxicated him so that the sinister forces he had set in motion no longer oppressed and terrified him. The only reality was Marta, and he had to have her, all the time, entirely for himself.

"Barry—you mustn't—he might—"

But his kisses stifled her protests. With an inarticulate cry she yielded to his insistent embrace. He snapped off the light, and like two drunken persons they fumbled their way back to the lounge . . .

This might force the issue. Let Ostrom find out. Then Marta would no longer have any choice. That would be the logical goal of all this witchcraft.

"We're crazy," she sighed, "but I don't care . . . and I love it . . ."

Later, she sat up, and smoothed her rumpled dress. "It's so simple, darling," Marta said. "I won't see you any more."

"What?"

She laughed softly. "Wait! I said it was so simple. Aisha has twisted our fate into knots to bring us together. I don't know what bargain you made, but something is keeping her to her bargain. Now, if I refuse to see you, there is only one way she can carry on—give Allan a break, so I can leave without quitting him when he's down."

"Club fate into line?"

He spoke the words slowly; their meaning was expanding in his fancy. Actually, he had already done just that when he had ignored Aisha's warning; his will and his persistence, it seemed, had compelled her to weave a new pattern for three destinies. And Marta's opposition to one detail would compel Aisha to vary the pattern.

He remembered the hundreds of rugs he had bought in his years in Persia; he remembered the many whose design had changed its motif during the many months of weaving. Weavers did diverge from their original plans; certainly Aisha could.

Baylor rode across the moon-drenched plain and then into the mountains which towered high above the plateau. Snowcaps gleamed; the wind whined and wailed, penetrating his sheepskin jacket. But the thaw had started, and for all the chill, great masses of snow tore loose from the upper heights, thundered down the steep slopes with an express train rumble.

Aisha was not alone in the cavern. A slim and shapely girl sat cross-legged on a mat beside the hearth. She made a pretense of raising her veil, but the gesture was slow, and she gave Baylor time to see her striking beauty. And when the transparent gauze did dim the smooth contours of a face the color of old ivory, her dark eyes still peered over the edge, incredible and fascinating eyes whose depths amazed Baylor.

One tiny foot peeped from the folds of her embroidered tunic. The garment snuggled about her bosom, outlining its roundness; the collar was high, concealing her throat, but the entire effect was to make a tantalizing display which challenged the eye.

The exquisite stranger fascinated Baylor. The faint slant of her eyes suggested a Turki, but her cheek bones were not quite prominent enough. She was a lovely riddle; and he wondered what complaint against destiny brought her to this eerie spot.

"Wait, I will call her," the girl said, and went back into the darkness of the cave.

Presently, Aisha came out, alone, and greeted him; Aisha, uglier and greasier than ever, was giving her talons a rest from their task. She gave him no time to explain his mission. She gestured toward the looms. "O Man, with all these fates to weave, I must hear your impatience? Go back! Or must I tell you what to do with the golden hoard you found?" She rose, claws raised, and cursed him.

Baylor retreated before the repulsive hag. That she knew of the gold dispelled any lingering doubt as to her powers. He dared not risk her wrath, lest she weave some devilish symbol into the web of his fate.

As he rode back toward the plain, he realized that his problem was simple enough. A well placed bribe, no more than the top layer of that buried treasure, would put Ostrom back in command. Baylor wondered why he had not thought of that before. That would settle Marta's last scruple.

~ ~ ~ ~ ~

FOR the next few days, he called on Persian dignitaries. Bribery was a matter of finesse rather than blunt proposi- tions. There were ceremonial calls, and return calls; intermi- nable tea drinking, and dinners which lasted until dawn. But long before Baylor was anywhere near the bottom of his pot of gold, Ostrom was reinstated, and with a thousand polite- nesses.

There had been an error. A reconsideration. The company could not do without his distinguished services. So he went out again, supervising the route and its many stations.

Meanwhile, Marta was holding to her resolution. Night af- ter night, Baylor waited, and vainly. She was forcing Aisha's hand, forcing the weaver of destiny.

And Aisha's magic, he finally began to believe, must have failed. Where for a while events had dizzied him, now noth- ing was happening. Then it occurred to him that far from be- ing inactive, Aisha was hitting back at Marta and her way of forcing a change in the design.

That her absence was deliberate made Baylor's loneliness and his desire for her overpowering. Finally he decided to upset the agreement which he and Marta had made at the very start: that he would never enter the house during Os- trom's absence.

Baylor knew every angle and corner of Ostrom's villa. It was simple enough for him to find crumbling masonry which gave him a toehold; and in a moment, he had scaled the wall.

Then he picked his way across the garden, and into the shadows of the plane trees which shaded the house.

There was a light in Marta's window. He climbed into the nearby tree and worked his way out on a limb. In spite of the hour, he was taking no chances on meeting a restless servant.

Since Marta was awake, her maid might be on duty. Then, as he came nearer to the stuccoed wall, Baylor saw that she was alone, stretched out on a couch. Beside her was a tray full of cigarette butts, most of them half smoked. She stirred restlessly as he crouched among the leaves, watching the play of light that brought glints of white skin through the sheer chiffon of her gown. High breasted, slim and lovely, and little more than a yard away: the long, luscious sweep of her legs, the rise and fall of her bosom behind the lace panel of the neck yoke, all this tempted him, egged him on; but most of all, there was the somberness of her eyes, the strain which puckered her brow, that told him how difficult it was to keep to her resolution.

The branch dipped a little. Twigs brushed the sash. Marta started, sat up. He said, in a low voice, "I had to see you."

She hurried to the window. "Oh, Barry! You mustn't! Go back home. Suppose he returned?"

"Come down into the garden."

She took her head. "I'm afraid."

"Then I'm coming in."

"Oh, no! Don't—"

The branch dipped under Baylor's weight. He leaned forward to reach the sill. "Watch out!" Marta cried in dismay.

"It'll hold. Nothing to it."

By all reason, Baylor was right. Yet there was a crack, a lurch; the limb yielded suddenly. He just missed his hold, and crashed from branch to branch. He thumped to the ground; the impact stunned him. He could not catch his breath, nor could he move, but he was fully conscious, and hoping that Marta's cry of dismay would not arouse any of the servants.

In a moment, she was in the garden and beside Baylor and the branch which had followed him to the ground. "Barry, darling, are you hurt?"

"I'll be—all right—in a minute," he said through clenched teeth, and tried to sit up.

She slipped an arm about him. A sharp twinge of pain cut into his effort. He groaned, and for a moment, his head was pillowed against her bosom. But before he could make a further effort, a flashlight blazed. Reaching through Marta's thin gown, it picked out her bare legs and shoulders, gleamed from her streaming hair.

Allan Ostrom had returned. He cursed, whipped a pistol into line. "Lucky I came back tonight, you son of a bitch!"

Baylor knew that Ostrom would fire; the broken branch told what had been going on, and in Iran, no one would question the right to cut down an intruder. Aisha's magic had tricked Baylor.

"Shoot and be damned to you!"

4. Daughter of a Witch

BAYLOR'S body was paralyzed, and what followed numbed his wits. Marta flung herself in front of him, more to distract Ostrom than from any chance of shielding her lover. But that was not what checked Ostrom's fire.

A gray mist, coming from nowhere, swirled about him. The haze thickened, blurring the outlines of his face and form. There were bands of mist, ribbons of mist, gray serpent forms which licked and lapped and twined, layer after layer; the tenuous bonds multiplied until Ostrom seemed to sag and crumple under their force. They could not possibly have weight, Baylor told himself, yet such was their effect on the man with the gun.

The hate-twisted face was blurred, it became more and more remote. Fear and utter amazement now shaped Ostrom's features. He let the gun drop and clawed at his throat, straining as he did so. His mouth worked but there was no sound.

Then the haze thinned, and once more the two faced each other. Baylor's sense of time was entirely warped. There was no expression for the duration of this weird thing; he could be sure of nothing other than that Aisha's uncanny power had reached from the cavern of destiny.

With a painful effort, Baylor sat up. Ostrom said, in the voice of a person still numb from shock, "I'm glad I didn't fire. That's not the way. Come in, I have to talk to you. Both of you."

Baylor rose and limped into the house. With each step he was regaining a bit more control; he had not suffered more than a nasty impact.

Marta picked up the pistol. She seemed quite unaware that what she wore was scarcely a token garment.

"You were spying," she accused. "Well, now you know. I don't have to tell you."

"Hardly spying." Ostrom turned to Baylor. "I lost my head. You practically bought her, or tried to. That is quite intolerable."

Deliberate, precise, poised Ostrom was himself again.

"Bought her?" Baylor echoed. He nearly added, "That wasn't necessary!"

"Bribing those officials to reinstate me. Everyone knows that. Even I finally heard, on the road. And soon there will be guesses as to why. That is infinitely worse than if you had taken her outright."

Baylor nodded. Ostrom was right. There was no use trying to tell this logical man how it had all started. Baylor could only say, "She couldn't leave you after you'd been double-crossed by the official crowd. And she wouldn't see me. So I fairly broke in."

"I was assured, along the road, that you would be doing something of the sort, so I contrived to return unexpectedly. Not spying, but acting on almost certain knowledge. The knowledge of everyone but myself. And there is only one way of settling this."

"How?"

"We will go into the mountains by separate routes. We will meet, and only one of us will return. My disappearance, or yours, will settle things nicely for the survivor."

Marta cried, "You sound like a movie thriller! Can't you be grown up? You're planning murder—for him or for yourself—because you feel you've lost face, because you think he tried to buy me. And then you turn around and propose making me the prize of a duel!"

Ostrom said, coldly and deliberately, "You really do not enter into this. The point is that I've been put into a false position."

Marta turned on Baylor: "You don't have to accept this insane challenge! Don't you dare accept—I'll never look at you again if—if—good God, don't you see what he's trying to do? If you did win, you'd still lose! He's my husband, and if you killed him—Barry, don't you see how impossible, how horrible that'd be?"

Ostrom brightened, perceptibly enjoying his triumph; it was clear that he was pleased by Marta's having caught the full meaning of his challenge. Win or lose, he would have his vengeance.

Baylor said, after a long silence, "I'm in the wrong. Pointing a gun at you would be difficult, even in self defense."

"I'd thought of that," Ostrom admitted.

"Something cheated you out of your chance a few minutes ago. But you're entitled to it." He ignored Marta's cry, and shook her hand from his arm. "So, to keep it from being formal and deliberate, you come from the north on the Takht-i-Khosru trail, and I'll head upgrade to meet you, around noon, when the light won't blind either of us. We'll fire on sight."

"Barry! Regardless of what happens—"

Baylor sighed. "He's entitled to his chance."

He turned his back on the two, and left.

Within the hour, he was riding up the Takht-i-Khosru trail, toward Aisha's cave. While he had a trick for evading the issue which Ostrom in pride and stubbornness was trying to force, Baylor was afraid that Aisha's devilish magic would upset the plan.

The entire chain of circumstance was now quite beyond any stretching of coincidence. The pattern of the web was forcing him and Ostrom and Marta, warping the judgment of each. Thus Baylor feared to decline the challenge, feared to risk persuading Marta to pack up and leave Iran, and not because of the stigma of cowardice, for that would not matter once he was out of the country. His apprehension was deeper. He felt now that any attempt to evade the weaver's magic would end fatally. Each time he thought of flight, he pictured an accident to Marta.

When he reached the cave, he found the lovely Turki girl sitting by the fire. She lowered her veil a little, and smiled, and said, "Mother is not here."

"Mother?" he echoed, perplexedly.

"Yes. I am Shireen, the daughter of Aisha. I have been in Mosul, studying magic. When she goes to the mercy of Allah, I will weave in her place. The fallen angels, Harut and Marut, taught her, many years ago, and now they have taught me."

Shireen was exquisite. However much the close fitting and high necked tunic concealed her body, its gleaming surface betrayed the splendid curves beneath. An invitation lurked at the corners of her mouth, and it was reflected in the depths of her great dark eyes when she said, "Be pleased to wait, and welcome, though only Allah knows when she returns."

She made room for him on the hearth rug. Her perfume was heady, and when her satin sleeve brushed his arm, the thrill made Baylor tingle from head to foot. Though her mother was incredibly ugly, Shireen was young, and lovely as Lilith; the speculative gleam in her eyes gave Baylor hope.

But Shireen had read his thought.

"You came to change the pattern of your web. You forget that I will remind her, and Allah alone knows what punishment my mother would think of!"

"But you're her daughter. After all—"

Shireen shrugged. "You want the red-haired Ferinshi woman, but you do not wish to pay the price of destiny. A man must die, and you shrink from that. Since you love her so little, you might love me instead. And then there would be no blood guilt, and all would be well."

"But I'd lose her—" He made a helpless gesture. "There would be no point to it all, the web had best never been started!"

"You do not care for me, yet you ask me to break the law?"

"Two women—that is not our custom," he protested.

Shireen sighed. *"Ya khudayal* Against such love, there is no answer. But the study of magic is long and lonesome . . ."

Baylor could not be sure who made the first advance. All he knew was that he had Shireen in his arms, and that her eager lips pressed against his mouth, that her breast flattened against him.

The embers dimmed, and weird mists swirled from the further depths, blotting out all the many looms, shutting out all but the ruddy glow of the hearth. Finally Shireen stirred languidly in his embrace and smoothed out her rumpled tunic.

"Now I will weave so that you will have your heart's desire, and without blood guilt on your hands, and more than that is not permitted."

She took his hand, and he followed her into the mist veils through which he could barely distinguish the web of his fate: and for a long time, he watched her as she unraveled certain knots, and rewove with other colors and in other lines. And all through the intricate Shirazi pattern, he could pick the shapes which symbolized himself, and Marta, and Ostrom: though these things were beyond his reading, he knew that all would be well.

It was nearly dawn when he left the cave. Shireen's eyes were somber, and she sighed, then said, "We will meet once more, and then I put the seal to your fate."

Baylor mounted and rode up the trail of destiny. The plan which he had shaped before he met Shireen could not fail, now that he had persuaded her to offset her mother's devilish irony.

5. All Is Illusion

IT WAS nearly noon when he reached the region where he was to meet Ostrom. Water from melting snow caps trickled across the trail and down the steep banks into the ravine below. Here and there, boulders which had fallen from the upper slopes dotted the way. Baylor dismounted, drew his pistol, and marched on.

He was breathless, though more from excitement than from the altitude. Though the sun would not shine into the eyes of either combatant, the glare from snow patches would make for difficult shooting, and this was what he needed.

Presently, as he approached a brow beyond which there was a long, level stretch which snaked along the brink of a steep drop, he heard the laboring of an engine. Someone was driving from the north, coming up the grade which led to the further end of the level zone.

From a distance, he recognized the car. Ostrom was at the wheel. Baylor halted, waved. The car pulled up, well beyond accurate pistol range, and Ostrom advanced on foot. He shouted something which the wind distorted, so that Baylor could not understand the words, but the glint of metal and the accompanying gesture made it clear that Ostrom had recognized him and was ready.

Baylor advanced perhaps twenty paces. Then he halted, leveled his weapon. It was very simple, after all. Trick Ostrom into shooting prematurely, with not one chance in a thousand of scoring; then refuse to return his fire. Having had his chance, he would be satisfied. His own wits and the hours spent in persuading Shireen would avert what Aisha had devised.

When Ostrom halted, Baylor's life hung on another man's trigger finger. The distance was appallingly short. For an instant, every instinct urged him to defend himself. He was dizzy. The rocky trail seemed to billow beneath his feet. There was a rumbling in his ears.

Ostrom's arm jerked. The pistol bounced up. A slug whacked past, a few inches wide of Baylor's head, and zinged from the rocky wall. Ostrom sagged. He yelled, hoarsely, "Fire! Get it over. Come closer if you're afraid you'll miss!"

True to his word, he was shooting only once.

Then it occurred to Baylor that his gesture would have to be decisive, and beyond misunderstanding. He raised his pistol and fired almost straight up. Then he started forward, pocketing his weapon. Ostrom's crazy sense of honor should now be satisfied.

Ostrom's expression changed. He started, gestured, whirled about to dash for his car. The roaring in Baylor's ears became louder. In an instant, he realized that the rumbling was real, and not illusion. Rock fragments peppered the trail. The pistol concussion, perhaps the impact of the bullet, far up on the snow-laden ledge, had started an avalanche. And Ostrom, steady enough when facing a gun, was now gripped by panic. He was running toward the spot where the main force of the snow slide would strike, instead of in the opposite direction.

Ostrom stumbled. That gave Baylor a shred of hope. He raced toward the man, shouting at the top of his voice; he had to check him. Marta would never believe that an avalanche, and not a bullet, had settled the issue.

Too late, Ostrom understood. He regained his feet, turned. He was within arm's reach of Baylor when the fringe of the slide enveloped them. Its further limit engulfed the car.

The seconds which followed were a choking darkness which roared and drummed and thundered; a flailing, a pounding, a crazy whirling and spinning from which nothing could emerge whole and alive. Yet Baylor did not quite lose touch of Ostrom. Once a tree checked their descent. And then, as the slope tapered off, a larger tree deflected the rush of snow and earth and rock.

Baylor managed to crawl clear. Though with difficulty, he could still move; but Ostrom was finished. Shireen, though keeping her word, had played a trick worthy of her mother. Baylor was exonerated. Since he could not extricate Ostrom without help, there would be witnesses to clear him in Marta's eyes.

Painfully, he worked his way up the steep slope and toward the car, which had not been swept over the side. But when he reached the top, he saw that he would have to ride his horse. The wheels were hopelessly fouled with debris.

And he learned then what he had not theretofore suspected—Marta had accompanied Ostrom. Rock fragments weighted the robe which almost concealed her in the back seat. She cried out at his touch, then looked up, eyes charged with pain. Her lips were bluish, her face was paper white.

"You'll have to get help," she gasped. "You can't move me by yourself. I couldn't stand it."

He knelt on the littered running board, wiped her forehead, wiped the red froth which trailed from the corner of her mouth. "Marta, my God! Why—how did you—?"

"I was afraid—he'd ambush you—I hid—under the robe—I saw the slide—but I thought—oh, I guess I was too shocked by what had gone before—I didn't start to move till—too—late."

He knew now that he could not, single handed, help her in any way. Neither was there time to be wasted in bringing a doctor all the way from Shiraz. The thing to do was get a litter and have porters carry her. He said, "I have to leave you here. There's something wrong with your back. I'll get porters. We'll tie you to a litter. Anything else and you'd hurt yourself even more."

"I know, Barry. I'm not afraid. I'm glad I came. I saw what you did—I know why, too—it's part of the game, darling—we're free, now—everything's worked out, and this is just part of what we have to pay—but I'm not afraid, the pattern's finished—"

He made her as comfortable as he could, arranged the robe as a shelter from wind and sun, then fought his way across the stretch of debris.

Perhaps pack animals could drag the car clear, once men with shovels and levers pried away the rocks and mud. But everything was impossible. The quickest relief he could get would take far too long. Staying with Marta was useless; so was leaving her. He spurred his horse, charged crazily down the slope up which he had so slowly crawled.

It all hung on the witch pattern. Whatever was woven into the web of wizardry was what would happen. Aisha and her daughter were the nearest help. Were it not for that, he would surely stop and empty his pistol into them. And then his agony of rage, lacking any nearer object, turned back against himself. The impact numbed him. He had done all this himself. This was the result of his effort to unbind himself and two others from their destinies.

And since he now hated himself as much as he did the weird woman and her daughter, he became calm, riding with skill and ferocity he had never imagined possible. Somehow, he kept from throwing his horse; or perhaps there was the web of wizardry to keep him on the road.

"They'll help—they have to help—"

Whether with magic or with mundane device, he did not know. This time he would force them to change the pattern. Twice he had failed in his purpose, twice he had compromised, but now he would succeed.

He flung himself from the winded horse and ran the last dozen yards. Shireen, hearing the hoof beats, came to the entrance of the cave. He thrust her aside, and demanded, "Where's Aisha?"

"She returns when she will."

"Then change the pattern! Now! Don't ask me what you've done—you know, you know too well—you said that I'd be back, and you knew why you said it."

Shireen retreated before his fury. He advanced a pace, but did not quite manage to seize her arm. "Change it! Weave life and help for her! Now!"

Shireen made a helpless gesture. "I had nothing to do with it. I was lonely, and you pleased me, and so I tied knots to please you."

This might well be the truth, but Baylor was beyond reason or compromise. He drew his pistol. "Get to work."

Shireen made a fluent move which tricked his eye. The satin tunic spread back over her shoulder, lingered at her breast, slowly sank to her hips, and then cascaded in a shimmering heap about her ankles. "Do you still threaten me, strong man? Fire, I am waiting."

A moment passed. His jaw ached from the grimness of his tension. He dared not waver. He forced his hatred to grow until it blotted out all that sleek beauty before him. Until he was filled with the will to destroy her, she would mock him; more than a threat was needed.

And the girl still smiled sadly and shook her lovely head. "You were warned, O Man! Warned according to the law. She will live, but who knows how long you will love what is left of her? This is not my doing, this is not my mother's doing, this is the law. No man may outstep his destiny without paying a forfeit. You asked that there be no blood guilt on your head, and there is none. And if your pistol can change the law, do with me as you please."

His fierce glance wavered. For the first time, he dared to look past Shireen. He was the slave of the web, rather than of her will. Cutting her down—

He shouted his triumph as he knocked her asprawl in his haste to get at the completed web which shimmered on the little loom. He slashed the warp threads which held it to the beam, and bounded toward the hearth.

Shireen screamed and scrambled from the rocky floor.

"Don't! Don't do that!"

She clawed him, clung to him. He stumbled and they rolled against the wall. There was no understanding what Shireen gasped. He kicked himself clear of her, seized the web and flung it into the glowing embers.

"There—damn you!" he croaked. "That'll settle it!"

He expected a stench of burning wool, the blackening, the oily exudation from the nap; but this blazed with a curious violet flame, and the scent was pungent, bittersweet, like a strange incense. The pattern stood out in fiery relief, then subsided.

Shireen regained her feet. "Fool," she screamed, and lurched toward him, but he knocked her aside, and she lay there, unable to rise.

Then she laughed, and her face and her bare body became horrible. This was not Shireen, this was Aisha, with snaggled teeth and a shapeless body that seemed patched together of well-worn saddle leather.

"Now you know!" she mocked. "And soon you will know all! I am Shireen, Shireen is me, we are all illusion. And for illusion you have flung yourself into the fire!"

Then Baylor felt the burning of the web. Intolerable pain ate into him. The redness and the fierce glow ended with the crumbling of the ashen skeleton of the web, and it was as though he fell through a chilly blackness. Anything was welcome, as long as it got him out of that accursed cave.

There was a period of non-sensation, and then, strangely, he was approaching the landslide. Marta ran from the car to meet him. This was not quite believable. Ostrom, unruffled and unharmed, came with her.

He hailed Baylor; and Marta took his arm. Her touch was friendly, like a sister's, rather than possessive.

Ostrom said, "We've been damn' fools, we three."

Baylor sighed. "I was talking to a native girl. When she said everything was illusion, I thought she was crazy, but it makes sense, somehow."

They set out walking. None of them had any thought for the car, or for the distance to Shiraz. Baylor did not quite understand until they met a caravan. The mule drivers apparently did not see the trio, and utterly ignored their presence on the narrow trail, but one shivered, and made a curious sign with his hand. He recited, *"I betake me to Allah for refuge from Satan . . . and from the evils of the night; and from the spells of women who blow on knots; and from the envy of the envier when he envieth . . ."*

SELENE SLAYS
BY NIGHT

By E. Hoffmann Price

SHE HAD GORGEOUS LEGS, and her skirt was high up over her knees. But it was her eyes that nailed me; they kept me from noticing garter clasps or what-have-you, of which last she had lots.

Her smile said, "It's awfully lonesome out here, every afternoon, I wish you wouldn't hurry away . . ."

Anyone can *say* that, but this gal could *look* it.

Her eyes were hazel, with greenish glints in them. I don't know why I thought of cats then, but I did. Women with cat-eyes aren't awfully scarce. I mean the kind with drooping lids, longish and with a slant. This dame out in the hills gave me that notion from everything about her.

Every move she made was cattish, particularly when she looked down and smiled a little, and let her skirt drop. She purred almost when she said, "I'll take a dozen pair, Mister—?"

"Uh—Clay," I stuttered, like I'd just met myself.

Legs weren't a treat to me, not even when they're part of a Grade A gal who looks lonesome. They were long and slim and sleek, but punching doorbells to sell Tru-Silk Hosiery is not conducive to sustained enthusiasm. Particularly not since the company sent out that gadget so the customer can figure out the exact length and thigh measurement for a perfect fit.

That just made more work; but it quit being tiresome when this dame moved like a cat trying to rub up against someone it liked, and said, "Oh, I never was any good at figures, you could do it better, couldn't you?" Well, she wanted a dozen pair, and her name was Selene Felice Brown. A queer combination, but the first two fit like the hose she was wearing at the time. I hadn't the foggiest idea why they fit. They just sounded like she looked. I wondered if I'd spelled them right. Before I could check it back, she swayed closer, with a move that made me think of a friendly cat; so much so that I didn't know whether she was or wasn't getting familiar.

I hoped she was. This business is not what people think it is. It's as bad as peddling brushes, and let me tell you, the ice business has been way to hell-and-gone overrated. I've tried them all.

She could have reached to sign the order blank, but she leaned over. A light touch, but a lot of it. She was flexible, silky. Somehow, I got a picture of everything from knee to shoulder, and I was wondering how a fellow would keep his paws off of something like that.

Selene didn't sign the blank after all. She looked up through her lashes and said, "That's not necessary, is it?"

There was a twitch to her lips. They were red and her teeth were small and white and pointish. She smelled like a foreign garden; the odd perfume came from her hair, and oozed out of the vee of her lacy sweater. That sweater, I meant to remark, was filled with more than just perfume. Not too much, not too little, but just—

Just right. I had an armful of her. For a second I was wondering what I'd do if she squawked and called headquarters and said I'd gotten fresh. A fellow ought to have a little finesse. The way I grabbed was plain dumb. I was about scared into letting go and stuttering something about slips not counting, when she slunk up closer, so much like a pleased cat that I pretty nearly jumped a foot.

"You mustn't," she purred; but she wiggled a little closer, begging to be kissed.

I was getting dizzy. A fellow can soak up just so many sensations per second and more than that leaves him dopey. Selene slipped out of my arms just in time.

She laughed when I stood there, looking at my empty hands. "I'm terrible, teasing you. I'm a cat, I'm afraid." She laid a red-nailed little hand on my arm. "I'm sorry. We can't have everything, can we? But cats want everything, everything they see, don't they?"

"Say—listen here!" Selene was a mind reader, playing up the thought I'd had ever since she gave me that first eye-smile. "You got cats on the brain?"

She nodded. Lights danced in orange-brown hair. It was sleek against her head like a copper helmet. It was as smooth as her white skin. "I like them." She caught my hand, and then she rippled into a chair, with me sitting on the arm. "I think you do, too."

I watched her stretch those legs out and park her feet on the needlepoint footstool. She had a dainty way of making the move. "Yeah, I do. Honest."

"I knew that." She yawned; no, it was really a stretch, and it lifted my blood pressure, seeing that it was sleepy vitality. Lots of it, in reserve; not a bit like these peppy persons that haven't really anything but who work twenty-four hours a day to pretend they have. "Mind opening that door?"

She pointed. When I got away from her, I began to notice that peculiar smell. A tiny whisper of an odor, all over the house. It wasn't the big Boukhara rug. They have a goaty tang, and it takes a hot climate to bring it out. Then I got it: *cat.* Toned down, but no mistaking it.

I opened the door. There were a dozen or more of them. Long-haired Persians, short-haired alley cats; blue, striped, black, orange, pure white. Some of the toughest customers you'd ever find, even along the water front. Their ears were in ribbons. The fur was raked off their cheeks. Their purring sounded like a far-off airplane. It wasn't until they pretended they'd just noticed me that I woke up to the size of the granddaddy of them all.

I bet he weighed twenty pounds or more. He was as big as a mountain bob cat, the kind with fringed ears. His face was hard, with big rolls of muscle at the base of his jaws. He had bull dog shoulders, and the hind end of him was lean. If he'd come toward me with his tail swaying sidewise, I'd slammed the door in a hurry.

He was muttering and mumbling in his throat. Once he meowed, a hoarse, rasping bass. The cat smell in that glassed-in porch was heavy, though the place was spotless. Selene said, "I knew you liked them! Captain is awfully fussy, he hates strangers."

The rest of the horde crowded around me. For a second, I felt squeamish. Ten-fifteen of them together pretty nearly outweighed me. I began thinking, "What if they got mad or hungry and teamed up?"

One is nice and harmless and soft, even if he's a feline mug like Captain. But suppose a lot of them did gang up on a man, hanging on with those fingerlike claws? Ever notice, front and rear, how they have everything a human hand has, except a thumb? A man might conk a few, but by then he'd be nuts from panic and blind with blood. Crazy thought, but I think we all feel that way, from the old days when we wore tails and dodged saber-tooth tigers.

Captain was the only out-size in the crowd; but the standard models were big and tough. Their yellow eyes never blinked. They lined up, with more than just a hint of order, waiting their turn to come up and rub against my leg. Those that waited studied me in the way a cat does: getting an answer, and then keeping it to himself.

Selene came out of her chair. She was smiling like a woman whose brat you've just called a handsome young man who'd undoubtedly be President some day. Then she began speaking to the brutes.

No, not baby-talk, no "muzzer's-itty-bitty-kitty-kittens" stuff. It startled me. Her lips hardly moved. Just enough to show a little more of her teeth than with her mouth closed. The sound came from the hollow of her throat, one of the second or third places to kiss. It was that chirping a cat makes when he's not meowing or squalling or spitting.

Captain answered her. Selene's tone was liquid, silky, rounded; the rag-eared giant sounded like far-off buzz saws hitting knots. If I hadn't actually seen it, if I'd just been lis-

tening from a distance, I'd have said, "She's got an outlandish foreigner working for her." It was almost articulate.

I must have jumped a foot and looked scared and silly. Selene said, "Oh, they *do* like you."

Captain turned away from me, and all his gang turned
with him. They marched back into the sun parlor. I couldn't
help believing she had told him to take them away, and he'd
answered, "Okay, sister."

Now that the other cats had made room for Selene, she
snuggled close to me. "Lots of people hate them, and it's
mutual. I know you and I'll be friends, won't we?"

"Love me, love my cats, huh?" She nodded, smiled. I
went on, "Long as they don't get jealous, I'm not kicking.
Say, did you train them?"

She shook her head. "Did you ever try training one?"

Well, whoever did? It can happen, but not often enough to
count.

We ended up on the chesterfield. It had lots of cushions.
The sun was setting, and the hills threw long shadows across
the patio, and into the low-ceiled room. The taste of Selene's
lipstick filled my mouth. She purred something about it getting late. "Please—you mustn't—do go away, I've been
foolish—"

A door creaked. I sat up with a jerk and let go. Her lids
nearly hid her eyes, and there was a lift to her breast, and she
was shaking all over. She didn't want me to leave. I didn't
either, but that hinge creak—

Well, it might have been the wind, and not her boy friend.
Only, it wasn't either. It was the sun parlor door. The cats
were filing out like soldiers in a column. Captain led the parade. I leaned over again to keep Selene from getting too far
out of that heap of cushions. She didn't try to stop me. She
was slipping, fast.

But the cats swarmed over us. A hundred and fifty pounds
of assorted cats. It was like a living stream swamping us.
They got between us, purring and squirming. She tried to
push them away, but there were too many. I shoved one, and
then changed my mind. Captain had his two big paws on Se-

lene's bare shoulder. He just gave me a personal look and showed his teeth, and let hell blaze from his eyes.

"Sister, you win!" I said, getting sore, because they'd gotten my goat. "I'll send your hosiery by mail."

They always came by mail, direct from factory to the customer; I was just cracking off. Selene got up. The army was swarming around her ankles, purring and rubbing against her calves. Both stockings had new runners. With all those devils, she'd need hosiery by the gross, not by dozen.

"I didn't—I couldn't help—" She was breathless, pushing me toward the door. "Honestly, I didn't, but it's best—he'll be home—soon—But bring them, don't mail them."

I slammed the door. It was too late to make any more calls. If it had been ten A.M., it'd still have been too late. For all Selene said, and I couldn't help believing her, those cats had busted in to keep her in line. She meant she'd not called them in. Remembering the way she'd been hanging on, it'd be silly to say she hadn't started playing for keeps. But her cats read something, way back in her mind, and thought she'd be sorry. Subconscious, I guess is the word. Or were they just jealous, and if *that* was it, what had I run into!

I'd hardly driven around the first curve of the narrow road that snaked through the hillside suburb of San Mateo when a big cream-colored coupé with a sharp-beaked radiator grille came swooping up to meet me. I damn' near ran into the ditch. I killed my engine, and before I got it going, the bus was swinging into the drive of Selene's bungalow. That was plain from the mirror.

On the way to town, I was wondering, "Is she psychic or are the cats, or, was that just the fellow's regular time to come home?"

~ ~ ~ ~ ~

TRYING to figure that out began to get me down. The fact that I was thinking of such a screwy thing instead of dismissing it was what really worried me. Next day, I punched doorbells and blinked like a toad in a hailstorm. I had Selene on the brain. I didn't get inside a single door. I guess I looked punch drunk. The gals eyed me and froze up. Some of them looked like they smelled something.

That worried me. "They smell those cats."

I sent my clothes to the cleaner and put on the other suit. No go. I spent all night trying to figure out why Selene made me think of cats. Worse than that, Selene's legs began winking at me; *me,* and I was so used to this business that legs were just things you stuff into Tru-Silk.

No, I couldn't make any sales even when I did crash a door. I began to eye my reflection in door panes to see if I really looked goofy. I began looking just that way from trying to see if—this is getting complicated, but a state of mind does double up.

After a couple days of it, I decided to see Selene. I had crazy notions, such as the one that she was a cat in human form, and no wonder her oversize cats pushed prowling salesmen around. I had to see what that other guy did when he came to the house. Believe it or not, that's why I went to peep.

I parked my bus at the city limits, and hoofed it into the hills. There were lights here and there along the narrow road, and the windows of cottages winked from dense growths of oak and laurel and buckeye. Selene's place was somewhat beyond the development that had a road lighting system. It was dark, but I could have found my way with my eyes closed. Like a cat, huh?

The day I was there, I hadn't had time to size up the layout of the house. Gravel walks are noisy, so I slipped along the patio wall, and ducked some cactus, and came to a lighted window.

Out there, people naturally are careless about shades. By day, it'd make no difference. At night, it was—man, man!

Selene was at her dressing table, powdering her shoulders. She wasn't wearing much more than some of her powder. The big fluffy puff didn't hide much. I gaped. Not at what you'd think. It was the *way she moved.* Sure, I did see things, but I wasn't looking for them.

Watch a cat dolling itself up, slicking out its fur, and there's Selene; except, she used a puff.

I backed away. First, it was lousy, standing there looking. Second, that slinky cat-motion wasn't helping a bit. I heard a man's voice, a man's feet clumping around. For a while, I thought they were getting ready to go out.

But they weren't.

The fellow was in the living room, pacing up and down. I could tell by his impatience that while he might drop in every evening after work, he did not have a mortgage on her.

A good looking chap. Big, husky, not hard-faced, not pretty, either; his gray suit went well with his black hair and tanned skin. The way he clamped down on his cigar showed he had definite ideas about everything.

Then Selene came out, and the way he grabbed an armful proved the cigar stance hadn't lied. She wore a blue chiffon robe and blue mules; both were silver-shadowed.

There were cats asleep all over the living room. The door of the sun parlor was open. "Darling," Selene wrapped slinky arms around the handsome fellow. "Let's stay home this evening . . ."

Well, they stayed home. It was nice and quiet in the hills, and the crickets sounded loud and the stars were real close. Selene and her boy friend had moved out of my view. That was okay, too. It also seemed okay with the cats.

Selene was getting hell kissed out of her. All I could see was her silver and blue mules, but they told a lot. One fell off. The cats didn't even wake up. One raised his big head, slowly opened his eyes, slowly closed them, and went back to sleep . . .

I checked out, quick!

That proves I wasn't peeping for the usual reason. I'd learned something. Selene's cats didn't mind Mr. Garner. I got the name from his car registry papers. I heard so much "Darling, I've missed you so," that I figured he didn't show up every night, and she wanted to know why not. He was a chump for ever missing a chance.

But what was settled? That the cats ganged me when I was trying to get familiar with Selene; and that they didn't move in on Garner. That proved nothing. Cats do things and only cats know why; and they aren't telling. Here were ten-fifteen of them, all doing the same thing. There was a "so-what" that worried me.

The payoff was that scent from Selene's bedroom. Per-fumed odor that a well kept woman's wardrobe finally gives to a room. That was all there, and just a shade more. Yes— *cat.* I had known it right along; a tailor-made perfume to blend with, not drown out a cat scent.

Sure, that could be explained a dozen ways. Look at what perfumes are made of. Civet, from a kind of skunk. Musk from the glands of an Asiatic ox. Ambergris from a sicken-ing by-product of a sick whale. A perfume is something that narrowly missed being a stench.

Cat scent is rank; the bigger the cat, the ranker. Try hang-ing around a tiger cage. Selene's room had a tang which was cat odor that had crossed the borderline and become sweet-ness.

I mulled that over all that night. She was making me dizzy. At the morning conference, I went to sleep and the sales manager gave me a dirty look, also some dirty remarks when he saw I'd not sold a thing for nearly a week. They meet every morning in the big town, listen to an hour of pep talks, and pep-songs. I used to laugh that off and say, "Nuts, I sell 'em, don't I? Go ahead and sack me for missing these conferences. But now I wasn't selling them.

I was waiting for Selene's order to come from Chicago. I was hanging around in the laurel clumps that grew from the canyon and half way up the hillside. After trying all day to keep from coming out to the house, I finally went in the eve-ning. Then I got cold feet, fearing Garner would show up.

But he didn't. It got late, and still no Garner. Owls began to hoot, and somewhere a wild cat began to howl. First like a woman moaning and then like nothing on earth. The hills behind San Mateo have plenty of wild life, even with San Francisco only twenty miles away.

Selene was alone. She was sitting there, not fidgeting like most impatient people do, or even looking at the clock. She was looking at the door, with that intent way a cat watches a gopher hole. Waiting. She'd cock her head, just a hair's width. A moment or two later, I'd hear an engine, the one she'd already heard. By that time, she'd straighten up, knowing it was not Garner's car.

Why didn't I push the door bell?

Nuh-uh. Not afraid Garner would drop in and she'd land behind the eight ball; just afraid to break in on a hundred and twenty pounds of hostile cat! She had everything but fur and pointed ears. By now, I'd sold myself on the idea that Selene was a cat goddess.

The next day, the hosiery arrived. I'd had it sent to my own address, so I could bring it to her house.

She was glad to see me. She mixed me a drink. We sat there on the chesterfield and I could feel that we were both thinking things. Selene got up, made that curious, throaty chirping, and five or six of her cats went into the sun parlor with the others. This time she made sure the door was latched.

Then she gave a slow little smile and shook her head.

I said, "What the hell?"

Selene looked at me for a moment. I was sure now that some feline scent came from human skin. The breeze had shifted and it came through her bedroom window. Finally she said, "I told you I was a cat. But I wasn't playing with you."

I believed her. "Maybe not."

"You understand cats, don't you?"

"Yes, some."

"They stick to their house, don't they?" She was saying something we both knew. That doesn't hold for town, but it does in open country. When people move and leave a cat to shift for himself, he doesn't follow them. He hangs around, and when someone else takes the house over, he comes back, looks the new owner over. If he likes him, he moves in.

Cats are opposite in every way from dogs. When they're fighting mad, they wag their tails. You can't browbeat them and make them like it. They don't give a damn if they please you or not. People think they're dumb because they won't do tricks. That's wrong. They do what they want, and nothing else. I knew all that, and I knew what Selene was. She had a human shape and mind, but the rest was feline.

Like in every woman, only a lot more so. She was a super-woman, with an extra touch of cat.

"So you stick to your house?"

She nodded. "I belong to it, and you don't."

This was getting close to telling me about Garner, and I wanted to change the subject. She was sitting so close that that was easy, but the kissing didn't get very far. About the time we were both whirling, we heard the beasts in the sun parlor. They were clawing at the glass of the French doors. They were rearing up. Captain showed his teeth. He was working at the latch, and looked like a small tiger.

What if he did work it open? I didn't want any of it. He was just too big to seem real. Everything was crazy. Selene jumped up. She "talked" to them, but Captain snarled. She caught me by both arms. "You'd better go. Don't you see, I'm a cat and I have to stick to my house."

"I'll buy the damn' place! Listen, is it that Garner guy? Where does he come in? Does he own you or the house, or what? Look here—"

But she edged me to the door. She had a silky way of using all her weight, without trying to. I couldn't have gotten rough with her if I'd wanted. I couldn't have gotten a hold of her against her will. Supple, wriggling out of any grasp.

"You idiot!" I flared up. "He's making a sap of you, I saw you waiting the other night, I—"

"Shhh . . . Wait . . . *everything* will be all right . . . This is his house, but it can be yours . . . come back tomorrow. Tomorrow afternoon."

I was over the threshold before I knew it. Selene stood there, smiling through the panes. I took a step and then looked back. She'd turned away, but I could see enough of that smooth face to know that hell must be in her eyes.

Tomorrow! The boss had told me if I didn't snap out of it, I was through. I didn't blame him. But I couldn't explain. Imagine, saying I was off my feed account of wondering how a cat could become a woman? That I was saying her name to myself, over and over, till the words became a part of me? Selene Felice—Selene Felice—

Selene was some kind of myth, a moon goddess. Felice, that's the female for Felix, which means fortunate.

~ ~ ~ ~ ~

THAT night there was a full moon. Selene coming over the hill. Selene looking into my window. A lunatic is a fellow who's moonstruck. That antique idea isn't silly. Ever try sleeping with moonlight in your face? Sometimes you succeed, and sometimes you wish you hadn't. I finally got up and drove down the Peninsula.

To the hills behind San Mateo. To find out what Selene was doing about Garner. She was going to do something; but when, and what? I couldn't wait any longer.

So I parked and walked. A car the age of mine is as conspicuous as a bombing squadron in that hill quiet. The moon was high. The early red had looked like a prediction of war. Now she was high and white and the shadows were black, with all the slopes dancing in glimmer. I felt more a fool, the closer I got to Selene's bungalow. Each time I reached the last curve, I backtracked.

Something told me to check out while the checking was good. Who could put up with a dame whose cats began to lift the roof when someone took an armful or two? Garner—he got away with it—and that kept me wondering why. Wondering how much longer the cats would keep on sleeping. The way those beasts guarded Selene got under my skin as bad as the thought of Garner pawing her.

No job, no Selene. A grain of sense. I was back at the wheel of my car when I saw Garner's long coupé coming toward me. A twelve cylinder job with red enameled centers on the hub caps. They make not many limousines of that kind, and the coupés are scarcer yet.

There were two people in that bus. I had snapped on my headlights, so I saw plainly enough that the girl was not Selene.

The tail lights winked around a curve just opposite to the direction to Selene's house. There is a network of dead end drives and private roads, but only two main lines went from the wide spot where I was parked.

Sunrise services at Christmas and Easter are a hobby out on the Pacific Coast; a chamber of commerce gag to make blizzard-bound middle westerners wish they were dead. Either Garner's new girl lived along the road, or she was heading for the wooded spot near the bowl. There weren't any religious doings scheduled for months to come, but that didn't mean the place went to waste.

It was not far. I followed without even a parking light. My hunch was right. He swung off toward the bowl. I was grinning all over. I'd give Selene something to think of. I'd pick her up, and we'd use my flashlight, over the edge of the amphitheater. A heel's trick, but I wanted Selene cured of her crazy idea of belonging to Garner's house.

They wouldn't hear my gears when I made a U-turn, for I had not tailed them closely. It was tricky work, on that narrow winding road, so I lost time. I was shaking and sweating, though I might know that Garner would spend more than five or ten minutes with his new dame, out under that moon.

Then I saw the green eyes in the gloom. At first I thought it was one of the big wild cats that still live just behind the settlement; a whopper. Next came a long row of green eyes. A column of cats marched along without a sound. When they reached a place where the moon blazed down on the road, I saw the even lashing of their tails.

The craziest thing you can imagine: all kinds of cats, holding their heads high, as if they were sniffing the air before a fight. When they finally passed me, I was shaking my head. I

had not driven over a quarter of a mile when another gang of
them came down a trail that cut into the narrow road.

"Convention, huh?"

The past week had been screwy enough for anything as
sensible as a feline congress. The hills were full of them.
Some had long gone native. Anyone knows how two-three
house cats sometimes disappear the same day and stay away
for a week and come back around the same time. And not
during mating season, necessarily. They know where and
why they go, but they don't tell.

The lights were on at Selene's house. The door was ajar. I
knocked. No answer. I stepped in. I did not hear a sound.
The sun parlor was empty. Captain and his gang had checked
out. Selene's car was in the garage.

Maybe she'd strolled to see some neighbor. A lonesome
person would, with so much moon flooding the canyons and
the open hillsides. Selene goes for a stroll, doesn't latch the
door. Cats head for a convention.

But I made sure. She was not in her bedroom. On the floor
was a pair of moccasins, some Tru-Silks, a rumple of underthings, and a brassiere. A skirt and sweater was over the
foot of the bed. She'd changed and checked out.

I was good and sore. The prime chance to settle Garner
was all shot! Could I go around punching doorbells and asking for Selene?

Then I got it. I'd go back to the bowl, tail Garner, and find
out where his new girl friend lived. He'd just found her, I
figured, hence this moonlight stuff. Later, he'd be spending
time at her house, or a place he'd get for her.

The way to play it was to hide out in the turtle back. Better than trailing in a slow, noisy bus like mine. I parked some
distance from the road fork and went on foot.

Then I heard the cats. The awfullest howling, and more of
it than I'd ever imagined, much less heard. And you know
what one feline courtship sounds like, or one good duel with
well matched contenders. I wondered if any bob cat had
come down from the further range.

There could have been a dozen, and you'd never have heard them in that screaming. Up—up—up—and still no ceiling. I ran, figuring at first that that riot would hide any noise I made lifting the turtle back. Ten to one it wasn't locked, and if it was, his keys were in the ignition, where they should be, with girl on his brain.

The nearer I got, the louder the screams. I quit running. There were noises no cat ever made. Captain, that monstrous fellow of Selene's, did have a raucous voice, like an old time sea captain. But I quit running. Those howls, that threshing in the thicket near the bowl . . .

It stopped. My knees began to shake. My mouth got dry. There were sounds like those a cat makes when he has a big mouthful and is impatient; tearing, shaking his head, sinking his fangs. The very same, only, many times more of it.

"Hell," I said aloud.

I walked on. Gravel crunched under my feet. Then leaves. I stumbled in spite of myself. Ahead, two tail lights stared from the clearing. When I reached the big coupé, no one stirred anywhere.

I did not get the score until I finally went toward the clearing. The smell might have warned me, but it didn't. It was not until I looked and saw that I got sick and scared. The bones were new, white. The moonlight made that clear. A doctor could have told which were a man's and which a woman's. But I'm no doctor. I just needed one.

I turned and ran. There was one question I had to ask, and I knew that Selene could answer it. By looking at her cats when they came home. If her menagerie was lean, I'd know it hadn't happened.

I stumbled half a dozen times, running up to my car. I nearly went over the bank, trying to make a U-turn. Getting to her house was a job. My feet pounding in the patio brought Selene to the door. Her eyes widened further than I'd ever seen.

Then she smiled and sighed and reached out with both arms.

"Darling, you did get impatient, didn't you?" Her blue robe was not made to hide much. Now it trailed straight down from her shoulders, and what she wore beneath it wasn't much. "It's so nice. I'm glad you did."

Her voice was contented, and her eyes were sleepy. She was warm and sleek in my arms. There was not a trace of make-up on her. Her hair was damp and mussed. She had stepped from under the shower only a minute ago. So she had neither cosmetics nor perfume.

Then I saw the cats. Captain was washing his face. So were some of the others, though half of them were asleep. And they all bulged. Their stomachs would have dragged the carpet if they had tried to walk. Selene's warmth seemed to distill a cat scent from her skin and hair. That, and the thought of what made her animals look overfed made me break loose. "Uh—something I ate—where's—?"

"Anything I can get you—?"

Captain got up. He gave me a knowing look. He arched his back and rubbed against me. So did the others. I stood there gulping. Selene purred in my ear, "You've hurried too much—"

She sat on the lounge. There was a decanter on the end table. I took a hefty one. I told myself I had a bad case of jitters. That I was moonstruck. I pulled myself together. She curled up against me and whispered, "The house will be yours, if you want it ... I go with the house . . ."

I must have looked like myself again, but I was all wrong inside. Her eyes had a contented expression. She stretched back among the cushions.

"I've been terrible, but that's all over, darling."

Then she looked puzzled. She knew it was long past the time for me to take an armful. Her cats were purring, sleepy. I could not explain why I wasn't kissing her. I muttered, "It just doesn't seem real—can't believe it yet—dashed like crazy—an impulse like that—"

She thought she understood. After all, it made sense, a fellow walking in circles for a week or two, then breaking in and finding there's nothing more to argue about. "I'm dizzy." I got up. "I'll wash up a bit."

The water in the bathroom was cold. It should have done the work. In another few minutes, I'd know that it was a hallucination, out there by the bowl. But those minutes had not a chance.

Not when I saw the bottom of Selene's tiled shower.

A tattered bit of satin; coral-colored where it wasn't soaked with blood, and earth. It was clawed to streamers. I knew it must have been torn from Garner's girl. That was bad enough, but what followed was worse: a question. Did Selene tell Captain to round up his pals, or did she lead them herself?

That was when I made a dive from the window. My yell and the slamming sash brought Selene on the run. I landed in a heap and did not notice the cactus. She cried out, but I didn't answer. I couldn't. I scrambled to my feet and tore up the slope.

Nothing was following me. It wasn't *that* that I was afraid of. I was afraid of what I remembered, at the bowl. So I hit the road and somehow stuck to the curves. Black clouds gathered. A freakish rain pelted down. The windshield wiper couldn't handle it all.

~ ~ ~ ~ ~

I KNEW there'd be no footprints left around the bowl. But I was wrong.

I sat around with a bottle all night, and didn't feel the stuff at all. An afternoon radio newscast spilled the story. Someone had found the car and the bones, and scraps of coral underthings. Mr. Garner and girl friend; jewelry and dental work clinched that. No one explained how skeletons could be picked clean so quickly.

I could have explained one mystery: why, in the sheltered spot near the blood-stained blanket, there was a big paw print, ". . . *as if a leopard weighing a hundred pounds or more had killed the couple.*"

All the others had been washed out by the rain, and the cops couldn't follow any trail. I am still wondering if she had that bloody satin in her claws, or whether Captain brought it back to show her what a job he'd done. Her name was a give-away from the start. I had spelled it Felice. It should have been *felis,* which sounds the same.

Yeah, that's Latin for cat. I don't know who owns the house now, and I'm not going out there to ask. I got a new job. No more measuring dames for hosiery. I am twisting a gas pump. But every time a gal drives up I hope it is, and I pray it isn't, Selene . . .

THE MAN FROM THE MOON

By Otis Adelbert Kline

WE STOOD on the eastern rim of Crater Mound—my friend Professor Thompson, the noted selenographer, and I. Dusky shadows lengthened and grew more intense in the great, deep basin before us, as the Sun, his face reddened as if from his day's exertions, sank slowly beyond the western rim.

Behind us, Alamo Edwards, the dude wrangler who had brought us out from Canyon Diabolo two weeks before, was dividing his time between the chuck wagon and our outdoor cookstove in the preparation of our evening meal, while our hobbled horses wandered about near-by, searching out clumps of edible vegetation.

"How is the story progressing, Jim?" asked the professor, referring to a half finished novel I had brought out with me to occupy my time with while my friend puttered among the stones and rubble in the vicinity. "I've reached an impasse—" I began.

"And so have I," rejoined my friend dejectedly, "but of the two, mine is far the worst, for yours is in an imaginary situation, while mine is real. You will eventually solve your problem by using your imagination, which has no fixed limitations. I can only solve mine by using my reason, which is limited to deductions from facts. If I do not find sufficient facts either to prove or disprove my theory, what have I? A hypothesis, ludicrously wobbling on one puny leg, neither able to stand erect among established scientific truths nor to fall to dissolution among the mistaken ideas of the past."

"What single, if weak, leg supports your theory that the craters of the moon were caused by meteorites?" I asked.

"You are standing on it," replied the professor. Then, seeing me look around in perplexity, he added: "Crater Mound is the only known Terrestrial formation that exactly resembles in shape the great ring mountains of the moon. If Crater Mound was caused by the impact of a gigantic meteorite with the earth, there is a strong probability that the numerous ringed craters of the moon were created in a like manner."

"But was it?" I asked.

"That is something I can neither prove nor disprove," he replied. "The evidence I have thus far discovered leads me to believe that many relatively small meteoric fragments have fallen here. But they could not have fallen singly, or by twos and threes, to make this dent three-quarters of a mile in diameter and more than four hundred feet below the surrounding earth level, to say nothing of throwing up the ring on which we now stand to a mean height of a hundred and fifty feet above the plain."

"Then how could they have fallen?"

"If this great earthen bowl was caused by them, they must have struck this plain in an immense cluster at least a third of a mile in diameter, probably more."

"In that case, what has become of the cluster?"

"Part of it is probably buried beneath the soil. Part of it, exposed to the air, would have been burned to a fine ash, having generated a terrific heat in its passage through the atmosphere and still having, before it cooled, an opportunity to unite with oxygen. There should, however, be an intermediary residue which I have been unable to find."

"Maybe it was carted off by prehistoric Americans for the metals it contained," I feebly ventured to suggest.

"Improbable as that statement may seem," said the professor, "there is a small amount of evidence in favor of it, for I have found a number of meteoric fragments miles from the rim of the crater. By Jove! We appear to have a visitor!"

He clapped his powerful binoculars to his eyes, and looking in the direction in which they pointed, I saw a tall, bent figure, apparently attired in a robe or gown, leaning on a long staff and carrying a bundle of poles under one arm, slowly descending the slope opposite us.

"Seems to be a Chinaman," he said, passing the glasses to me. "What is your opinion?"

I looked and saw an undeniably Mongolian face, with slanting eyes, prominent cheek bones, and a long, thin moustache, the ends of which drooped at least four inches below the chin. The voluminous garments, though badly tattered, were unquestionably Chinese, as was the cap with a button in the center, which surmounted the broad head.

"A Chinaman or an excellent makeup," I replied. "Wonder what he's doing out here in his native costume?"

Our speculations were interrupted by the clarion supper call of Alamo from the camp behind us:

"Come an' get it, or I'll feed it to the coyotes."

"You go down and eat," said the professor. "I'm not hungry anyway, and I want to stay here and watch this curious newcomer. Bring me a bacon and egg sandwich and a bottle of coffee when you have finished."

Knowing my friend's disposition—for once he had made up his mind, a fleet of tractors could not drag him from his purpose—I did not argue with him, but descended to the camp.

While Alamo grumbled about dudes that were too interested in rocks to come for their chow while it was hot, I finished my evening meal. Then, taking my binoculars, I carried his light snack to the professor as requested.

The last pink glow of the sun was fading in the west, and the moon was rising when I reached the top of the ridge.

"Sit down here beside me," whispered the professor. "Our visitor seems to be preparing for a religious ceremony of some sort, and I dislike disturbing him."

While my friend munched his sandwich and sipped his coffee, I used my binoculars to watch the Chinaman. He had erected four poles supporting four others which formed a square above a low, flat-topped rock near the center of the crater. Suspended from the horizontal poles by cords were many small objects which were apparently very light in weight, for they stirred like leaves in the breeze. A lighted taper stood in the center of the flat rock, which was surrounded by a ring of thin sticks that had been thrust into the ground. The Oriental was on his knees before the stone, immobile as the rock itself, his face turned in our direction.

"Seems to be keeping his eyes on us," I said.

"I think he is waiting for the moon to rise above the crater rim," replied the professor, once more applying his eyes to his own binoculars.

My friend was right, for as soon as the first shaft of moonlight entered the crater the kneeling figure was galvanized into action.

Bursting into a singsong chant, quite audible, if unintelligible to me, the Celestial applied the flame of the taper to each of the thin sticks he had planted around the stone, all of which were soon glowing like burning punk. Then he stepped beneath one of the objects suspended from a horizontal pole, made a short speech in the direction of the moon, and lighted it with the taper. It burned out in a few seconds, casting a weird, yellow light over the scene. Stepping beneath the next suspended object he made another speech and lighted that object also. This one burned with a blue flame. He continued thus for several minutes until all the dangling objects had been consumed—each with a different colored flame. Then he extinguished the taper and knelt once more before the stone, resuming his chant, and prostrating himself from time to time with his forehead touching the stone. The breeze, blowing in our direction, was laden with the sweet, heavy odor of burning sandalwood and musk.

A half hour passed with no change in the ceremony. Then the burning joss sticks winked out, one by one. When the last went dark, the kneeling man made a final obeisance, then rose, took down his framework of poles, tucked them under his arm, and leaning heavily on his long staff departed toward the west.

"Show's over," I said. "Shall we go back to camp?"

"Hardly," replied my friend. "I'm going to follow him. In this bright moonlight it should be easy. By Jove! What has become of him? Why the fellow just now disappeared before my eyes!"

"Maybe he fell into a ditch," I hazarded.

"Ditch, fiddlesticks!" snapped the professor. "I've explored every square foot of this crater and know there is no depression of any kind where he was walking."

"Eastern magic," I ventured. "Now you see it, now you don't."

"Rot! You stay here and watch the western slope with your binoculars. I'm going down to investigate."

I watched, while the professor stumbled hastily across the crater and frantically searched the vicinity of the place where he had declared the Celestial had disappeared. After a twenty minute hunt, he gave it up and came back.

"Queer," he panted as he came up beside me. "Deucedly queer. I couldn't find hide nor hair of the fellow—not even the burnt ends of his joss sticks. Must have taken everything with him."

We returned to camp, squatted beside the fire, and lighted our pipes.

Alamo had stacked the dishes, putting off to the last the one camp job he hated—washing them—and was picketing the horses. Suddenly we heard him sing out:

"Well, look who's here! Hello, Charlie. You wantee come along washee dishee, gettee all same plenty much chow?"

Looking up in surprise, I saw the tall, ragged Oriental who had disappeared so mysteriously a few moments before, coming toward us. He was still leaning on his long staff, but minus the poles he had previously carried.

The professor and I both leaped to our feet from places beside the fire.

The Chinaman paused and looked at Alamo in evident bewilderment.

"I beg a thousand pardons," he said in excellent English, "but your speech is quite unintelligible to me."

"Well, I'll be damned!" Alamo tilted his broad Stetson to on side and scratched his head in amazement.

By this time my excited friend had reached the side of our Celestial visitor.

"He was only inviting you to sup with us, in the patois of the West," explained the professor.

The Chinaman bowed gravely to Alamo.

"Your magnificent hospitality is duly appreciated," he said, "but I beg to be excused, as I may not partake of food in the presence of the mighty Magong." As he uttered the last word he extended his left hand toward the moon, then touched his forehead as if in salute. There was something majestic about his bearing that made one forget the tattered rags in which he was clad.

"We accept your excuse without question," said the professor, quickly. "Permit me to welcome you to our campfire circle."

Our guest bowed low, moved into the circle of firelight, and laying his staff on the ground, squatted before the fire. Then he took a long-stemmed pipe with a small brass bowl from one of his capacious sleeves, and the professor and I both proffered our tobacco pouches.

"I'll use my own, with your indulgence," said our visitor, filling his pipe from a small lacquered box he carried. Before closing the box, he threw a pinch of tobacco into the fire, raised his left hand toward the moon, and muttered a few words unintelligible to me. Then, after touching his forehead, he lighted his pipe with the glowing end of a stick from the fire.

After puffing in meditative silence for a few minutes, he said:

"As I have thanksgiving devotions to perform, my time is limited. I will therefore, as briefly as possible, explain the reason for my visit, and convey to you the communication of the great one, whose humble messenger I am.

"Twenty years ago I was a Buddhist priest in T'ainfu. It was expected of every member of our order that at least once during his lifetime he should make a pilgrimage to a certain monastery in Tibet, there to perform mystic rites in a secret sanctuary, where a sacred stone of immemorable antiquity was kept. I made the pilgrimage, fully expecting to return to T'ainfu, as my brother priests had done and take up the duties of my humdrum existence there for the term of my natural life.

"There are things which I may tell you, and things which I may not disclose, so let me explain, briefly, that the whole course of my life was changed when first I viewed the sacred stone. It was graven with mystic characters, similar to yet unlike Chinese writing. According to tradition, none but a living Buddha could decipher this sacred writing, which might not be transmitted to any of his followers, however great or wise.

"Now I had, from the days of my youth, made a study of our ancient writings, and had learned the meanings of many characters since wholly obsolete, as well as the former meanings of those whose significance had been entirely changed. I firmly believed, with my fellow priests, that none but the living Buddha might translate the writings on the stone. You may judge, therefore, of my surprise, when I found myself able to translate several of the ideographs graven on its sacred surface. I instantly believed myself the true possessor of the *karma* of Buddha, and that the living Buddha of my order was an impostor. On attempting to translate other characters, I found the majority of them unintelligible to me.

"One of the requirements of my pilgrimage was that I was to spend four hours a day for a period of seven days alone on my knees before the sacred stone. A guard, posted outside the door, saw to it that but one pilgrim was admitted at a time. On the day following, I secreted writing materials in my clothing, and spent the time allotted to me on that day, and the five days following, in carefully copying the writing on the stone.

"I carried my prize away without detection, but did not return to T'ainfu. Instead, I wandered from monastery to monastery, from temple to temple, conversing with the learned men and reading the ancient records to which I, as a pilgrim priest, was usually given access without question. The task of translation, which had at first appeared easy, took me ten years to complete.

"When it was finished I knew that it had not been written by God, as was supposed, but by the first earthly ancestor of my race, and I found myself charged with a trust which appeared as difficult of fulfillment as the translation itself. The crater which you have been investigating was described to me—yet its location was unknown to the writer. I was charged to find it and to find you. It took me nine years to find the crater, during which time I visited thousands, none of which exactly fitted the description. It took me a year more to find you and to receive the sign."

"May I ask what sign you refer to?" inquired the professor.

"My illustrious ancestor, who charged me with the task of conveying his message to you, said in the writing that his spirit would be watching me from Magong. He prophesied that you would appear at this place, and when you did, he would flash a brilliant signal to me from his Celestial abode."

"And you have the signal?"

"I have and do, for it is still visible. Look!" He pointed toward the full moon.

The professor looked, then raised his binoculars to his eyes and focused them.

"By Jove!" he exclaimed. "You have unusually sharp eyes. There is a brilliant, star-like light in the crater, Aristarchus. A rare occurrence, too."

"I have studied Magong for many years," replied our guest, "and have trained my eyes to see things hidden from the sight of ordinary mortals. I could have used a telescope or binoculars, but for my purpose I have no need of them."

"Remarkable!" commented the professor. "And this light fulfills the prophecy?"

"To the letter. Permit me to deliver my message, therefore, and depart, for I have much to do before Magong veils her face once more."

Drawing a large, bulky envelope from his pocket, the Oriental arose and handed it to the professor with a profound bow.

Springing to his feet with alacrity, the professor accepted it with a bow as low and dignified as that of the donor.

"Man of science," said our guest. "Use this message as you will, for that is your privilege, but you will confer a favor on the illustrious sender and bring manifold blessings on yourself and your descendants if you will use it to advance the knowledge of mankind."

"I will endeavor to use it as you ask," replied the professor, "and thank you for it, and for the trust you have placed in me."

"Do not thank me," was the answer, accompanied by a significant gesture skyward. "Thank P'an-ku."

"I will, and do. May we not have the pleasure of your company tomorrow?

"A thousand thanks, and as many regrets, but my task will have ended when Magong veils her face, and I am weary and would return to T'ainfu. So farewell."

He took up his staff, and without a further word, stalked majestically out into the moonlight. The last we saw of him was when his tall, gaunt figure was silhouetted against the sky for a moment on the crater rim.

With trembling fingers the professor broke the seal of the envelope and drew therefrom a neatly written manuscript. It was in English, and he read it aloud to me, while Alamo snored lustily from the folds of his blanket, several yards away.

With Professor Thompson's permission, I publish it here for the first time, making it clear at the outset, that while it seems to explain many matters which have puzzled our leading scientists for hundreds of years, and is not, in the light of our present knowledge, either susceptible of proof or refutation, we cannot vouch for its veracity.

THE STORY OF P'AN-KU

HAVING attained the advanced age of two hundred and ninety-eight earthly years, and feeling the hands of San-miau, the devourer, grim messenger of the Supreme God, T'ien, ever closing tighter on my throat, slowly squeezing out my soul from this old shell of a body, I, P'an-ku, lord of thousands, founder of a new race, and last survivor of an old, have retired from my manifold duties and pleasures—the ordering of the affairs of my subjects, the company of my wives, my children, and my children's children, who will someday be numerous as the stars of heaven—to write this history of my own people for those to come who will have the intelligence and the desire to understand it.

For a million historical years, men of my race inhabited Magong when she was yet a planet among planets, a free, rotating sphere with her own undisturbed orbit, midway between the orbits of this planet and that of the terrible, devastating war-world, Mars. For a half of those million historical years, an ancestor of mine—a P'an-ku—sat on the imperial throne of Magong and held dominion over all her lands and seas.

When I was born, Crown Prince of Magong, my people had reached an advanced state of civilization, for much can be accomplished in a million historical years. For more than ten thousand years, Magong had been in communication with Mars, the only other planet inhabited by intelligent beings. For over five thousand years, our interplanetary ships had visited their planet, and their ships had made friendly calls on Magong, carrying passengers, manufactured merchandise, and raw materials. A colony of their pale, white people, whose faces I wish we had never seen, was founded on one of our continents and treated with every friendly consideration by our rulers: that is, my ancestors. A colony of our stalwart yellow people had also settled on Mars, and had been received with every appearance of good will.

Before I was sixteen years of age I had learned to navigate an ether ship, and when I had demonstrated to my father's satisfaction that I was a thorough master of interplanetary navigation, he permitted me a leave of absence of two years for the purpose of visiting the inner planets—Earth, Venus and Mercury. This trip was mostly for my own education, as all three of the planets had been explored thousands of years before, and had subsequently been visited at regular intervals by our scientific expeditions for the purpose of tabulating the evolutionary changes taking place on them. Mercury had developed nothing but the most lowly vegetable organisms. Venus teemed with life, ranging from the microscopic, unicellular animalcules to gigantic, four-footed reptiles, which roamed through her great forests of fern and fungi, some of them feeding on these and other primordial thallophytic growths, some preying on these herbivora or on the lesser creatures coexistent with them on that planet. Some of them had evolved membranous wings with which they flapped clumsily from place to place, but there were no birds or mammals. Among the plants, none flowered or bore fruit or seeds. All reproduced by spores or spawn or by simple fission.

On the Earth, a higher order of evolution was in progress. Many of the plants, having developed specialized sexual organs, flowered and bore fruit. Birds forsook the ways and forms of their reptilian ancestors—evolved a thousand shapes and hues—cultivated glorious plumage and melodious voices. Mammals suckled and reared their young, and man, the greatest mammal of them all, was slowly battling his way to world supremacy with crude weapons and implements of wood and stone.

On my return to Magong, alter visiting the inner planets, I importuned my father to permit me to visit Jupiter. This he flatly refused to do. The trip, he said, was too long and dangerous for one of my years. Furthermore, only one, out of a thousand of our most skillful and experienced navigators who had attempted the trip, had returned to tell of it. I had to be content, therefore, with several trips to Mars, where I, as Crown Prince of Magong, was always received with such pomp and splendor that I wished I might be permitted to go incognito and mingle with the common people—but even this small pleasure was denied me.

At twenty-five, I was made commander-in-chief of Magong's interplanetary navies. Shortly thereafter, trouble developed between my father and Lido Kan, Supreme Ruler of Mars. It seems that a number of Martians, jealous of the economic progress made by our colonists on that planet, had gone to Lido Kan with tales of woe, insisting that they be deported. So strong was the pressure they brought to bear on him, that he finally took the matter up with my father. The reply of my father was courteous but firm. He insisted that if his people were to be deported from Mars, the Martian colony must also leave Magong. Lido Kan argued that his people had created no disturbance on Magong, and no dissension among the subjects of my father, which was true enough, and my father naturally retorted that his subjects were too courteous to even think of bringing up such a matter.

One word led to another, and things went from bad to worse, until a group of Martians attacked and massacred the inhabitants of one of our settlements. My father instantly demanded an imperial apology from Lido Kan, complete punishment of the perpetrators of the crime, and indemnity for relatives of all the massacred people. Lido Kan delayed his reply for several days, but was eventually swayed by the jingoists of his realm, and replied that he would neither apologize, pay indemnity, nor punish any of his subjects, as my father had received fair and timely warning. While my father debated what to do in this crisis—for he had always been a man of peace—word came that an army of Martians had completely wiped out our colonies on that planet.

A short time thereafter, the commander of one of our large interplanetary passenger ships ether-waved me that the Martians would not permit him to leave port, and that several hundred of our ships were being held in a similar fashion. I immediately left Magong with a fleet of battleships, intending to demand their release or fight, but was met half way by a fleet of Martian warships.

The contest that ensued was short and disastrous. My fleet used the cold, energy-decreasing green ray of condensation, which we had developed—the enemy fleet, the hot, energy-increasing red ray of dispersion. We had developed our inter-rotating green rays to such a degree that any substance touched by them would contract to less than one-hundredth of its normal size with a corresponding increase in density. The toughest metals, under this ray, would become as brittle as egg shells and more dense than pure lead.

The effect of the red rays of the Martians was the opposite, but fully as devastating, as these rays, rotating in receding spirals, tore the atoms apart on contact, making the heaviest metals less dense than the atmosphere in an instant. When a green ray met a red ray of equal intensity, they neutralized each other.

By superior maneuvering, I managed to wipe out the last Martian battleship when I had lost all but the flagship of my fleet. This had been badly crippled by a red ray, and after making temporary repairs, I limped sadly back to port.

On the face of my father, when I reported to him in the throne room that day, was a look sterner than any I had ever seen him wear.

"My son," he said. "War is a terrible thing—the worst affliction that can come to humanity—but it is at hand and we must meet it like men. The Martians have made a start by wiping out our colonies and attacking our fleet. Now they are determined to eliminate us entirely from the solar system. At this very hour they are preparing to use their most terrific weapon of all against us."

"What weapon is that, O my father?" I asked.

"Come with me, my son, and I will show you."

He led me up to the great observatory on top of his palace. We passed through the general observation room, where a hundred enormous telescopes were in constant use—a thousand trained men observing, recording, and manipulating the instruments. Going into his private observation room, my father himself trained his huge telescope on a distant object.

Then he called me to look. I saw what appeared to be a huge spiral of nebulous matter forming near Mars.

"They are clearing interplanetary lanes for the passage of a huge fleet," I said. "See, they are collecting all the meteoric bodies for millions of miles in all directions."

"They are doing more than that, my son," my father replied. "'That matter-condensing and projecting apparatus which they formerly used to clear the way for peaceful ships is going to be used for a horribly deadly purpose. Have you noticed *where* they are condensing the meteoric mass?"

"It seems to be on a line between Magong and Mars," I replied.

"It is. Have they ever condensed material in that position before? You know full well they have not. They have always concentrated it in a position where it could be projected out into space without harm to anyone."

"Why, Father, what do you mean?"

"I mean that as soon as that synthetic nebula reaches a sufficient degree of cohesion and solidity it will be projected at *us!*"

"What will it do? Will it burst our planet asunder? Will everyone be killed?"

"No. It is not large enough for that, but it can do incalculable damage, and if their aim is good and they are not stopped in some way, they can collect enough of such matter from the meteoric belts of the solar system to depopulate this planet."

"Can't we dodge them? What about the new gravity control plant?"

"The thing is still in the experimental stage. Besides, it is a terrible and a dangerous thing to disturb or attempt to change the orbit of Magong. Every body in the solar system is in perfect balance with every other body, and too great a change, even in the orbit of our own relatively small planet, may cause untold damage—some upset of the scheme of things, which we cannot possibly foresee. True, we have slightly perturbed the motion of Magong, just as an experiment, but it has been done cautiously, and always with a counter-perturbance sufficient to bring it back to the proper place in its orbit."

Once more my father looked through the giant telescope.

"The projectile is formed and on the way," he said gravely. "Where it will strike, no one can tell—not even those who are sending it. It may crush this palace, destroy this city. It may kill nobody or wipe out a million people. It may miss Magong entirely, but this is not probable. We are too large a target. Let us go below. There is nothing more we can learn here at present. I will show you the only efficient aggressive weapon to which I can turn at present. By this, and by the remaining interplanetary fleets under your command, the question of our very existence will be determined."

We descended to the main floor and entered a compression tube car, in which we were shot to one of the numerous physics laboratory stations of Magong. My father presented Wang Ho, the venerable chief scientist of the institution.

"Wang Ho," he said. "Is the atmosphere disintegration ray ready?"

"It is ready, your majesty," was the reply.

"Then train it on Mars. They insist on war, so we will give it to them in earnest. They are determined to destroy the face of our planet, therefore let us remove the atmosphere from theirs."

"Your majesty is aware, I hope, that a continuous use of this ray will be suicidal. For every ten cubic parsads of their atmosphere we send out into space, we also send out one cubic parsad of our own. If your majesty would wait, and have a number of these ray projectors made in portable size, they could be fastened to ether ships and used without destroying our own atmosphere."

"Unfortunately," replied my father, "we cannot wait. The war is on. It may be decided in a few days. Several weeks would be required to fit out ether ships with these ray projectors. No, we must fight now or be forever beaten. Turn the ray on them, and keep it going as long as they are in range.

Our other projecting stations will take up the duty, one by one, as the planet revolves on its axis."

He turned to me.

"My son," he said. "The entire war fleet of Magong is in your keeping. Save the fleet if you can, yourself with it, but remember—it is only a barrier. It is one of the protections of Magong. If the barrier must be destroyed in the line of duty—then do not attempt to save it at the cost of that which it was set up to protect. Do you understand?"

"Fully, father. I will be wary and circumspect, but I will not fail in the line of duty."

Once more we entered the compression tube and were shot back to the imperial palace. Alter bidding farewell to my mother, I said a last goodbye to my father, and went out to my flagship. There were tears in the eyes of my mother as she called her last farewell to me. My father was too much of a man of iron, however, to betray his emotion at such a time.

My fleet of ten thousand ether ships was ready for action, awaiting only my word of command. I had formed a daring plan which, if successful, might mean the destruction of the fleet and my own death, but would make it possible for Magong to win the war.

Leaving half of my ships to guard the planet against enemy craft. I took the other half and made straight for Mars. Shortly alter we started, the first huge missile of the Martians passed us, and a few minutes thereafter it struck Magong with a brilliant flare of light, leaving a great dark pit in the ground where it had fallen. Referring to my charts I found that it had alighted on a small village of about two hundred souls. What a sudden and terrible end for them!

As we pressed onward, I saw another large nebula spiraling into shape, and knew that it would not be long until a second projectile was on the way to Magong.

Presently I saw a huge enemy fleet put out from Mars, evidently with the intention of meeting and giving battle to my fleet. This did not fit in with my plans at all, so I immediately gave secret orders to all of my commanders, then bade them disperse.

There were nearly a thousand magnetic wave stations on Mars, most of which were in continuous use because of the terrific efforts the Martians were putting forth to crush Magong. These stations were sending out powerful, man-directed magnetic lines of force, which drew all relatively small particles of matter with which they came in contact, toward the stations from which they were projected. This procedure would have been dangerous to the Martians themselves had they not been clever enough to cross the lines of force and form contracting vortices, hundreds of thousands of miles from their planet. Under the direction of the central station, these vortices were combined and recombined at regular intervals, until visible nebula: resulted. The nebulae were condensed by extra and special lines of force from the central station, then projected at Magong, close-knit, spherical clusters of stone and metal. When the central station was turned away from the target by the axial rotation of the planet, a duplicate-control station on the other side carried on the work under the control of the same operators.

During the progress of my ship toward Mars, six of these huge clusters were projected at my world. Five of them struck the target and one missed, to shoot out into space and become an asteroid with an orbit of its own around the sun.

My plan was simple and direct. Each of my ships carried a chart showing the location of the thousand enemy wave stations. Each station was numbered, and five ships were assigned to the attack of each.

My ship, together with four others of the most powerful of my navy, each carrying a battery of twenty huge ray projectors, was to attack the central magnetic station.

While we neared Mars I watched the movements of the enemy fleet, and saw that it was heading straight for Magong, evidently pleased at the fact that my first fleet had dispersed. This exactly suited my plans, as I knew that Hia Ku, my able lieutenant, would give them a warm reception with the five thousand ships I had left under his command, and I would be free to carry out my attack.

When I drew near the central wave station of the Martians I saw that my other four ships had arrived on schedule, and ordered the attack. We were discovered almost instantly, and a thousand red rays were flashed at us, but we were able to neutralize these by laying down a barrage of green rays. Then a number of Martian ether ships, reserved to guard the central station, arose and attacked us from above. One of their rays pierced our upper barrage and one of our ships, with her controls destroyed, plunged dizzily groundward, but was disintegrated by the red rays before she had fallen half way.

With this ship gone my barrage was weakened, and I knew that it would only be a matter of minutes until we should all meet a like fate. As certain death faced us, I thought quickly, and as quickly gave orders, resolving that in our passing we should at least cripple the central wave station of the enemy. My ships instantly responded to my command, and in a moment all were plunging directly downward, temporarily protected above and below by our green ray barrage—our objective the glass dome of the central wave station. It was my hope that when we crashed through this dome to our death we might destroy, or at least cripple this station, and thus hamper the Martians and give my father the time he needed to fit out other ships with atmosphere destroyers, thus assuring the victory of Magong.

But the Martians were too wise for me. They must have suddenly focused their lines of magnetic force on our ships, forming a contracting vortex a short distance above the dome, for we lost control of all of them simultaneously. They revolved about each other for a moment, and then crashed together. With that crash I lost consciousness . . .

When I recovered my senses once more I was lying on a metal, bench to which my hands and feet had been bound. Standing over me with a sneering smile on his pale face was Lido Kan, Supreme Ruler of Mars.

"What happened?" I asked, bewildered. "Where are my men?"

"All died but you," he replied, "when we brought your ships to the ground. I had thought to bring them down gently, but the rage of my operator got the better of him and he wrecked all four. I cannot understand how it happened that you lived through that crash. It was a miraculous escape."

"Perhaps I have been saved for a purpose," I replied. "The Supreme Ruler of the Universe is all-knowing."

"I, at least, have kept you for a purpose," replied Lido Kan, savagely. "Lying here on your back, you shall witness the destruction of your world." He pressed a lever and a curved metal plate slid back from the ceiling, disclosing a great dome-like lens which looked out into space. "The empire of P'an-ku is doomed," he continued. "While this side of our planet is turned toward Magong, you shall witness its destruction through this lens. As soon as we turn away the lens will become a mirror which will give you the battle scenes as witnessed from our station on the other side. I pride myself that this is a rather clever invention of mine."

I made no reply, but looked eagerly out toward Magong. Already the once fair face of my planet was growing pock-marked and ugly from the cruel disease called war.

"You are a clever whelp," continued my captor, watching my features closely, "but not clever enough for Lido Kan. Your ships destroyed two hundred of my magnetic wave stations, but it will not take long to rebuild them, and in the meantime the others are functioning quite successfully, as you will observe. At least half of the population of Magong has already been destroyed by my projectiles."

"Don't be too sure of victory," I replied. "By the time you have destroyed Magong, you may find yourself without an atmosphere."

"Hardly. It will take many days for your father to destroy our atmosphere. One week is all I require to silence all of his ray projectors and exterminate his people. But enough of this idle talk. I must to the grim work before me. I leave you to the pleasant contemplation of the dissolution of your heritage—the empire of Magong."

Left quite alone in the small, bare observatory room, I lay on my back and watched the progress of the battle. High above me the Martians were forming an enormous cluster of meteoric material. Already it was at least ten times as large as any they had projected at Magong, and they continued to add to it. Presently I saw that it was ready to be projected. There was a terrific roar from the machinery in the building around me, and the huge globe shot outward, but not in the direction of Magong. It described a short curve and began to fall directly upon Mars. Once more there was a roar from the projector machinery, and once again the sphere shot outward, only to return, drawn by the terrific pull of Mars' gravity on its great mass.

A feeling of exultation came over me, as I saw that my enemies failed, again and again, in their efforts to project the sphere. It appeared to me that they had brought destruction on their own heads. But Lido Kan was not without resource. Suddenly I heard a more terrific roar from the machinery than had occurred before. A great section was split from the mighty sphere, and simultaneously, the larger and smaller pieces were projected obliquely out into space. This time they did not fall back, but continued to travel in curved paths. The smaller, moving much more swiftly than the larger, soon disappeared from view, but it reappeared again in a few hours. The larger, moving more majestically across the sky, appeared to travel in a direction opposite to that taken by the smaller, because of its slower motion and the axial rotation of the planet. I had witnessed the formation of the moons of Mars.

Foiled in his attempt to hurl so huge a projectile, Lido Kan once more turned his attention to the firing of smaller ones. Hour after hour I watched, my lens presently turning to a mirror as Mars turned her face away from Magong, and each hour added to my sorrow as I saw the surface of my planet turning to enormous ringed pits. Presently an attendant brought me food and drink. Afterward, I slept at fitful intervals.

Days passed, and I detected new tactics on the part of my father. He evidently decided to risk all in an attempt to dodge the projectiles, for I saw that Magong was shifting out of her orbit—moving in closer to the sun in an eccentric fashion that would make it difficult for an operator to properly aim and time a projectile intended to strike her.

Soon I saw that he had moved into the orbit of Earth, then beyond it, between the orbits of Earth and Venus. At first I could not fathom his plans, but gradually they dawned on me, as I saw Earth come along and Magong fall in behind her. It was his intention, I felt sure, to use the larger planet as a shield against the devastating Martian projectiles.

Something must have gone wrong with his control station, however, for Magong presently fell behind the Earth in her race around the sun, then rose, crossing her orbit behind her, and hurried forward to catch her once more—this time outside Earth's orbit, between Earth and Mars. Something, also, had happened to Magong's rotation on her axis. Whereas she had previously revolved once in every twelve hours, she now turned with exceeding slowness. Rushing on past Earth, she continued for some distance, then paused and fell back once more to wait for the larger planet. Magong, I could clearly see, was caught in the gravity net of Earth. Thus she had become a satellite of that planet, even as the huge broken projectile of Lido Kan had become two satellites of Mars.

Lido Kan kept up his pitiless bombardment of Magong, once he had grown accustomed to her new orbit, with deadly accuracy. Once, and once only, did I see him miss, the projectile, which was a relatively small one, passing Magong and striking somewhere on the planet Earth—I could not tell just where because of the silvery cloud envelope that hid her surface from view.

Although fully four-fifths of her population must have been wiped out by this time, I knew that Magong still kept up the fight, as the atmosphere in my room grew rarer each day until breathing was a painful effort.

One day Lido Kan entered my room. Strapped to his back was an apparatus containing concentrated air, from which he took mouthfuls from time to time.

"I come to take leave of you, young whelp of P'an-ku," he said. "My people are dying by the millions for want of air, thanks to the infernal rays which your father has managed to keep trained on us. Our dissipated atmosphere cannot be brought back, nor could we manufacture a new one from the elements locked in the soil in less than a thousand years. I am leaving, therefore, with the five hundred large ether ships I still possess, for the purpose of colonizing the damp, unhealthful and savage planet Earth. My wave projecting stations, I will leave manned, each being provided with a supply of concentrated air, and committed to the task of continuing the bombardment of Magong until death overtakes them.

"I will have one of your hands unfettered, and will leave you plenty of food and water so that when death finally overtakes you, you will be slain by your own father, as he continues to dissipate our atmosphere. And so, farewell."

He went out, and shortly thereafter, my attendant came in, placed a tank of water and a large basket of food within reach, and unlettered one ol my hands. Then he, too, went out, and I was left alone, gasping for breath, as the atmosphere continued to grow more rare.

Presently I saw the fleet of Lido Kan set out. Instantly, with the thin point of one of my eating sticks, I set about picking the locks of my fetters. Within an hour I had freed myself. Finding my door unlocked I rushed from the room. Presently I blundered into the great deserted room from winch the official Martian ether visiphone messages had formerly been sent to Magong. Opening a switch, I found that the power was still on, and signaled the station of my father. My heart gave a leap of joy when his face suddenly appeared in the disc before me.

"Have you any ether ships left?" I asked him, after we had exchanged greetings.

"Not quite a thousand."

"And does Hia Ku still live?"

"He lives, and command the fleet during your absence."

"Then dispatch him at once to find and destroy the fleet of Lido Kan, who has just left here with five hundred ships, purposing to colonize Earth."

"Then the atmosphere is nearly dissipated?"

"It is."

"But what about you, my son? Are there any ships left in which you can return?"

"There are none near-by, and I have not the strength left to go out and search for more. My death is only a matter of hours, and I am resigned to my fate."

"Do not despair, for I, your father, will save you. I will shut off the atmosphere-destroying rays at once, and will have a small, swift ship there to bring you back in less than four hours."

I returned to the room where I had been imprisoned to watch for the ether ship, and true to the word of my father it appeared in less than four hours—a tiny, one-man craft. I hurried to the roof, reaching it just as the ship alighted. A man stepped out—an old and faithful servant of my father.

"The ship from His Majesty, your father, Highness," he said.

"But why a one-man craft?" I asked.

"Hia Ku took all the others when he left to attack the fleet of Lido Kan," he replied. Then, before I could prevent him. he took a small, green ray projector from his belt and pressed the muzzle to his abdomen. With a gasping "Farewell, Highness," the brave and loyal fellow dropped dead at my feet.

Hurrying below once more, I entered the ether visiphone room and signaled my father. His face appeared in the disc. I told him what his messenger had done, and tears streamed from his eyes.

"Just another sacrifice to the rapacity of Lido Kan," he said. "Get into your craft now, and I'll turn on the rays once more."

I lost no time in getting back to the little craft and away from Mars. I was making swift progress toward Magong, when suddenly I happened on the remnants of the two battle fleets. There were only three of our ships left, and they were beleaguered by four enemy craft. Both flagships were still intact, and at the time, dueling with their enormous ray projectors—green against red. As I approached them, one of our ships was cut in two by a red ray, the halves hurtling out through space.

I had one small ray projector on my forward deck—a puny weapon indeed against those of the huge battleships, but I determined to enter the unequal contest. Selecting the helmsman's turret of the nearest enemy ship, I plunged toward it. My approach in the tiny craft was apparently unperceived, and I did not turn on my green ray until within less than a thousand feet of my target. When the ray struck it, the turret instantly collapsed, and the ship, out of control, swung broadside, scattering her ray barrage and leaving her hull unprotected. I instantly turned the nose of my craft upward and passed over her, noting as I did so that she had been broken up by the huge green rays from our two remaining battleships.

Without pausing to give the enemy a chance to understand just what had happened, I quickly plunged at the helmsman's turret of the next ship. Once again my tiny ray threw a mighty ship out of control, and it was destroyed by the green rays of Hia Ku. This time, however, I did not escape unscathed, for one of the red rays of the second ship, shooting wildly upward as she went out of control, had carried off part of my forward deck.

I tried to close the safety plate beneath my instrument board, to keep my air and warmth from escaping into outer space, but it stuck, and a cold that closely approached absolute zero swept over me. With numbed hands I pulled frantically at the recalcitrant plate, and in a moment more had it in place. In the meantime, however, my small, swift craft had hurtled away uncontrolled to a position nearly a thousand miles from the four remaining combatants.

I swung her to, and steered for the battle scene once more. Then I saw something which wrung a gasp of horror from my lips—a huge meteor cluster from Mars rushing straight at the four ships. I had no time to signal them—to do anything, in fact. A moment later it struck them, and all four combatants disappeared in a blinding flash of light without appearing to have had the slightest effect either on the path or the mass of the projectile.

With a heavy heart I turned my ship toward Magong. A short time later I saw the projectile strike. There was a small chart on board, and on referring to it, I found that it had destroyed one of our atmosphere disintegrating ray stations.

A two-hour run took me to Magong, during which time, four more enormous projectiles hurtled past me on their death dealing errands. As I steered toward the palace of my father a fifth shot past me, hurling my tiny craft through the thin atmosphere like a leaf caught in a whirlwind. When I succeeded in righting it, and looking downward once more, a chill of horror crept over me, for this last messenger of death had dug a huge pit more than sixty miles in diameter, and the center of the pit marked the spot where my father's palace had stood. My beloved parents were no more. P'an-ku, the mighty monarch, was dead. I was P'an-ku, ruler of a desolate waste that had once been the mighty, flourishing empire of Magong.

I alighted near the rim of the enormous crater and stepped out of my craft. A moment later, gasping for breath, I hastily sprang back inside and closed the door. The atmosphere of Magong was nearly gone. With her huge ray projectors still going, she was committing suicide in order that her hated enemy might be destroyed.

Rising, I made for the nearest ray projector station. Circling close to it, I peered in the windows. Not a living soul greeted my gaze, but there were many dead bodies on the floors. The projectors, however, were still working—pointed by machinery set to keep their rays on Mars until they should fail to function for lack of power.

An occasional meteor cluster struck Magong from time to time, but they grew smaller and fewer in number—a sure sign that their projectors were succumbing, one by one, to the death-dealing rays our people had left trained on their planet. Rising, I made for the nearest world which would support human life—Earth. It was a good two hours' journey, and I noted with alarm that I had only a small supply of concentrated air in my tank—enough to last me about forty-five minutes by using it judiciously.

Pressing my speed control lever to the highest notch, I rushed Earthward with super-meteoric swiftness. Forty-five minutes passed, and still the Earth, although looming big ahead of me, was many thousands of miles away. Glancing at the indicator on my air tank, I saw that it registered zero. I closed my foul air escape valves, and breathed as lightly as possible. Presently I felt a deadly lethargy creeping over me. By exerting my will power to the utmost I managed to retain control of my senses for a few minutes longer.

Suddenly my waning consciousness registered the fact that my instruments showed I had nearly reached the outer limit of the Earth's atmosphere. To have entered it at the speed at which I was traveling would have meant a sudden, flaming death. Two things I managed to do before my senses fled—set my control lever at low speed, and unfasten the door beside me. Then came oblivion.

When I regained consciousness I was lying on the earthen floor of a large, mud-walled hut. Standing around me was an awe-stricken group of light-skinned, half naked savages. I sat up, and as I did so, the earth shook beneath me and a portion of the mud wall collapsed, crushing three men and a woman. The remainder of the savages prostrated themselves around me with every indication of superstitious fear.

I signed that I was hungry, and food and drink were instantly brought me—a huge chunk of scorched meat and a white sour beverage which I afterward learned was the fermented milk of some animal. I ate and drank, and feeling stronger, arose and stepped out of the hut, walking as if my body had been weighted with lead because of the planet's tremendous gravitational pull. As I did so, the earth quivered once more, and the hut collapsed completely.

By signs I finally made the terror-stricken savages understand that I wished to know the whereabouts of my ether ship. One of them, who appeared bolder than the rest, led me to a place where an enormous fissure yawned in the hard ground. Far down in this fissure I saw the craft wedged. I was casting about for some means of rescuing it, when the earth trembled and the crack closed over it.

Thus cut off from interplanetary travel—for I did not know how to construct another ether ship—I found myself earthbound. I immediately set about learning the simple language of the savages, living in a dwelling of skins tied to light poles because of the frequent earthquake shocks. These, as well as the many volcanic eruptions, terrific electrical storms, meteoric showers and electromagnetic displays from the polar regions, I knew were the results of the recent constant proximity of Magong to Earth, and that things would, in time, reach their proper balance once more. The savages, however, believed that the coming of "The great night light" and the subsequent terrifying phenomena, were due to some magic power which I possessed, and I was consequently worshiped as a god.

Propitiatory offerings of food, flocks, and animal skins poured in to me from neighboring tribes for hundreds of miles in all directions. Gradually the earthquake shocks subsided, the volcanic eruptions ceased to be continuous, the meteoric showers grew less frequent, and the elements less destructive. After a year had passed I married a daughter of the chief of the tribe among which I had fallen. Other chieftains, learning that the god married women, quickly tendered the hands of their daughters.

One of these, I married from time to time, thus making alliances with tribe after tribe which none might wish to break. I grew immensely wealthy, as the wealth of these people was reckoned, and built me an immense palace of hewn stone, personally supervising the work of my horde of unskilled laborers. I also built a temple for the worship of the great god, T'ien, Supreme Ruler of the Universe, and taught my people to worship Him, and to regard me only as His earthly vicar.

Most of my numerous wives bore me children, and I was grateful for the fact that all of them, instead of resembling their mother's people, had the yellow skins, straight black hair, and slanting eyes of my race. My children grew up and married savage women and men, yet there was slight modification in the physiognomy of their offspring. As the years passed, I learned that these people, my children and descendants included, rarely lived longer than a century, their average life span being about seventy years. When I passed the century mark without showing any signs of senility, it was noised about that I was an immortal. This belief increased my power, and consequently I neither denied nor affirmed its truth, although I knew I should be middle-aged at two hundred and would probably be dead before I had traveled far in my third century of existence, as three centuries was the average life span for my race, and a total of four centuries rarely attained.

Having now reached my two hundred and ninety eighth year, I am ready to return to my maker, leaving a hundred thousand descendants—a proud race who have long since ceased to intermarry with the white-skinned savages. They are known as the Celestial People, and I have made them lords over the lesser races of my mighty empire.

This record, which I have graven on age-defying stone with my own hands, will be sealed in the cave in which I am cutting it. I have calculated that, not less than five thousand years hence, the door of the cave will be revealed by erosion.

As the end approaches I feel the gift of prevision—the urge to prophesy. When my message is found, my descendants will be numbered by millions. They will not be scientists, but religionists. I see this tendency persisting in them, up to this day, and it will continue. Although I have taught them to read and write the language of my people, and to worship T'ien, I have long since abandoned the attempt to teach them science. My every effort to get them to grasp even the rudiments of astronomy and physics was unavailing. My simplest statements along these lines were interpreted as symbolic religious utterances and wound around superstitious beliefs.

The pure language of my forefathers, together with the characters I have taught them, is undergoing a gradual change. It may be that, five thousand years hence, this writing will be unintelligible to my descendants. Time, however, should raise up a man among them, who will have the intelligence and the persistence necessary to decipher it. I picture him, however, as a studious man of religion, and therefore uninterested in its scientific aspects—and my scientific mind yearns to communicate with others of its kind—minds that will understand.

To my descendant, I therefore give this charge:

Translate this writing into the languages of the leading nations of Earth. Then journey hence, to a place where you will find a pit three-quarters of a mile in width and more than five hundred and fifty feet deep. It will be ringed about by a wall a hundred and fifty feet in height. My figures are approximate because they are only calculations based on the size and speed of the meteoric mass which Mars projected to Earth.

Because it is unique on Earth, and exactly resembles the pits on my native planet, men of science who are interested in Magong will eventually visit it. When you have found it, you will secrete yourself in the neighborhood and observe these men. Each time you see a true scientific visitor, watch the face of Magong for a sign. When a bright light appears, you will know that my soul has recognized the right person, and signaled you from its celestial abode.

Hand him a translation of this writing in his own language, and go about your own affairs with my blessing, for it is to him and to his kind that I, as a scientist, address this message.

And now, as I bring this, my life story, to a close, I look back over a long, and fairly happy existence spent on Earth, yet each time I view Magong, I cannot help thinking of what might have been, had it not been for that horrible, man-made plague called war. Nor can I repress a feeling of sadness at sight of my once-proud world among worlds, now a lowly satellite, her war-scarred lifeless face forever turned sadly and submissively toward her new master, Earth.

RAMBLE HOUSE's

HARRY STEPHEN KEELER WEBWORK MYSTERIES
(RH) indicates the title is available ONLY in the RAMBLE HOUSE edition

The Ace of Spades Murder
The Affair of the Bottled Deuce (RH)
The Amazing Web
The Barking Clock
Behind That Mask
The Book with the Orange Leaves
The Bottle with the Green Wax Seal
The Box from Japan
The Case of the Canny Killer
The Case of the Crazy Corpse (RH)
The Case of the Flying Hands (RH)
The Case of the Ivory Arrow
The Case of the Jeweled Ragpicker
The Case of the Lavender Gripsack
The Case of the Mysterious Moll
The Case of the 16 Beans
The Case of the Transparent Nude (RH)
The Case of the Transposed Legs
The Case of the Two-Headed Idiot (RH)
The Case of the Two Strange Ladies
The Circus Stealers (RH)
Cleopatra's Tears
A Copy of Beowulf (RH)
The Crimson Cube (RH)
The Face of the Man From Saturn
Find the Clock
The Five Silver Buddhas
The 4th King
The Gallows Waits, My Lord! (RH)
The Green Jade Hand
Finger! Finger!
Hangman's Nights (RH)
I, Chameleon (RH)
I Killed Lincoln at 10:13! (RH)
The Iron Ring
The Man Who Changed His Skin (RH)
The Man with the Crimson Box
The Man with the Magic Eardrums
The Man with the Wooden Spectacles
The Marceau Case
The Matilda Hunter Murder
The Monocled Monster

The Murder of London Lew
The Murdered Mathematician
The Mysterious Card (RH)
The Mysterious Ivory Ball of Wong Shing Li (RH)
The Mystery of the Fiddling Cracksman
The Peacock Fan
The Photo of Lady X (RH)
The Portrait of Jirjohn Cobb
Report on Vanessa Hewstone (RH)
Riddle of the Travelling Skull
Riddle of the Wooden Parrakeet (RH)
The Scarlet Mummy (RH)
The Search for X-Y-Z
The Sharkskin Book
Sing Sing Nights
The Six From Nowhere (RH)
The Skull of the Waltzing Clown
The Spectacles of Mr. Cagliostro
Stand By—London Calling!
The Steeltown Strangler
The Stolen Gravestone (RH)
Strange Journey (RH)
The Strange Will
The Straw Hat Murders (RH)
The Street of 1000 Eyes (RH)
Thieves' Nights
Three Novellos (RH)
The Tiger Snake
The Trap (RH)
Vagabond Nights (Defrauded Yeggman)
Vagabond Nights 2 (10 Hours)
The Vanishing Gold Truck
The Voice of the Seven Sparrows
The Washington Square Enigma
When Thief Meets Thief
The White Circle (RH)
The Wonderful Scheme of Mr. Christopher Thorne
X. Jones—of Scotland Yard
Y. Cheung, Business Detective

Keeler-Related Works

A To Izzard: A Harry Stephen Keeler Companion by Fender Tucker — Articles and stories about Harry, by Harry, and in his style. Included is a compleat bibliography.

Wild About Harry: Reviews of Keeler Novels — Edited by Richard Polt & Fender Tucker — 22 reviews of works by Harry Stephen Keeler from *Keeler News*. A perfect introduction to the author.

The Keeler Keyhole Collection: Annotated newsletter rants from Harry Stephen Keeler, edited by Francis M. Nevins. Over 400 pages of incredibly personal Keeleriana.

Fakealoo — Pastiches of the style of Harry Stephen Keeler by selected demented members of the HSK Society. Updated every year with the new winner.

Strands of the Web: Short Stories of Harry Stephen Keeler — 29 stories, just about all that Keeler wrote, are edited and introduced by Fred Cleaver.

RAMBLE HOUSE's LOON SANCTUARY

52 Pickup — Two thrillers from 1952 by Aylwin Lee Martin: *The Crimson Frame* and *Fear Comes Calling*

A Clear Path to Cross — Sharon Knowles short mystery stories by Ed Lynskey.

A Jimmy Starr Omnibus — Three 40s novels by Jimmy Starr.

A Roland Daniel Double: The Signal and The Return of Wu Fang — Classic thrillers from the 30s.

A Shot Rang Out — Three decades of reviews and articles by today's Anthony Boucher, Jon Breen. An essential book for any mystery lover's library.

A Smell of Smoke — A 1951 English countryside thriller by Miles Burton.

A Snark Selection — Lewis Carroll's *The Hunting of the Snark* with two Snarkian chapters by Harry Stephen Keeler — Illustrated by Gavin L. O'Keefe.

A Young Man's Heart — A forgotten early classic by Cornell Woolrich.

Alexander Laing Novels — *The Motives of Nicholas Holtz* and *Dr. Scarlett*, stories of medical mayhem and intrigue from the 30s.

An Angel in the Street — Modern hardboiled noir by Peter Genovese.

Automaton — Brilliant treatise on robotics: 1928-style! By H. Stafford Hatfield.

Away from the Here and Now — A collection of SF short stories by Clare Winger Harris.

Beast or Man? — A 1930 novel of racism and horror by Sean M'Guire. Introduced by John Pelan.

Black Hogan Strikes Again — Australia's Peter Renwick pens a tale of the 30s outback.

Black River Falls — Suspense from the master, Ed Gorman.

Blondy's Boy Friend — A snappy 1930 story by Philip Wylie, writing as Leatrice Homesley.

Blood in a Snap — The *Finnegan's Wake* of the 21st century, by Jim Weiler.

Blood Moon — The first of the Robert Payne series by Ed Gorman.

Calling Lou Largo — Two hardboiled classics from William Ard: *All Can Get* (1959) and *Like Ice She Was* (1960)

Chariots of San Fernando and Other Stories — Malcolm Jameson's SF from the pulps are featured in the first book of the John Pelan SF series.

Chelsea Quinn Yarbro Novels featuring Charlie Moon — *Ogilvie, Tallant and Moon, Music When the Sweet Voice Dies, Poisonous Fruit* and *Dead Mice*. An Ojibwa detective in SF.

Cornucopia of Crime — Francis M. Nevins assembled this huge collection of his writings about crime literature and the people who write it. Essential for any serious mystery library.

Crimson Clown Novels — By Johnston McCulley, author of the Zorro novels, *The Crimson Clown* and *The Crimson Clown Again*.

Dago Red — 22 tales of dark suspense by Bill Pronzini.

David Hume Novels — *Corpses Never Argue, Cemetery First Stop, Make Way for the Mourners, Eternity Here I Come*. 1930s British hardboiled fiction with an attitude.

Dead Man Talks Too Much — Hollywood boozer by Weed Dickenson.

Death Leaves No Card — One of the most unusual murdered-in-the-tub mysteries you'll ever read. By Miles Burton.

Death March of the Dancing Dolls and Other Stories — Volume Three in the Day Keene in the Detective Pulps series. Introduced by Bill Crider.

Deep Space and other Stories — A collection of SF gems by Richard A. Lupoff.

Detective Duff Unravels It — Episodic mysteries by Harvey O'Higgins.

Dime Novels: Ramble House's 10-Cent Books — *Knife in the Dark* by Robert Leslie Bellem, *Hot Lead* and *Song of Death* by Ed Earl Repp, *A Hashish House in New York* by H.H. Kane, and five more.

Don Diablo: Book of a Lost Film — Two-volume treatment of a western by Paul Landres, with diagrams. Intro by Francis M. Nevins.

Dope and Swastikas — Two strange novels from 1922 by Edmund Snell

Dope Tales #1 — Two dope-riddled classics; *Dope Runners* by Gerald Grantham and *Death Takes the Joystick* by Phillip Condé.

Dope Tales #2 — Two more narco-classics; *The Invisible Hand* by Rex Dark and *The Smokers of Hashish* by Norman Berrow.

Dope Tales #3 — Two enchanting novels of opium by the master, Sax Rohmer. *Dope* and *The Yellow Claw*.

Double Hot — Two 60s softcore sex novels by Morris Hershman.

Dr. Odin — Douglas Newton's 1933 racial potboiler comes back to life.

Evangelical Cockroach — Subversive fare from Jack Woodford

Evidence in Blue — 1938 mystery by E. Charles Vivian.

Fatal Accident — Murder by automobile, a 1936 mystery by Cecil M. Wills.

Ferris Wheel Hussy — Two from Aylwin Lee Martin: *Death on a Ferris Wheel* (1951) and *Death for a Hussy* (1952)

Finger-prints Never Lie — A 1939 classic detective novel by John G. Brandon.

Freaks and Fantasies — Eerie tales by Tod Robbins, collaborator of Tod Browning on the film FREAKS.

Gadsby — A lipogram (a novel without the letter E). Ernest Vincent Wright's last work, published in 1939 right before his death.

Gelett Burgess Novels — *The Master of Mysteries, The White Cat, Two O'Clock Courage, Ladies in Boxes, Find the Woman, The Heart Line, The Picaroons* and *Lady Mechante.* All are introduced by Richard A. Lupoff who is singlehandedly bringing Burgess back to life.

Geronimo — S. M. Barrett's 1905 autobiography of a noble American.

Hake Talbot Novels — *Rim of the Pit, The Hangman's Handyman.* Classic locked room mysteries, with mapback covers by Gavin O'Keefe.

Hollywood Dreams — A novel of Tinsel Town and the Depression by Richard O'Brien.

Hostesses in Hell and Other Stories — Russell Gray's violent tales from the pulps. #16 in the Dancing Tuatara Press horror series.

I Stole $16,000,000 — A true story by cracksman Herbert E. Wilson.

Inclination to Murder — 1966 thriller by New Zealand's Harriet Hunter.

Invaders from the Dark — Classic werewolf tale from Greye La Spina.

J. Poindexter, Colored — Classic satirical black novel by Irvin S. Cobb.

Jack Mann Novels — Strange murder in the English countrysice. *Gees' First Case, Nightmare Farm, Grey Shapes, The Ninth Life, The Glass Too Many, The Kleinert Case* and *Maker of Shadows.*

Jake Hardy — A lusty western tale from Wesley Tallant.

Jim Harmon Double Novels — *Vixen Hollow/Celluloid Scandal, The Man Who Made Maniacs/Silent Siren, Ape Rape/Wanton Witch, Sex Burns Like Fire/Twist Session, Sudden Lust/Passion Strip, Sin Unlimited/Harlot Master, Twilight Girls/Sex Institution.* Written in the early 60s and never reprinted until now.

Joel Townsley Rogers Novels and Short Stories — By the author of *The Red Right Hand: Once In a Red Moon, Lady With the Dice, The Stopped Clock, Never Leave My Bed.* Also two short story collections: *Night of Horror* and *Killing Time.*

Joseph Shallit Novels — *The Case of the Billion Dollar Body, Lady Don't Die on My Doorstep, Kiss the Killer, Yell Bloody Murder, Take Your Last Look.* One of America's best 50's authors and a favorite of author Bill Pronzini.

Keller Memento — 45 short stories of the amazing and weird by Dr. David Keller.

Killer's Caress — Cary Moran's 1936 hardboiled thriller.

Lady of the Yellow Death and Other Stories — Tales from the pulps by Wyatt Blassingame. #14 in the Dancing Tuatara Press series.

League of the Grateful Dead and Other Stories — Volume One in the Day Keene in the Detective Pulps series. In the introduction John Pelan outlines his plans for re-publishing all of Day Keene's short stories from the pulps.

Man Out of Hell and Other Stories — Volume II of the John H. Knox pulps collection.

Marblehead: A Novel of H.P. Lovecraft — A long-lost masterpiece from Richard A. Lupoff. The "director's cut", the long version that has never been published before.

Master of Souls — Mark Hansom's 1937 shocker, introduced by weirdologist John Pelan.

Max Afford Novels — *Owl of Darkness, Death's Mannikins, Blood on His Hands, The Dead Are Blind, The Sheep and the Wolves, Sinners in Paradise* and *Two Locked Room Mysteries and a Ripping Yarn* by one of Australia's finest mystery novelists.

More Secret Adventures of Sherlock Holmes — Gary Lovisi's second collection of tales about the unknown sides of the great detective.

Muddled Mind: Complete Works of Ed Wood, Jr. — David Hayes and Hayden Davis deconstruct the life and works of the mad, but canny, genius.

Murder among the Nudists — A mystery from 1934 by Peter Hunt featuring a naked Detective-Inspector going undercover in a nudist colony.

Murder in Black and White — 1931 classic tennis whodunit by Evelyn Elder.

Murder in Shawnee — Two novels of the Alleghenies by John Douglas: *Shawnee Alley Fire* and *Haunts.*

Murder in Silk — A 1937 Yellow Peril novel of the silk trade by Ralph Trevor.

My Deadly Angel — 1955 Cold War drama by John Chelton.

My First Time: The One Experience You Never Forget — Michael Birchwood — 64 true first-person narratives of how they lost it.

Mysterious Martin, the Master of Murder — Two versions of a strange 1912 novel by Tod Robbins about a man who writes books that can kill.

Norman Berrow Novels — *The Bishop's Sword, Ghost House, Don't Go Out After Dark, Claws of the Cougar, The Smokers of Hashish, The Secret Dancer, Don't Jump Mr. Boland!, The Footprints of Satan, Fingers for Ransom, The Three Tiers of Fantasy, The Spaniard's Thumb, The Eleventh Plague, Words Have Wings, One Thrilling Night, The Lady's in Danger, It Howls at Night, The Terror in the Fog, Oil Under the Window, Murder in the Melody, The Singing Room.* The complete Norman Berrow library of classic locked-room mysteries, several of which are masterpieces.

Old Times' Sake — Short stories by James Reasoner from Mike Shayne Magazine.

One Dreadful Night — 1940s suspense and terror from Ronald S. L. Harding

Pair o' Jacks — Two works by Jack Woodford: *Find the Motive* and *The Loud Literary Lamas of New York.*

Perfect .38 — Two early Timothy Dane novels by William Ard. More to come.

Prose Bowl — Futuristic satire of a world where hack writing has replaced football as our national obsession, by Bill Pronzini and Barry N. Malzberg.

Red Light — The history of legal prostitution in Shreveport Louisiana by Eric Brock. Includes wonderful photos of the houses and the ladies.

Researching American-Made Toy Soldiers — A 276-page collection of a lifetime of articles by toy soldier expert Richard O'Brien.

Reunion in Hell — Volume One of the John H. Knox series of weird stories from the pulps. Introduced by horror expert John Pelan.

Ripped from the Headlines! — The Jack the Ripper story as told in the newspaper articles in the *New York* and *London Times.*

Robert Randisi Novels — *No Exit to Brooklyn* and *The Dead of Brooklyn*. The first two Nick Delvecchio novels.

Rough Cut & New, Improved Murder — Ed Gorman's first two novels.

Ruled By Radio — 1925 futuristic novel by Robert L. Hadfield & Frank E. Farncombe.

Rupert Penny Novels — *Policeman's Holiday, Policeman's Evidence, Lucky Policeman, Policeman in Armour, Sealed Room Murder, Sweet Poison, The Talkative Policeman, She had to Have Gas* and *Cut and Run* (by Martin Tanner.) Rupert Penny is the pseudonym of Australian Charles Thornett, a master of the locked room, impossible crime plot.

Sand's Game — Spectacular hard-boiled noir from Ennis Willie, edited by Lynn Myers and Stephen Mertz, with contributions from Max Allan Collins, Bill Crider, Wayne Dundee, Bill Pronzini, Gary Lovisi and James Reasoner.

Sand's War — The second Ennis Willie collection

Satan's Den Exposed — True crime in Truth or Consequences New Mexico — Award-winning journalism by the *Desert Journal.*

Satan's Sin House and Other Stories — Dancing Tuatara Press #15 by Wayne Rogers – Gore and mayhem from the shudder pulps.

Gelett Burgess Novels — *The Master of Mysteries, The White Cat, Two O'Clock Courage, Ladies in Boxes, Find the Woman, The Heart Line, The Picaroons* and *Lady Mechante.* All are edited and introduced by Richard A. Lupoff.

Sam McCain Novels — Ed Gorman's terrific series includes *The Day the Music Died, Wake Up Little Susie* and *Will You Still Love Me Tomorrow?*

Sex Slave — Potboiler of lust in the days of Cleopatra by Dion Leclerq, 1966.

Shadows' Edge — Two early novels by Wade Wright: *Shadows Don't Bleed* and *The Sharp Edge.*

Sideslip — 1968 SF masterpiece by Ted White and Dave Van Arnam.

Slammer Days — Two full-length prison memoirs: *Men into Beasts* (1952) by George Sylvester Viereck and *Home Away From Home* (1962) by Jack Woodford.

Sorcerer's Chessmen — John Pelan introduces this 1939 classic by Mark Hansom.

Star Griffin — Michael Kurland's 1987 masterpiece of SF drollery is back.

Stakeout on Millennium Drive — Award-winning Indianapolis Noir by Ian Woollen.

Star Griffin — 1987 SF classic from Michael Kurland gets the Ramble House treatment.

Strands of the Web: Short Stories of Harry Stephen Keeler — Edited and Introduced by Fred Cleaver.

Suzy — A collection of comic strips by Richard O'Brien and Bob Vojtko from 1970.

Tales of the Macabre and Ordinary — Modern twisted horror by Chris Mikul, author of the *Bizarrism* series.

Tenebrae — Ernest G. Henham's 1898 horror tale brought back.

The Amorous Intrigues & Adventures of Aaron Burr — by Anonymous. Hot historical action about the man who almost became Emperor of Mexico.

The Anthony Boucher Chronicles — edited by Francis M. Nevins. Book reviews by Anthony Boucher written for the *San Francisco Chronicle,* 1942 – 1947. Essential and fascinating reading by the best book reviewer there ever was.

The Best of 10-Story Book — edited by Chris Mikul, over 35 stories from the literary magazine Harry Stephen Keeler edited.

The Black Dark Murders — Vintage 50s college murder yarn by Milt Ozaki, writing as Robert O. Saber.

The Book of Time — Classic novel by H.G. Wells is joined by sequels by Wells himself and three timely stories by Richard Lupoff. Lavishly illustrated by Gavin L. O'Keefe.

The Case of the Little Green Men — Mack Reynolds wrote this love song to sci-fi fans back in 1951 and it's now back in print.

The Case of the Withered Hand — 1936 potboiler by John G. Brandon.

The Charlie Chaplin Murder Mystery — A 2004 tribute by scholar, Wes D. Gehring.

The Chinese Jar Mystery — Murder in the manor by John Stephen Strange, 1934.

The Compleat Calhoon — All of Fender Tucker's works: Includes *Totah Six-Pack, Weed, Women and Song* and *Tales from the Tower,* plus a CD of all of his songs.

The Compleat Ova Hamlet — Parodies of SF authors by Richard A. Lupoff. This is a brand new edition with more stories and more illustrations by Trina Robbins.

The Contested Earth and Other SF Stories — A never-before published space opera and seven short stories by Jim Harmon.

The Crimson Query — A 1929 thriller from Arlton Eadie. Perfect way to get introduced.

The Curse of Cantire — Classic 1939 novel of a family curse by Walter S. Masterman.

The Devil Drives — Odd prison and lost treasure novel from 1932 by Virgil Markham.

The Devil's Mistress — A 1915 Scottish gothic tale by J. W. Brodie-Innes, a member of Aleister Crowley's Golden Dawn.

The Dumpling — Political murder from 1907 by Coulson Kernahan.

The End of It All and Other Stories — Ed Gorman selected his favorite short stories for this huge collection.

The Fangs of Suet Pudding — A 1944 novel of the German invasion by Adams Farr

The Ghost of Gaston Revere — From 1935, a novel of life and beyond by Mark Hansom, introduced by John Pelan.

The Gold Star Line — Seaboard adventure from L.T. Reade and Robert Eustace.

The Golden Dagger — 1951 Scotland Yard yarn by E. R. Punshon.

The Hairbreadth Escapes of Major Mendax — Francis Blake Crofton's 1889 boys' book.

The House of the Vampire — 1907 poetic thriller by George S. Viereck.

The Incredible Adventures of Rowland Hern — Intriguing 1928 impossible crimes by Nicholas Olde.

The Julius Caesar Murder Case — A classic 1935 re-telling of the assassination by Wallace Irwin that's much more fun than the Shakespeare version.

The Koky Comics — A collection of all of the 1978-1981 Sunday and daily comic strips by Richard O'Brien and Mort Gerberg, in two volumes.

The Lady of the Terraces — 1925 missing race adventure by E. Charles Vivian.

The Library of Death — By Ronald S. L. Harding, Dancing Tuatara Press #20.

The Lord of Terror — 1925 mystery with master-criminal, Fantômas.

The N. R. De Mexico Novels — Robert Bragg, the real N.R. de Mexico, presents *Marijuana Girl, Madman on a Drum, Private Chauffeur* in one volume.

The Night Remembers — A 1991 Jack Walsh mystery from Ed Gorman.

The One After Snelling — Kickass modern noir from Richard O Brien.

The Organ Reader — A huge compilation of just about everything published in the 1971-1972 radical bay-area newspaper, *THE ORGAN.* A coffee table book that points out the shallowness of the coffee table mindset.

The Poker Club — Three in one! Ed Gorman's ground-breaking novel, the short story it was based upon, and the screenplay of the film made from it.

RAMBLE HOUSE

Fender Tucker, Prop. Gavin L. O'Keefe, Graphics
www.ramblehouse.com   fender@ramblehouse.com
228-826-1783 10329 Sheephead Drive, Vancleave MS 39565

Made in the USA
Monee, IL
26 July 2021